THE TREES

THE TREES

Ali Shaw

B L O O M S B U R Y
NEW YORK · LONDON · OXFORD · NEW DELHI · SYDNEY

Bloomsbury USA
An imprint of Bloomsbury Publishing Plc

1385 Broadway   50 Bedford Square
New York   London
NY 10018   WC1B 3DP
USA   UK

www.bloomsbury.com

BLOOMSBURY and the Diana logo are trademarks of Bloomsbury Publishing Plc

First published in Great Britain 2016
First U.S. edition 2016

Extract from *Dante's Inferno*, The Indiana Critical Edition, Dante Alighieri. Translated and edited by Mark Musa, Copyright © 1995 by Indiana University Press. Reprinted with permission of Indiana University Press.

This is a work of fiction. Names and characters are the product of the author's imagination and any resemblance to actual persons, living or dead, is entirely coincidental.

No responsibility for loss caused to any individual or organization acting on or refraining from action as a result of the material in this publication can be accepted by Bloomsbury or the author.

ISBN: HB: 978-1-63286-283-9
ePub: 978-1-63286-284-6

Library of Congress Cataloging-in-Publication Data is available.

2 4 6 8 10 9 7 5 3 1

Typeset by Integra Software Services Pvt. Ltd.
Printed and bound in USA by Berryville Graphics Inc., Berryville, Virginia

To find out more about our authors and books visit www.bloomsbury.com. Here you will find extracts, author interviews, details of forthcoming events and the option to sign up for our newsletters.

Bloomsbury books may be purchased for business or promotional use. For information on bulk purchases please contact Macmillan Corporate and Premium Sales Department at specialmarkets@macmillan.com.

For Inka

Midway along the journey of our life
I awoke to find myself in a dark wood

Dante Alighieri, *Dante's Inferno*

I

I

The Night the Trees Came

He stood in the corner shop with rainwater dribbling off his anorak, looking for the cheapest box of beers. The checkout girl thought him a drunk, he knew, so he paid on his shiny new credit card in the hope it somehow proved him otherwise. He walked home with his back straining under the weight of the beers, puffing as he went, the box supported on the ledge of his belly. Tepid August rain splashed freely at his face and hair, often hitting the bullseye of his bald spot. After he had dumped the drink on his doorstep to get out his key, he paused for a moment and gazed along the empty street. The rain watered the world so heavily that he wondered if it might rinse it away. He did not think he would mind if it did.

This was a part of his ritual whenever Michelle was away from home, just as later he would watch reruns of westerns until the small hours and stagger to the takeaway for his sweet and sour chicken. Like all good rituals it summoned the same old feelings, every time. First the squalid glee (increasingly unbecoming, he knew, in a forty-four-year-old man) of slouching alone in his armchair with a meal of grease to scoff. Second, when the beer had kicked in, the self-righteous thrill that made him spring to his feet and rant at the world beyond his door as if he were some cowboy with a six-shooter, capable of riding it down. Third, and it would last until he dragged himself to sleep, the comedown ache of his self-loathing.

Inside, he changed into dry clothes and began his first beer. The opening scenes of the western rolled. Horses raced across the Mojave, their hooves beating cracks into the dirt. Gunshots fired, brittle and easy, like the sounds of twigs snapping. He cracked open his second beer and sprawled back in his armchair with a happy giggle.

Later, he staggered to the takeaway and got drenched all over again and came back with battered chicken balls and a red congealing sauce in a polystyrene pot. Walking home, he marvelled at how many worms had crawled up from the earth that evening. Scores upon scores of them, squirming in the flowerbeds. There were millipedes and woodlice too, and a legion of slugs pulsing across the road. A car rushed past, its headlamps filling every raindrop yellow, and when it was gone there were crushed trails of slime on the tarmac.

Had not the alcohol already gone to his head, he might have paused to be troubled by such a slithering multitude. Instead, he trotted home eager to appease his rumbling stomach. When he reached his front door he fumbled his key in the lock, dropped it to the path and had to stoop to retrieve it. There were worms on the paving slabs too, narrow rosy ones and the thicker kinds with crimson saddles. There were beetles big as grapes. There were wrinkled black slugs with toxic orange undersides.

In his surprise, he lost hold of his takeaway. As if in slow motion, the pot of sauce slid out of its bag, rotated as it fell, and splattered the garden path sweet and sour. He dropped to his knees to save what he could, but already the sauce was pitted by the downpour. When he staggered inside to inspect the damage done, he had saved only half an inch of the precious red substance. In that a caterpillar was drowning.

He ate his chicken balls with tomato ketchup. He started another western. Cowboys wisecracked and shot each other off the roofs of buildings. Later, his anger seized him and he sprang to his feet, cursing his bad luck to be rotting here in this box of a house, on the kind of ordered street loved only by bureaucrats, in a town like every other town in the country, and why did nobody make good westerns any more?

Later still, he felt crushingly alone. There was nothing for it but to slope upstairs to bed. He felt stuffed full of his own ridiculousness, force-fed another dollop with every step he struggled to ascend. He drew the curtains and undressed in the yellow gloom of his bedside lamp, averting his eyes from the mirror on the wardrobe door lest he see his complexion or the sag of his gut. At last he squirmed into bed, face down. Then came the final act of this ritual of his: the prayer of abject desperation. Said to nothing, except perhaps the stuffing of his pillow, since he believed in no higher powers. Said all the same, said to *anything*, just in case there existed some presence out there in the cruel world that was bigger than his disbelief.

His name was Adrien Thomas.

He fell asleep with a whimper and a snore.

And somewhere out in the darkness, something creaked.

It was a night of whispers, and of pattering claws.

The rain fell for many hours, and did not relent until the flower-beds swam with it and the verges were a mush. The trees spaced along the suburb's roadsides hissed in unison with the breeze. It was a night when no cats fought, for any animal that owned a basket had already hunkered down. It was a night when bats flew in unseen frenzies, around and around the satellite dishes and the television aerials.

Someone's pet rabbit died, in its hutch, of a stopped heart.

Someone arriving home late from an evening function slipped as she left her car, fell and sprained her ankle. When she looked to see what she had slipped on she found a pasty slime covering her drive, such as she had only ever seen on rotting logs in the dankest of woodlands.

The night smelled of mildew and resin. Rainwater seeped into the sewers and the soil. Along Adrien Thomas's street a fox trotted, its head nodding, its jaws hanging ajar. It paused outside his house for a full minute, green eyes shining in the lamppost light.

Worms and millipedes crawled in their masses. Twigs shivered on roadside trees. And then, from somewhere underground, a yawning creak began.

Those who heard it dismissed it for the soughing of a branch in the wind, or of a telephone mast in need of repair. Yet both its sound and its source were deeper than that. It was a moan as of some lumbering presence stirring, as of something drawing towards consciousness from overlong hibernation.

The people of the suburbs slept. Adrien Thomas slept.

There was a silent moment when the rain had stopped falling and the fox was long gone and the bats had flocked out of sight.

Then the trees came.

The forest burst full-grown out of the earth, in booming upper-cuts of trunks and bludgeoning branches. It rammed through roads and houses alike, shattering bricks and exploding glass. It sounded like a thousand trains derailing at once, squealings and jarrings and bucklings all lost beneath the thunderclaps of broken concrete and the cacophony of a billion hissing leaves. Up surged the tree trunks, up in a storm of foliage and lashing twigs that spread and spread and then, at a great height, stopped.

In the blink of an eye, the world had changed. There came an elastic aftershock of creaks and groans and then, softly softly, a chinking shower of rubbled cement. Branches stilled amid the wreckage they had made. Leaves calmed and trunks stood serene. Where, not a minute before, a suburb had lain, there was now only woodland standing amid ruins. Some of the trees were flickeringly lit by the strobe of dying electricity, others by the fires of vehicles that had burst into flames. The rest stood in darkness, their canopy a gibbet world hung with all the things they'd killed and mangled as they came.

2

Cockcrow

Adrien flung himself upright in bed, the room reverberating around him. Only when it stilled did he begin to hear all the other noises that might normally have woken him. Car alarms and burglar alarms. A spitting like a fountain of sparks. Even his own heartbeat, hammering in his ears. Then with a groaning lurch something huge collapsed outside, and he clutched his blankets to his chest.

He could tell this was no nightmare even as he slid out of bed. With the digits of his alarm clock vanished into powerless black, he stood in the darkness clasping and unclasping his hands. He had no idea what could have happened but, outdoors, people were beginning to scream, and the noise made a cold feeling curl up in his belly.

Adrien felt for his glasses on the bedside table and thumbed them onto his face, useless though they were without light. Then he found his wristwatch and pushed the button that lit up its face. Now he could see the warping of the floor and the splits in the walls and ceiling. In the greenish glow of his watch's light he turned around and around, taking shaky breaths of air that newly smelled of herbs and cinders, noticing for the first time the branches that had entered through the fissures in the walls. One had burst in at ankle height, and was a hump-backed spine arching in and out of the carpet. Another had knocked the wardrobe sideways and cracked the mirror like a surface of ice. 'What on earth . . .' he began, just as, with a slam, something heavy hit something else out in the street. There was a brief human cry, cut short no sooner than begun.

Adrien pressed his fist to his teeth and tried to think straight. Still as naked as when he'd slid into bed, he crept across the room and opened the bedroom door.

Bark blocked the way.

It was the cracked rind of a tree trunk, grown up through the floorboards and on into the ceiling. From there it would unfold its branches through the attic and the rafters above. Following its upward lines with his eyes made Adrien swoon, and for a moment he thought he would faint.

He steadied himself, then found the strength to reach out and touch the bark. Grains of soil cloyed its recesses. Torn wires dangled from twigs.

Adrien snatched back his hand. For a minute he could only stare. Then, spurred by sudden indignation, he lunged forward and shoved at the tree with all his might. It did not budge. Again he snatched back his hand.

'Jesus,' he whispered, 'Mary and Joseph.' Then, just to be sure, he added, 'Michelle.'

Might he have died and gone to some kind of hell? He did not know what he had done to deserve it, save for having done nothing particularly saintly either. He wanted to turn tail and flee from the tree but there was nowhere to run except in circles around his room. After half a minute, he thought to try the window. He tore back the curtains and the street was overcome with trees.

'Oh my God.' He pressed his hands to his head.

It was a night wood clogged with the rubble of all the walls, gardens and pavements that had preceded it. Headlamps and rear lights shone through the foliage and the devastation. Cars had been flipped vertical, or else were suspended by the branches. One still sounded its alarm with its indicators blinking orange auras. A van hung on its side in the high fork of a trunk, beaming two spotlights at the ground, its driver sagging inert against his safety belt. Torches and the square lights of mobile phones flashed and swayed at ground level as people staggered out of their ruined houses, each as stunned as the next. The trees had ejected every last obstruction from the soil. Pipes and cables and the contents of basements. Clipped lawns ripped to shrouds of turf.

Sweat tickled the small of Adrien's back. 'Michelle,' he croaked, as if to say his wife's name could somehow rush her all the way back here, across the Irish Sea, to save him. When it did not, he tried to think what she would do in his place. She would rally in no time. Her neighbours' screams, growing more frequent now, would compel her into action. Michelle could face anything down, brave whatever life threw at her.

But he was not Michelle and she was not here. He was Adrien, and people had always cited their marriage as proof that opposites attract.

He tried the bedroom light but the bulb did nothing, so he dressed in a dark and terrified hurry and found his mobile phone in the pocket of his jeans. It had no signal, and he wondered how long it would be before he could call Michelle. He craved the reassurance of her voice right now, even if it were raised at him in one of their daily arguments. After a minute he dared to lean out of the window (the pane had vanished) to see what had become of the rest of his house. Branches hooped and hooked out of the front wall, and it appeared that one tree had grown up through the kitchen and another through the bathroom. When the floor groaned under him he had the sense that his bedroom was only held intact at the trees' mercy, a kind of treehouse balanced on their shoulders.

Shade by shade now, Adrien's eyes were adjusting. In the canopy something small crept then bounded. A grey leaping streak of fur that he realised was a squirrel going about its everyday habits, as if the trees had stood there for all time. Something about that made Adrien's stomach wobble, and he had to hug himself tight to stop himself from vomiting.

'At least,' he thought out loud, when the sickly feeling had passed, 'I've done my homework.'

He began to strip the bed.

On many nights, since moving to this house, he had lain awake imagining some crisis that would require him to abscond through the window. Often the mere act of imagining disaster could convince him of real danger, and he would nudge Michelle in the dark and whisper something like, 'Can you smell that smoke?'

'No. It's nothing. Oh, Adrien, not this again. Go back to sleep.'

Instead of following her advice he would envisage flames raging on the landing and begin to plot their escape. He would attempt to work out how many sheets he'd need to knot together to make a rope long enough to descend from the window. Michelle, noticing him tense in the darkness, would ask him what was wrong.

'Nothing,' he would say.

'Something must be. Your eyes are open.'

'It's nothing.'

And in the earlier days of their marriage she would press herself closer to him and lay her hand on him and stroke his chest until he dozed back to sleep.

He finished stripping the bed and took from the gaping cupboard all of the spare sheets. He tied their corners together with the only knot he knew, which he lost faith in after having fastened two sheets. It looked too simple to dangle his life from, even though he tested it by tugging with all his might.

When he had tied a good enough length, he found his keys and threw some clothes into his bag, supposing that he would not be able to get back into the bedroom until the fire brigade or whoever the government sent arrived to put things right. He licked his fingers and used them to smooth his hair down. For a second his fingertips touched the balding crown of his head and his heart sank familiarly, then he tied the rope of sheets around the bed's headboard and again around its legs. At the open window he paused and could only gape at the canopy. Behind it the sky was just becoming visible, a masked grey that seemed to agitate the leaves into life.

When Adrien yanked the rope all of the knots held firm, but looking down from his first-floor bedroom felt like teetering out of a high-rise. 'Help!' he called. 'Up here!', but the new foliage absorbed his voice and none of the people wandering dazed into the ravaged street heard him. He flung the tied sheets from the window and was briefly satisfied that the quantity required was exactly what he'd deduced it would be during those nights lying awake beside Michelle. Then he turned, heart thumping, and squashed his belly across the sill, pivoting until his head was in the bedroom and his feet kicking open air. He seized the rope and lowered himself a knot, then another, then one more.

A frightened shriek popped out of his throat, like an air bubble escaping a plughole. The rope had held but Adrien panicked regardless. He clung to the string of sheets with his eyes clenched shut, until the muscles of his arms began to strain. Then with gritted teeth he looked up at the criss-crossed branches, and longed to climb back to his room and wait to be rescued there.

When he tried to lock his ankles around the rope it only swayed dizzyingly side-to-side. His own weight was stretching his wrists and shoulders and, finally, pain and terror forced him into action. Scuffing the wall with his toes, he steadied himself as best he could and tried to abseil down, his palms burning from the friction. He misjudged the last few metres and fell with a back-quivering thump.

For a minute he just lay there on his front lawn, waiting to discover which bones he had broken. When the pain of his landing lessened, he was surprised to find they were all intact. Regaining his breath, he climbed to his feet and surveyed the disaster he had once called his address. Other people stood here and there, stunned into silence. Some were bleeding, others covered in dust. Over them all the trees cast their shadows, although now and then the wind chanced an opening and a star shone through. Then, briefly, a pale glow edged the leaves and they were like sharpening knives.

Adrien tried his best to take stock of it all. It was clear that other houses had fared far worse than his own, and his next-door neighbour's was one such casualty. Its owner, Mrs Howell, was an elderly dear who seemed to spend her every waking moment clipping her verges and manicuring her flowerbeds. She would not be doing that again. Mrs Howell's front wall had fallen away completely and the contents of her bedroom had been offered up to the air on arms of timber. Adrien's throat tightened when he saw her bed, and hot tears swelled on his eyelids. The bed hung above the street, punctured by three long branches that had scattered mattress foam among the twigs like misshapen blossom. As for Mrs Howell's body, Adrien could see little of it, wrapped as it was in her bed covers. Just like the bed, it had been skewered. Only a liver-spotted hand and one lock of hair showed between the folds of the sheets.

Adrien turned away, holding his forehead, but there was no relief to be had in any direction he looked. 'Why has this happened?' he muttered, but the forest gave no answers. It only enclosed him in its towering prison. Smells of bark and mosses filled the air, as well as some syrupy scent that was faint but ever present, like blood in the tongue. Somewhere in the distance a building rumbled its collapse. Somewhere somebody was weeping. The sun, beginning to rise, edged with an emerald glow the leaves overhead.

A dog barked. A cock crowed.

And out of sight, on the highest of branches and in the most secret of hollows, stranger creatures went about their business.

3

Elm

Half an hour before the trees came, Hannah woke and slid out of bed, perfectly awake in a matter of seconds. Since childhood she'd been the briefest of sleepers, springing up as soon as her body was rested. Although she loved to doze off sometimes in a sunny glade, or curl up catlike on the sofa at the end of a hard day's work, she only ever took what her body needed from sleep. Life was too precious to spend it under covers and behind walls.

Hannah's bed was a narrow thing she rarely bothered to make. It filled her tiny room, since Seb had the bigger of the two in their house. That seemed only fair, when her sixteen-year-old son hardly ever wanted to leave his desk.

Hannah tiptoed onto the landing, where she gave Seb's door a gentle push. The teenager lay face down on his bed, his duvet and sheets piled over him despite the warmth of the night. At the start of the summer, Hannah had suggested that he try sleeping under the stars. 'Go on an adventure,' she'd said. 'Go away for a fortnight with your friends, or even ask along some girls you like. Go somewhere wild and take the guitar I bought you and a tent and your swimming shorts. Go and . . . go and skinny-dip in a lake, or . . . or cook over a campfire. *Shout* stuff from the top of a mountain, Seb. This could be a summer you remember all your life.'

After she had said all that, Seb had only looked at her as if she'd asked him to go to jail. He was too busy, he'd explained, for any of that stuff, having already organised some online gaming thing that

Hannah didn't pretend to understand. She didn't pretend to understand much about Seb.

She left him sleeping and padded downstairs, where she pulled on a favourite jersey whose cuffs were too long and full of holes. The kettle hiccupped and burbled as she waited in the dark for it to boil. Hannah loved to be awake at night, when vision ceded to the subtler senses. When the kettle whistled she could taste its steam rolling in the air, and she held her breath to better hear the glugging water when she poured it into her mug. She added a teabag and leaned close and *listened* to the quiet work of its brewing, grinning at every miniature pop of a bubble, and at the hot condensation forming against her ear.

Once the teabag was out and the soya was in, she slipped out into the garden, holding her drink in both hands. She took a seat at the outside table and relished the warmth of the mug against her palms. Some mornings, up early doing this, she'd seen a vixen streak across the far end of her lawn. One time she'd even spied an owl, perched on her neighbour's cherry tree. Its face had rotated to meet hers, and they'd stared at each other for what had seemed like hours.

Hannah's garden table had been carved from wood, and she often liked to trace her finger along the maze of its grain. Her brother Zach had built it from an elm and, instead of giving it legs, had fitted it to the very stump of the tree he'd sawn its planks from. It was a monument as well as a piece of furniture, since like most elms in the country Hannah's had committed a kind of suicide. Elms had been doing that for years. When she and Zach were just kids, beetles had spread a parasitic plague from tree to tree. There had been an elm in Hannah's childhood garden, from which her parents had hung a swing, but not long after her mother died the beetles had come upon it and its leaves had drooped like autumn come early. Zach, thirteen at the time and four years Hannah's elder, had already learned enough about trees to explain its decline. 'It's a fungus, see, a parasite on the beetles that's doing it. And what the elm does is it tries to block it off. That's why you see all these bulges of wood, *here* . . . and *here*. They're the elm making walls in

14

itself. Problem is, they work too well. They block the food coming up from the roots. The elm starves itself to death by accident.'

Zach, by far the biggest boy in his school year, had felled that elm with an axe. Just like Hannah, he had grown up ahead of his years in those strange months following their mother's death, when their father had done nothing but sit at his window seat and grieve. Only when Hannah and Zach cremated the swing along with the elm did their father rise, and come staggering into the garden as if he hoped to rescue the wood from the flames.

Hannah clenched her fist around the handle of her mug, and waited for the memory's stab to fade. A stag beetle ran across the table, coming within a horn's length of her finger, and at once Hannah embraced the distraction, delighting in the insect's top-heavy wriggle. Then she laughed doubly to see another two following it, a duo scuttling past with the waddle of slapstick clowns. Then three more rushed after them, and Hannah's smile began to vanish, and then a half-dozen more swarmed by and she rose uneasily to her feet. Feathers rustled, further down the garden, and Hannah frowned to see the dim outline of a blackbird hopping about, its beak tapping manically at the grass. All over the lawn, worms were oozing out of the soil. Bees, who should have been tucked up with their honeycombs at this hour, were in flight. The flowerbeds were pebble-dashed by snails.

Hannah backed away from the table, her tea still steaming where she'd left it. Pillbugs had begun to mill there along with the beetles, and ants and chafers and a rabble of weevils each the size of a lentil. Something fine and threadlike touched her cheek, and when she brushed it aside she found her fingers strung together by spidersilk, and looking up saw hundreds of them hurrying this way and that on their tightropes. A gruff yap snapped Hannah's attention away from them and, in a burst of leaves, the vixen she had seen on past occasions rushed across the bottom of the garden and was gone again through her neighbour's hedge. But had that been (Hannah shook her head even as she thought it) something tiny *riding* on its back?

15

Perhaps she would have dwelled on that last thought had not, at that moment, something else happened, something that expelled all else from her mind.

The trees arrived.

Each plant burst from the ground like a geyser, an upward torrent of thickening bark and branches that thwacked each other flailing as they grew. Hannah threw herself aside just in time to duck the sweep of a bough that would have knocked her head from her shoulders. Instead, it crashed into Zach's elm table and all the planks and struts were smashed at once, just as the stump base was ejected from the earth by another tree rising. The remains of the table were buffeted left and right by the skyward punches of the forest, dead roots trailing in their wake. Hannah's mug of tea was lobbed aside and whirled out a spray of hot liquid before it shattered off a trunk. Then it was done. The trees had arrived, and Hannah, slowly, stood upright beneath them.

'What the . . .' she whispered, 'what . . .' but she didn't know what else to say. Stray leaves flaked from the treetops, and Hannah gaped at what had become of her garden.

Then a thought burst into her mind like one final, late-coming tree.

'Seb!' she yelled, and was at once sprinting towards what remained of her house. The back wall was a dust cloud and the roof was spread like a net across the treetops. Hannah had no time for that. She charged inside, tripping and stumbling, only to find the staircase twirling in pieces like a child's mobile. She didn't hesitate, having climbed more trees in her lifetime than she could count, and was at once scrambling upward, thinking of her son and nothing more.

'Mum! Mum, where are you?'

His voice was such a powerful relief that Hannah nearly lost her grip and fell. Instead she swung herself the final distance, on to what had been the landing, and with a shout of 'Seb!' threw her arms around him. They embraced in the spot where Seb's bedroom doorway should have been.

16

'Mum?' He looked as bleary-eyed and helpless as he'd been when he'd wailed in the night fifteen years ago. 'Mum . . . am I dreaming?'

'Seb!' was all she could gasp, pressing her face into his hair.

'But, Mum,' he said, 'what's happened?'

'I don't know.' She took a deep breath. 'I've no idea. You're okay?'

'Yeah. I think so. But . . . but . . . the house . . .'

'As long as you're okay, Seb, so is everything else.'

He drew back from her and looked fearfully around them. '*Is it? Is this a forest?*'

Hannah couldn't answer. She knew that forests could not be conjured out of nothing, and she knew more than most about the power nature had. Nevertheless her bedroom had vanished and a tree grew there now, and beyond it the road had filled with more of the same. With a bang and a sizzle a van's engine exploded into flames. Incinerated leaves wriggled away in fiery streaks, and the air smelled of burning rubber. The trees withstood the heat as if it were nothing. They cupped the van's inferno as casually as they might a bird's nest.

Hannah supposed she was in some sort of shock, and might think differently later, but now that Seb was safe she felt more awestruck than terrified. It was a more reverent kind of fear, one she had felt only a few times in life, such as when she'd stood on the edge of a vast canyon with her toes poking over the brink, or when on a trip to Oregon she'd seen a mountain lion prowl across her path.

'Oh my God,' despaired Seb. 'I can't believe this . . . Our house, Mum! All of our things!'

Hannah wasn't listening. She was, in fact, beginning to smile. The burning van across the street was held in the arms of an oak, and nearby stood beeches and limes, but by the roaring light of the fire she could make out the leaves and patterned bark of the trees that had demolished her house.

They were neither oak nor beech nor lime.

They were elms.

4

Murderers

At first Adrien found himself habitually sticking to the pavements, even though the trees had grown up through them as often as they had through the roads. Other people did the same, when they were not milling around in shock or rushing this way and that bellowing the names of loved ones. Their shouts echoed through the forest, which replied with low and straining creaks or occasional shivers that ran through the foliage. Adrien swigged on his hip flask, even though his head ached from last night's drinking. Right now he needed whatever kind of courage he could come by.

The rising sun had found the many dead among the branches, their bodies flapping with crows and jackdaws. Adrien had already looked into the lifeless eyes of one poor woman who was slowly being licked away by housecats, the bells on their collars tinkling as they ate. He had wanted nothing more than to run from that sight, but for a long half-minute his disbelief had transfixed him. When he had finally wrenched himself free he had rushed in the opposite direction, running until he was breathless, which had not taken him very far. Then he had filled his mouth with whisky and somehow found the will to carry on.

He was currently heading for the centre of town, although all he really wanted was to draw clear of these new woods. Trying to stay composed, he pictured the reception awaiting him once he'd escaped. Perhaps he would be cheered like one pulled from an earthquake, then wrapped in a blanket by an aid worker and handed hot food to help him overcome his ordeal. Perhaps journalists would wish to interview him. Perhaps he would appear on the news. After that, he could find a working telephone and contact Michelle.

The trees made the world seem smaller. At some thirty yards they drew shut a branching curtain that crossed out everything beyond. Adrien heard things long before he saw them, such as two dogs whose barking preceded them by a full minute and continued into the distance long after they had chased each other past. Most other sounds were strangled noises he could not place. Human voices warped by the forest, or the moans of buildings coming down. Sometimes there were whispers, but if Adrien dared to look up he'd invariably see another corpse among the leaves. Other times what he took for bodies were in fact just lengths of wood, with offshoots jutting out like human limbs. Once, his imagination even tricked him a step further. He thought he saw a kind of figure, an emaciated thing no bigger than a monkey, watching from above. A moment later he realised it was just a coincidence of the way the sticks and foliage grew, yet he quickened his steps all the same.

He took a shortcut through the grounds of a primary school, where the trees were full of tiny chairs. Hanging from twigs in a wrecked classroom were pictures drawn by the pupils, and at once Adrien wished he hadn't come that way. The pictures showed childhood monsters with many limbs, and among them enthroned fairy queens and wolves that walked on their hind legs.

He had no sooner left that classroom than he jumped from fright. Ahead of him stood a small child, boy or girl he could not tell. It had bare feet and cartoon pyjamas and its hands were folded behind its back. Its face was pressed against a tree trunk and it stood so still that for a cold moment Adrien took it for another of the dead. Then it bounced twice on its heels and peered around the edge of the trunk, away from them both. Adrien cleared his throat to alert it to his presence, at which it turned and stared up disinterestedly. A little girl, who ran giggling to another tree and pressed her face against it as before.

There was no one else in sight so, much to Adrien's dismay, it fell to him to try to help the girl. 'What are you doing here,' he asked nervously, 'and where are your mummy and daddy? Are you playing hide and seek?'

The girl held a finger to her lips.

'What are you doing? Do you think this is a game? You're . . . you're going to have to trust me. I'll try to help you find your parents.'

The girl laughed and sprang away between the trees, where Adrien lost sight of her. 'Wait!' he cried, stumbling in pursuit, but he did not see her again. The trees seemed to close ranks in the direction she had run in, and only her laughter continued as if it were a thing alive unto itself. Adrien leaned against a trunk and felt not much older than the girl, and certainly less capable. He mopped his forehead with his cuff and puffed out his cheeks, unsure how much more of this he could shoulder. 'Come on,' he urged himself, 'pull yourself together. There can't be much further to go.'

The trees in the town centre were the biggest Adrien had yet seen. Here and there people stared up at them, slack-jawed, and Adrien overheard someone suggest that the trees had grown that large to match the height of the buildings they'd replaced. He didn't like that idea, and shuddered and doubled his pace, trying not to breathe too deeply the dust-filled air. All around him, the ground floors of office buildings smoked with the ashes of their upper floors' collapse. Several men were braving the ruins to look for, as far as Adrien could tell, some folders full of papers. Two women were helping a wheezing man to walk out of another wreck of a building, his body dun with powder head to toe. 'I can't see!' he kept exclaiming. 'I can't see *anything*!'

Adrien could feel the ash settling in his own lungs and lining the insides of his nostrils. It tasted by turns like metal and paper, and he spat out as much as he could. When he got clear of the office blocks and was again among smaller buildings that had not been so crushed by their own collapsing weight, he felt perversely thankful, even for the returning smells of sap and woodland flowers.

He stopped. He stared. Then he picked his way into a building whose walls had all been lifted away like the lid of a butter dish.

It couldn't be, and yet it was. Here were the maps of Italy, now tattered and slug-tracked. Here were the magazines whose cover photos showed families lazing on beaches or in olive groves, their holiday smiles made to look leering and tasteless by their new surroundings.

The language classes Michelle had taken, and forced Adrien to attend along with her, had been her gift to herself following her big promotion. And here, still standing, covered as it was in dropped leaves and scraps of ceiling, was the very desk at which the two of them had sat. Adrien reached out and touched it, and the cool of its veneer and the right angles of its frame made it seem like some object from the distant future, beamed down to this place of tangles and jagged wood.

Adrien hadn't really wanted to learn Italian, but could hardly refuse when Michelle's gift to him had been so much more generous. 'I want you to take a career break,' she'd said. 'We'll have to be strict, but with this new job we'll have enough. You hate teaching and I can't bear to see you so miserable. Take some time, Adrien. Work out what you really want from life.'

With a grunt of dismay, Adrien staggered out of the other side of the building. *Work out what you really want from life.* How vile of chance and memory to bring that up right now, as if he had no more urgent problems. It was an easy enough ask from someone like Michelle, someone who could sit down and assess her wants and drives as if they were items on a restaurant menu, but over the course of the nearly twelve months since he'd quit the school, Adrien had made only this progress: he wanted to be a good man, ideally a great one. A man who would go down in history as the solver of some global crisis or the architect of some peace treaty (he didn't much care which). Yet he also wanted to get up late. He wanted, if at all possible, to sit for most hours of the day in his boxer shorts, eating junk food and watching leathery men spur horses between cacti. He had quickly learned to dodge Michelle's

21

question. His career-break had become one long exercise in avoiding it.

He kept on walking, and did not at first notice that he had entered a churchyard. There were no walls left to mark its boundaries but there was a graveyard in which the trees had peeled back the turf, bringing to light what lay beneath. Now bones jutted among the branches like barkless growths, and a skull gawped from the end of one bough. To Adrien's relief, these were the oldest graves. The newer ones were further off, and fresh flowers in the treetops warned against going near.

'Oh Jesus,' he mumbled, coming to a stop and wishing that Michelle had not been out of the country on this of all mornings. He couldn't wait to speak to her, even if their last conversation had been yet one more ugly row. He had no friends in this town, probably through fault of his own. After taking up Michelle's offer, he didn't even have colleagues.

'Hey!' yelled a woman, from somewhere nearby. 'Hey! Please help!'

The woman who was hailing him stood in the shadow of the church's battered steeple. Adrien headed towards her, glad in that moment to be in anyone's company. The woman didn't seem to be in any obvious danger, but as Adrien drew closer he felt that there was something odd about her, something different from all the other people he'd passed that morning. She was roughly his own age, albeit in far ruder health, with square shoulders and an abrupt jawline, and the kind of wild sun-bleached hair that came only from a life lived outdoors. The knees of her jeans were grass-stained and she wore a tatty jersey whose sleeves were too long, so that the cuffs were torn full of holes. Her face was bronzed, blunt, weathered, and her eyes were Adrien's new most-feared colour: green.

'Please help,' she asked again.

Adrien glanced ahead, towards the place where the fresh flowers hung. 'I don't know,' he said, 'whether I'm the sort of help you're looking for.'

'You're the only person who's stopped. I'd started to think that nobody would.'

Truth be told, Adrien was already wishing that he hadn't. He wanted to get clear of the trees. 'What's wrong?' he asked urgently. 'You don't look hurt.'

'We need to save the yew.'

Adrien looked around in confusion. 'I beg your pardon?'

'The graveyard yew. It's eight hundred years old.'

Behind her grew a tree so ungainly that Adrien could well believe it had lived eight centuries. Its trunk stood thicker than his arm span and its base was fattened by woody bunions. Its old bark was pronged with crooked twigs and at its highest point it split into five spines, each fraying out a spread of needled leaves. Yesterday it would have been imperious here, but today it was humbled by all the new growth. The nearest new tree, in fact, had with one muscled feeler levered half of the old yew's roots out of the ground. Now they hung limp in the air, a display cabinet of worms.

'This yew's been here longer even than the church,' said the woman. 'They're going to kill it if we don't do something.'

'Who's going to kill it?'

She gestured to the new trees towering above. 'They'll starve it. They've already blocked out all of its sunlight, and stolen all its soil. It must be some kind of mistake.'

He scratched his head. 'A mistake? Whose?'

She didn't answer that question, only assessed the roots of the yew with a determined expression. Adrien watched her with gathering suspicion. Now he knew what was different about her. She *was* distressed, but her distress was unlike anybody else's. 'You're actually *upset*, aren't you,' he began, 'because a tree is dying?'

The woman nodded, missing all of his insinuation. 'I used to come and sit here,' she said, 'on a bench. It was attached to the back of the yew. I can't even find that bench any more. I used to bring a book, or the newspaper, or just think, you know?'

Adrien licked his lips. He too had once frequented a favourite tree to read beneath, although for some reason he had long since stopped. A park chestnut, which often in the autumn would jolt him from his book with the drop of a conker. Sometimes, and only when nobody was watching (he didn't like to be thought of as childish), he used to prise apart the conker shell and collect the polished nugget from within.

'Look,' he said, 'it's just a tree. You can find a new favourite one. There are more than a few to choose from.'

She turned and glared at him. 'It's not just *any* tree. It's living history.'

Adrien took a step back, cowed by her sudden conviction. 'Sorry,' he mumbled, 'I know it's really old.'

And he did know. It was not only westerns that he watched on television. If this yew was as old as she said it was it would have been a sapling at the time of medieval kings. It would have grown fat in its infancy off soil stacked full by the bubonic plague. Troubled Catholics would have prayed around it, wondering what would become of their souls when their king rejected Rome. The crude props and theatre of the mummers would have played in its shadow, as might the fresh recited verses of a feted Elizabethan bard. It would have been marched past by the hard boots of Roundheads and the fine shoes of Cavaliers. Its leaves would have tried the first smog, sucked in the first fumes of the first factories. Young women would have sneaked into its quiet churchyard imploring heaven to keep safe their sweethearts, who ducked from the whistling artillery in the mud-sunk ditches of Europe. Time had trampled through this churchyard and left behind, as time always did, the sense that just because things had progressed, they were progressing towards a goal. For thirty seconds at least, Adrien was persuaded that it would be the right thing to save the yew. Then, gently, he said, 'Look . . . it's obviously doomed. Even if it wasn't, whatever could we hope to do? We'd have to tear down all these other trees, for a start, with diggers or something, and even then . . . just look at its roots. Too much damage has already been done. Even I can see that.'

The yew was in short supply of leaves. Those it still had grew in serried strips along the twigs, like the teeth of broken combs. Its bark was as grey and eroded as the graveyard's headstones, as if the aim of its long growth had been to turn itself into yet another monument to the dead.

'I can't bear to just give up on it,' said the woman.

'There's no shame in giving up,' said Adrien. 'I give up on all sorts of things. But . . . maybe this yew has served its time. Been around too many people. If it had a bench attached to it, well . . . that makes it almost a piece of our furniture. Maybe there's not enough *tree* in it, any more, for it to . . . for it to . . .' He looked up and around him and then snapped his mouth shut. He had been about to say *for it to be spared*, as if some judge had decreed what the forest could and could not destroy.

'Not enough tree in it any more,' repeated the woman, then simultaneously laughed and sighed. 'Maybe you're right.'

Even if she was some sort of crazy hippy, and Adrien had little time for hippies, he was pleased to have made her smile. A breeze hissed through the canopy. The yew's exposed roots shivered pitifully.

The woman nodded and turned away from the uprooted tree. At the same time a tear sped down her cheek and Adrien's pleasure turned to alarm. He had enough to worry about this morning, without a stranger crying on his shoulder, so he whipped out his hip flask and offered it to her.

'But it's eight thirty in the morning,' she said.

He took a swig of the whisky and was about to return it to his pocket when she laughed. 'That doesn't mean I don't want any.'

When she took it and her fingers touched his they were rough-skinned and warm. She drank more than he felt he had been offering, then gave it back with a grin. 'Thanks. This was kind of you.'

Adrien liked being told that he was kind.

'You must think I'm some sort of crazy hippy,' she said.

Adrien wasn't quick enough to deny it.

'That's okay,' she shrugged. 'Most people think that about me. But I'm not. My name's Hannah . . .'

'And I'm Mr Thomas,' he said by habit. 'I mean, ugh . . .' He trailed off in disgust because it was his teacher's moniker, even if it was also his surname. 'Just Adrien. Just call me Adrien.'

'Alright, Adrien, where are you headed?'

'I don't really know. I only planned to get away from my street. Out from the trees. But they just go on and on. And on.'

Hannah nodded. 'I think they might go on for ever.'

Adrien took another backward step. He didn't know what he found more disturbing: that idea, or the hopeful way in which Hannah had suggested it. He cleared his throat. 'I don't know about that. They can't go on *for ever*, can they?'

'If they can appear as suddenly as this, who knows?'

He tried not to think about it. 'I'm going to try to find a working telephone. I thought perhaps I'd try the police station. Maybe someone there will have some answers.'

'Mind if I tag along?'

Adrien hesitated. Already he was becoming dispassionate about the yew. Pleased, even, for its impending death. One less tree to fell. Likewise, he might rather be alone again now. Other people always made life so complicated.

'First I need to fetch my son,' said Hannah, as if his silence was agreement, 'and then we can head to the station. My house is only a few minutes away. Mind stopping there en route?'

Adrien did mind, but could also never bear to look ungracious, even when he felt it. He hung back a pace or two behind Hannah as she led the way. The last thing he wanted was to meet her son, and he considered dashing off. There wasn't much chance of bumping into her again, so he would never have to explain himself. The only thing that stayed him was the indignity of it.

'So,' Hannah asked as they went, 'what did you do for a living?'

For a moment Adrien wondered how she knew that he'd stopped at the school and was on a career break. Then he realised that she had simply made a correct assumption: that whatever he had done before he would not be returning to any time soon.

'Uhh . . .' he said, 'I was a teacher.'

'Wow, good on you. My dad was a music teacher, so I know a bit about that. It must be hard. Standing there in front of all those kids . . . the very idea gives me the shivers.'

'You'd get used to it,' he said, although he never really had. All those bored, pubescent faces and their intimidating chatter at the back of the class. All they wanted to do was flirt with each other and spring pranks on him.

Adrien didn't return her question as they walked, and ask Hannah what she had done for a living, simply because he was too busy being immiserated by her good cheer. Everyone else they passed looked stunned or distraught, but Hannah was in no short supply of smiles. Noticing something in the middle distance, or perhaps pausing to touch a particular leaf, her face would light up with childlike glee. Twice already she had directed the full force of that smile at him, and he had shrivelled like a bug under a lamp.

When Hannah stopped and laughed out loud it seemed the strangest sound beneath the whispered friction of the leaves. Coarse, almost vulgar, to laugh in the face of the smashed world. She was laughing at a town house whose walls the trees had carefully unshuttered. They had been pulled open like the front face of a doll's house, putting all of the rooms and fixtures on display. Slender shoots had unpicked every chair and every fitting, refurbishing them with threads of green and the occasional flower. To these a morning haul of insects had buzzed, and lured in turn countless birds of all sizes. They whirled about the building in colour and song, for in truth it was a house of perches now, fit for birds alone. Blue tits and great tits and coal tits bounced from mantelpiece to picture frame, while pigeons loped in the kitchen and chaffinches swirled through the bed chambers. On the top floor a sparrowhawk joyfully unravelled the stringy insides of a starling, while crows bobbed at its clawed feet, quarrelling for its table scraps.

'Isn't it beautiful?' asked Hannah. 'Like everything made right?'

Adrien tried his best to see it like she did, as some sort of happy restoration, but then a croaking magpie bounded out of the pantry and shook an emptied crisp packet in its beak, admiring its greased reflection in the foil.

'We've needed something like this for a long time,' whispered Hannah.

'I don't know,' said Adrien, also in a whisper. 'I really don't know about that.'

'Cheer up,' she said, and nudged him with her elbow before setting off again. He stayed put for a moment, astounded that she might demand such a thing of him. Then the magpie cawed like a vulture, and he scampered after Hannah.

The two new acquaintances moved on, leaving behind them the house full of birds. Heedless of their departure, that house's feathered tenants continued to sing that the building was their own. A rabble of sparrows squabbled over berries put forth in the master bedroom. A starling had found a snail in the bathtub and cracked its shell over and over against the enamel. The sparrowhawk on the top floor finished its meal and beat wide its wings before take-off, swooping away to leave what bones remained to the crows.

Now and then, other townspeople wandered by that house. The birds paid them no heed, although often those passersby stopped to listen to the squabble of song emitting from every floor. Thus distracted, nobody saw or heard a tiny figure, an emaciated thing no bigger than a monkey, creeping head-first down the trunk of a tree.

The figure was green and sticklike, as if it were made out of twigs and leaves. Its eyes were two round and empty sockets and its mouth was a criss-cross of thorns, giving its head the overall appearance of some squirrel or rabbit skull hewn out of wood. It moved in the stop–start fashion of a mantis, and when it reached the forest floor, raised itself on two crooked hind limbs.

The breeze blew. The forest creaked.

The little figure waddled unseen, except perhaps by a swivelling pair of avian eyes, following Adrien and Hannah.

5

Wolves

When they reached Hannah's house, she introduced Adrien to a tree that had crushed her car into sheet metal and burst rubber. To Adrien's deepening disquiet, even this did not arrest her smiles. 'Don't you think it's an improvement?' she asked, with her hands on her hips. 'I've never liked cars anyway. And the funny thing is, I've spent years trying to grow one of these in the back garden.'

Adrien scowled at the destruction. 'A tree?'

'A black poplar.'

He squinted at the plant. Its leaves like arrowheads, its bark the brown of bog water. 'You must be really pleased,' he said.

'Seb!' she called out, as she led Adrien inside. 'Sebastian!'

No reply.

'How old's your kid?'

'Sixteen.'

Adrien might have known it would be the worst age. He thought of all the sixteen-year-old boys he'd taught, their grease and zits and toilet humour. It had been despair at all that which had, in part, led him to so fear having children of his own.

They found Seb in what had once been the sitting room, but which was now a kind of cave made from plasterboard and branches. His ears were covered by a large pair of headphones and his eyes were fixated on the screen of a laptop. He was skinny and pale, and either his T-shirt was too small for him or else his arms were too long, or both.

'Hey,' said Hannah, 'hey, Seb.'

Seb didn't hear beneath the headphones.

Hannah made her way across the room, but before she reached her son his laptop beeped a battery warning. Seb stared horrified at the red light that accompanied the noise.

'Come on,' said Hannah. 'We're going to the police station.'

'What?' Seb asked. 'Why?'

'To find things out.'

'Okay . . . I'll be right with you, Mum.' But he neither moved nor looked away from the screen.

'I liked it better before computers had batteries,' said Hannah, turning to Adrien. 'When I could just pull the bloody plug out if I needed his attention.'

Adrien laughed awkwardly. He too was at odds with technology, although he maintained that technology had started it. He moved closer until he could see the laptop's screen. The boy was copying files onto a memory stick, muttering, 'Come on, come on,' as a progress bar inched towards completion.

'Seb,' said Hannah, 'this is Adrien. I met him this morning.'

For a horrified moment, when Seb looked up, Adrien thought the boy recognised him. His mind filled with the mugshots of all the teenage boys he'd taught in recent years, but he did not catch Seb's among them. Then the boy gave a distracted nod, said, 'Oh, hi,' and returned his attention to the screen, on which the animated hourglass kept spilling its digital sand.

Adrien cleared his throat, relieved not to have to be Mr Thomas. 'Um, hello, Sebastian. I don't suppose you have an Internet connection on that thing? Or any way to contact people? My wife is in Ireland.'

Seb shook his head balefully. 'The Internet's down. Everything's down.'

'Oh,' said Adrien. 'Oh, that's a shame.'

The laptop's progress bar crawled. Hannah, restless, gazed through the empty window frame at the world without. She had changed subtly since the moment they'd entered the house. Her smiles had left her and she'd begun to fidget. When a squirrel ran a helix along a branch, she half-reached in its direction. Then she turned back to her son with renewed impatience. 'We should be outdoors. We should be experiencing this.'

Seb only looked aghast. 'All I want,' he said, touching the memory stick as if it were a charm, 'is to save my stuff. And then you can have me.'

'You can do it later.'

'There's hardly any battery left, Mum!'

'I don't think it will take very long,' offered Adrien, at which Seb glanced up at him gratefully. Adrien wasn't about to start empathising with teenage boys, that much was certain, but he could not help but think of all his own photographs and videos, and documents kept like household junk, every electric memento reduced now to the thin reality of a powerless chip-set. After he had left his job he had, as one of his projects to distract himself from that awful assignment Michelle had given him and then funded ('Work out what you really want from life . . .'), scanned and digitised every old snap and film from his past so that he could file away in the attic yesteryear's cumbersome albums and video cassettes. He wondered what had become of those hard copies. Probably flung out through the roof by branches.

'Ready yet?' asked Hannah.

'One more minute,' whispered Seb, and the laptop immediately beeped. With a downward whirr it powered off, and Seb groaned and pressed the *on* button. The laptop powered up but died again before it had booted. With the next press nothing changed and Seb covered his face with his hands.

'Come on,' said Hannah. 'Put your shoes on.'

Glumly, the boy unplugged and pocketed his memory stick. Adrien offered him a sympathetic shrug, but Hannah had already found Seb's shoes and was handing them to him to drag on. When they left the house, she didn't bother to lock the front door behind them.

Outside the police station a single mounted officer did all he could to placate both his shying horse and the gathering crowd. They had come still in their night hair and faces, packing into the gaps between the trees so that Adrien had to go up on tiptoe to see the policeman and his flustered animal. Behind them a squad car lay smashed against the entrance to the station, its chassis smeared with mud and leaves. Much of the rest of the building had been carried high into the branches, where the early morning sun found the hard square windows of the cell doors.

The officer was a young man, not far into his twenties, doing his best to yell answers to the crowd's questions. What had happened that morning? He did not know. How much of the town had been affected? All of it, as far as he could tell, and as much of the area beyond as anyone had ventured to. Where was the council or the government or the United Nations, and what were they going to do about this? He did not know.

Adrien tried to elbow his way forward, to hear things better, but then a man shouted something in a high pitch that turned every head. A middle-aged businessman in suit and spectacles clawed his way towards the policeman. He stopped when faced with the horse, which stamped and puffed hot breath into his face. 'I saw it!' he exclaimed, poking his glasses up his nose, 'hardly an hour ago!'

The businessman was shaking, so the policeman raised a calming hand. 'Steady,' he said, to horse and man both. 'What did you see?'

'A . . . a . . .' The man wrung his fingers and looked from side to side as if with stage fright. 'A wolf!'

The horse swung sideways and its hooves clopped against the broken road and it took all the policeman's efforts to calm it. While he struggled, the businessman raised both arms aloft to the crowd, his tie askew beneath his unbuttoned collar and his shirt untucked and ripped in several places. 'A wolf!' he yelled. 'A wolf!'

Many among the crowd whimpered. A child was crying, and Adrien felt like joining in. Yet the leaves shook soothingly overhead and the policeman brought his horse under control. 'Calm down,' he ordered. 'It was probably just somebody's dog. I saw a fair few running loose as I rode here.'

One or two of the crowd concurred in murmurs. 'Too big!' proclaimed the businessman, then again raised his arms to shout, 'A wolf! A wolf!'

Eventually someone took his hand and he was led away, glancing left and right as if something still prowled out there between the trunks. Hannah grinned at Adrien, and he hoped like hell it was because she found the idea of a wolf improbable, not exciting. He did what he could to smile back, because he didn't want to look cowardly, but he wished somebody would take his hand and lead him away as they had the businessman. He could well believe in wolves and bears now, and who knew what other beasts besides, stalking through the darkness under the trees.

'Go home,' the policeman advised the crowd. 'I know nothing more than you do. Return at the same time tomorrow and I'll pass on whatever I can learn between now and then. Ration your food and tell your neighbours to do the same. It may be some days before we can begin to fix this.'

'They're not going to fix this,' muttered Seb as he, Hannah and Adrien left the police station.

'They might,' protested Adrien, although he was beginning to believe otherwise.

Seb shook his head. 'They're fooling themselves if they think that can be done.'

Hannah put an arm around her son and gave him a sideways squeeze. 'Don't worry, Seb. They might not need to *do* anything. I know this all feels . . . I know it feels scary, but give it time and we might see a blessing in disguise.'

'People have died,' said Adrien, with a touch of indignation. 'My next-door neighbour was impaled by a branch.'

Hannah frowned. 'Oh . . . I'm sorry, Adrien, I didn't mean to sound flippant. I mean, I know people have died, and I'm sorry about your neighbour. I'm just . . . trying to see the bigger picture, that's all.'

'You're not the only one,' proclaimed Adrien, 'and all I can see is endless bloody trees!'

33

'Mum, you heard what the policeman said. The whole town is covered. Didn't you hear that man who said he'd ridden here from his village, on his bike? He said it was all forest, all the way in.'

Hannah nodded, not even slightly alarmed. 'Who knows? Maybe the trees have covered the whole country.'

Adrien tensed. 'You sound like you *want* that.'

'All I'm saying is that it could have been something much worse.'

'What could possibly have been worse than this?'

'When nature gave her answer,' Hannah said simply, 'to all the things going wrong.'

Adrien cleared his throat. He might have no choice concerning the trees, but lunatic hippies and teenage boys were the two things he needed least in a disaster of this magnitude. 'I'm very tired,' he announced in a tight voice. 'I think I'm going home now. It was nice to meet you both.'

'Oh.' Hannah looked disappointed. 'Well we could come with you as far as—'

'No! No need to trouble yourselves.'

'But you said you live in—'

'Bank Street, yes. Which is in the other direction to your place.'

'Is it? I thought that was not so far from us.'

'I should know,' Adrien insisted. 'I'm the one who lives there.'

Hannah nodded slowly. 'Ri–ight. Okay. Well . . . sorry. Um, and good luck. And goodbye, I suppose.'

'Adrien . . .' It was Seb.

'Yes?'

'Have you got enough food?'

The boy sounded genuinely concerned, but Adrien didn't let his expression betray that no, actually, he had next to nothing in his kitchen, and that was why he had been living off takeaway since Michelle went to Ireland. At the mere thought of food, his stomach gave a conspicuous rumble. He hoped neither of them had heard. 'I'll be just fine, thank you,' he said,

34

'On our way here you said you hadn't eaten breakfast . . .'

'All the more reason to head back now.' He waved at them force-fully. 'Nice to meet you!'

And with that he turned and marched away.

Instead of walking straight home, Adrien headed to the nearest supermarket, reasoning that if people in faraway places were allowed to go looting in the wakes of typhoons and tidal waves, he was allowed to do so now. If he could just get one decent meal inside him, he might find the fortitude to confront the awful thought teasing his mind: if the forest covered more than just the town, if the forest stretched on for such a long long way, how was he going to contact Michelle?

He wondered if she knew yet about what had happened. Perhaps she was sitting, even now, in her hotel room in Ireland, dressed in the business attire she always managed to make look artful, ready for a day at her conference, watching the news on the television. Somewhere in the middle of England, the reporter would say, a horrid little town had been pulverised overnight by a forest. And then she would recognise it as her town, and think at once of all the people she knew there, and of her husband, and then . . .

And then he was not sure what she would think.

Adrien groaned and hung his head, ashamed of how he'd behaved on the morning that Michelle had left for this trip. She'd woken him on the sofa, where he'd slept the night, and after he'd rubbed his eyes he'd seen that she was already wearing her work clothes, with her packed suitcase at her side.

'I'm going now,' she'd said. 'I've got to catch my plane.'

As steadily as the daylight, Adrien had begun to remember every hurtful thing he'd shouted the night before. Yet Michelle's posture, and the way she'd just hovered there as if there were one last thing she'd forgotten to pack, had suggested she wanted to make peace before she left.

Adrien had rolled over and faced the cushions, and not said a word.

The supermarket was already full of people, all bustling and squeezing for their ransacking. They bumped and dragged trolleys over the busted tarmac of the car park, none of the goods in them bagged. One man's collection of wines reassured Adrien that nothing had been paid for either, and when he joined the press of bodies inside he shouldered his way first towards the off-licence aisle. To his dismay this had been emptied entirely, although it still stank of alcohol drained from smashed bottles. Adrien moved on, through all of the aisles above which the roof had not caved in. Nigh on everything had already been taken, and most of what remained had overflowed from earlier looters' spoils, or tipped off the shelves and been trampled against the floor. A bent old man fought his back to collect trodden beans. A child, egged on by her father, crawled with frightened concentration into a cold grotto of freezer compartments, where the twigs dangled with glass as if it were a hoarfrost.

When at last the tide of looters flowed him out of the supermarket, Adrien's only trophy was a sack of ice cubes, its contents melted into bagged slush. He told himself that any clean water was a godsend, but his gut clenched with hunger and disappointment.

He got lost three times on his way back home. The world looked so different now, and the vegetation seemed to distort paths and turn straight ways crooked. When he finally found his house, he supposed he ought to be grateful. It had survived the forest's coming far better than most, and in his kitchen there were even cupboards still mounted on the walls. All he could find in them, however, were packets of flour and sugar, and one out-of-date cereal bar. He ate the bar immediately, curled up into a single soft morsel, then washed it down with half the slushed ice cubes, which he'd poured into a mug.

Many times Michelle had suggested he grow vegetables in their garden, and now he dearly wished he had done so. She had even cleared the space for him, a few years ago, unearthing and replanting the flowers she had tended there before, choosing him the best fertiliser and bordering the plot with stones selected on a trip to the seashore. In a garden centre they had purchased the seeds and the bulbs, and he'd fed off her excitement at imagining their first crop. 'By day we can garden together,' she'd said, 'and in the evening eat the vegetables you've grown.'

But on his first attempt at tending them he had put down the trowel and looked at the dirt lining the creases of his palms and thought how precious and fleeting life was, and how he worked long hours all week in a job he loathed and that the sole reason for doing that, as far as he could tell, was to receive a salary that enabled him to purchase and not farm his own food. How he hated gardening. The falseness of it. Digging out a weed because it wasn't pretty enough. Coming upon the slugs who had melted after digesting pellets. One time blindly reaching into a spray of withered daffodils and finding a bird bleeding to death from someone's pet cat. 'Mother Nature is a psychopath,' he'd told Michelle, 'and I won't spend my weekends on my hands and knees, painting her toenails.'

'Now you say that,' she'd said, tears springing down her cheeks, 'after we've been to so much trouble. What else are you only pretending to enjoy?'

In his ruined kitchen, Adrien took off his glasses and wiped his eyes with his sleeve. He understood full well that he'd been an awful husband. What he had never understood, and in fact still could not, was why Michelle had stuck with him for so long.

Leaves dangled from the kitchen's light fittings, and Adrien could see up to the bathroom through a hole in the ceiling. He discovered that he had, absent-mindedly, reached across and begun to play with a protruding branch. It had broken through the wall behind the cooker, pushed open the oven door and unfurled as if it were something baked there.

Adrien plucked one of its leaves and tried to eat it, but it tasted bitter as pith. He spat it out and washed the taste away, then noticed which mug he was drinking from and didn't know whether to smile or to cry. Michelle had brought it back from her last big trip, as a jokey kind of present. *Kisses from Egypt*, read the caption, and the picture was a close-up of a camel's slobbering mouth.

Adrien was just about to take another sip when he saw, standing in the kitchen doorway, a figure made out of sticks and leaves.

It was no more than a foot tall, with an oversized head that weighed to its left. For a face it had only a deformed knot of wood with a hollow in it, which might have been a single eye socket or a mouth. Its ears were two tatty leaves, angled towards him as if listening.

Adrien yelped and on instinct flung the mug at the monster. Yet no sooner had the handle left his grip than he realised his mistake. The breeze, blowing in through smashed openings, sifted apart the figure's body. It was nothing but a chance arrangement of twigs and greenery, and the mug missed it and shattered off the door-frame, water spraying in every direction.

Adrien stood motionless for a minute, biting on his thumb. Then he tiptoed over to the mound of sticks and nudged it with his foot. It was as innocent a collection of natural litter as might be found anywhere in any forest.

'Nothing to be worried about,' he told himself, although, for some reason, he still was. He unscrewed the cap of his hip flask and sniffed the remaining contents with suspicion. Then he downed them, and began to wish he had not scorned the company of Hannah and her son.

6

Whisperers

Hannah was just a little girl when she fell in love with the woods.

One summer of pale sun days, when the light hung plentiful and brittle but never warm, her parents took her and Zach for what would prove to be their final family holiday. The journey was a time-stretching, seat-rattling voyage from traffic jam to traffic jam, onto the motorways and the dual carriageways and at last the country lanes, beyond which the trees lay in wait.

Of course Hannah had left the city before that. She had watched the countryside pass by en route to grandparents, uncles and aunts who lived in other towns. She had spent a few weekends at the seaside, instantly disliking the slabs that were the ocean and the blunt cliffs, along with the sand that she found in her clothes for days to come. Her last time there she had stood on the beach with her hands on her hips, blowing raspberries at the water, resolute that she hated oceans and was a city girl with an urban heart.

Yet that summer, in the forest surrounding a petite cottage blushing with dog roses, she'd had her first chance to *roam*. The same was true for Zach, and he took on the role of her guide in the wild. While their mother sipped wine and reclined in the cottage garden, and their father tinkled the keys of the piano that took up half the floor space in the sitting room, Hannah and Zach were free to claw their way from bush to bush, to snap off what flowers and cones they fancied and to be scratched and stung in return, to choose from an endless supply the best broken branches to use as adventurers' staves. In the afternoons they carried hatfuls of nuts and berries back to the cottage and their mother would hum and hah as she consulted a guidebook and threw some fruits away and washed others at the sink and declared them fit to eat. They climbed taller and taller trees, not even thinking about falling, sitting side by side on high branches and swinging their legs in unison. They built a den out of fallen timber and, when they returned to it the next morning, found a weasel preening there before it hopped away, with each leap bending its spine as curved as a horseshoe. Then, in the evenings, they would sit on the floor and watch the log fire crackling, and recount all they had seen that day, and their father would coax long beautiful melodies out of the piano, and their mother would watch him adoringly, trying not to blink and miss a note.

Although Zach kept a watchful eye on his sister, he was never condescending or brusque, as other girls' older brothers could be. That summer he led her through that arboreal realm hung with that month's eerie light, and stood at her side in a fairy ring of red toadstools, and marvelled with her when she found a magpie's nest with an earring and a tin soldier and a silver key inside. Hannah kept that key in her pocket from that moment forth, trying it now and then in cracks in the bark.

On the last day of that holiday, feeling something like grief about leaving, Hannah asked Zach if fairies dwelt in the woods. To her surprise, he abandoned his usual pragmatism and paused to consider it. 'Fairies, huh?' he said, and looked around as if he might actually spot one. 'I dunno, Hannah. Little people dressed in flowers just don't seem like nature's thing.'

'I didn't mean like *that*. I just meant . . . you know . . . I meant . . . that if Mother Nature had servants, what would they be? And I thought they might live in a wood like this.'

Zach mulled it over for a minute, then said, 'There are already such things, Hannah. Right *here*.'

He pointed to the ground, then swept his hand away to their left, where against a tree an ants' nest was stacked. Back and forth from it ran a trail of the tiny insects, oblivious to Hannah and Zach's shoes in their path.

'Ants,' said Hannah, disappointed.

'These and the worms,' said Zach. 'And the bees and the spiders and all the other bugs. Servants, just like you said.'

Those words of her brother's had stuck with Hannah down the years, although she'd never really known why. Perhaps, like so many memories of that fortnight with her family, it had wedged in her mind because that holiday had been their last. During the December that followed, Hannah's mother was murdered.

All these years later it was still hard to even think it. Murdered. Hannah's mother was still the bravest and most confident woman Hannah had ever known. After spending the first half of her career rising up through the ranks of a shipping company, she had ended up well paid but dissatisfied. Never one to sit back and indulge her frustrations, she had quit her job and become an aid worker, and brought her logistical expertise to bear on delivering help wherever it was needed. That December she had been abroad, travelling with a mobile vaccination station. She was due home on the twenty-third, the day after the Yuletide concert in which Hannah's father always played. When that concert came around, Hannah and Zach sat in the audience unaccompanied by any adult, feeling terribly grown up for doing so. They applauded the hardest in the hall when their father took his bows, for they knew how nervous he had always been about performing, and how only their mother could calm him.

The news came when they arrived home that night. The telephone was ringing when they opened the front door, and their father picked up the receiver with his bow tie undone and a smile still on his face. Then the smile faded, and faded further, and never truly reappeared.

The leaves of the brand-new forest fanned in a roving breeze. Hannah roved too, wandering through the woodland, the magic of its sudden appearance tempered only by the long distance between her and her brother. Even though she felt guilty for admitting it, she would have loved to be sharing these days with Zach instead of Seb. Zach would see the good in it and delight in being at her side, whereas her son just wanted to hide in the shell of their house. Hannah had run out of energy trying to persuade Seb of the forest's grandeur. Even as a small boy, when she had painted his room into a jungle the envy of his peers, he had sought out only the nearest screen. On every camping trip he'd treated every hike, every firefly she'd helped him capture in a jar, every tree she'd cajoled him to climb, every wild animal she'd performed her impression of, as she might treat a night in front of the computer. He had politely pretended that he did not find it all a colossal waste of time.

She worried about him often, especially when rising waters were mentioned on the news, or the death of a species announced, or noises made about ice caps slipping into oceans. She thought of Seb leaning over his laptop, and what kind of world he was growing himself up in. And when the news brought tales of louder disasters, and to her shame Hannah found them easy to forget in her day-to-day rush, she feared a flood or a tidal wave of heart-stopping magnitude sweeping through the landscapes of Seb's future, and him having simply no idea of how to cope.

And *that* was why she could not help but see some hope in the coming of the trees. They were as much a promise as they were an apocalypse, and she had the means to show Seb how to live amongst them.

Hannah had been letting her feet lead her, and in so doing had wandered into a building that until two days before had been a post office. Larches queued in it now, their crowns ruffling full of envelopes. Occasionally a letter, sparrow-brown or white as a dove, flapped free of the twigs that held it and sped off on the breeze, while beneath it on the forest floor the parcels and bubble-wrapped packages sat in flightless heaps. The tills had been smashed open, but other than that it didn't look as if anyone had been in here since the trees came. Anyone human, that was . . .

Three portly forest hogs were nosing through the mounds of parcels to get to the soil beneath. Hannah could not help but clasp her hands and grin as she watched them, laughing 'Pignuts!' when she saw what they were unearthing. As if to prove her right, one hog looked up at her with a joyful squeal, and she saw white kernels mushed across its tusks.

For years now, Zach had kept pigs outside his lodge in the forest. Hannah had greedily learned all she could about them, wishing she had a way to tend her own. These three were of a smaller species than his, coloured and patterned like fat little fawns, and Hannah supposed they were escapees from someone's private paddock, since they were nothing like large enough to be livestock. For a happy moment she entertained the notion that they were some wilder breed, restored just like the elms from a bygone era.

Holding her breath, she crept closer to the pigs, who continued to dig unheeding. Soon she was within touching distance where, resisting the urge to reach out to stroke, she crouched alongside them. A burping sow was to her left and a squealer to her right, and she joined in as they combed the soil. Her fingers passed through soft dirt already raked by the animals, until simultaneously she found a pignut in her left hand and a roll of posting tape in her right. The pignut must have been overlooked by the hogs, so she offered it to the nearest one as a thank you for letting her take part in its sport. As if there were no reason on earth to be fearful of humans, the hog grubbed it off her palm. Its damp, tickling whiskers sent a thrill shooting up her arm.

When, eventually, Hannah left the hogs and strode onward through the town, she didn't wipe her hand clean. She let the strands of the hog's slobber dry against her skin, thickening as they cooled, reminders of the curly-tailed friends she had made that morning. She was in no hurry, and often paused at the sound of some other animal passing through the undergrowth or shaking the branches. She called out hellos to squirrels and birds aplenty, and one time when she thought she saw something thinner passing

43

overhead, stopped to try to see it better. After five quiet minutes there had been no further sign of it. She didn't think she'd imagined it, although she'd also thought it had moved on two legs, and *that* had to have been imagination. She had the suspicion that, whatever it was, it was still up there, camouflaged and watching, but she left it to its privacy and walked on beneath evergreens and birches, limes and oaks, until she came to Bank Street, where Adrien lived.

'Oh,' Adrien gasped, when he answered his door. 'Hannah, it's you!'

He had a breadknife clenched in his fist, bags under his eyes, and was wearing a shirt creased as crepe paper, which nevertheless he had buttoned all the way up to his collar and tucked into his trousers. Hannah did her best not to laugh. 'I've not come to mug you,' she said. 'I found your house number in the address book. Actually I've come to apologise.'

Adrien looked confused. 'For what?'

'For pissing you off yesterday. I sometimes let my enthusiasm get the better of me.'

Adrien shook his head, and laid down the knife. 'Forget about it, honestly. *I* sometimes let my lack of enthusiasm get the better of me. Do come in. Please come in.'

His house was not quite as wrecked as her own, but his efforts to repair it seemed to have made matters worse. After Hannah had followed him inside, he pushed shut the door and turned the key in the lock. Again Hannah suppressed a smile, although Adrien would never have noticed it, mesmerised as he was by the contents of the paper bag she was carrying.

'I brought you some food,' she said, and offered it to him.

The bag was full of knobbly apples that had dropped from a tree in her garden. They were some of the best Hannah had ever tasted, with a crisp flavour like a glass of white wine. Along with them was a piece of cake wrapped in film, which Adrien lifted out in trembling grip.

'This is . . . this is all for me?' he asked.

'Of course. Actually, only the apples are from me. The cake is really from Seb.'

He stared at her for a moment as if she were playing some trick. '*Seb* baked this?'

'Is that surprising? It's a few days old, but it should still taste alright.'

'No, it's just . . .'

'Seb's not an obvious baker, I suppose.' She felt a pang of pride over her son. 'He's actually really good at lots of things, once he gets away from the bloody Internet.'

Adrien licked his lips, and Hannah could hear his stomach growling.

'Do you mind if I . . . ?' he began.

Hannah grinned and nodded. Adrien tore off the film, beneath which the cake glistened with buttery moisture. He shoved it towards his mouth as if to eat the whole slice in one bite, then instead restrained himself to make it last, chewing with his eyes closed and relief wrinkling his forehead.

When he had finished (and picked every crumb off the film, and licked each finger) he selected an apple and gazed at it as if it were an orb of gold.

'I know,' she laughed. 'Can you believe it?'

'In what?'

'These apples!'

'Er . . . I suppose I can, yes. Why is that so strange?' He looked at the apple with sudden distrust. 'Wait . . . what are you saying? That these apples are . . . new?'

'If by that you're asking me whether the apple tree that dropped them wasn't in my garden before yesterday, then yes, they're new. But what's amazing is that the trees don't seem to know what season it is. Coming here I've seen some in blossom and some in fruit! I guess you can hardly blame them. They've not been around long enough to know any better.'

'I think I do, actually. Do blame them. For plenty of things already. But, umm . . . thank you. For thinking of me. I suppose you're wondering what happened to all that food I said I had?'

She shrugged. She had her suspicions.

'Umm . . .' he said, rubbing the back of his neck. 'The thing is . . . urrrh . . . I sort of . . . miscalculated. Turned out I had less than I thought I had. Turned out that I, actually . . . that I lied. Sorry.'

She laughed. 'You've no need to apologise. We all want to be self-sufficient.'

'Well . . . yes, I suppose . . . I suppose that's one way of looking at it, yes. All the same, it's very kind of you to bring me this. Especially now that food is going to be so hard to come by.'

'We've a whole forest's worth of food to eat now. Don't worry so much. Nature will provide.'

She was about to mention the cluster of mushrooms that had already bulged up through the cracks in Adrien's floorboards, but he followed her glance, and the sight of them made him look queasy. 'Well then,' she said, 'are you going to the police station again today?'

'I guess so. The officer said he'd be back. Perhaps he'll tell us what to do.'

'Bet you he's not going to be there.'

Adrien looked alarmed. 'But he said he would be!'

'He won't. People are going to realise that they can't use telephones or emails or anything like that to reach their loved ones. They're going to have to go and *find* them. That's what Seb and I will be doing, anyway.'

'You . . . you're leaving town?' There was a forlorn tinge to his voice.

'You're sweet, Adrien. And yes, we're leaving.'

'Where for?'

'My brother's house. It's something like a fortnight's walk west of here. Zach's a forester. He'll have taken all this in his stride.'

Adrien nodded grimly. 'So . . . this is goodbye, I suppose. And . . . and all the best. Although I'm sure you'll fare far better than me. I'm quite certain I shall be eaten alive.'

She watched him for a moment. 'Forgive me for bringing this back up, but . . . it doesn't have to be such a disaster.'

This time Adrien didn't bite back. He only looked grey with worry and reminded her, in doing so, of her fraught-hearted father. Perhaps that was why she felt so sorry for him.

'Adrien, how about . . . how about I give you a field guide? I've got loads, and I'd only be leaving them to rot on my bookshelves. It'll show you what you can eat and what's poisonous.'

'That would be very kind of you,' Adrien said glumly. 'Books are something I *can* understand.'

'I could give it to you tonight.'

'But you said you were leaving for your brother's house.'

'That's tomorrow. Today we've got a few goodbyes to try to say, and bags to pack, then tonight we're going to cook whatever food we can't take with us. Should be quite a feast. I built a clay oven in the garden last summer and have barely had the time to use it. Somehow it's survived, so . . . what do you say? Would you come over for dinner, to wish us on our way?'

When Adrien arrived at Hannah's house that evening, wearing a tie along with his creased shirt, Hannah covered her mouth with the back of her hand, and bit hard on her lip to stop herself from giggling. 'Hello,' she said, 'come inside. Wow! You have turned out smartly!'

'Well, you know,' Adrien huffed, 'you didn't specify a dress code. I didn't want to look out of place. And I'm sorry I couldn't bring you a bottle of wine or anything. I got you this instead.'

It was a tiny sapling, inexpertly dug up and replanted so that it leaned from the pot at a wonky angle. 'I saved it,' said Adrien, 'from my neighbour's garden. She . . . wasn't going to miss it.'

'An apple tree!' Hannah took it from him. 'That's very sweet of you. Come through and I'll show you its new big sister.'

He followed her across the remains of the ground floor, which she had enjoyed clearing of all her smashed furniture. When she looked back at him he blushed, caught in the act of loosening his collar and untucking his shirt. She suspected that he actually rather liked wearing a tie, just as her father had used to. Her father had always said that it helped him feel held together.

Seb greeted them in the back garden, and Adrien met him with a grimacing sort of smile and mumbled, 'Thanks, uhh . . . for the cake.'

'Glad you liked it,' said Seb, then gestured to a picnic rug laid out on the ground. 'Have a seat.'

Adrien hesitated, then did as he'd been asked, while over them all the giant apple tree held court, its limbs ample and wide, as if it were the true host there that evening. While Adrien settled beneath it, Hannah opened a box of matches and struck one into life. With this she lit a candle, then drifted between several glass lanterns she'd already hung from the surrounding branches. In each was another candle, soon winking with light and kindling the yellow out of the apples hanging on the tree. She stepped back and admired the effect, which befitted a warm evening that smelled of sugar and charcoal. Only when she turned back to the others did she see Adrien fidgeting and glancing from flame to flame, and Seb inspecting his knuckles, absolutely unenchanted by the lights.

'Er . . .' Adrien began, 'er . . . is that safe? I mean, might not those candles cause a forest fire?'

Hannah laughed. 'This is a temperate forest, Adrien. You could attack these trees with a flamethrower and they wouldn't burn down. They're full of water.'

Adrien arched his neck to look at the surrounding plant life. 'Michelle always used to insist on having candles at dinner,' he said. 'I had to blow them out when she wasn't looking.'

'Michelle was your wife, wasn't she?' asked Seb, suddenly gaining some interest.

'Still is,' said Adrien, frowning.

'Oh . . . sorry. Something about the way you said it made me think you two were—'

Adrien shook his head quickly. 'Still is.'

'Well I can promise you,' said Hannah, 'that there'll be no raging infernos this evening. The closest thing you'll get to that is in my cooker.'

48

Nearer to the house stood the clay oven Hannah had built. When she opened it, out shone a rosy glow that played across the roots and scattered leaves. From amid this heat, she removed char-cooked sweetcorn, and kebabs of aubergine and marrow, bracketed with roasted peppers and red onions.

'We're vegetarians,' explained Hannah, 'did I mention that before?'

'Er . . . no,' said Adrien, a carnivore's disappointment writ large across his face. 'But of course you are, of course. And that's fine. Of course it is.'

Hannah allowed herself a private smile, having seen expressions such as his a thousand times before. She would let her recipes do the persuading.

Seb served up, and while they ate, Hannah kept sneaking looks at Adrien, who was evidently astounded. The molten flesh beneath the black blistered skin of the vegetables tasted too good to leave room for any talking. Adrien finished first, almost gasping for more.

'Help yourself,' laughed Hannah. 'There's no need to go hungry.'

Adrien did just that, and after he had eaten another portion as large as his first, they all reclined satisfied in the flickering light. Adrien asked what Hannah had done for a living, and she told him about the nursery, five miles south of the town, where she'd tended the contents of plots and greenhouses and helped grow bright flowers to supply to florists.

'So that's why you're so at ease with all this,' he remarked. 'You had green fingers, all along.'

'Maybe,' Hannah said, 'although I suppose I have felt, for a long time, like I've been . . . waiting for something. And now . . . here we are. A restart. All we have to do is make the best of it.'

Adrien looked unconvinced but, before Hannah could try to reassure him, Seb changed the subject.

'So,' began the boy, 'are you going to tell us where she is?'

'Where who is?' asked Adrien.

'Michelle.'

'Oh.' His face fell. 'Michelle is in Ireland.'

'Ouch. That must be tough.'

'Yes . . . I'd really hoped to have spoken to her by now, but there's still no phone signal. No way at all to make contact.'

'I'm sure she's trying to reach you, even now,' said Seb.

'Maybe. It would be nice to think so.'

'If you could just get some signal, you'd see all the missed calls and the messages she's left you.'

'Unless,' suggested Hannah, 'the trees have appeared in Ireland too.'

Adrien turned to her, looking mortified. 'Do you really think they've spread that far?'

Hannah did, but wished at once she hadn't said so. 'I might be wrong,' she backtracked. 'Sorry, Adrien, I know that was the last thing you wanted to hear. Sometimes I don't think before I open my mouth.'

'It's okay,' said Adrien.

'But if you don't mind me asking . . . what are you going to do?'

'Do? How am I supposed to do anything? I just have to wait. Until people fix things.'

'But how long will you give it? How many mornings will you go back to the police station and wait for help to show up?'

'I . . . I . . . *pfff*. How many will it take?'

'Was the policeman there today, like you thought he'd be?'

After a moment, Adrien shook his head.

'Listen,' she said, as gently as she could, 'you can't stay here much longer. Things are going to get worse before they get better. There are going to be problems with sewage, disease, all that stuff. We need to get out, into the proper forest.'

Adrien looked alarmed. 'The proper forest? What the hell is *this* one?'

'I mean the one that's grown up beyond the town. The one that isn't full of all our old junk.'

He shook his head. 'There's not going to be a phone line out there, either.'

Hannah conceded that, although she was serious about her warning. She had tried to deliver such advice to several neighbours that day, but all were too shocked by the trees' arrival, too busy salvaging what remained of their lives, to pay her any heed.

'I don't know,' said Adrien. 'I'm not really the sort for it. I'll just . . . just batten down the hatches and—'

'Go west, then,' interrupted Seb. 'At least you'd be going towards her.'

Adrien flapped a hand dismissively. 'Come off it. Michelle is in Ireland.'

'Which is west of here.'

Adrien sighed. 'Look . . . it's more complicated than that. If, uhh . . . even if I found a way to speak to Michelle . . .'

Hannah and Seb both waited, but Adrien didn't continue.

'Even if you could,' Seb concluded, after a minute, 'the two of you aren't really speaking.'

Adrien nodded. 'You could put it that way.'

'How bad is it?'

'The last time we saw each other, we didn't talk at all. I mean, Michelle tried, but I . . . I was still angry. At myself, as much as anything. The night before that we'd argued, you see. We've been arguing more and more. For, uhh . . . quite a while.'

'What are your arguments about?' asked Hannah.

Adrien took a deep breath. Maybe it was just the way the candles cast their lights, but Hannah thought she saw tears forming on his eyelids. 'Me,' he said. 'Me, mostly. What I'm doing with my life.'

'And what are you doing?' asked Seb.

Adrien gave a short, artificial laugh. 'If I could answer that question, there might not be arguments.'

Seb raised an eyebrow. 'So she picks a fight with you about that?'

Adrien wagged a finger. 'No, no, she doesn't pick a fight. She only tries to help.'

There was an awkward silence, during which Adrien stared into his wine glass. Then he took a swig and gave another artificial laugh. 'You two don't want to hear about this. It'll bore you both to tears. Why don't you tell me what *you're* going to do? You said you were going to find . . . Zach, was it?'

'Yes,' said Hannah. 'My brother. He'll have hardly even noticed this has happened.'

'And where does he live, then?'

'West of here. He's west of here, like Michelle is.'

Hannah tried to catch Seb's eye, but Seb was watching Adrien too closely. She hoped her son would support her in what she was about to suggest. She couldn't bear how defeated Adrien looked by his predicament. He seemed very prone to despair, and she knew all about that. Despair was a pit her father had flung himself into. It was one of the great regrets of Hannah's life that she had been too young at the time to lift him back out.

'Adrien,' she said, 'why don't you come with us?'

He frowned. 'I beg your pardon?'

'Come with us. West. Towards Zach. Sometimes having something to head towards makes everything else seem clearer.'

Now at last she caught Seb's eye, hoping that he didn't object. He only looked thoughtful, and beyond that she couldn't read his expression.

'I couldn't possibly,' said Adrien, sounding stunned. 'You said you were leaving tomorrow.'

'That's right. Is that a problem?'

'Well . . . I haven't planned for it. I haven't worked out all the particulars.'

'There's not a lot of planning you can do. Pack a bag and you're ready.'

Adrien shuffled about uncomfortably. 'You'd think that, wouldn't you? You'd think it would be that easy. But, uhh . . . when actually you start getting into the nitty-gritty of *any* journey . . . suffice to say that you need to put some hours in, to make sure you're prepped for every eventuality.'

Seb cleared his throat. 'I know it's scary. But I think you should go one step further.'

'What does that mean?'

'Don't just come with us. Go and find Michelle.'

Hannah clapped her hands, and was delighted with her son.

'But . . . that's simply impossible,' said Adrien. 'There's the Irish Sea between us, for one thing.'

'Cross it,' said Seb.

Adrien looked seasick at the very proposition, but Hannah couldn't stop smiling. Sometimes, just when she thought Seb was made out of wires and circuit boards, he came up with ideas so romantic that she wanted to throw her arms around him and bury a kiss in his hair. Were he only her little boy again, the one he had been not so many years ago, she would have done so there and then.

Adrien still looked perturbed, and Hannah did not want to put him off. 'You don't have to do anything, of course,' she said. 'Only think about it. But it would be no trouble for us. We'll call past your place before we leave, about nine in the morning. It's en route anyway. Then, if you've decided you can come, we'll all head west together.'

7

Forest Law

There was no way on earth that he was going with them. That was what Adrien told himself as he hurried home, clumsy from the wine, through woods very dark. No, he would not be leaving with Hannah and Seb, no matter how easy they made the journey sound. He didn't have it in him. Michelle was the driven one, the one in whose nature it was to try to fix things. Adrien was the one who tried to weather life from the safety of his armchair, or a thoughtful stroll around the block, or a long evening bath until the water got cold.

Throughout the wooded ruins of the town, campfires were burning. Some were so far off that the tree trunks hid their flames and their lights showed only in faint circles, strung across the distance like particles of lens flare. Some were nearer and roaring, and at one such blaze Adrien paused, hidden behind a tree, and listened for a moment to those gathered there arguing over who best deserved a sleeping bag. They came to blows a moment later, while around them the lazy embers left their fire and settled sometimes on the bark before winking out. That was one more reason, he thought as he scurried away, why he should not go with Hannah. They would end up arguing, probably over something he'd done. Everybody argued, in the end, even lovers who had taken oaths. Adrien did not think he could bear any more arguments in his life.

The fires were more frequent in the town's main shopping streets, but Adrien felt like he was walking through a refugee camp. The newly homeless had congregated here with what possessions they had salvaged, and now sat in the firelight covering their faces when the smoke rolled towards them. Above them hung the stock of the high street. There were all kinds of clothes, torn to ribbons. There were coat hangers clinking against twigs. There were upturned fast food fryers, whose cooking fat had poured down the bark and cooled there into a lard that glistened back at the flames.

When Adrien came to the end of the road, and had just passed its final campfire, he heard something whisper overhead. He'd grown used to the hushed tones of the foliage, so why this one sound stopped him in his tracks and raised the hairs on his neck he could not tell. Then, when it started again, he realised that it wasn't coming from throughout the treetops, like the noise of the leaves normally did. It was coming from a single point, directly above him.

He didn't know whether he even wanted to look up. The whisper was a sandpaper song of rustles and tiny exhalations. Hardly the intimidating growl of a wolf or even a dog, but something about it made Adrien sweat all the same. He looked around and saw, not a stone's throw behind him, five young men trying to roast a bird on their fire. He should be safe enough, with them nearby. After taking a deep breath, he looked up.

A thousand eyes stared back down at him.

Adrien instinctively raised his arms to protect himself, but the treetops were full of too many glinting stares to oppose. From every twig they watched him, and some even peered out from cracks in the trunks. He staggered backwards, full of cold adrenalin, trying to find the coordination to turn and run. Then, from behind him, there came a deep and echoing laughter.

It was the men at the campfire, who were watching him with glee. A moment later, their firelight found a piece of broken signage in the branches above. The first letter was missing, but the rest spelled *pticians*, and no sooner had Adrien read it than all of the eyes in the branches became squares and circles of glass. He hung his head and wanted to sink into the dirt with embarrassment. When he trudged away, the sniggers of the men followed him into the darkness, and only when he had gone some distance and the night could hide his blushes did he begin to feel uneasy all over again. What he had seen might have been nothing but spectacles, but he had never heard of any spectacles that *whispered*.

Back home that night, lying in the spare bed because he could not access his own, Adrien tried to think of anything but wolves and whispers. He thought about Hannah, and wished he had the courage to prettify the ruins of *his* house with candles in glass lamps. He wished he had the knowledge to build an outdoor oven that could roast vegetables as satisfying as hers, but as soon as he imagined himself doing so he imagined the flames escaping. In an instant he was engulfed in a forest fire, choking on smoke, waiting for the brilliant blaze to consume him.

'Sleep,' he chided himself, slapping his cheeks. 'Think about something *good*.'

He thought about Michelle, and tried to guess what she'd be doing right now. No doubt, if what Hannah seemed to hope for was true and the trees had appeared in Ireland, Michelle would be busy rescuing people. Perhaps she would even be planning to rescue him. Unless . . .

Adrien had not told Hannah and Seb about Roland. There was no way to do so without feeling humiliated. Laughing, handsome Roland, who even now would be with Michelle in Ireland. He was her supervisor, a man with a soft Irish accent and eyes full of cool intellect, who had pushed hard for her big promotion and insisted she accompany him to all those thrice-accursed conferences. Adrien had met him at her work's Christmas dinner party, one of those yawn-inducing occasions to which 'better' halves were invited, and sat in silence eating cabbage while the bastard openly flirted with his wife. He had no evidence that the two were now conducting an affair, but he suspected it regardless because, were he in Michelle's place and offered a choice between an unemployed, overweight no-hoper and a chiselled charmer whose life was just so goddamned put together, he knew what he would choose.

'*Sleep!*' he hissed, and slapped his cheeks again. Yet the house was darker than ever he'd known it, and its walls full of cracks and new entrances. He began to wish he had curled up by one of the fires in the high street, for it seemed like lunacy to want to be unconscious, all alone and hidden away in his house. He felt like a sacrifice laid on an altar, plump and juicy for any wolf to accept.

Something clattered against the windowsill and he sat bolt upright and stared in its direction. He could see nothing but trees and stars, but he did not find that reassuring. As a child he'd been an avid stargazer, but tonight they only reminded him of the winking glasses he had mistaken for eyes. When nothing further moved on the sill, he persuaded himself that the clatter was only the branches of a tree, and lay back down with a sorrowful exhalation. 'How the hell am I ever supposed to sleep again?' he asked of the night. Then his nostrils started to twitch. What was that smell? Was that the musk of *fur*? Or was that just himself, sweaty with fear? 'Nothing,' he said to himself, 'it's nothing. Just go to sleep.'

The leaves whispered, indoors and out. The forest was a hundred unoiled hinges. Yet at some point Adrien must have slipped out of consciousness, for later he woke with a start from a nightmare and beheld a high moon whose white glow filtered through the canopy. He gazed through bleary eyes out of the window, as the foliage puckered for the lunar light, and thought for a moment that he saw something small and bow-legged standing on the sill. Then his nightmare reached out to reclaim him, and he sank willingly into its embrace.

A knocking on his door in the morning. Hannah and Seb were fifteen minutes earlier than they'd said they'd be.

'So you're coming!' Hannah said happily, when she saw Adrien's packed bags lying in the hallway.

'Err,' said Adrien, after a deep breath, 'I think I might be, yes.'

He had climbed out of bed that morning with fear congealed in his stomach and lungs. Then he had realised that he had no choice. He wasn't brave enough to lie at home night after night, hoping that when at last he heard footsteps in his room they were Michelle's and not a wolf's. That didn't mean he was going all the way to Ireland, certainly not, but he could set off west with Hannah and travel as far as her brother. Perhaps he could even stay with him there, for as long as he could get away with, and learn a thing or two about woodcraft from Zach (already Adrien had pictured himself with an axe slung over his shoulders, sauntering beneath the trees as fearlessly as he imagined the forester doing). Then, when it was time to move on, he would wave his goodbyes and *look* like he was the brave husband striking west, only to loop back on himself and return here, by which point he was sure the government or the army or whoever it was would have made some progress towards putting the world back together.

Packing had been tough. The things he'd always said he could not travel without were a freshly pressed shirt, some polished shoes, a slim briefcase and a Shakespeare, but now they all seemed redundant. He did not own walking boots, so he had chosen his never-used jogging trainers. As for clothes, he had no idea how long it would take to walk to Zach's and he supposed he would have to find the means to do laundry en route. Seven pairs of everything seemed about right. Seven favourite shirts (a pity they couldn't be ironed), seven pairs of briefs, a spare pair of briefs, seven pairs of socks, a spare shirt, two spare T-shirts to be on the safe side, two pairs of corduroy trousers because he wasn't sure which shade he preferred and did not want regrets, a spare pair of jeans (he would set out in his other pair) and four sweaters of varying thicknesses. Added to this a wash bag containing shower gel (he pictured himself showering beneath waterfalls), toothpaste, comb, soap, shampoo, razor, shaving brush and stick, then plasters in case his jogging shoes blistered while he broke in their heels. As an afterthought his eye-mask for sleeping, and of course a pillow, and his sleeping bag and a spare blanket in case the sleeping bag proved too thin.

He had managed, with the aid of some stamping and swearing, to squeeze all of these things into a backpack and the biggest holdall he owned. He couldn't help but notice that Hannah and Seb each wore only one small rucksack, but neither passed comment on his luggage.

'Right then,' said Adrien, and clapped his hands. 'I suppose I'm ready.'

'I'm really pleased you're coming with us,' said Hannah, and turned to lead the way down the garden path. Adrien, however, did not move. Hannah and Seb looked back at him from the roadside. 'What's wrong?' called Hannah. 'Have you forgotten something?'

Adrien looked back over his shoulder at the tatters of his house. Not a lot had survived of his hallway, except for a floor clock inherited from his father, which Michelle had always hated with a passion. Adrien hadn't much cared for it either, but had insisted that they keep it out of some troubled sense of duty. Now he was in love with it. He was in love with the torn-up carpet and the hanging strips of wallpaper. Of course he would be coming back, he knew he would. He and Michelle would be living here again before too long. Yet the start of this journey felt more like an end than a beginning.

'Okay,' he puffed, 'okay.' And he followed Hannah.

Both the town and the woods were quiet that morning. Where, in the days before, they had been filled with cries and sobbing and the sounds of things crashing into the dirt, now there was just the simmer of the leaves, and grey faces watching the three new travellers without expression as they passed. Adrien's final sight of the place where he had lived for so many years was an electricity hub fished off the ground, dangling its cables like a jellyfish caught in a net. Then the town was gone, and he was walking after Hannah down a ruined route of tarmac, and trees were leaning over him from every direction.

'We've got a choice,' said Hannah, 'of two ways to do this. One is to follow the roads, and I've packed a road atlas for doing just that. The other way, the better one I think, is to use my compass and try to travel as the crow flies.'

'We'll get lost if we do that,' said Seb immediately.

'Not if we stick to the compass. We want to go almost due west, anyway. Going in a straight line would be quickest.'

'There'll be rivers and things. We'll get stuck.'

Hannah flapped another map she'd brought with her. 'We can use this one to find the crossings. It won't be hard, I promise.'

'What do you think, Adrien?' asked Seb. 'I think we should stay on the roads.'

Adrien swallowed. He had absolutely no desire to plunge at once into the deeper forest and leave all signs of civilisation, but nor did he want to look like a coward. He was grateful to Seb for doing the fretting for him.

'I don't want you to be uncomfortable,' he assured the boy, 'so I think we should stick to the roads for now.'

Hannah didn't try to hide her disappointment. 'I suppose I'm outvoted,' she said, 'but let me know if you change your minds.'

They followed the coloured lines of the road atlas west. Sometimes they overtook fellow groups of evacuees, although more commonly they only heard them, for the forest grew too tangled to see far ahead or behind. Disembodied voices reached them often, snatches of conversation heard beneath the wind that rippled the leaves, and sometimes they were sure they were about to catch up with a large group of travellers only for the voices to fall silent for another hour or more. More frequent than the wandering living were the stationary dead. They marked the road like milestones, some stuck to the steering wheels or doors of vehicles that had burned black, others still strapped in their seats wherever their cars had collided with risen trunks. Several times Adrien had to pause and hold his head at the sight of them, waiting longer each time for the cold and dizzy feelings to pass.

That their deaths went so undisguised was his only protection. Afforded no dignity or final respects, their passage neither recorded nor relayed to their loved ones, sometimes the dead seemed too unreal to have been actual people. If, however, some identifying mark was on display, be it a wedding ring or the contents of a handbag turned out by a carrion animal, Adrien would skip on past as quickly as he could, and focus on keeping his stomach in check.

Progress was slow, mostly because of Adrien's luggage. His rucksack weighed him down and his holdall unbalanced him whenever he shifted it grip-to-grip. How the hell, he wondered, did explorers travel the length and breadth of deserts and arctic wastes? Bastards had husky dogs, he supposed.

Eventually Hannah stopped him. 'Adrien, you shouldn't be carrying this much.'

'Thank you,' he said, impressed by her kindness. 'It's very good of you to offer. Perhaps if you could each put just three or four of my things into your packs . . .'

'No, Adrien. Seb and I have already got the tent and the sleeping bags, the cooking gear and the rest of it. I meant that you should leave some stuff behind.'

He gaped around him at the trees. 'What? Here on the road? How would I ever find it again?'

'You wouldn't.'

'But . . . these are my things!'

'And yours to dispose of. Do you really need, for example, that pair of polished shoes dangling from your straps?'

He hung his head. Then, item by painful item, he set aside over half of his luggage, and the holdall itself, piling everything neatly at the foot of a tree. 'Although I don't know,' he moaned, 'whether I'll have enough clothes to get by. We'll need to do laundry in the next few days, else I'll have nothing left to wear.'

'We'll make what we've got last longer than that. We can rinse stuff in a river when we cross one. Don't look so horrified. It's your own smell, Adrien, and nothing to be ashamed of.'

61

They pressed on, and it was true that Adrien found things easier with a lighter load. The road became even grimmer as the day warmed, and in places they walked with their sleeves across their noses and mouths. They all stopped mid-stride when the bloodied driver of a minibus lurched out of his seat and raised an arm to hail them, but a moment later they realised he was just another traveller, with a bandaged wound in his arm. He said he had been resting on the padded seat, and was heading from another town towards their own. After they had bid him farewell and good luck, Hannah turned to the others and said, 'Are you still sure you want to do this on the roads? It will be much less gruesome going cross-country.'

Adrien and Seb remained unwilling. 'I'm scared, to be honest with you,' admitted Seb, and Adrien was grateful not to have to say so too.

Resolved as they were to stick to the road, it seemed that in places the road itself had other ideas. For long stretches it was broken into so many pieces that it was hard to discern its original contours. Slabs of tarmac lay scattered in every direction like the slates of some volcanic wasteland, or wedged sometimes into tree trunks like hard black fungi. In one such place there was no sign of anything but the woods, until Adrien felt something wet splatter his hand. He was surprised to find a streak of white liquid dribbling over his knuckles, and when he looked up saw a milk tanker groaning in the branches. They walked in the direction it had been driving, and both Adrien and Seb sighed with relief when they again saw bent lampposts and some cat's-eyes still embedded in asphalted ground.

Another hour passed. Fairy-tufts of cotton began to blow out of the deeper forest, swirling round their heads without ever alighting. Then Hannah stopped in her tracks and clapped her hands. 'Oh my *God*. Look!'

Without warning, she swerved off the road. Adrien and Seb did their best to follow, while she raced over a driveway and then a fence flattened against the earth. Beyond it they found themselves surrounded by flowers at every level, not only on the forest floor but strung like bunting through the canopy. None of them grew wild, every stem belonging to a flowerpot or grow-bag held at a jaunty angle by the branches.

'This,' Hannah explained, gesturing to all the colour, 'is where I work.'

The nursery had consisted of a wide yard and car park, then three ranks of greenhouses and polytunnels. The panes had been smashed from the greenhouses and their frames swatted against the tree trunks, leaving legs of metal dangling from the bark. 'I didn't recognise it,' she laughed, 'I thought we must have missed it.'

She carried on into the middle of the nursery, turning around and around with her neck arched to better take in the destruction. 'Ten years,' she said. 'That's how long I worked here!'

'I'm sorry,' said Adrien. 'It must be hard to see all that effort gone to waste.'

Hannah laughed. 'Don't be silly! Do you think I liked it that much? I mean, I used to, but . . . last year we got a new boss, and she and I had . . . differences of opinion.'

'You hated her,' clarified Seb.

'I didn't *hate* her, Seb. Diane is just . . . she just . . . started to put profit above everything.'

'Doing what's good for business,' shrugged Adrien.

'She put all the flowers into rectangles. Red flowers over there, yellow over there, just blocks and blocks in neat rows. Before Diane we grew all sorts of things, wherever they grew best. Even if we made a few hundred pounds less each year, we still made enough to get by.'

Adrien had to admit that the trees appeared to prefer Hannah's system. They had jumbled all of the nursery's flowers into a jarring mess of colour.

'Is there anything you want from here, Mum?' asked Seb.

'No,' said Hannah, 'let's leave it as it is.'

'What about that bike? Who does that belong to?'

Adrien and Hannah turned to look in the direction Seb was pointing. A bicycle with a wicker basket leaned against a tree

63

trunk, and at the sight of it Hannah's breath caught. 'That's Diane's bike!' she said, then headed towards it.

'Diane?' she called out. 'Diane, are you here? Hello, Diane? It's Hannah!'

'Mum . . .' said Seb, urgently. He had not followed her towards the bike. Instead he was pointing at something else now, and his arm was shaking.

It was Diane.

She lay in the shade of a hornbeam tree, a curly redhead with one or two locks of grey in her mane. Now her hair was the only way to identify her.

Adrien shut his eyes, but it made hardly any difference. The sight before him had seared itself instantaneously into his mind. A crow cawed overhead, and with that sound revulsion kicked in. Adrien veered away and clung to a tree trunk for support, his fingernails digging into the bark. He vomited across its roots, then vomited a second time.

He did not know what possessed him to turn and look again. Perhaps it was that same disbelief that he'd felt at the horrors along the road, perhaps some sort of need to pay respects. Hannah was looking, too, and Seb had his arms wrapped around her.

Diane's body had been opened wide as a flower, with her bones its jutting stamens. It was obvious that there was less of her than there should have been, although pieces of something streaked the undergrowth.

'Wh-what . . .' began Adrien, under his breath.

Hannah gave a long, dry groan and gripped Seb's arm for support.

'What's happened?' asked Adrien, louder this time.

'Eaten,' said Hannah, very quietly.

'Eaten?' gasped Adrien.

Hannah held one hand to her head. 'It must have been wolves.'

Adrien thought at once of the businessman outside the police station, who had claimed he'd seen a wolf running through the forest, just hours after the trees came.

64

'Diane!' sobbed Hannah, crumpling up so quickly that it was all Seb could do to lower her gently to the ground. The boy crouched with his arms around his mother, to block her view of the body, but at once Hannah strained to look over his shoulder and gave another anguished cry.

'Don't look,' whispered Seb urgently, while strands of Diane's hair blew against the roots. 'Don't look, Mum.'

All Adrien could say was, 'Wolves . . .'

'We should get out of here,' said Seb.

Hannah shook her head. 'We have to do something for Diane.'

'Seb's right,' said Adrien, coming to his senses. 'Let's just go.'

'But . . . we've got to bury her or something.'

'We can't,' said Adrien, grabbing up his bag.

'We have to! We can't leave her like this!'

'No, Mum,' insisted Seb.

'We'll pay our respects somewhere else,' said Adrien, and with that Seb pulled Hannah back to her feet. They retraced their steps, back through what had been the nursery's car park towards the road. None of them spoke, but Adrien could tell that the other two were likewise listening to the noises of the forest, and praying not to hear a growl or gruff bark among them. They kept their heads down and moved as briskly as they could. Every bright flower was a reminder of the red they had just witnessed. Every tree was a thing of bones beneath its costume of foliage.

'This isn't right,' said Seb, stopping after a few minutes.

'Don't stop,' pleaded Adrien. 'Let's just get back to the road.'

Seb shook his head. 'I mean . . . this is wrong. The way we're headed. We never came this way.'

'We did,' said Hannah, checking the compass. 'We have to have done.'

Adrien had been so preoccupied with what he'd just seen that only now did he realise they were walking on soil. They had crossed a tarmac driveway and a car park to get to the nursery, but had trodden on nothing but dirt on their return. 'It doesn't matter,' he said. 'The road *has* to be in this direction.'

They kept walking, but after a few more minutes had seen not an inch of tarmac.

'You know your way, right?' Adrien asked Hannah. 'I mean, you said you'd worked here for ten years . . .'

Hannah looked like someone coming down with a fever. 'Of course I know my way.'

They kept walking. No road appeared, nor any sign of one.

'We've got to go back,' said Seb. 'We must have walked in the wrong direction.'

'We can't have,' said Hannah, looking again at the compass.

'But we've been walking for ten minutes now.'

Hannah chewed her lip and looked at the woods to left and right. 'We should have seen something. There was a construction yard next to us. There were farm buildings.'

'We've missed them,' said Adrien. 'We've just missed them, because we're too preoccupied. It's understandable. Let's just keep going, and get away from where the wolves were.'

They set off again, but after a further ten minutes had found not one single piece of asphalt. It was all roots and dirt and dead leaves.

'I don't recognise this,' muttered Hannah. 'Not any of it.'

Adrien listened to the noises of the woods, his entire body primed with fear. He could feel it tingling on his flesh like static electricity. Any second now, he expected to hear a bone-chilling howl.

It did not come, but neither did the road.

8

Unicorn

The three travellers' only option was to follow their compass west. They saw nothing but woodland for the rest of the day, and no other walkers and no built things of any kind. By the time the light began to fade it was difficult to tell what kind of progress they had made, and they pitched their tent in uneasy silence.

That first night of their journey was full of strange hoots and cries, as if every nocturnal being was celebrating the trees' arrival. The forest creaked like an antique stage, and now and then a screech or a snort came so loud that it sounded as if it were underneath the canvas with them.

Hannah lay wide awake, her sleeping bag still open, trying to process what had happened to Diane. She listened to Seb's breathing as it gradually steadied towards sleep, then to Adrien as he adjusted and readjusted his sleeping mask until he too caved in to dreams. After that, she listened to the busy gnats and insects outside the tent, then to a single childlike scream from a vixen. All the while, all that she thought about was wolves. How they could go for days without a kill. How when at last they fed they did so in a frenzy, gorging on every last morsel. They didn't even wait for their prey to die. They ate as soon as it was defenceless.

Hannah might never have seen eye-to-eye with Diane, but she would not have wished her fate on anybody. It made her feel cowardly that her memory had already sanitised much of that awful scene. Her mind had blanked what scraps the wolves had overlooked, so that Diane was nothing but a redheaded wig and a tattered, empty outfit. It was as if she had left behind her hair and clothes, vacated them for a world less cruel than this.

How heartless, Hannah thought, she must have sounded in these last few days. All those poor men and women along the road, burned and broken, while she had just prattled away about how beautiful the woods were. She hadn't a religious bone in her body, but she felt a sinful sort of guilt at not having buried Diane. They should have at least said some words. They should have turned back for the town and sought out Gareth, Diane's husband. 'Does he even know?' Hannah whispered to the night. 'Is he even still alive?'

Suddenly unable to bear the confines of the tent, Hannah grabbed her coat and let herself out, barefoot into the night. For the first time since the trees had arrived, since she'd rushed to find Seb with her whole world in the balance, she felt shaken. Adrien was *right* to be as petrified as he was. Seb was right to want to stay on the road.

With the cloud cover keeping the woods very dark, Hannah's feet were her only way of knowing the world. The grass beneath her soles felt like damp hair, and each root was a bone massaged through skin. A deathly whisper passed through the leaves of tree after tree, and when a thistle sparked the tip of Hannah's toe she hopped away from it with a sharp intake of breath.

It took some time for her eyes to accustom to the darkness, and even then she could only faintly make out the worming lines of the branches surrounding her. She wondered what Zach would say about Diane's death, and whether he was awake or asleep in his part of this forest. She could at least smile to think that, in a few days' times, she and Seb would be reunited with him.

As if in sympathy with that hopeful thought, a firefly lit up the bulb of its tail. Then another began to shine, and another. In less than a minute the undergrowth was twinkling with miniature lights, but Hannah folded her arms and refused to be moved. Diane would never see such sights again.

The fireflies' light was not very powerful, and could only illuminate other fragile things. It showed off the blur of a flying bug, or the shimmering weave of a spiderweb, or in one place both: a silver moth imprisoned in thread. When Hannah stepped closer, the moth's eight-legged captor fled out of sight, but Hannah guessed it had not run far. It would be watching from the edge of vision, waiting to devour its prey alive.

It was a plump enough spider to forgo this one meal. Hannah reached out finger and thumb and broke the links of the silk. The moth stepped into her waiting hand and preened itself on her palm, its antennae soft and white as pillow feathers.

The moon split the clouds and the woods were splashed as silver as the moth. With a puff of Hannah's breath the insect took to the air. It darted left then right, then upwards. Just when she expected it to vanish it came to another flapping halt, opening and closing its wings several times. Their pattern was a woman's eyes, and the mascara was running.

Weightless as the light, the moth took off again and looped twice around Hannah's head, tickling her ear. She did not allow herself to smile, even when a breeze combed the branches and the trees, like the insect, seemed to beckon her to follow.

She found a smooth seat on a log, and lowered herself onto it to try to think of some fitting way to remember Diane. Without prayer to believe in, some time in silent contemplation was the best she could offer, yet she found with frustration that none of her thoughts would stay still. They strayed from Diane's death to another, and Hannah bowed her head when they did so.

There had been three press photographs of the site of her mother's murder. She and Zach had seen them only many years later, for their father wanted the two of them to be older before he showed them his copies. When he did so he confessed that he had looked at them far too often in the intervening years, out of a failed hope that to do so could help confront what had happened. Grainy and monochrome, they were not at all gory. The bodies of Hannah's mother and her two colleagues had been removed and all you could see was the aid truck parked at an angle across the dusty road. In the first and second photographs, if you leaned in close, you could just make out the bullet holes in the truck's doors and windshield. In the third you could not, but that picture had always seemed to Hannah the most violent. It showed the open back of the vehicle, to demonstrate what had been stolen, but unintentionally the photographer had captured a lizard as it basked on a roadside rock. It was a tiny animal, hardly in focus, but that it could be so relaxed in that place as to sunbathe had filled Hannah with an unexpected fury.

After showing them those pictures, her father found it impossible to discuss them, but she and Zach had done so often. Over the course of years, and many conversations, her brother had convinced her to see that third photo in a new light. 'Who knows what a lizard thinks?' he'd said once. 'But when I look at it I'm glad it's there.'

'Not me,' Hannah had replied. 'How can it just carry on as if nothing has happened?'

'Carrying on is what nature does,' said Zach. 'And that, I find, is about the only thing I have any faith in.'

Something brushed Hannah's hair, and she looked up with a startle. The moon was retreating behind the clouds and the woods were again too shadowy to see details, but when she heard a whirr of wings stop suddenly on her shoulder, there was no question that the moth had returned. It took off once more, and looped away down the same route it had taken before. The last of the moonlight traced the forest floor in that direction, and Hannah fancied that it lit up a trail, perhaps made by badgers or deer. She stood up and followed.

She saw no further signs of the moth as she went, but soon heard running water. Then the trees parted wide enough to see a hurrying brook, and the moon came out again and its waters took glittering leaps over pebbles and dead branches. The closed heads of white flowers lined the far bank, and dotted the undergrowth as far as Hannah could see.

She froze.

There was a gigantic animal on the other side of the water.

Asleep under the gloom cast by a willow, it was an enormous beast the like of which she had never before seen. Even though the leaves drooped around it and their shade concealed much of its body, Hannah could tell from the steady rise and fall of the animal's ribs that it was no boulder or misshapen log. It had the bulk of a rhinoceros, and at first Hannah tried to persuade herself that it must be one, escaped from a zoo. Yet instead of leathery skin it was covered in a long pelt of fur like that of Highland cattle, and instead of the armoured neck of a rhino it had something longer and more elegant like a horse's. Its face was hidden in the grass, but Hannah could hear the rhythmic growl of its breathing and a grinding rumble from its stomach. A breeze rippled the willow leaves and white moonlight dappled the beast's coat. Only then did Hannah see its horn. More like a dorsal fin than a tusk, it grew from the animal's nose jagged and slender. At the sight of it Hannah could not help but clasp her hands to her head, not out of fear but out of wonder. If she had ever seen anything like this, it was in some picture book of giant animals extinct since the Ice Age.

To her own great surprise, Hannah felt oddly at ease in the company of this beast. Perhaps that was due to how deeply it slumbered, as if it had been dreaming beneath that willow for millennia. Forgetting all else, she let herself admire it, and as the minutes passed she did not move or think, only beheld. When at last a thought came, it was a clear one and untangled. Bestial things and beautiful things could be as one, she thought. Indeed, until they had found Diane she had always believed that wolves were beautiful creatures. Now, looking at the massive animal snoring on the other side of the stream, she knew she still did. She hoped the ghost of Diane would forgive her, but she could accept that the wolves had only done what the world had made them to do.

Hannah settled down on the bank. The waters of the brook sang to her. For an hour or more she sat there, gazing at the horned animal. Then, too gradually to notice, she drifted off to sleep.

Next morning the animal was gone, but Hannah's spirits were restored. They packed down the tent and followed the compass through woodland just like that of the previous day, with no buildings and no fellow travellers in it. Hannah said nothing of what she had seen, suspecting that the boys would think it only something new to be afraid of, but that didn't stop her from smiling whenever she recalled it.

Many trees they passed that morning were heavy with fruit, so Hannah stopped to shake their branches and gather up everything that dropped. Other trees looked as if they had burst from the ground in deep autumn, dank pillars of bark that bulged all over with fungi and lumpen mushrooms. These too Hannah harvested, breaking off slabs of mould the colour of crusts. 'Wonderful,' she whispered to herself, and wrapped them up in a spare T-shirt.

At noon they came upon a road, and Adrien looked so grateful that Hannah half expected him to kneel and kiss the tarmac. For her own part she gave a quiet sigh, as if a cloud had covered the sun. 'I never want to let this out of my sight,' Adrien said, raising his finger with a flourish, 'Never, ever, *ever*.'

Seb seemed inclined to agree to that, but Hannah thought again of the horned animal she had seen, and wished they had chanced upon *that* instead of yet more crushed cars and tarmac.

Soon they met a large group of walkers following the road in the opposite direction. Hannah stopped to make conversation with some of them, trying to ascertain where they'd come from and what lay ahead. Most said they'd only set out a few hours before, having abandoned a nearby town. 'Everybody's leaving,' explained one woman. 'Everyone who can, at least.'

Upon finding out the name of the place, Hannah reopened the road atlas that had been so useless in the deep forest, and after a minute of searching found their coordinates.

'Wow,' said Seb, once they had taken it in. 'That doesn't make any sense at all.'

'And yet here we are,' marvelled Hannah.

Adrien said nothing, only looked ill.

Their position was some fifteen miles west of where they had begun their journey. That in itself was of no great surprise, but according to the map they had crossed both a motorway and a gushing river. They had seen neither.

A few hours later, they reached the town that everybody was departing. It didn't take long to understand why. 'Our town will probably be the same by now,' explained Hannah. 'This one just looks a lot worse because we've already spent two days in the woods.'

In every street, sinkholes had opened in the ground. These were places where so many roots had stuffed the soil that it had collapsed, and into such pits the trees had tossed the remnants of the buildings. Sewage had risen to mush the earth and stinking pools of it lay everywhere, as did lampposts bent like jewellery wire and spaghetti piles of cables tugged out of the ground. A tall statue of some famous son of the town lay face-down in the dirt, and here and there were less monumental bodies. Some of them had been draped by a conscientious curtain or sheet. Others had not.

Hannah led them at a brisk pace, and they covered their noses to avoid breathing the rot and faeces. What townspeople they saw were packing their things, but many buildings already seemed deserted, save by rats and droning flies. On the main road out of the town, a steady exodus trudged west. The road was an avenue of tacky soil trodden deep by so many passing footsteps, and among the obstacles the worst were the people themselves. They sweated and struggled to push wheelbarrows and shopping carts full of their possessions across tall roots and through mud that sucked at wheels, while others carried as much in their packs as Adrien had when first he'd set out. Everybody delayed everybody else, and at times they moved so slowly that they might have been queuing.

'None of them know what's coming to them,' whispered Adrien. 'They think it's going to be so goddamned easy to get where they're going. And then — *poooff!* — the forest will vanish the path out from under them!'

'You needn't be so pessimistic,' said Hannah. 'We've still made good progress west, haven't we? I hadn't begun even to work out how we'd cross that river, and now the woods have arranged things so we never have to.'

Adrien's mouth opened and closed in disbelief, but Seb was the one to respond. 'We won't find Zach's lodge this way, Mum.'

'What makes you think that?'

'Because the compass can only get us close. After that we'll need the landmarks on our maps to actually exist.'

'Let's just try to have a little faith,' said Hannah. 'And, for now, why don't we take a shortcut? This is like being in a traffic jam.'

They headed down a side street, then took another after that, choosing in accordance with the compass. Along the way their feet found, always with a telltale crunch, everyday objects half-buried in the leaves. A toothbrush with dirty bristles, a phone charger still plugged into its phone, the front half of a kettle with its spout raised like the tail of a cat, a tin of black shoe polish, a candle. Upon the trees' arrival all things had been divided between junk and treasure, and the candle Seb grabbed and showed them like a trophy. Adrien pulled a disgusted face when he saw it, and turned away as if it were a lump of gristle.

'Thank God that's over,' said Hannah, when they finally left the town behind them. At once the air freshened, and they could look around without fear of the dead.

'Don't get too excited,' said Seb, who was trying to make sense of where they were on the road atlas. 'There's another town not far from here, and slap bang on our route.'

'Cross your fingers, then,' Hannah grinned, 'that we never see it, just like we never saw that motorway or river.'

Neither Seb nor Adrien laughed along with her, so she sighed and led the way along a quiet route that had once been a country road, high-banked and meandering beneath beech trees. They followed it for an hour until, without warning, it terminated. Hannah only noticed when she'd taken a few steps on softer footing, but when she looked back Adrien and Seb were

74

stationary on the last foot of tarmac, both staring at the soil beyond as if it were hot coals. 'There was a junction not ten minutes ago,' Adrien said. 'Why don't we go back there and take the other path?'

'That junction led north,' said Hannah.

'The last time we left the road we were swallowed up by these bloody woods. I say we were lucky to get out again. Let's just go back and follow the paths we know. So what if it heads north? There'll be another after that. One of them will go west, eventually. Roads join up. That's what roads do.'

Hannah sighed and looked into the woods. 'It just doesn't feel like we have a choice.'

'Of course we have a choice,' huffed Adrien.

'But if the trees want to take the road away, I don't see—'

'The trees don't *want* anything,' snapped Adrien. 'They can't, because they're trees.'

'I didn't really mean the plants themselves,' said Hannah, trying to keep her voice even. 'I meant the forest.'

Adrien held up one shaking forefinger. 'The *forest* doesn't want anything, either! The forest . . . the forest is just a bloody plural!'

Seb stepped between them with his hands raised. 'I'd rather not leave the road, either,' he said, 'but I'm starting to think Mum's right about us having no choice. Why don't we just vote on what to do? There are three of us, so we can't fail to get a majority. All those in favour of leaving the road . . . ?'

Hannah raised her hand victoriously, assuming she had Seb's support.

'All those for staying on it . . .' said Seb, and raised his hand alongside Adrien's.

'That settles it, then,' said Adrien gleefully, and spun on his heels to march back the way they'd come.

Hannah crossed her arms and glared at Seb, whispering, 'Why did you just trick me? Can't you ever try to see things my way?'

Seb looked back at her with an expression of such weary impatience that Hannah felt as if *she* was the child being reprimanded.

'Give me a chance, Mum. This is the best way to see if you're right.'

'But now we're going to have to go all the way back to—'

'Give me a chance,' he repeated, and with that set off after Adrien.

They had only been retracing their path for a few minutes before the road vanished again. Adrien drew to a sudden halt at the end of it, then took a few backward steps. 'Wait . . .' he began. 'This can't be happening. We just walked this way.'

Seb laid a hand on his shoulder. 'It's because of the forest,' he said.

Adrien stared at the earth as if willing a road to materialise out of it. Then, after a minute of looking close to tears, he gripped tight the straps of his rucksack and said, in a tiny voice, 'Oh bloody hell. I wish I was braver.'

'You already are,' said Seb, turning him around. 'Now come on. Back the way the compass shows.'

They headed west again. Hannah shot a smile at Seb when Adrien wasn't looking, but her son looked no happier than Adrien. She didn't know what to make of it. During the last year especially, she'd got used to Seb changing at an almost daily rate, be it in his height, his voice or shoe size. This was a different kind of maturity. She couldn't decide whether she thought it was a good thing.

Unlike the last time they had lost the road, this time they saw occasional reminders of civilisation. When they came upon a lattice of steel bars that filled a glade from root to treetop, they didn't at first understand what they were seeing. The branches had grown in and out of the laddered metal, sometimes wrapping themselves around it like hands around rungs. Then Seb spotted a yellow sign with a picture of a zigzag striking a man in the chest, and Hannah said at once, 'It's a pylon.'

'And it still goes up,' said Adrien, as if that were some sort of victory.

After that they saw only forest for several hours, but come evening they arrived at a country cottage abandoned by its owners.

Two muscular trees had demolished the place, although they grew on either side of the building. Where their boughs had met they had done so like the punches of boxers, and remained outstretched in jabs and hooks. The cottage's centremost rooms had been bludgeoned the hardest, but there was shelter to be had in half a sitting room, secure on the leftmost side of the house. Agreeing to stay for the night, they made themselves comfortable on the sofa and two armchairs. From the moment they did so they felt exhausted from walking, and as a breeze blew and the glassy remains of a ceiling lamp tinkled, one by one they fell asleep on the furniture.

9

Whisperers

The moon rose gradually into the night sky, and after some hours had climbed high enough to peek its light into the cottage where the three travellers slept. Many leaves stroked against the ruins, sometimes coming loose and drifting lazily downwards, until they came to rest on the sitting room floor. Neither Adrien, Hannah nor Seb noticed. Theirs was a deep sleep, and they did not even stir when some prey animal screeched in its death throes, somewhere not too far from the cottage.

A tree trunk groaned. A slug bunched and stretched across the floor. Then paws came padding, and a hedgehog snuffled along the trail of the slug. It grabbed hold of it and ate it like a slice of watermelon, taking its time to slurp up all the good slime and now and then push the slug back straight when it tried to curl up and protect itself. It ate until a badger grunted outside, upon which it immediately abandoned its meal and fled in the opposite direction.

Time passed. The slug died. The night conducted its affairs with growls, hisses and cool silence. Then, from one of the cottage's shadowy recesses, there came a sound as of paper being scrunched into a ball. Another sound followed, this time something like fingernails scraping over a board. The leaves held their breath. Onto the moonlit sitting room floor came a far stranger creature than a hedgehog or a badger. It stood no taller than a foot, but moved with the bent difficulty of the very old, its footsteps tapping like walking canes. Its head was a lump of broken bark, its eyes and mouth were woodworm holes. For hair it had spider silk, and indeed a spider tensed on its brow like a brooch. Stick-thin arms hung from its shoulders, and they were mismatched in length and one of them had three consecutive elbows.

The little figure paused in the centre of the room and slowly turned its head, as if it was studying each of the three sleeping travellers in turn. Then, ever so quietly, it whispered.

For a full minute nothing happened. The figure stayed still as a statue. Then, after a minute more, its whisper was returned from somewhere in the rafters. Another figure crept down from the ceiling, coming head-first like a lizard descending a rock.

This second creature was much like the first, except it had a hooked nose that filled up its entire face and left no room for nostrils beneath or eyes above. For ears it had only two lank leaves, wilting where they stuck to its shoulders. It swung itself off the wall and touched down on a bookcase. From there it headed to the floor, its claws tiptoeing over the books' spines. Hannah drew a sharp breath but did not wake. Neither Adrien nor Seb moved. And now a third and similar creature, an ungainly thing with twiggy quills poking out of its back, crept in through the door and approached the armchair where Seb was sleeping. It took hold of the boy's trouser leg and began to climb, even as its hook-nosed companion crossed the floor and clambered up the side of the sofa where Hannah lay. The first crept to the foot of Adrien's armchair and made its way up the leg, and the spider on its head wriggled excitedly.

The quilled figure had by now reached Seb's lap, and used the folds of his hoodie to clamber all the way up to his shoulder. When one of its spines prickled Seb's chin and he startled, the figure twitched and lost its shape, and at once became like nothing but a clump of dead twigs. Seb mumbled something, blew one of sleep's raspberries and relaxed. A minute passed, and another. Then, with a scrape and a hinging whine, the twigs reassembled and were the little monster again. The other two had likewise disassembled, but now they too came back together. The first made its way up Adrien's shirt, until it reached his collar. From there it used his parted lips and then his nostrils for handholds, to raise itself onto his face. Adrien slept on oblivious, while the thing made some silent, motionless assessment. Then it crawled on, up over Adrien's forehead and scalp onto the top of the armchair, and from there onto a branch and into the treetops. The others followed suit and, once they had climbed out through the roof of the cottage, began again to whisper.

Adrien woke, stretched, and smelled something fragrant on the morning air. Hannah was already awake, crouching just outside of the cottage and putting some breakfast together, but Seb remained out cold in the other armchair. When Adrien stood up, all the muscles in his legs twanged from the day before's walking. He waddled outdoors, wincing with every step.

'That smells potent,' he said, nodding to what Hannah was making.

'Oh, good morning, Adrien. And really? It's just last night's leftovers, mixed with some mint to freshen things up.'

Adrien frowned. It didn't smell like mint to him, more like the green inner fibres of a twig. 'Hang on a minute,' he said, and rubbed his nose. Something stringy came away on his hand, but he did not think it was mucus. It was a strand of spiderweb, with a bead of aromatic sap caught in its silk.

'Ugh,' he said, and flicked it away.

For the first hour of walking that day, Adrien's legs and hips ached like he'd run a marathon. Come mid-morning things improved, but once again he struggled to match Hannah's strides. Seb took it in turns to walk alongside his mother or hang back and keep him company. 'How on earth does she have all this energy?' Adrien asked him, on one such occasion.

'Who, Mum? She's always had it. And it's only going to get stronger, once we join up with Zach.'

Adrien mulled that over for a minute. He thought he'd detected a hint of regret in Seb's tone. 'Your uncle,' he fished, 'sounds like a bit of a superhero.'

Seb frowned.

'You don't think so, then?'

'Oh, he is. He is. I mean, he's everything Mum says he is. If ever you need someone to tell you stuff about trees, Zach's your man.'

'But . . . ?'

'I didn't say but.'

Adrien shrugged. 'Okay. I just thought you sounded—'

'*But* if you try to tell him about films or music or, for example, the website you made, he couldn't give the slightest shit.'

'Ah.'

Seb folded his arms. 'He's just like his sister, in that regard.'

Adrien paused to clamber over a low-growing branch that Hannah had vaulted with grace. His legs couldn't get high enough for such acrobatics, so he had to lay his belly on the bark and wobble over to the other side. 'That's your thing then, is it?' he puffed, once he was safely across. 'Websites and so on? You still have that memory stick tied around your neck.'

Seb climbed over the branch as if he had hardly even noticed it was there, then touched the memory stick like a locket. He had threaded a shoelace through a clip on its lid, and not taken it off since he'd first hung it there. 'It was, until all this happened. I don't suppose it can be any more.'

Adrien nodded. 'What will have become of it? The Internet, I mean, without any electricity?'

'It'll be like everything else. In ruins. Bits of it will have survived, and you might be able to rebuild them. But most of the data will have been destroyed along with whatever it was stored on. You couldn't access it without power, anyway.'

'Dead and buried, then.'

'No point pretending that it isn't.'

'So why do you keep that stick around your neck? What good is that now?'

Again Seb touched his makeshift pendant. 'I suppose it's like . . . keeping something in a safe you've lost the code to. This drive contains everything I could copy before the battery on my laptop died. Images, html files, that sort of stuff.'

'Things for your game? That kind of thing?'

Seb raised an eyebrow. 'What game?'

'Your mum told me you've spent all summer playing a g—'

Seb cut him off with a laugh, although he didn't sound very amused. 'Of course that's what she'd think I was doing. It wasn't a game, it was a project. In her eyes everything is time-wasting, unless I end the day covered in mud and scratches.' He sighed, and tucked the memory stick out of sight, beneath the collar of his T-shirt. 'Anyway . . . it doesn't matter any more.'

Adrien was surprised to see the boy's eyes moistening, and as Seb stared resolutely ahead of him he wore the expression of one recalling a real place, some quiet beach or restful meadow long since lost to tides or the cement mixer.

'Tell me about it,' said Adrien. 'Tell me about your project.'

Seb returned a grateful smile. 'Some other time, perhaps. But thank you for asking. That's Adrien Thomas one; Zach, Mum and Callum nil. And *they've* been playing all my life.'

'Wait . . . who's Callum?'

Seb looked amazed for a minute. 'Huh? You don't know?'

'I don't think you've ever mentioned someone called Callum . . .'

'But Mum would have . . .'

'She hasn't.' Adrien paused for a moment. 'Oh, wait, hang on . . . he isn't . . . ?'

'Yes.'

'So you don't even call him your f—'

'No.' Seb clenched his fists. 'He's just Callum. Because he's never done anything to deserve being called anything else.'

'Callum,' repeated Adrien, stooping to pass beneath a meeting of branches. 'Are we allowed to talk about him?'

Seb made a big act of indifference, but his pace quickened and his lips were tight. 'Talk about him all you want. He's as good as a stranger to me.'

'Do you ever see him?'

Seb shook his head. 'He tries now and then. He phones once in a while. *That's* something that can dent Mum's enthusiasm, I assure you. I don't speak to him, though. I tell Mum to say I've gone out. He emails me sometimes, but it goes straight to my junk folder.'

'Are you not tempted to at least—'

'No. Why should I be? He booted Mum out of Handel's Wood and never did a thing to help her raise me.'

'What's Handel's Wood?'

'The place he founded. You'd have hated it. It's where they met, when they were young. She hasn't told you about that yet, either? It was a hippy place in the woods. Growing all their own food, using their own sewage for fuel, that kind of thing. I would have hated it too, I'm sure. But you only have to see the photos to know how happy Mum was there.'

'And she left because . . . because . . .'

'Yeah,' said Seb. 'Yours truly came along.'

Adrien remained adamant that he did not like teenage boys, but nevertheless he felt a tug of concern for this one. Seb was trying hard to smother his anger, just as Adrien could remember doing during his own youth.

'It doesn't matter anyway,' said Seb, with a sweep of his arm. 'It's normal. I read on one site that fifty per cent of all parents split up.'

Adrien thought of all the schoolkids he'd watched struggle to cope with their families' break-ups. 'Statistics,' he said, 'are never much good at making you feel better.'

'I don't know. It's just the way the world is. Relationships come to an end.'

Adrien thought impromptu about Roland. He could imagine him presenting that same statistic to Michelle, trying to pry her away from her husband. If the chances of saving his marriage were as good as fifty per cent, Adrien supposed he was a lucky man.

'Are you okay?' asked Seb, who must have picked up on his sudden aura of gloom. 'I didn't mean to imply that you and Mich—'

'My own relationship is doing just fine, thanks,' said Adrien in a hurry.

Seb said nothing.

'Look,' said Adrien, 'you're too young to know about this, but the thing about falling for someone is . . . is that because you don't know it's happening until you're already head-over-heels, you can't . . . you can't be as prepared as you'd like. And it . . . you know, it goes very fast. In ways you're not used to. You just hang on for dear life, and you haven't got a clue how to steer it, and then all of a sudden you realise that at some point way back there the whole damned thing came off its wheels. You mess it up, that's all I'm saying. You never really know what you're meant to be doing, and you mess it up.'

'And that's what's happened to you and Michelle?'

Adrien watched a lone pink petal flitter through the air, then ruin the secrecy of a spiderweb. 'Something like that.'

'What are the chances of fixing it?'

He hung his head. 'Honestly . . . I've no idea.'

'You should tell me something about her. So I can picture what she's like. Tell me something from the beginning, when things were easier.'

'Why would you care about something like that?'

Seb looked faintly offended by that question. 'I like figuring out how things came together.'

'Uhh . . . you know, actually, all I can really remember about our first meeting is . . . panic.'

'Panic? That's all?'

'Well . . . we met in an art gallery. I was bored, to be frank with you. I don't get much out of looking at paintings. I was there as cover on a school trip, and I was sat on a bench in front of a Van Gogh when this lovely woman in a business suit sat down beside me and only then asked if the seat was free.'

'You liked her even then.'

Adrien blushed. 'Something like that.'

'I could tell. Go on.'

'I told her the seat was free, and she said isn't that painting beautiful. I said it was. I didn't really think so but *she* was beautiful and . . . I remember she smelled so intoxicating . . .' Adrien paused for a moment, and his steps faltered. 'She told me . . .' he cleared his throat, 'about the things she admired in the painting. I told her that I liked the way the spirals foretold Van Gogh's mental degeneration, which was something I'd overheard a stranger say in passing five minutes before. I didn't really know what it meant, but Michelle clapped her hands and looked at me as if I'd read her mind, and I wished . . . I really wished that I had. Then just when I hoped that moment would go on for ever, one of the schoolgirls bounced up to me and asked what time the bus was leaving and . . . and after I'd told her and she'd gone off with her friends, Michelle looked disappointed and asked if the girl was mine. No, I said, oh-no-no-no, of course not, I'm not even married, I'm a teacher, I'm on a trip. Then she said *Ooh, an art teacher?* And I thought God, that's what she wants me to be.'

Seb raised his eyebrows. 'You didn't tell her that you were?'

'Of course I did. And I managed to bluff through that first encounter. And then she kind of smiled in this adorably sexy way and asked me, as if it were the cheekiest, most adventurous thing in the history of the world, whether she could have my email address. I gave it to her, and she arranged a meal, and after we had eaten that meal she asked me out.'

'Even after you'd admitted you knew nothing about art?'

Adrien winced. 'I didn't. I'd read and read and boned up on all kinds of artists so I could prolong the bluff. Just to get through that meal with her. And by the end of it I was so besotted that I couldn't bear to tell the truth.'

'When did she find out?'

'Not right away. Our dates were a kind of torture. Wonderful torture, of course. I had so much art homework I barely slept. After maybe our sixth time seeing each other, after I walked her home to her flat, she told me she knew. She said she'd known the instant I lied about being an art teacher in the gallery. She said she'd fallen in love with me for being such a bad liar. That she loved me for trying so hard. Whatever that meant. And then she invited me in.'

Seb was grinning from ear to ear. 'It's so good to hear you talk about the happier side of—' He stopped. The smile left his face and he never finished the sentence.

The woods had turned pink.

It was as if with one step they'd gone backwards from late summer into spring, for in the canopy the usual greenery had met a sudden wall of trees in flower. The air foamed with blossoms, thanks to a breeze that tore the petals off the twigs and streamed them through the forest.

'Isn't it pretty?' asked Hannah, when Adrien and Seb caught up with her. 'Even the floor is pink!'

Adrien looked back at his footsteps, crushed fuchsia trails in a carpet of blossom. He didn't think it was pretty at all.

'Look at you two,' laughed Hannah. 'What does it take to make you enjoy nature?'

A stream of blossoms flowed along with them as they walked, like the train of some elegant dress. Here and there a scrunch of its petals hitched on a sprig, but they soon unravelled and blew free again. Everything was so soft and satiny that none of them realised, until Adrien spotted the broken edge of a building rising out of the flow, that they had arrived on the edge of the next town, its wreckage strangely lit beneath a sifting roseate ceiling.

'This must be the place I saw on the map,' said Seb.

'Yes,' agreed Hannah, suddenly a lot less cheerful. 'I was hoping we'd dodge it.'

'Me too,' said Adrien, remembering the decay of the last town. Compared with that other, this one at least seemed eerily at peace. Its population appeared to have evacuated it entirely, although Adrien supposed there could easily be a thousand people within earshot and he would never see them behind the blowing petals. Everywhere smelled cherry-sweet, even a surfaced sewage main he glimpsed when the blossoms parted to reveal it.

'This is a horrible place,' he muttered, sticking close to the others.

'At least it's a spectacle,' said Hannah. 'We should try to enjoy it.'

Adrien folded his arms. Every time he managed to see through the blossoms, his disgust was vindicated by a glimpse of something awful beneath. In one place he saw a corpse so encrusted in pink and white flakes that it looked like a man made from coconut ice. Likewise the blossoms' perfume hid another smell, something as elusive as it was repulsive. Adrien did not think it was silage or death or any of the other bold odours he'd become all too familiar with since the trees came. Still it made his stomach turn, especially when the breeze blew stronger and whisked up the air.

Hannah led them towards the town centre where, when they reached it, every shop and office was lathered in petals. Still they saw no residents, although here and there isolated hunks of masonry loomed hard out of the cloud. The smell Adrien had no word for lingered on the air, and when they found themselves in the forecourt of a petrol station he wondered whether it might be from the diesel, some of which was still dribbling from the pipes. The trees had smashed the pumps and doused themselves in petrol, to which stained circles of blossom had stuck like scales. Adrien leaned closer to one and took a sniff.

No, the smell was something else.

'You know what?' asked Hannah, grinning now, 'I think places like this are a message for us.'

Adrien stood up straight and rolled his eyes. 'A message,' he repeated sarcastically. 'And what message is that?'

Hannah stopped smiling. 'That we don't need oil any more.'

'Oh for heaven's sake, Hannah.'

'Heaven has nothing to do with it. I'm talking about nature.'

'If nature is in the business of sending us messages,' said Adrien, 'I wish it had started by sending an email. Instead of, you know, destroying the whole fucking world.'

Hannah put her hands on her hips. 'How many messages do you need? She sent us more warnings than anyone could count.'

87

'You see,' said Adrien, raising a finger, 'I'd have accepted your point if you hadn't said *she*.'

'It was just an expression.'

'It was telling, that's what it was. You think nature is some big happy fairy sitting on her mushroom throne.'

'Can I squeeze past?' asked Seb, before Hannah could respond. He had opened his pack and pulled out his drinking water, which he now drank until the last drops were gone from the bottle.

'Seb, what are you doing?' asked Hannah.

Some of the petrol pump's diesel had welled in a gnarl of the trunk that had displaced it, and into this Seb dipped his emptied bottle. The fuel glugged into the container. 'I'm keeping out of this argument, Mum, but people *will* want this. It will be worth far more than water.'

'Good thinking,' said Adrien, pouring his own water onto the dirt at his feet, 'we might be able to barter it for something.'

Adrien followed Seb's lead, then recapped the bottle full of oil. 'Hannah,' he said, 'you should fill yours too.'

When he turned back to her, she was red in the face. 'Why on earth,' she seethed, 'would I want to do that?'

'Because, like Seb says, other people will value it, even if you don't. We'll be able to trade.'

'But people won't *need* it, will they?'

'Yes they will,' said Adrien. 'To light fires and things.'

Hannah threw her hands in the air. 'We're in a forest! There's tinder underfoot, everywhere we go.'

'That's all very well for you to say. Not everyone knows how to light a fire from scratch.'

'Then they need to *learn*! Winter will get here eventually, and by then they'll freeze if they haven't figured it out. We certainly won't be helping them by delaying that lesson.'

Adrien was just about to retort that one less person would freeze with a bottle of oil to burn, and that Hannah could be bloody hectoring at times and he didn't appreciate it, when what she'd just said hit him full force. How did *he* expect to survive the winter, if he did as he planned and slipped home after they'd reached Zach? He had not yet learned how to start a fire, let alone which mushrooms did and did not kill you. He could barely even put up the tent without bashing his thumbs with the peg mallet. What exactly, he asked himself, *did* he know how to do? He knew how to see the bleak side of every situation, that was one thing. He could recite a few lines of *Hamlet* and *A Midsummer Night's Dream*, that was another.

He took off his glasses and pinched the bridge of his nose. 'This is a nightmare.'

'No,' said Hannah, 'it isn't.'

Adrien stared down at the forest floor made blurry by his short-sightedness. For once he was glad of his weak eyes, for they blotted the woods into a smudge of brown and pink.

'Come on, Adrien,' said Seb, gentler than Hannah. 'It isn't so bad.'

Adrien took a deep breath. 'Isn't it? Because when I look around me, it bloody well looks like it is. What about all those corpses along the road, were they not *so bad*? What about my house destroyed by the trees, and everything I ever owned gone with it, and Michelle in another country with the bloody sea between her and me? Is none of that *so bad*? And what do you think about Diane, and a pack of fucking wolves on the loose? Are you insane? This is the end of the world.'

Hannah shook her head. 'If the world had ended, we wouldn't be standing in it. Like I've told you, this is a fresh start. I'm determined to prove that.'

Adrien thumbed his glasses back on. 'Are you really? Well, it will never work. I'll never see things that way because it's . . . it's . . . *wilfully* optimistic. People like you think that just because something's pretty and green, it's not going to do its level best to kill you.'

'People like me? What's that supposed to mean?'

Adrien flung his hands in the air. 'Hippies! And do you know what? I liked things the way they were before! I bloody well preferred a suburb to the countryside. All you want is for things to be wild and natural, but I want them to be safe! The only wolf I want to see is a wolf on television, a million miles away. God damn, I miss my television. I miss westerns! I miss the takeaway at the end of my street! I *liked* eating crappy chicken in a crappy sauce that was probably made out of plastic! I'd have plastic everything back in an instant, and tarmac and petrol, and anything else that would get me away from all these fucking trees. But *you* . . .' He took a deep breath. 'It's like you're pleased that this has happened. It's as if you wanted all those people to die.'

Hannah's expression was icy. 'How on earth could you think that, Adrien? When all I've done is help you.'

But Adrien was angry now, and the blossoms danced around him and he was terrified too. He'd been so damned terrified ever since the forest arrived. Ever since long before that, in fact. Ever since years ago. *Work out what you really want from life,* but he was too damned terrified to even begin. 'You *shouldn't* have!' he spat. 'The only way to help me is with a chainsaw and a demolition truck. If you don't have those I'm fucked, don't you see? You should have just left me alone to be eaten like Diane!'

'I don't appreciate this, Adrien,' said Hannah, in a voice trembling to control itself. 'Why don't you apologise so we can try to move on?'

He stared at her, and as he stared he heard a kind of echo in his mind of all the things he'd just said. He shrank. A part of him immediately wanted to do as she'd asked, to apologise and accept her help and perhaps sort out the mess that was himself, but the other part of him was still in control. *That* part was the side that had roused itself for every clash with Michelle, the side that always wanted something more perverse. It was the part of him that whipped itself into a bitter fury at the end of every evening spent watching westerns drunk and alone, and it seethed inside of him just as it despaired.

'I never asked for your help,' he said.

'And I never forced you to take it,' said Hannah.

90

'There isn't any helping someone like me. I'm a loser, Hannah. A lost cause. Go on and find your precious brother. Be happy with your plants and your murderous animals. I'm going home.'

'You haven't got a home to go back to,' said Seb, with concern.

'That's not what Adrien thinks,' said Hannah, every word shaking with anger. 'Adrien thinks he's better off digging around for tinned food in the rubbish than being in the woods with *people like me*.'

Adrien set his teeth, his heart hot with despair. 'Just fucking leave me to it, alright? Go and be with Zach and leave me here to take care of myself.'

'We're not going to—' began Seb.

'If that's what he wants,' interrupted Hannah, 'then I'm not going to stop him. Far be it from me to stand in the way of a man taking care of himself.'

Seb looked from Adrien to his mother. 'Mum, he doesn't . . .'

'Come on,' she said. 'Maybe Adrien can barter his bottle of petrol for a tent and a compass, or maybe just a road atlas. Maybe he can use it to pay for foraging lessons.' And with that she marched off westward.

Adrien had begun to tremble, both with residual fury and the fear of what might happen next. Seb lingered, troubled. 'I've got to go with Mum,' he said, after a moment.

Adrien tried his best to give an indifferent shrug. Instead it was a flinch and a desperate grimace.

For a moment Seb looked the angriest of all three of them. 'What about Michelle?'

He thought of his wife in Ireland, and in his picture of her the sun was shining and Roland was at her side, and their hands were joined in happiness. 'She'll be just fine without me,' he said.

Seb shook his head. 'Why are you doing this?'

'Fuck off,' said Adrien, half-heartedly. 'Fuck off with your mother and forget you ever met me.'

'This isn't what you want.'

'How the hell would you know what I want?'

'I'm going to bring Mum back,' resolved Seb. 'Don't you move from this spot.'

Again Adrien tried to shrug. Seb watched him for a moment, then pressed his own bottle of fuel into Adrien's free hand. 'And in case I don't manage to convince her, take this. I still think it might be worth something.'

Then he went after Hannah.

10

Wolves

Adrien stayed put in the petrol forecourt, wondering if Seb would come good on his promise and return with Hannah in tow. After ten or fifteen minutes, neither the boy nor his mother had come back, and Adrien began to feel loneliness gnawing away at him. He tried to square his shoulders and stand up straight, but it was as if his skeleton would not allow him to do so.

He could remember Michelle comforting him in the rain, in their front garden, after one of the first almighty rows of their marriage. That one had started because of dirty dishes. Michelle had found him knelt on the kitchen floor one rainy November evening, with the washing-up sponge clenched so tightly in his fist that a puddle of soapy water had formed on the lino beneath it. 'Adrien,' she'd asked, 'what on earth?' and he'd stabbed a finger in the direction of the grimy cups and plates in the sink and tried to explain that the constant wiping clean and resoiling of the crockery had come to seem to him, on that terrible evening, like the embodiment of life's futile struggle.

'That's really silly,' Michelle had said, and although he'd known she meant it kindly he'd received it as mockery. He'd said something spiteful and she'd defended herself, then before he knew it he was storming out of the house and deciding to leave her for her own sake, to save her from him. The rain, however, had been pelting, and Adrien had been wearing only the shirt he'd left in. He'd stood in the garden getting soaked, agonising over the indignity of returning for a waterproof.

'Why do you do this?' Michelle had asked when, ten minutes later, she'd come out under an umbrella to find him. 'It can't really be because of dirty dishes.'

'I don't know,' he'd said. 'I can't stand myself for it.'

'Little things overwhelm you. Sometimes it's as if everything overwhelms you.'

'You're right,' he'd said, wiping tears and rainwater alike from his cheeks. 'But in those times the world just seems so damned formidable.'

With one arm she'd held the umbrella over his head. With the other she'd reached around his waist and held on to him tight. 'I want to help you, Adrien. But you mustn't give up. You can't wait for the world to be perfect before you start living in it.'

Adrien began to walk through the woods again. He reckoned Michelle had been far too charitable, but he sighed with gratitude all the same. He headed back the way they had come, back through the blossoms flowing against him, one arm held high like someone walking out in a blizzard. At least, he was certain, Hannah and Seb would make swifter progress without him. He could picture Hannah embracing her brother, just a short week or so from now, and he managed to smile.

He did not know how he'd find his way home, but he plodded on with his arms kept aloft against both the blossoms and the weight of his own self-loathing. The forest air was heavy, weighed down by pollen and that smell he still could not name. Petals danced on every puff of the wind, and Adrien felt the distance between himself and Hannah stretching like a band of elastic about to finally snap.

Then he saw a tree trunk with a stain up its bark. It did not glisten like the petrol, but it certainly stank. Its tang seared the air like venom.

'Oh,' he said, sniffing it again. 'That's what it is . . .'

It was the smell that had been nagging at him since arriving in the town. Piss. It was an animal's piss, a canine's territorial marking, all acid and ammonia. No petal's sugar could pamper it out. Adrien hoped that only a dog had made it.

A moment later, from somewhere very nearby, a wolf howled.

At once Adrien turned and ran for Hannah. Back past the petrol pumps he raced, back past the spot where Seb had left him. The blossoms spurred close all around. Did he dare to hope they might shield him? No sooner had he done so than they swirled apart before him and he dug in his heels. Up ahead, standing on the roof of a car like a lookout, was a brown wolf with pale eyes. For a half-second that felt like an eternity, Adrien could only stare. Then, with a squeal, he shed his backpack and veered the other way, forcing the stiff muscles of his legs to run their fastest. He pelted over root and tarmac, at any moment expecting to be brought down, to feel the weight of the animal landing claws-first on his back. Cars blocked his way as often as tree trunks, and he zigzagged between both, through what had been a motor showroom now full of punctured wheels and smashed chassis. For a moment he saw the wolf to his right, and hurled himself left with glass crunching under his feet. When he glanced back over his shoulder there was no sign of it, but the petals conspired and he could see only a few metres. On he rushed, colliding with the side of an estate car then hurtling away, ignoring the bruises of the impact to charge headlong as fast as he could.

Coming out of the showroom and into a street, he was amazed that he was still alive. He raced along the road, dodging tree after tree, and was just thinking he might have escaped when the wolf sprang out in front of him. Adrien skidded to a stop, but the wolf did not attack. It watched him with yellow eyes and its snout lowered, except when it twisted its head sideways and sent a bark into the distance. From somewhere in that direction, a gruffer bark answered it.

At once Adrien realised what was happening. The wolf wasn't even panting, for it had been no great effort to chase an unfit man over a short distance. A yowl cut back through the woods from nearby, and then another, and Adrien knew that he had been momentarily spared. This was a kind of generosity shown between the wolf and its pack. When the rest of the animals arrived, then they would eat him alive.

Something crashed into Adrien from the side, and he fell under its momentum wailing with what he supposed was his death cry. Then he was being pulled back up not by teeth but by hands, and it was Seb. The wolf sprang forward to put a stop to the escape, but then it squealed and yapped the air and fell back. A stone had struck its flank, and there was Hannah flinging another.

'Run!' yelled Seb. 'Run, Adrien, run!'

Adrien did as he was told, and Seb and Hannah raced after him. Moments later, Seb grabbed him again and yanked him into a nearby building. Hannah piled in too, and at once she and Seb were dragging something heavy across the door. It was a shelving unit, and they were in the ruins of a shoe shop. Boots and loafers and plimsolls lay scattered everywhere, and Hannah grabbed a high heel and flung it with all her might through the smashed shop window. A yelp and a snarl met it, then Seb yelled, 'This one too!' and Hannah helped him heave another block of shelves across the window.

Adrien could only stand in the middle of the shop, chewing on his knuckles and trying to calm his racing heart. Seb and Hannah added chairs and part of a counter to their barricade, then all of a sudden sprang back. A flash of fur had passed close to the other side.

'Grey,' murmured Adrien. 'That one was grey.'

Neither Seb nor Hannah heard. They resumed the building of their barricade.

'The first one was brown,' said Adrien.

'There are five,' said Hannah over her shoulder.

Seb tipped vertical a block of seats, and shunted them across the last hole in the window. The shop was temporarily secured, slices of sunlight shining through the gaps in the furniture blockade.

Some of the sunny gaps winked out. Then some more. Then the first lit up again. The wolf pack prowled the length of the barricade with hunger grinding in their throats. When Adrien held his breath, he could even hear their nostrils sniffing.

One of the beasts howled, and the noise sucked all the warmth out of the air. The return howl was even more awful, since it answered from further away. 'Even more are coming?' whimpered Adrien, pressing his hands to his head. Now he understood why they hadn't seen another soul in the town.

'This isn't good,' said Seb, who had turned pale. Hannah was thumping the barricade to test it, and it didn't seem anything like as secure as Adrien would have hoped. He looked around for an escape. Much of the shop had caved in, and blossoms scudded in the gloom. Shoes were worn on the ends of bent branches like feet at the end of chewed-up limbs. Whatever fire exits and storerooms the place had once had were buried now under rubble, and there was no way out.

'We're trapped!' said Adrien.

'He's right,' agreed Seb.

'We'll think of something,' said Hannah, although she didn't sound like she believed herself.

A wolf thumped against the barricade. Then there was a snarl and another thump, and the shelves shook and budged an inch. Claws scrabbled against the wood, and Hannah and Seb threw their backs against the furniture to stop it from falling away. Meanwhile Adrien willed some tunnel or secret hiding hole to open itself in the rubbled back half of the shop. What he saw instead was a mound. It was tucked into the furthest recess, four feet high and made from rags and squares of carpet dragged into place. Bones surrounded it, as did bird carcasses picked of their meat. Adrien sniffed the air and knew what the smell was.

'Oh my God,' he said in a tiny voice. 'Oh sweet Jesus.'

'What is it?' grunted Seb, forcing his shoulders against the barricade.

'This is their *den*!' He pointed to the mound, which began to stir even as he did so. 'There's one in there right now! We're dead! We're dead!'

In that moment the other wolves threw themselves at the barrier with coordinated force. Hannah and Seb both gasped at the animals' strength, and were knocked back from their posts. That bought enough time for the alpha wolf to shove its head through a resulting gap, then barge it wider with the muscles of its shoulders. It slipped inside and six more followed, slinking into the shoe shop with the leisurely airs of conquerors. At the same time, the mound of rags lifted and slid apart, and the sleeper within stepped out.

It was a teenage girl.

She was Japanese, and her jeans and T-shirt were covered in damp earth, as if she had swum through a bog. Mud was in her hair as well, cloyed lumps of it like braided beads, and blossoms unintentionally stuck there too. She wore a hunter's belt, with a knife and a slingshot attached to it, and tall boots strapped up like a soldier's. She was perhaps a year older than Seb, drawing herself upright and glancing urgently from the three travellers to the failed barricade and the wolf pack.

Adrien backed towards her, since there was nowhere else to back. The alpha wolf watched him do so with its ears erect and its mouth hanging parted, as if amused by the sight of him. Grey-furred and paler at the belly, it had a white arc across its forehead like a crescent moon. Adrien could not help but stare into its eyes. Eyes that were cracked like lovers' lockets, the halves of the irises pale gold compressing a black slit.

In unison, the beta wolves peeled back their lips and extended their teeth diagonally into growls. They were taking their time, Adrien supposed. They had their kills cornered and he realised that, even though it was appetite that drove them and not malice, they were still going to enjoy the coming meal.

Twung. A noise like a plucked guitar string, and something whistled through the air. The alpha wolf squealed and flinched its head to the side, a spray of blood squirting from its nose. The other wolves hesitated and looked to their leader. *Twung.* The alpha yelped again as something struck its nostrils, ripping bare the raw pink flesh beneath the leather of them. It gnashed the air, as if fighting an invisible hornet, then (*twung*) its eye imploded.

98

Something pulped the eyeball into jelly. *Twung.* One of the betas wailed as its nose in turn split open. *Twung.* Another beta flinched and was bleeding from the lips. With a guttural cry, the alpha turned tail and dashed out of the shop, and the betas followed swiftly behind, howling their curses as they fled into the woods.

The girl unstrung a stone from her slingshot and said nothing.

Adrien clasped his hands. He very nearly prostrated himself at her feet. 'You!' he exhorted. 'You! It was you! Thank you, thank you, thank you so much!'

The girl looked at him with perhaps a hint of a smile, but still did not say a word.

'Bloody hell,' said Hannah, wiping her forehead. 'And thanks. You just saved our lives.'

'You . . . you shot them!' said Adrien, suddenly full of adrenalin. 'You *nailed* them!'

Clearly the girl didn't think much of it. She had dealt with the wolves so bravely that it took Adrien a moment to realise she was cold, and shivering almost imperceptibly.

'Here,' said Seb, in a sudden hurry, producing from his pack his spare hoodie. The girl hesitated before taking it, then nodded and put it on.

'Thanks,' she said.

'No, thank *you*,' said Seb, staring at her.

The hoodie was baggy on her and its cuffs covered the girl's hands entirely. She raised the hood, and between the shadow of its brim and her fringe her eyes were hidden.

'That was incredible,' said Seb.

She shrugged. 'Difficult to miss at that range.'

Her voice was quiet but assured. A stealthy sort of voice, Adrien thought.

'You ripped those wolves apart!' he declared triumphantly. 'You destroyed them!'

She spared him the slightest smile. 'You're funny.'

'Come with us,' asked Seb, breathlessly, then looked as surprised as the rest of them that he had suggested it.

'Hang on a minute, Seb,' said Hannah, suddenly wary. 'She doesn't even know us. Why would she want to come with us?'

'Because . . . because . . .' said Seb.

'Where are you going?' asked the girl.

'West,' said Seb in a hurry. 'Barely a week from here is my uncle's house.'

'But,' added Hannah, 'no doubt you have family of your own you're heading towards.'

The girl shook her head. 'Not on this side of the planet.'

'Are you American?' asked Seb.

'No,' she said. 'Japanese.' But her accent was American.

'Oh . . . so . . . where *are* you going?'

She shrugged again. 'Anywhere.'

'Then come with us!'

There was an awkward pause. The girl headed back over to the ragpile she'd emerged from, and from there picked up a rucksack, which she slung onto her back. 'I'm not really a people person. I'm better off alone.'

Seb looked glum. 'Well, you can keep my hoodie. That's the least I can do.'

'Hold your horses, everyone,' said Adrien. He had spotted two pheasants hanging from the girl's pack. At the sight of their red cheeks and banded tail feathers, something had dropped open in his stomach, a sudden hunger that only meat could satisfy. 'Why don't you hear us out?' he said, licking his lips. '*I'm* not really a people person either, but those wolves are still out there, and God knows what else. Surely there's strength in numbers, right?'

'Steady on, Adrien,' said Hannah, gravely. 'Last time I checked, *you* weren't coming with us any more.'

He gaped at her. 'I thought you . . . I thought we . . .'

Hannah folded her arms. 'Just because we didn't want you to be eaten by wolves, doesn't mean we're going to put up with you behaving like you just did.'

'But . . . but,' he gasped. Their argument of earlier seemed a million years ago now. 'I *will* be eaten by wolves! I didn't mean any of that stuff, Hannah!' He clasped his hands. 'None of it at all. I'm so sorry! I'm a shit, I know, an ungrateful little shit. But I'll make it up to you, I promise. I'll . . . I'll carry all of your bags. I'll pick all the mushrooms and the berries you want me to.'

'You're not strong enough. And you'd poison yourself.'

Adrien looked imploringly to Seb, but it was as if Seb had forgotten him and had eyes only for the girl. Adrien wetted his lips, his mouth drying out with panic. He felt entirely sure that, were he left alone, the wolves would come back for him. They would have their revenge on *him* for the wounds the girl had inflicted.

He sank to his knees. If ever in his life there had been a time to beg, this was the moment. 'I am so, *so* sorry, Hannah,' he grovelled. 'I'll do anything, and if there's nothing I can do I'll *learn* something. I'll be your dancing monkey, if that's what it will take.' He took a deep breath. Hannah looked unmoved. 'Goddammit, Hannah, I'll die! I'll die if you leave me alone! If those wolves don't come for me then the trees themselves will.'

Hannah's arms were folded. 'This is pathetic.'

But the girl had covered her mouth with the back of her hand, and behind it she was giggling. 'He makes me laugh,' she said. 'Maybe I will come, after all, as long as he does.'

'Deal!' pronounced Seb before his mother had a chance to speak.

Hannah looked pained for a second, then said, '*Fine*. But you'd better mean it, Adrien, if we're going to get along again.'

'I mean it,' said Adrien, climbing light-headed to his feet. He did, and he hoped he sounded like he did.

When Hannah turned her back on him he looked at the girl and mouthed, 'Thank you.'

She grinned back at him with such a predatory smile that it was itself almost something canine. Adrien bridled a little then, an ounce of pride returning to him. It suddenly didn't feel so good, to have been saved from exile just because he was ridiculous.

Seb was still staring at the girl. 'I'm Seb, by the way, and this is Adrien and my mum, Hannah.'

She nodded. 'A family?'

'Not Adrien. He's just a . . .' he glanced at his mother, 'a friend.'

'And your dad is . . . ?'

'Not around.'

'Is he dead?'

Seb frowned, but the girl had asked it so matter-of-factly that Adrien did not think she'd intended offence.

'No. Probably not, anyway. Just gone. Years and years ago. Don't much care where.'

She nodded for a moment, reflecting on this. 'My dad is an asshole too.'

Girl and boy looked at one another. Then, briefly, they shared a smile.

'Can, er, can we get moving now?' asked Adrien, still conscious of the odour of wolves. 'I'd really love to get out of here.'

'You haven't told us your name yet,' said Seb.

The girl smiled at him again. 'My name is Inoue Hiroko.'

II

Slingshot

Seb tried to talk to Hiroko as they walked, but for the most part she responded monosyllabically, or with dead-end answers, and eventually he stopped trying. She stalked along with the hood of his borrowed top pulled up like a cowl, and from what Adrien could glimpse of her face she remained deep in thought at all times. When they stopped to eat that night, and upon hearing that Hannah and Seb were vegetarians, she sat at a deliberate distance and piled up sticks for a small cooking fire all of her own. Hannah offered her some of the mushrooms she had gathered that day, but Hiroko only shook her head and opened her rucksack. In it were all kinds of useful implements, the sorts of tools Adrien wished he'd had the sense to pack or even own in the first place. Among them was a tinderbox, which she used to ignite some old newspaper she had found for kindling.

While the flames gathered Hiroko selected one of the pheasants she had been carrying and began to pluck it with nimble fingers. Now and then, when a brand in the flames cracked and fizzed up sparks, the orange firelight revealed her face beneath her hood. She looked by turns stoic and bitter. Adrien supposed that he might look like that, too, were he in Japan and his home so very far away.

Some time later she used her knife to tease out the last entrenched quills of the pheasant. By now the fire was in full blaze, and she pierced the meat with a metal rod and placed it over the flames. As the pheasant cooked, the smell of charring game tormented Adrien. He lost all appetite for the carrot he had been chewing: he would rather inhale smoke for his supper. Eventually he could bear it no longer and approached the girl's fire, not daring to meet Hannah's disapproving gaze.

'May I,' he asked, 'um . . . I know you're the one who caught it, but . . . may I have anything that's spare? Of the pheasant? Just anything that's left when you're done. I could trade you, I guess, um, some carrot, for some . . .'

She jiggled loose one pheasant breast with the tip of her knife, then tore off a leg and held both cuts out to him balanced on the flat of the blade. 'Thank you!' he exclaimed when she tilted the metal and the hot succulent meat slid into his cupped hands. His eyes streamed gratefully as he devoured it, enjoying the grease that smeared his cheeks and whiskers. When, with messy chops and meat stuck between his teeth, he tried to thank her more formally, with a stiff bow such as he had sometimes seen people from Japan exchange, she laughed at him as if he were a jester.

For a moment he was indignant, but then conceded that he would do handstands and cartwheels for her if it bought him more meat. He grinned, and turned over the bones to check for final morsels. 'So,' he asked, 'how come you know how to do all this stuff? I mean, I'm in my forties and I can barely follow a trail of breadcrumbs through the woods.'

Again that made Hiroko smile. 'My dad taught me. An old trapper taught me.'

'Your dad's an old trapper?'

She shook her head.

'Whereabouts was this trapper, then?'

'California.'

'You *are* American.'

'No.'

'You sound it.'

'I'm from Iwate Prefecture in Japan.'

'Do they speak with American accents there?'

She frowned. For a moment she looked less like a fierce fighter of wolves and more like a teenage girl a long way from home. 'I guess I haven't spent much time there.'

'But that's where your family comes from, right?'

Hiroko nodded.

'After you saved us from the wolves, you said your dad was an asshole.'

She flinched for a fleeting second.

'My dad was an asshole, too,' he said softly. 'And Seb said his was, so that makes three of us. We'd better ask Hannah what her dad was like.'

Hannah stoked her fire with a branch.

'I suppose it must be hard,' said Adrien, 'being this far from home.'

Hiroko folded her arms. 'It's fine. Everything's fine. And, Adrien? I don't want to talk about it.'

The next day, Hiroko caught a wood pigeon. They were walking through birch woods when she did so. There the black cores of the trunks were bandaged with silvery bark and their slender columns had caged and pierced the cars along the road. One elderly driver lay curled up in a ball on the back seat of his vehicle, barred in by the trees. Hannah yelled to him but he did not move, and they heard flies buzzing on the vehicle's bodywork. Later, they saw a roadside café crammed with slender birches, their serrated foliage spilling from the open windows and the door's letterbox. The tables within were wedged between the narrow trunks, still balanced with ketchup bottles and salt and pepper pots. Four young men were trying to break in, but the birches grew so close together that they could find no way between them, and when Hannah shouted a hello they turned back from the café with hungry eyes.

'Thieves,' whispered Hiroko, hands on her slingshot at once. 'The fat one has a woman's backpack.'

'That doesn't mean they're thieves,' said Hannah as the men started to pick their way back through the maze of birches.

'I think they might be,' said Seb, and Adrien was more than happy to agree. They hurried away before the men could reach them, and Adrien was glad of the enfolding woodland that quickly shielded them from sight.

An hour later, Hiroko made a loud hissing noise and they all stopped and looked at her in surprise. It was the only sound she had made since her warning about the men at the café.

Through the silence that followed cut the throaty purr of the wood pigeon, and the girl nodded towards it and selected a triangle of stone from her ammunition pouch. She fitted it to her slingshot's rubber, aimed, and the sling flicked out and knocked the pigeon off the branch. Hiroko strode across the leaves and picked it up, then nodded to them to carry on walking.

For a minute they all stared at her: Hannah horrified; Adrien wanting to pump his fists in the air; Seb somewhere else in between. How simply, Adrien thought, the pigeon had presented its life to her. How casually she had reached out and accepted it and tied it with the dead pheasant still hanging from the straps of her backpack. Hiroko could stay as closed a book as she liked, if she kept claiming food for them like that.

In the afternoon they found a road that led them through a valley of broken villages. People watched them pass with blank expressions, and although sometimes they stopped to exchange small talk, Adrien always got the impression that such folk would be happiest once they'd taken their leave. In between such ruins, they hardly saw another soul. They heard them, sometimes, laughing or shouting or conversing on the edge of hearing, but it was as if such sounds stemmed from a parallel woodland, ever out of sight of their own.

Sometimes Hiroko walked in front, with Seb hovering as close as he dared. Sometimes she dropped back and watched the undergrowth with keen eyes. Adrien took one such opportunity to fall in alongside Hannah, who acknowledged his presence with a cursory nod.

'Hey,' he said. 'Are you still mad at me? Because I've got something for you. I mean, I found it, but it's yours now, if you want. It's meant to be a kind of present.'

He held it out to her and she took it. It was a silver box, only big enough to fill the centre of her palm, but with a large keyhole in its lid. He had discovered it in a doll's house destroyed by a sapling.

'What's in it?' Hannah asked, trying to open it. The lid didn't budge.

'Don't know. Nothing, I think. It's locked. But if you shake it, you don't hear anything inside.'

'So you're giving me an empty box that I can't even open.'

'Ye-es,' he said.

She offered him a sheepish smile. 'You're an idiot,' she said. 'But I can't stand to be mad at you. And thank you for the box. It's funny, it reminds me of something . . . When I was a little girl I found a silver key in a magpie's nest. Back then I thought it could unlock fairy doors in the woods. Now I'm going to pretend it was always meant for this.'

She slipped the box into her pack, and Adrien returned her smile with interest.

For that night's meal, Hannah cooked a soup of sorrel and wild garlic. She made enough for all of them, but Adrien ate his tormented by the smell of the next pheasant smouldering on Hiroko's separate fire. They were camped beneath a broad beech, whose curtain of branches rippled in time with the rising smoke. Adrien willed himself to remain alongside Hannah, but no sooner had he swallowed his last spoonful of soup than his stomach rumbled its loud dissatisfaction. He tried to ignore it, chewing on the inside of his cheek, but when he looked at Hannah she only looked amused by his sufferings. 'You're an idiot,' she told him anew, 'but a sweet one. Go on, you don't have to sit here on my behalf. Go and eat some meat, if Hiroko will let you.'

With a grateful duck of his head, Adrien sprang up and scurried across to Hiroko's fire. The girl met him with the same amused look as Hannah, and began to carve the meat into portions.

Seb stood up and crossed from his mother's fire to Hiroko's.

At once all mirth left the camp. Both Adrien and Hiroko froze as Seb knelt down between them, and when Adrien dared to look back at Hannah she was staring wide-eyed at her son.

'Please,' said Seb, nodding from Hiroko to the pheasant.

Hiroko pulled down her hood and brushed back her fringe to look Seb in the eye. Seb met her gaze, and offered out his plate. Adrien cleared his throat. He should say something, he knew. He glanced at Hannah and saw she'd turned her back on them. He looked back to Hiroko and didn't know if he was brave enough to pick a fight with such a girl.

'Um,' he said, 'now you two listen . . .'

Hiroko ignored him. She cut out the choicest part of her pheasant breast and placed it on Seb's plate. 'This is your first time?' she asked.

'In my life,' said the boy.

'Now then, Seb,' advised Adrien, 'think about what you're doing.'

Seb closed his eyes and opened his mouth, as if taking a breath before diving into water. He placed a pinch of flesh on his tongue and, after a moment's hesitation, began to chew.

Adrien had the sense that even Hannah was watching somehow, through the back of her head.

Seb swallowed and did his best to smile. 'It tastes . . . it tastes . . .' His lips curled both from the flavour and a loss for words. 'Gross.' He considered the rest of the meat on his plate. 'I think I prefer vegetables. But, you know, maybe it will grow on me. You can't expect to like everything first time.'

Hannah was quiet all the next day, which was hot from morning until dusk, with every leaf basking in sunlight. Carrying rucksacks and the tent in such weather was thirsty work, but Hannah still insisted that they boil any river water before drinking it. It made

Adrien miserable to watch the crystalline liquid they hauled from a stream bubble up and lose its freshness in the heat, but he knew there was no use arguing, and he drank it in its tepid state.

Unlike every day before that one, Hannah did not halt them to point out rare flowers or edible shrubs. Sometimes she did stop unannounced, to pick leaves or prise out roots, but often the others had already walked ahead some distance before they realised she was crouched far behind them in the undergrowth.

Towards the end of the day's walking, Adrien summoned the courage to talk to her. Seb and Hiroko were some way in front, leading the way with the compass, so there wasn't any need to lower his voice. 'Am I in trouble again?' he asked.

Hannah didn't say anything.

'I should have done more to dissuade him.'

She sighed. 'Of course you're not in trouble. And thank you for saying *something*. This is about Seb, not you. This was his decision.'

On they plodded, and after a minute Adrien cleared his throat. 'Can I help you carry some of those fruits you've been gathering? It could free you up to pick some more.'

'I don't need any more, do I? I only need enough for myself, now.'

'Umm . . . Hannah, look, if it means anything . . . I think you're the best cook I've ever met. I didn't think anyone could make vegetables taste as good as you do.'

She scowled. 'Is that a compliment or a concession?'

Adrien winced. 'Just try to remember that what Seb did last night wasn't about diet, or principle, or anything of that sort. Seb's a boy and Hiroko's a girl. It's what happens.'

'He's only just met her. *You've* only just met her, and both of you are in awe of her.'

'I'm not in awe of her.'

'You are. All because she knows how to kill things. As if it's *difficult* to kill things. You don't even know the first thing about her.'

'She said . . . she said she'd learned some things from park rangers. And that her dad was an asshole.' Adrien scratched his head. 'That's a start. Look . . . she seems like an alright kid, to me. And believe me I've seen my share of horrid ones. Isn't it good for Seb to have someone his own age to talk to?'

But he could see that it was too soon to try to persuade Hannah of anything. She looked crumpled by what had happened, and he would have preferred her to be raging, even at him. For his own part he did not know what it must be like to see a dearly held principle rejected by a child. He had never even managed to keep a New Year's Resolution, let alone a decision about ethics. He was about to try again to cheer her up when, out of the corner of his eye, he saw something dart through the undergrowth.

'What's wrong?' asked Hannah, when he stopped dead still and stared after it.

'Did you see that?' he whispered back.

'See what?'

'A . . . a something.'

'What do you mean? I didn't see anything. And I hope you're not going to call Hiroko back here to try and catch it . . .'

Adrien shook his head, only half listening. Nothing moved in the undergrowth, save for the slow nodding of a few pillars of foxgloves. Yet he was sure that whatever he'd seen was crouched there in the tangles, observing.

'What is it, Adrien?'

He took a step towards it and at once it fled from him. It hopped up and sprang along the forest floor, running very fast. Weeds obscured it, thistles and ground ivy, but he saw enough to know it moved on two legs, was about a foot tall and as skinny as a grass-hopper. He lost sight of it in the middle distance, and his eyes scanned the forest for one last glimpse. Then, instead, he saw the thing it had been running towards.

It was a huge tree, standing on the edge of vision. Just another tree, perhaps, but grand and dark and as bare as midwinter. It had only two lower branches, which grew horizontal like the arms of a chair. Its other branches fanned out higher up, as leafless as the rest of the plant. Despite its distance, its bulk seemed to superimpose itself on the surrounding forest. To look at it for long made Adrien's eyes strain, as if it were in the foreground and the background at the same time.

'Adrien?' asked Hannah. 'What's going on? You're white as a sheet.'

'Don't you see it?' He pointed a shaky finger.

'See what?'

He turned to Hannah and tried to find the words to describe it, then could not and simply pointed all the harder at the giant tree and whatever creature had rushed towards it. Yet when he looked again, both had vanished. It was as if neither had ever been there.

Hannah laid a hand on his arm. 'You look sick.'

'You . . . you didn't see that, did you, Hannah? You didn't see it at all.'

'I saw . . . maybe I saw the undergrowth shaking. I might have seen a rabbit, or something like that. It was hard to tell.'

Adrien shook his head. 'It definitely wasn't a rabbit. It was a . . . a . . . it was running towards a . . .'

'Towards what, Adrien?'

'A tree,' he mumbled, after a minute, confused and embarrassed. 'I suppose it was nothing. Let's go and catch up with the kids.'

Zach

Her brother had always warned her about moving into Callum's community at Handel's Wood, but Hannah was young when she was drawn there: twenty-five and high on ideas. On the night before she'd been due to relocate, when the contents of her rented flat were all packed up in cardboard or zipped away in her luggage, Zach had appeared on her doorstep unannounced.

'You've come at the eleventh hour to try to dissuade me,' Hannah said, with a smile, when she invited him in.

'Something like that,' Zach said. 'In the end I just had to jump on a train.'

They ordered takeaway and ate it off a table made from a cardboard box, sitting opposite each other on suitcase chairs. Hannah was pleased to see him, as she always was, even when he did his best to dissuade her from moving into the community.

Zach's best had never been very persuasive. He didn't have much of a way with words. The most moving thing about his plea was that he'd written so many cue notes, crossed out and redrafted on sheets of lined paper. When she teased him about it, he admitted glumly that he'd been up all night revising them, and that he'd spent his train journey doing the same. The gist of his argument was that it was too soon after their father's death to be making big life decisions.

'Look,' Hannah sighed, 'you're wrong. This isn't about Dad. This is about moving on.'

Too soon, in Zach's opinion, was just over five months since the funeral. It didn't sound like a long time, but it had felt like five years. *Every* month had felt like a year, ever since their father's diagnosis. That the cancer took two years to kill him had surprised both Hannah and her brother, for their father had seemed to give up on life no sooner than he heard the doctor's verdict. Perhaps he had been waiting for an excuse, ever since what happened to their mother. In contrast, the five months following his death had been full of changes, and sudden spans of time on Hannah's hands, and a chance to enjoy life again, albeit guiltily.

'I just think this guy . . .' said Zach, 'this Callum of yours . . .'

Hannah folded her arms. 'Are you always going to be this over-protective, Zach? I know you're my big brother, but I'm not so small any more.'

'Men like him . . . men like him are . . .'

'He's a good man. A very principled man, in fact.'

'But men like him . . .'

'A man who cares about the planet, for one thing. I thought you two would get along famously!'

'He's just . . . I dunno, he's just . . .'

She looked at Zach. Giant, meditative Zach, who had been able to grow a full beard since he was sixteen, who had the frame of a wrestler but the thoughtfulness of a hermit. Men and women alike were drawn to him as if towards a campfire. He could have been an alpha male in most any company, should he ever have wanted to keep any, and should he have given a damn. Hannah had fool-ishly thought that he and Callum would become friends. That they would find much common ground in their love of nature and their antipathy towards what Callum called the rat race. Yet when, in the veggie restaurant where Hannah had organised their meeting, Callum had espoused most lyrically the virtues of self-sufficiency, and decried those he collectively called *the man*, and talked at length about Handel's Wood and how it represented a dream come true and a model for a better kind of life, one lived in harmony with nature, Zach had just stared down at his napkin as if he were back at their father's funeral.

'What it is . . .' said Zach slowly. 'What it is, is . . .'

Hannah gave him time.

Zach frowned with concentration, as if words were sheep that needed to be whistled into place. Eventually, he managed to say it. 'Men like him are what's wrong with the world.'

She laughed, gobsmacked. 'Don't be so ridiculous. Callum isn't one of those sorts of men! What are you saying? That you think he's a charlatan?'

'He hasn't built that place to live closer to nature. I should know, Hannah. I live in the woods. He's not built it for self-sufficiency, either. He's built it to be in charge.'

'Someone's got to be in charge. Why not one of the good guys?'

'He wants to be in charge of *you*, too. You're grieving, Hannah. Better to remember it.'

She threw her hands in the air. 'You think I've forgotten? So this *is* about Dad, after all!'

Zach was about to object, but Hannah let him have both barrels. She shouted at him for the first time in years, and he took it in troubled silence, and she had to apologise afterwards.

The next day, she moved to Handel's Wood, and Zach helped her to transport all her things. His last words to her, before leaving her there, were, 'You can come and stay with me whenever you like. You know that anyway, but there it is: said. If you need to get away from him, my door is always open.'

She'd laughed that off, and a mostly happy eighteen months had followed. It had felt good to eat the food they'd grown themselves, to keep fires burning using only dead wood and sustainable stocks, to use sparing electricity from a biofuel generator. It *had been* good, and therefore easy to overlook those moments when Callum would appear out of nowhere to join a discussion and, within minutes, turn it effortlessly into a conversation about himself. Easy to overlook the way his eyes always lingered on the mirror, in the cabin she shared with him. After all, he was very good-looking and the sex was the best she'd ever had.

Whenever Hannah looked back on the moment she'd first told Callum about Seb, she always wondered what she'd been feeling beforehand. Had she been excited? Buzzing at the idea of sharing her big announcement? Dreamy with thoughts of how their future might play out? The memory had been obliterated by his subsequent reaction.

'Hey,' she'd said, that evening. 'Sit down for a minute. I've got something amazing I want to tell you.'

She could definitely remember smiling as she gave him the news. She could definitely remember stopping when she saw his face.

What she loved about Zach, when she ran to him four weeks later, was how unhappy he was to have been proved right. She had just endured a month of Callum's tantrums and black moods. Worse than that was the way in which, within days of her refusal to give up on the baby simply because he commanded her to, he had turned the entire community against her. His plan, it had seemed, was to force her out and forget about her. To a great extent it was successful.

On her first night in Zach's lodge, after fleeing Handel's Wood, her room there had smelled of moss and of pine needles and of mud, but also of something more lingering and familiar that went beyond the smells of her brother's house, way back to a simpler time. A woodland holiday when they were children, and both their happy father and their vibrant mother were still alive and with them, and life and the world she lived in were both so much simpler.

The next day brought a change in the air. The ground softened underfoot, and Hannah could smell the minty tang of herbs that loved the damp places. The pale stars of wild primroses ringed the earth, and through them ran long-trodden trails of muntjac and hare. They had crossed an invisible threshold into ancient woodland, forested since long before the trees came, and Hannah stopped them and said, 'This is the wood where Zach lives.'

It was clear to her that none of the others shared her excitement. Hiroko, of course, knew nothing of Zach and hadn't shown any interest in rectifying that situation. Adrien tried to look bright for Hannah, but he'd been twitchy ever since whatever had spooked him yesterday. Seb, on the other hand, she would have expected to show at least a drop of enthusiasm.

'Your uncle, Seb! We'll be with him in a matter of hours.'

Seb watched a crow flap past between the branches. 'Will we? How are we going to find him?'

Hannah wanted to stamp her feet. 'We *know* these woods. We'll just . . . look for something we recognise and make our way from there.'

Seb didn't appear convinced, but Hannah pushed past him and set a pace fast enough to always stay ahead. She'd relish Zach's company now more than ever, and reckoned she'd need his support to convince any of her companions to see the forest as a blessing.

The trees they now walked beneath did not branch until at great height, their trunks growing sheer and single-minded until they sprawled apart some thirty feet above. From there countless limbs spilled back towards the earth, forming leafy domes each of which felt like a private garden inside. In each Hannah hoped for a landmark she could use to guide them on to Zach, but most were full of nothing except leaf litter and logs, and once a hare that sat up straight and eyed them bravely. Then the rubber stretched in Hiroko's slingshot and it bolted out of sight.

In another of those green domes they found a perfectly intact bus shelter, and to start with this raised Hannah's hopes. 'There's been forest here for centuries,' she told the others. 'So these must be trees that have just filled in the gaps. We have to be standing on a road, no question about it.' She began to inspect the bus timetables. 'I bet I can find our way from here.'

Simply reading the names of the bus stops made her feel closer to Zach. These were the places where her brother bought groceries, visited friends, took her out for a pub lunch whenever she came to visit. One of the bus routes led so close to his lodge that Hannah was certain they'd be with him come the end of the day.

'Okay,' she said, striding ahead a few paces then crouching to part the leaf litter. There was tarmac underneath. 'Here's the road, just like I thought. All we have to do is follow it. It's going to be easy.'

They set out, but the road vanished after two minutes' walk. Hannah stood with her hands on her hips. 'That's okay,' she said. 'These are the same woods that have always been here. If all these trees were new, there'd be old ones uprooted everywhere.'

'Maybe they're on the same side as the new ones,' said Adrien morosely.

'But why would they want to stop us finding Zach? They'd have no reason to do that.'

Hiroko looked baffled. 'Trees don't take sides.'

Neither Seb nor Adrien rushed to contradict the girl, but Hannah was at least grateful for their conspicuous silence. 'Come on,' she said. 'This has to be the way. Let's all keep an eye out for other clues.'

For a while after that, all they saw was forest. Then, pushing through a curtain of leaves, they came upon another bus stop. 'Yes!' exclaimed Hannah. 'I knew it. Just let me work out which stop this is, and then I can tell you how close we are.'

The others waited as she examined the timetable, but it was as she was doing so that she noticed a peeling sticker on the glass, and then a scribble of graffiti on the frame. Both looked familiar.

'Hang on a minute,' said Seb, even as Hannah thought it. 'This is the same bus stop we found before.'

Hannah stepped out of the shelter and stared imploringly up at the trees, but they gave no sign of how to reach her brother.

Two hours later, they came upon the bus stop for a third time. They did not see it any more after that, but by the time the sun sank Hannah's spirits had gone down with it. At night the others conversed in low voices in the tent, but she did not join in with them. She closed her eyes and pretended she was a girl again, racing through a green world with her brother at her side.

Crunch.

Hannah opened her eyes. It was the night, and the others were asleep around her. The moon glowed so brightly that she could see a pair of wriggling earwigs silhouetted on the ceiling of the tent. Hannah yawned and tried to remember what dream had just woken her. There had been a heavy sound treading through the forest, a sound that went—

Crunch.

She sat up wide awake.

Crunch. It was the noise of something big as a log, crushing the twigs and leaf litter. Hannah held her breath and waited for it to come again.

Snorf. This time it was a huff of heavy breath, then something like chewing and something else dragging through the dirt. *Crunch.* It came from nearby, not far outside the tent, and Hannah slid out of her sleeping bag and crawled across to the door. She unzipped the inner tent as quietly as she could, reached through and opened the outer zip an inch. Then she pressed her eye to the opening, and peered out.

Snorf.

It was the horned animal she had seen sleeping by the brook, the night after finding Diane. It stood not a stone's throw from the tent, partially obscured by a thicket. At least as tall as a horse, it was nevertheless as bulky as a rhino and covered in a coat of tasselled silver hair. A loud and herbivorous rumble escaped from its gut, and it tore loose a mouthful of vegetation from a tree and stomped one foot with a *crunch*. It had a pug face, more wrinkled and squashed than a cow's, and broad nostrils out of which it gave a snort of breath so powerful that it could be smelled at once, even in the tent, an awful halitosis of cud and rotting vegetable matter. Hannah hardly noticed it, so transfixed was she by the animal's horn. Almost as tall again as was its bearer, it looked more like slate than ivory. A faint lacquer of iridescence coated its enamel, becoming almost a sheen at the tip. The animal snorted and walked away, leaving a trail of crushed and broken debris in its wake.

When the others woke in the morning, they found Hannah waiting for them, beaming from ear to ear. 'Look at this!' she said, and they all gathered round.

She was pointing to a footprint, a flattened circle of leaves and dented soil. Not far from that was another, and grey threads of hair snagged on one or two twigs.

'What made these tracks?' asked Hiroko, crouching over them. 'There aren't any animals this big in England.'

'Perhaps there used to be,' grinned Hannah. 'A very long time ago.'

'What do you mean?' asked Hiroko.

'It looked like something out of the Ice Age. Like a woolly rhino, only not quite as squat. It had a longer neck, you see, and the most beautiful horn . . .'

'Hang on a minute,' said Seb. 'You *saw* it?'

Hannah nodded enthusiastically.

'And you didn't wake us up?'

She folded her arms. 'I didn't think you'd be interested.'

'Did it look dangerous?' asked Hiroko.

'No! It had the bluntest teeth you can imagine.' Hannah shook the branch next to her, which was missing all its leaves and much of its bark. 'It was eating these. And it had thick silver fur all over, and did I tell you about its horn?'

'Like a kirin,' mused Hiroko, in a quiet voice.

'What did you say?' asked Seb.

It was a minute before the girl replied, for she was staring into the animal's footprint as if it were a wishing well. 'My grandmother,' she said eventually, 'lives in a house in the forest. It's an old house, the kind that creaks as you walk in it. It's full of woodwork and carvings, and byōbu that divide the rooms.'

'What are byōbu?'

'Screens. Folding screens. And hers are covered in paintings, even older than she is. They're of animals and beech trees and wildflowers . . . all the things from the wood where she lives, or the things people used to believe lived there. So . . . what Hannah just said made me think of that. A . . . a kirin. They're a kind of legend in Japan, although people draw them differently. They're our version of a unicorn, I suppose. My grandmother's favourite byōbu has one painted so big it fills three panels of the screen. She says a kirin is a good omen.'

'A good omen . . .' repeated Hannah, and above and around her the trees creaked as if with pleasure. 'Well, we're going to need a name for it, and I think *kirin* is a good one. Come on, then. Let's get packed up and follow it.'

'Follow it?' gasped Adrien. 'Are you kidding me?'

'I'm happy to hear any other ideas. The way I see it we were lost, and now this kirin has left us a trail.'

To that none of them had an answer, and although Hannah knew they didn't share one drop of her enthusiasm, she let herself enjoy the victory. 'That settles it, then,' she said with a beaming smile.

And they followed the kirin.

They trod the horned beast's trail all that morning, although they did not see the animal itself. It had too great a head start, but it had left clues to read, be they more prints in the soil or snapped sticks where its horn had cut a path. Hannah was just beginning to wonder what she'd say if it was leading them nowhere, when Hiroko pointed to something high in the branches. 'Look!' she exclaimed.

It was a picnic table, and another not far from that.

'Yes!' cried Hannah, 'I know this place.'

She began to dash about in the undergrowth, and one minute later found a painted post that marked the start of a bridleway. She had ridden this route on a mountain bike, not a year before, and remembered a smooth and tended track, with only the occasional root bumping her wheels. Now it was a line of saplings, squeezed between the older trees, but that only served to make her laugh. She was almost skipping as she led her companions down the path, feeling quite sure that the kirin, whose trail had vanished now, had led them here. Everything was right in the world, when the world was on your side. Best of all, she was about to be reunited with Zach. She couldn't help but walk faster, and faster and faster until the others struggled to keep up. Then, after another ten minutes, they reached her brother's lodge.

As the sheer euphoria of arrival faded, Hannah stood with her hands on her hips, taking in the sight before her. She could clearly remember her first happy visit here, when Zach had led her through each room almost on tiptoe, as if he could not believe his own luck to have moved to the place. Now she realised that she had, without questioning the idea, imagined her brother's house to have survived intact. Instead, branches ran amok through its two timber storeys and spilled awry out of its roof. They had used the wooden architecture to their advantage, fusing with the structure and bunching their roots into the foundations. In places it was impossible to tell where a trunk ended and the older wood of the walls began, and in this fashion the trees had warped all straight lines out of the lodge, bending the very shape of the place until it better resembled a stump than a human house. Fringes of moss hung from the eaves, and folds of bark shuttered up several of the windows. Hannah bit her lip to see it that way, then took a deep breath and grinned at the others. 'It's okay,' she said. 'I should think he's pleased this has happened.'

She led them up three steps to a wooden deck. There a bell hung, and she rang it and found reassurance in its familiar jangle, even as a breeze fluted through splits in the lodge's walls.

'Hey!' she yelled. 'Zach! Zach! Surprise!'

After a minute there was still no reply, so she jangled the bell again. Adrien cleared his throat, but smiled encouragingly when she looked at him for support.

She pushed the door open and let everyone into a wide hallway with jumbled coats and muddied boots scattered across the floor.

Illumination came not from the wood-shuttered windows but through higher openings in the ceiling. Through these and a veil of foliage the sun pushed its light, green by the time it reached the floorboards.

They opened a door to their left, and passed through a dining room with an overturned table. Another door led into a kitchen, where violets grew among the knives, forks and broken glass strewn around.

Nobody said anything, but Hannah began to feel a magnetic dread that pulled at her stomach. She held her breath. Adrien was the one who pushed open the next door, onto a plainly furnished sitting room.

There they found Zach. He sat in the corner, with his head cocked as if listening to some inscrutable sound. A giant man with a dense beard and brawny arms, he wore grass-stained jeans and a lumberjack shirt. A wound in his chest clogged the room with a reek of old meat, and had turned his shirt to rags with a dark circle across the heart of him. As the opened door disturbed the air, flies exited his body and swarmed for a few irked seconds, then touched down again to continue their egg-laying.

Hannah did not cry out or make any other noise. Only an arm against a nearby chair. A bend in her spine and a loll of her head as if nodding to sleep. Seb made the first sound, a succession of breaths sucked in faster and faster. He rushed out of the house. After a minute, Adrien staggered after him.

Hannah didn't leave. She could hardly even think. The sight before her emptied out her mind as if imparting something of itself. For a minute or two more she just remained where she stood, stunned by Zach's stillness and the wound where his heart should have been. Then she knelt. She was too shocked even for tears. It was as if her mind kept rejecting the news her eyes relayed. Look again, it instructed, look again, tell yourself how happy he is to see you. 'Zach?' she whispered, watching his lips, imagining perhaps some palpitation or twitch of life there that she knew she had not seen.

She was barely even aware of Hiroko, who pulled down her hood like one removing a hat in a church. 'Zach?' pleaded Hannah, shuffling forward on her knees to take hold of him. She did not care that the flies whined around her when she pressed her face against his. How soft his beard was. How strange the texture of the dead skin at his cheekbone, neither hot nor unduly cold, merely the temperature of air, or of unremarkable things.

'This is a gunshot wound,' said Hiroko.

'Zach,' whispered Hannah, shaking him by the shoulders, then stopping at once when that motion filled him with clumsy animation. His head drooped forwards and his chin rested on his chest. As delicately as she could, she lifted his head and made it upright again, leaning it back against the wall, then reaching up to shut his eyes, which were so dry. Her fingers trembled and she could not. Only then did she scream, as if that were some formality forgotten until now.

Hiroko crouched alongside her and reached out and slid Zach's eyelids closed. Although Hannah had wanted that to be done she cried out (no words, all breath) because she wanted to see the colour of those eyes again and she wanted them to smile at her, to greet her, sparkling, when he told her this is the world changed exactly how we always wanted, isn't this our dreams come true? And then she could do nothing except fall against Hiroko, who braced herself at the sudden capsize of Hannah's weight against her. The girl crouched there, tense as a fist, then reached out with uncertain arms and wrapped them around Hannah, who in turn wrapped her own around the girl. They held each other tight, and with Zach's eyes sealed all Hannah could look at was the gunshot wound in his chest, so rank and so dirty, and the heedless insects continuing their labours within.

II

I

The Night the Trees Came

On the night the trees came, Inoue Hiroko woke because of a fox. It climbed onto her chest where she lay in the youth hostel dorm, and woke her with a lick of her neck. Just one scratchy sheet between its black-booted paws and her nightshirt. It weighed less than she would have imagined, as it prodded at her nose with its own. Eskimo kisses that smelled of dog breath and damp fur.

No sooner had she woken than it sprang down to the floor and stood at the foot of the bed as if waiting there for her. Hiroko was on the bottom mattress of a bunk, in a dorm that slept all twenty schoolgirls on the European trip. Everyone else was still asleep. It was, after all, the dead of night.

In the dark, the outline of the fox's body scruffed into the gloom. Only its supermodel eyes were visible, fixed on hers. She had seen foxes hypnotise hens with such eyes.

'What do you want?' she whispered in Nihongo.

The fox pawed the floor with impatience.

'Go away,' she said, half-heartedly.

Instead it stepped forward and seized the corner of her bed sheet in its teeth. Then it backed off, tugging the sheet with it, and Hiroko gasped as her legs were bared. She slid out of bed, feigning sleepiness, then made a swift lunge for the blanket. The fox anticipated and yanked it out of reach, dragging it towards the door.

Hiroko grabbed a second time, but missed again.

No sooner had she done so than the trees arrived.

They smashed up through the floorboards, slamming the bunk she had just left into the one atop it. From there they crunched both against the ceiling, sandwiching Tanaka Manami, who had been sleeping above Hiroko, between furniture and plaster. Branches as thick as pythons thrashed as they grew, flipping aside mattresses, snapping every right angle of the bed frames. Then they had arrived, and were as still as if they had always been there, and all the movement in the dorm came from the waking school-girls, who quickly began to scream.

Hiroko remained where she stood, too astounded to move. Nearby Yamamoto Shiori called in pain for help, and Shimizu Natsumi bleated gruffly like a boy, and other girls called out questions or just let fly their voices. All the baggage of the trip had been strewn around the dorm in an instant. Uniforms hung unfolded on twigs. Neckties wrapped around the wood like striped ivy, a surreal opened wardrobe of blazers and white socks.

Hiroko looked for the fox, but it had vanished, her bed sheet gone with it. She had never before seen a fox so nose-to-nose, even in her grandmother's orchard where the animals came and went as they pleased, and it was perhaps this smaller amazement that kept her calm in the face of the larger one unfolding around her. Had a fox just saved her life?

She took a deep breath and assessed the dormitory. The biggest tree of all had impaled Oonishi-sensei. The English teacher was pinned two feet off the ground, still in her nightclothes. It was this that made many of the girls scream, flapping their hands at their faces as if their fingers were on fire. Hiroko felt a scream of her own coming, but she forced it back down her throat. You could overcome most anything if you refused to turn your face from it. She stood for one moment more with her head bowed, perfectly still amid the mounting chaos, then looked again and did not look away. Oonishi-sensei, who had been her English teacher for nearly a year now and who she had respected above all the other staff at the high school, had enjoyed conversing with Hiroko in the language that she taught. Often she would ask her to describe, as elaborately as possible, some place Hiroko remembered from California. Oonishi-sensei loved to hear about San Francisco's waterfront and harbour district, but Hiroko always preferred to tell of the national parks to which her father had taken her, for weeks on end, during every vacation. Sometimes the teacher struggled to keep up, and Hiroko had to slow herself down or repeat things in plainer English.

The delicate moonlight lit up one of the sensei's dangling palms. The other was obscured among the leaves. Her bare feet poked out from her pyjama bottoms, a strangely intimate sight, even in this scene. Her blood trickling down the bark looked colourless in the dark.

Hiroko slipped out of the dorm and into the shadowed corridor, where leaves flapped from the ceiling like the webbed wings of bats. She ducked beneath a wooden overhang and stood for a minute in the doorway to the boys' dorm. There the scene was much the same as in the girls', only with more screaming. Ito Ken caught sight of her, and his face was slicked with sweat and terror.

Look the world in the eye, Carter had always said. It keeps no secrets from you.

She smiled at Ken to try to encourage the fear out of him. He was in the grip of it and his lips quivered back around his teeth as if invisible fingers had pulled them. Hiroko turned away. She drifted down the stairs and through the hostel lobby, now pillared with trees. The table football's red and blue players lined the branches of a fir tree. A vending machine, which had been lifted off the ground, let fall a can of soft drink like a raindrop from a leaf.

Out in the street, people stood in shock and horror, regarding the bent lampposts, the cars high in the branches, the smashed house fronts and the roads torn up by roots. Everything had been burst and bent anarchically, but the scream Hiroko had stifled for Oonishi-sensei would be her only concession to panic. 'Look the world in the eye,' she whispered to herself. It had been a kind of mantra that Carter, that tough old trapper to whom her father had entrusted her in the wilderness, had repeated every day of his life.

'How do you expect to survive in the world,' Carter would drawl, 'if you turn away from the very sight of it?'

Hiroko did not turn. She looked around her at the lobed roof of leaves, the billboard levelled by an oak, the telephone mast shoved aside for a new and less sheer upright to claim its place. It did not surprise her to find she had an appetite for such destruction. She had always had that streak. Not for sustenance alone had she enjoyed learning to trap, to pluck and to skin and to butcher while Carter or her father urged her on. The parting of muscles had always engrossed her, the backwards jigsaw of the skeleton undone.

She could still hear screaming from within the hostel, and from elsewhere, so she kept walking and only paused when she had gone some distance. Not many more steps and she would be walking away from her fellow pupils, her teachers, her school in the city, from whatever effort they would make to return to it, return her to Tokyo and the life she did not know how to live there.

'Hey!' someone called. 'Hey, are you alright?'

Hiroko looked back over her shoulder to see a middle-aged English woman, still in her dressing gown, crossing the street towards her. One of her hands was held out and shaking. 'Are you alright, love? How badly are you hurt?'

Hiroko looked down at her arm and saw that there was blood on it. She did not know how it had got there. 'It's not mine,' she shrugged at the woman. 'I'm fine.'

The woman nodded. 'Are you looking for someone? Are you all alone?'

'I'm with a school trip.'

'And where are the rest of them, love? Are you lost?'

She pointed back towards the hostel. 'In there. And no, I'm not lost.'

'Would you like me to walk you back to them? I'm trying to help people.'

Hiroko considered it for a moment. Perhaps the senseis would be attempting to restore some calm to the other pupils. Perhaps they would be as blind with fear as the teenagers were. Apart from Oonishi-sensei, she had never respected any of them.

'No,' she said, 'but thank you for your concern.'

She began to walk away, between the trees.

'Wait,' said the woman.

Hiroko paused.

'It won't do to be all alone in the woods.'

'Won't it?'

'Where are your family, sweetheart? We have to find a way to contact them.'

'My father is in Tokyo with Saori. My grandparents are in Iwate Prefecture. That's all the family I have, and there isn't any way to contact them.'

'What about your mother? Where is she?'

Hiroko scowled, but it was not the first time a stranger had blundered into asking about her mother, and it would not be the last. 'Like I said, I was here on a school trip.'

'*Was?*'

Hiroko gazed back towards the youth hostel, and could think of no good enough reason to return to her classmates there. She supposed there might be some brief pleasures to be had from helping them survive. It would be easy, now, to prove that the girl they'd called a country simpleton or, worse, a *gaijin* because she'd lived so long in America, was actually the smartest among them, and that she wasn't stupid just because she struggled in exam halls or had been put back a school year for not knowing how to push numbers around paper.

'I'm sick of them,' she said. 'I'd rather be on my own.'

'But you can't just give up on your friends like that.'

Hiroko glared at the woman so fiercely that she backed away, tightening her dressing gown around her waist.

'They're not my friends,' said Hiroko. 'I don't have any friends now.'

That was the truth. She'd only really had two friends during the entire seventeen years of her life to date. Carter had been one of them, but the limping old trapper didn't even have a telephone and there was no way to keep in touch once she'd moved back to Japan. Her father had been the other. She had been best friends with her father, until he met Saori. A pang of regret shot through Hiroko at that thought, and it took her a moment to stifle it.

Branches swayed above them, or rattled clawed twigs against the frames of smashed cars. The woman was about to say something further when a blood-curdling wail cut the darkness and she clutched tight her dressing gown in alarm. Hiroko looked calmly towards the woods. She knew that cry well, for it was a kind of calling. The sound of the vixen, who lived in England just as it lived in Japan and her grandmother's orchard, just as it lived in California, just as it lived wherever human shadows were cast. That, at least, was something that she valued.

A propulsion of crows shot west beneath the canopy. In the distance an orange light waxed through smoke. Something on fire, the same colour as a fox. 'Well,' said the woman, backing away, 'I've only been trying to help.'

The vixen shrieked again, and Hiroko took a long deep breath of the air, rich as it was with the smells of exhaust and charred things and blossoms opening.

She followed the red animal.

2

Birch

Adrien dug the grave with Hiroko, who announced that the two of them would be doing it by presenting him with a spade. While Hannah and Seb sat huddled some distance away, he and the girl shovelled earth until dizziness stopped him. He was sodden with sweat and despair, but when Hiroko snarled something in Nihongo and drove her spade violently into the earth, he dug again despite his exhaustion. Sometimes they found a root in the hard ground, and had to kneel and hack at it with tools they found in Zach's shed. Hiroko dictated a relentless pace, attacking the soil with her shovel, but Adrien could not keep up and eventually flung his down. He held his hands to his head. What were they going to do now? He knew how much Zach had mattered to Hannah, but in the days since leaving home the forester had begun to matter to him too. This lodge was supposed to be a safehouse, where he could learn the secrets of a life in the woods. Then, if he ever saw Michelle again, he'd be a changed man. All of his bleak moods and melodramas would be things of the past.

He was still agonising about this when Seb retrieved his shovel. The boy followed Hiroko's steady lead until the pit was long and deep. Then Hiroko laid down the spade and wiped her brow. She had blisters on her palms from the labour, but ignored them as she motioned to Adrien to follow her. He did as he was told, trailing into the stinking lodge with his eyes rolling away from the sight of the dead man.

Hiroko took hold of Zach's ankles and waited. Adrien looked at her as if for a stay of execution, but she just glowered fierce and expectant and he steadied himself, then went and put his hands under Zach's elbows and felt the cold gelatinous blood there where it had clotted, and together they dragged him out and laid him in the grave with what reverence they could manage. Hannah looked on, with Seb's arm around her. Her face looked as if it had been splashed with scalding water.

Filling in the grave was easier, although Adrien found that his biceps throbbed with each scoop after the exertion of the digging. When the grave was full enough to cover Zach entirely, Hannah had such a fit of shaking that Seb squeezed her too tight and she spluttered and lay back shivering on the grass.

With all of that done, Adrien opened any of the cottage's doors and windows that could still be budged off their latches, and Hiroko scrubbed the place where Zach had lain. Yet still the smell persisted and they could not sleep indoors that night. Hiroko and Adrien pitched the tent in front of the lodge, allowing sister and nephew privacy at the grave of their lost one.

With the tent up, nothing but grief remained of the day. Adrien and the girl kept a respectful distance from Hannah and Seb, who sat talking in low voices.

'How did you get to be so fearless?' Adrien asked Hiroko as she stoked life into their fire. 'I mean, I wish I could deal with all this as naturally as you.'

For a minute he didn't think he would get an answer. Then she said, 'My friend Carter used to say that the world keeps no secrets. Look it in the eye if you can. Everything is there to see.'

Adrien considered this advice for a moment. 'Is that supposed to make it any easier?'

Hiroko lay back on the floor, her hands folded under her head. 'You can look away if you want. Lots of people do. You can make up a whole pretend world to look at instead.'

The fire clicked its fingers. The smoke made patterns. Adrien hung his head. He supposed that was precisely his own method, although he wasn't sure that his pretend world was any less frightening than the real one.

'I was looking forward to meeting Zach,' he said. 'He sounded like someone who knew how to cope.'

'Cope with what?'

'The forest. The way the world is now.'

Hiroko nodded. 'It's a shame.'

'You . . . you know how to cope, don't you?'

She only laughed.

'What's it like, Hiroko?'

For a minute he thought she'd say nothing. The gathering flames snapped and bit at the logs, while evening's gnats veered through the smoke. Then Hiroko closed her eyes and said, 'You'll feel better about things once you've found your wife.'

Now it was Adrien's turn not to speak, and to stare into the brightness of the fire. His plans had not changed. He was not going to struggle on alone towards Ireland, although there was no way he was going to confess that to Hiroko or the others. No, he would stride off in a westerly direction in two, maybe three days from now, then skirt back round the grounds of the lodge and strike east, and so home. The others would think it brave and romantic, he would think it small and gutless. Yet, if there was one thing Adrien Thomas had always known about himself, it was his limitations.

The next day, and the next, the crisp air sharpened the leaves, and they all agreed that the year must by now have slipped into September. It seemed to Adrien that the month was already recalibrating for its colder end, and after breakfast he took a brisk walk to work heat back into his bones. He lapped the lodge a few times and trampled through the surrounding woodland before at last he ventured inside, where the rank smell was lessening thanks to a chill wind that had scoured the place.

He found Hannah sitting at the kitchen table, which she had righted to spread with Zach's photo albums.

'Hey,' he said.

135

'Hey.'

She showed him a picture of two scruffy children on a bench, the boy tall with a gap between his teeth, the girl wearing plaits and craning her neck to look up in admiration at her brother.

Adrien pulled up a chair. Hannah turned a page. 'He had a portable generator,' she said. 'A petrol one that didn't need the mains. Out here in the woods his electricity often failed him, but he was never in a hurry to fix it. Sometimes when the lights went off I thought he'd knocked out the power on purpose.'

'And the generator's gone? Do you think that's what this is about?'

'No, it's still there, but . . . it's been used.'

'It was probably used by him.'

She nodded. 'Maybe, but he didn't like to. This all makes no sense, Adrien. Zach had no enemies. I'm trying to figure out whether anything's been stolen. I need something to understand, anything. I feel as if . . . I owe it to him to find out how it happened.'

Hannah had said such things several times the evening before, in between bouts of crying. Nobody tried to give her an explanation. Adrien reckoned that you didn't need enemies to be unlucky, or meet the wrong person at the wrong time. He had thought better than to say so out loud.

'Is there anything missing?' he asked. 'Maybe the generator was too heavy to steal? Has the fuel been taken?'

'It's still there. Most of it, anyway. The only things that are definitely gone are Zach's pigs.'

'He had pigs here?'

'In a paddock outside, although that's demolished now.'

'That might have happened when the trees came. They might have escaped.'

'Yeah,' she sighed, rubbing the sides of her head, 'I've thought of that too.'

He looked up at the branches coursing through the ceiling. 'Is it too early to ask what you want to do next?'

'No. We're going to stay here. Where else is there to go except back? I think Zach would have wanted us to keep the place going.'

'I'll stay for a bit. For a few days at least. To help get things back on track.'

'You don't have to. You have to get on. Find Michelle.'

Adrien looked away guiltily. 'Yeah,' he said, 'let's not worry about that right now.'

'I would really appreciate it,' said Hannah, 'if you stayed for a bit.'

He thought about going to hug her, but in the presence of her photographs the familiarity they had fostered during their journey left him and he felt too much a stranger. He thought about Michelle and tried to recall how he had used to comfort her when she was upset. He could not remember how he'd done it, although he could readily recall the countless times she'd aided him. And so he and Hannah sat in the cold silence of the rising morning and a bird rasped outside, and something rustled overhead through the wood.

'What exactly did Zach do here?'

'Looked after the trees.'

'I know that. I mean . . . do you know how he did it?'

'Some of it, of course. I used to help him when we stayed.'

'Then maybe we should do those things today.'

Hannah lightened a fraction. 'Yes. That would be . . . right. I'd like to live like him for a bit, do the day-to-day stuff he did. Try to feel what it was like to be him here.'

So that day they played at forestry management. They walked among the woods, and Hannah pointed out the spots where the deer had gnawed the bark, and then showed them a trick where just by crouching they could see much further between the trees, explaining that, 'This is the level the animals eat at, so it's much clearer. Once upon a time there would have been bigger animals in the forests, and the trees themselves would have been like shrubs and grasses to them. But now it's only the lowest few feet that get chewed back. I learned how to do this from him.'

Adrien looked up at the buckled canopy and imagined those long-dead larger animals she had mentioned: forest elephants and aurochs and maybe even kirins, all tearing up the vegetation with their giant teeth, and it made him shiver and feel glad for the extinctions of history.

Later in the afternoon they found a diseased branch rotting on a healthy tree. They sawed it off and applied a salve where they'd removed it, to save the rest of the plant from infection. They checked on stumps that Zach had coppiced. They repaired the protective mesh around a young sapling. Then they came upon some birches, and Hannah halted with a sigh.

'Oh bloody hell,' she said, and drew in a long, snorting breath. 'He called this glade his off-licence.'

Adrien did not know why, but he guessed it was something to do with the taps: black plastic taps hammered into the trunks, and a plastic container suspended below each. 'Nothing will come out at this time of year,' Hannah said, but turned one nevertheless. She gasped when a trickle of sap flowed into the container, a transparent substance with a green veneer.

'It only flows in March,' she said, wide-eyed.

The sap kept on coming, fast as tears.

'Perhaps you should turn it off again,' said Adrien warily.

Hannah dipped her finger in, to taste it. The others tried too, apart from Adrien, who stood back battling anxiety.

'It tastes good,' prompted Seb.

'It's just . . .' fumbled Adrien, 'you know . . .' He wanted to say that it felt provocative to bleed the trees and drink what was taken, but it seemed that to do so had raised Hannah's spirits. When he tried the sap, it had a cleaner flavour than he'd expected. He'd thought it would be sickly like too much maple syrup, but instead it was all clarity, only subtly sweet. The aftertaste was the faintest of things, like a fact eluding memory. Adrien swore he knew it from somewhere, even though he had never drunk sap before in his life.

He didn't enjoy it one bit.

On the way back to the lodge, the sap's aftertaste stayed tingling on Adrien's tongue. He followed behind the others and did not join in their conversations. Perhaps he was simply allergic to tree syrup, but he was beginning to feel even more uncomfortable in the forest than usual. The trail they were walking led them through glade after glade of birches, where bracken feathered the undergrowth. The peeling outer bark of every tree was quite beautiful, the colour of sunshine on snow, yet underneath the exposed timber was dark as grime. Adrien was once again worrying that plants such as these were bad things to drink from when, out of the corner of his eye, he saw something step out from behind a trunk.

It was small and bipedal. That was all he could tell without turning to look directly, which was something he was at first too terrified to do. He had fallen some way behind the others, and they had not noticed him stopping in his tracks. Whatever was standing there remained in his peripheral vision, and the birches creaked all around him and the twigs tapped without rhythm.

'Count to ten,' he told himself.

On the count of twenty-three, he managed to look.

Standing facing him was a little figure, just like the one he had thought he had seen in his kitchen, or the one on his windowsill, or the one in the woods on the way to the lodge. Its body was plaited out of stalks and twigs, and for a head it had a crest of frosted leaves like a thistle's.

It turned and ran with its arms outstretched like a scarecrow's. It tottered along like a child on the first run of its life, making a noise like a whisper as it went. Adrien was about to yell to the others to come back and save him when he saw what the figure was running towards.

It was a tree. Of course there was nothing remarkable about that in itself, but this tree grew giant and leafless on the far limit of vision. It was big enough to tell that it had only two lower branches, each a colossal thing that grew parallel to the ground without forking or putting forth so much as a sprout. Its higher branches all began some thirty feet up, where they forked and split into a hundred thorny tips and gave the entire plant a spreading kind of symmetry, like that of a high-backed chair. The tiny figure scampered towards it, and Adrien felt just as small as it was, and cold to the bone. He wanted to cry out but his jaw had tensed shut. Then he blinked, and the tree was gone. It and the figure had vanished in an instant.

After a few stunned seconds, all of Adrien's blood flushed back from wherever it had drained to. He turned and raced after his friends. When he reached them they had still not noticed his delay, and only glanced up at him without concern. Perhaps they were so used to his default state of anxiety that they couldn't tell it from his true fear, and he cleared his throat and was about to blurt out everything he had just seen when he realised that Hannah was telling a story about Zach. She was absorbed in it, as were the others, and tears were in her eyes. Adrien shut his mouth and looked back over his shoulder, but the giant tree and the figure both remained gone. Then Hannah finished her story and there was a sombre silence from the teenagers. Again Adrien opened his mouth to speak, but when Hannah smiled sadly for her brother he couldn't bear to interrupt her, nor to take that smile away.

Once they'd got back to the lodge, Hannah started looking through Zach's cupboards. 'Look!' she said, bringing out two dusty bottles from their storage beneath the stairs. 'And there are loads more.'

The bottles had no labels, but whatever was inside them was clear and lemon-hued. 'Birch sap wine,' Hannah declared, then crouched down and rolled a keg out of the cupboard. They lifted it onto the table, at which the woodwork shook and the wine bottles rattled glassily together.

'And cider!' she declared. 'From his apple trees!'

Adrien had always considered cider a crude drink, flavoured like a highway underpass. Likewise he had poured scorn on wine made from berries or flowers or birds' nests or heaven knew what else, saying that there was a reason why winemakers had spent millennia cultivating grapes and not blackberries. And yet, since his earlier fright with the tree and the little whispering devil, a fright he still hadn't found a way to tell the others about, even the sight of the barrel's brown dust made him itch for alcohol's confidence.

Hannah took some glasses from the cupboard and laid them beside the keg and the bottles. Then she gestured theatrically, every inch the maître d', and put on a wobbly customer service accent to ask Adrien which aperitif he required. He smiled at her, because in that moment she had tricked away her grief, and she grinned back at him before it came crashing back all the heavier for the guilt of forgetting.

'Just the cider, please,' said Adrien, and when Hannah reassured him that the sap wine was delightful he lied to her that he never mixed his drinks. Hiroko held up her hands in polite refusal, but Seb held out a wine glass and Hannah filled it. Then Hiroko got some water from her bottle, and they all toasted the absent master brewer as the sun shifted away behind the tree line.

The cider was bitter and salty both, like sea air cheering the senses just as it stung them. Adrien finished his quickly, where-upon Hannah offered him a top-up. Come the end of his third glass, he was drowsy and began to yawn. Seb, after an initial surge of energy, lolled to sleep, and Hiroko leaned back in her chair with her eyes closed. Hannah stared into her glass for a few minutes, and then began to talk about Zach, while Adrien nodded but said nothing, so that her anecdotes were bracketed by respectful quiet.

Then, after one such silence, Adrien realised that Hannah too had nodded off to sleep and, since this coincided with another topping up of his glass, took his drink outside to where the stars showed between the branches and the moon was a hairline crack in the sky. There he sipped the cider, letting his teeth bite at the glass as he did so, just to feel the act of drinking better. Despite his tiredness he did not wish to hurry sleep. He had a lot of thinking to do, and thinking was always less daunting with a glass in hand.

Adrien sighed. With no Zach to teach him otherwise, he supposed he was stuck being Adrien Thomas. Only now did he acknowledge what a fantasy his plan had been all along. No doubt he would have chopped his own arms and legs off before he managed to learn axework from Zach. No doubt he would have trapped himself in the first rabbit snare he built, and been caught and cooked and eaten by the rabbits to boot. Yet it was not, deep down, woodcraft that he had truly sought to learn here. It was how to be a man who wasn't weak, and who was sure of his place in the world.

He took from his pocket his photo of Michelle and marvelled at her smile and her wedding dress and the flowers in her hair. He fell asleep sitting against a tree, slumped with the photo in one hand and his glass tipping sideways in the other, the last of the cider dribbling out across his jeans.

It was an overcast night, cool and dank, but Adrien slept from one end of it to the other. In the morning the dew came and put droplets on every spiderweb and leaf, and on the lenses of his glasses. He woke to bright sunlight and the realisation that he was damp from top to bottom. After standing with a stiff groan he stamped about to get warm, and it was just as he was doing so that he noticed the concrete edge of an outbuilding.

He was some distance from the lodge here, but he vaguely recalled Hannah mentioning a garage Zach had never used. Adrien didn't remember whether or not she'd said she'd looked through it, so he picked his way closer to investigate.

Old leaves of ivy cloaked the building's frame, each like the battered metal of some knife from ancient times. It must have been years since that wiry parasite had sealed access via the garage door, but the trees had forced a new entry through one of the side walls. Over this a sheet of tarpaulin had been pegged, and weighed down at the bottom with stones. That had been done recently, and Adrien stopped in his tracks and stewed for a minute, wondering whether he dared investigate further. He watched a fly drone towards the tarpaulin, then another. Fat, inkdrop flies such as they had found on Zach's body. They landed on the edge of the plastic and raced each other over its hem to reach the garage interior.

He was about to turn back and find Hiroko when it occurred to him that there was no way that the pegs and stones could have been placed from inside. Whoever had sealed this opening had done it from out here, and that fact gave him courage to approach. He paused at the tarpaulin to listen for sounds of occupation, but all that he heard was the occasional stop–start whirr of a bluebottle's wings.

He removed enough pegs to peel back the plastic covers. The smell that rushed out yanked him back from the opening and made him stagger a few paces, expecting to vomit. A putrid stench such as the one that had greeted them when they'd first arrived at the lodge, although this was a different kind of putrescence. This had a salted, wooden quality like a butcher's workbench. Covering his nose with his sleeve, he again flapped back the tarpaulin and looked inside.

A pig had been lashed by its hind legs to a branch that grew across the garage ceiling. The animal's carcass looked pale as a salamander in the concrete dark, its entrails removed and all of its ribs welcoming the intruding daylight. Whoever had butchered it had done a haphazard job. Stringy tufts of flesh dangled from its wounds, where the meat had been hacked and not cleaved. The pig hung low enough for its snout to nuzzle the garage floor, and its head was bent at an awkward angle that showed off the crimson indent near its ear. It had been shot before it had been strung up there.

Back in the lodge, Adrien broke the news to Hannah as gently as he could. She said she wanted to see the pig at once, and charged off with him scurrying after, trying to advise her against it. She ripped the tarpaulin away entirely and stood in the opening with her arms folded, as if oblivious to the stench on the air.

After a silent minute, she said, 'Zach didn't keep the pigs for their meat. If he'd wanted to slaughter one he'd have taken it to an abattoir, or at least done it properly if he'd had to himself.'

She turned back for the lodge, and Adrien followed with one last gaze at the pig. It wasn't the animal's fate that disturbed him, even if he found that plentifully grim. It was the bullet wound in its cranium. It was whoever had fired it, who was out there somewhere still, in the woods.

3

Slingshot

When Hiroko found Seb, not far from the grove where they'd tasted the birch sap, she exaggerated the heaviness of her steps. Carter had taught her to walk in silence, but she didn't want to scare Seb by appearing unannounced. When he still didn't hear, she cleared her throat extra loud. He turned to look and it was obvious he'd been crying.

Seb dragged his palm across his eyes. 'Oh, hi,' he said, 'I was just stopping here to think. Just, you know . . . thinking. What are you up to?'

'Hunting,' said Hiroko.

'Oh. Oh yeah, of course.'

Seb was sitting cross-legged on an embankment, where rabbits had corked the soil. The trees grew with their arms horizontal, as if held out for balance on the burrowed earth.

'Have you got a minute?' asked Seb, in a quieter voice than before.

She took a seat there alongside him.

'The thing is,' he said, gripping his hands together hard, 'if I'm really honest, I never really liked Zach. And now I just feel so guilty.'

Hiroko didn't say anything.

'I was dreading coming to live with him, because we only ever did outdoors stuff when we came here, but now I'd give anything to set up our lives here. Isn't that stupid? Only now that he's gone do I miss him like crazy.' Seb rubbed his sleeve across his face. His eyelids were bright red. 'Sorry. I don't mean to unload on you like this. But I haven't got anybody else to talk to. Mum's got enough on her plate, and Adrien . . . well, he's Adrien.'

After a silent minute, a rabbit jumped out of its burrow and surveyed the pair of them, all heartbeat and twitching nose. Then it plunged down a different tunnel.

'It wouldn't have worked,' said Hiroko, 'if it makes you feel any better.'

Seb looked at her with confusion. 'What wouldn't?'

'Setting up your lives here. It wouldn't have worked out like you wanted.'

'What makes you so sure about that?'

She stared at the shadowed circles of the rabbit holes. 'Carter used to say that our lives are just fish out of water. We can't make them do what we want to. It's a wonder if we even manage to keep hold of them for long.'

Seb frowned. 'Who's Carter?'

'He was my friend.'

'Hm. Well, I wouldn't know about that. I've never tried to hold a fish.'

She laughed. 'You *should* try it some time.'

'Zach used to fish a lot. His stream is somewhere near here, I think.'

Hiroko wondered whether Seb had it in him to knock dead a fish when it had been reeled in on the line. 'You might enjoy it,' she said. 'It gives you time to think. And . . . you know . . . you *can* put a fish back in the river once you've caught it.'

'I think I'd struggle to catch it in the first place,' said Seb. 'Even with a rod and a net or whatever. Everything I know about is . . . is the Internet. Is computers and stuff. Things that have vanished in a puff of smoke.'

'Carter said the Internet was only ever smoke and mirrors, anyway.'

Seb smiled. 'Carter knew a lot about the Internet, did he?'

Hiroko crossed her arms. 'He knew about the things that mattered.'

Seb nodded, and reached beneath his collar to pull out his memory stick. 'This is the stuff that mattered to me. Most of it, anyway.'

'On there?' She stared at the thumb-sized strip of plastic. 'But that's just a piece of junk now.'

Seb laughed. 'You don't pull your punches, do you?'

'What would be the point?'

He turned the memory stick between finger and thumb. 'Of course I know it's nothing without electricity, but this stick is like . . . an old film reel I don't have a way to play any more.'

She unfolded her arms. 'Can I see it?'

Seb looked surprised. 'Er . . . sure.'

He handed it to her and it was warm from hanging against his chest. Hiroko held it up to the light and swung it like a pendulum. 'What's on it?'

'A website.'

'What's on the website?'

'Just ideas. A project of mine. I suppose you could call it a scrapbook.'

Hiroko handed it back to him. 'You'd have been better making an actual scrapbook.'

Seb retied it around his neck. 'Are you seriously telling me you've never had a keepsake?'

'Never.'

'You ought to give it a go.'

'No. They're a bad idea. An unnecessary attachment.'

'Did Carter say that?'

She shrugged.

'They help you remember things.'

'Help you be more hurt when they're gone.'

Seb watched her for a moment. She looked away at the nearest rabbit hole, and realised that she had folded her arms again.

'You told us your dad was an asshole,' said Seb. 'What did he do to be called that?'

'I also told you that I don't like talking about it.'

146

Two rabbits hopped from the burrow and crouched together in the scattered light. Hiroko wondered if they were always that frightened, even in their shadowy places beneath the earth. Then, out of nowhere, she remembered hunching in a ditch in a forest in California, her father alongside her. Both of them were trembling with fear and exhilaration, for a bear was loping towards them through the gorgeous cedar forest.

She forced the memory out of her mind. There would be no more days such as that, even were she with her father in Japan. They would be stuck in the metropolis and there would be no use crying about it. She had two pictures of her father in her mind. In the first he crouched with her in that ditch in California. In the second he was suited and groomed and gazing out of his apartment window, high up in the clouds in Tokyo, with Saori making tea in the background and their brand-new puppy playing on the floor.

'Thank you, by the way,' said Seb after a moment, 'for stopping here and speaking to me. This is, like, the longest you've talked with any of us.'

Hiroko's smile came and went in a flash.

'And, um . . . thank you for burying Zach. Adrien would have been of no use, without you. Thank you, well . . . thank you for just being such a badass.'

'I'm just a country girl with a slingshot.'

'I'm just a techie kid with a useless memory stick. We don't have to beat ourselves up about it.'

She looked down at her hands. 'Do you really think I'm a badass?'

Seb grinned. 'Yeah.'

'I don't feel very badass.'

'You're the baddest I've ever met.' He nodded towards her slingshot. 'Now my turn. Can I take a look?'

Hiroko unclipped it from her belt and tossed it to him. He tried to catch it but missed, and it landed in his lap.

'Carter could shoot cans out of the air with his,' she said. 'He could make them fly off in any direction you wanted.'

'And Carter was . . . your dad's friend, did you say?'

'In America. My dad kind of hired him, to be a sort of babysitter. This was back when my dad was different.'

Seb held up the slingshot and practised stretching back the rubber. Hiroko didn't reckon he'd have half the strength needed to fire it properly, and when he let go of the rubber it fell out of line without any twang. He threw it back to her and it was an overthrow but she caught it anyway, one-handed.

Another pair of rabbits hopped out of their burrow, twitching their noses left and right.

'Could you hit one of those, do you reckon?' whispered Seb. 'I mean . . . enough so we could eat it.'

Hiroko fitted a stone, pulled back the rubber, took a half-second to choose her target and then fired. The rabbit was dead before the breath had even caught in Seb's throat. The stone had clipped its skull back at a right angle and there was blood across its muzzle. Its companion bolted down the nearest hole, a white tail vanishing into shadow.

Seb had covered his mouth with his hands. 'You . . . you . . .' he spluttered, 'I didn't mean . . .'

'Didn't mean what?'

'Didn't mean actually kill it! Jesus! It was a hypothetical question! And you just . . . you just . . .'

She scowled at him. 'It was only a rabbit. Get over yourself.'

'It was a living thing!'

'And now it's not.' She folded her arms, suddenly feeling like she used to at school: the stupid one who answered questions wrong. *That* was the reason why she didn't do much talking. Talking was deceit, one of the games people played to keep themselves from looking the world in the eye.

'Hey,' Seb said, after a moment, 'hey, I'm sorry. I . . . I think I just . . . only said what my mum would do. On instinct, or something. I don't know if I actually meant that myself.'

She conceded a nod. Although she would never admit it, often she didn't know what she meant either.

'I'm just not used to things being shot, unless it happens in a game or a movie or something.'

Hiroko didn't play games and she didn't watch movies.

'It's not the same,' said Seb, standing up, approaching the dead rabbit. 'And yet it's kind of just as simple.'

He stood over it with his hands in his pockets. He looked lost in his thoughts, and Hiroko wished she could tell what they were. He seemed different from the other kids her age, and she almost reckoned she could trust him. Even if, when he said shoot a rabbit, he really meant *don't* shoot one.

'That was an amazing shot, by the way. I reckon your friend Carter would be proud of you.'

She bit her lip. 'It's nothing. Anything you do a lot of, you get good at.'

Seb crouched over the carcass. 'I'm liking this,' he said. 'Talking to you.' He lifted the rabbit gingerly by the hind legs and, when he stood up, it dangled from his grip with blood dripping from its mouth. 'Would you teach me how to skin it? How to . . . gut it and stuff.'

She was surprised. 'Do you mean *actually* teach you? If I cut it open, are you going to freak out again?'

He laughed. 'I said I was sorry, didn't I?'

'It's messy. You'll get blood all over you.'

'I'm sure I'll be really bad at it.'

She smiled. 'Alright. But I don't do anything fancy once it's done. I don't put herbs on it or anything like that.'

'Maybe I can help *you* with that. Mum's drilled herbs into me like times tables. I reckon I could concoct a mean dressing.'

Hiroko flapped a hand dismissively. 'Better if it's plain. Carter said things should taste like they really taste.'

'We'll see about that,' said Seb. 'Maybe I can surprise you.'

4

Gunman

Hannah said she wanted to get the lodge in order, so they spent the following day cleaning and tidying, chopping back branches, sponging the curtains and rugs where snails had crawled up them, and scraping the droppings of mice and wood voles off the floors. Then, in the afternoon, Adrien found her cross-legged on Zach's bed, playing with her hair in the manner of a girl. Alongside her were clothes: a narrow-shouldered suit jacket and a set of briefs.

'These aren't his,' she said, an edge of fear on her voice.

'Maybe a friend of his left them here?' Adrien hoped it was true more than he considered it likely.

Hannah shook her head. 'Did I tell you I found hairs on a pillow? Blonde ones.'

'A girlfriend, maybe?'

'No. He'd have told me if he had one. And besides, these are a man's clothes.'

'Perhaps a colleague? A friend you didn't know about?'

'No, Adrien.' She covered her face for a moment. 'This isn't right. Somebody's slept at least a few nights here. Recently. Probably since Zach died.'

He stared at the narrow suit jacket. 'Let's lock the back door this evening, and barricade the front one. For what good it can all do.'

Adrien slept badly that night. The forest was alive with nocturnal noises. The thud of wood on wood, the call of a bird and the parting of leaves as something scampered through. When the light of the morning arrived it did nothing to settle his nerves, for in a half-dream as he woke he fancied that the sun had broken like a shattered lamp, and had rained sharp glass onto the forest beneath.

In the evening they cooked outside on a campfire, using Zach's store of timber for fuel, but they ate inside at the table, which to Hannah's obvious distress had five chairs set around it. It was during their meal, when Adrien was in the middle of saying something, that Hiroko put down her knife and fork and looked up like a watchdog, alert. At once the others heard the footsteps, and no sooner had Adrien done so than he realised he had not locked the door as he had promised. The footsteps crunched along the outer wall of the lodge, heavy but cautious. Hiroko picked up her knife and slid out of her chair, creeping around the table with her eyes fixed on the unlocked door. Hannah took a deep, nervy breath and got up after her, taking her knife with less confidence. Seb followed last, obviously terrified, but Adrien remained in place, gripping his spoon as if it were a crucifix. When the footsteps paused, so too, it seemed, did the beating of their hearts. Nobody dared to breathe. Then came a noise of dead leaves crunching under the heavy step of whoever was out there. The wind fled through the eaves of the lodge. Hiroko seized the door handle, steeled herself, then flung it open.

For a moment they all stood in stiff poses, Hiroko poised with her knife and Hannah and Seb bunched up behind her. Then Hiroko lowered her weapon and Seb laughed. Sensing the danger was over, Adrien climbed out from his hiding place (he had slid beneath the table) and hurried over to join them. A pig was out there, snuffling along the foundations of the lodge, a natural grin on its whiskery lips. It had ears as big as handkerchiefs, which kept flopping over its eyes. It snorted merrily to see them, as if expecting a handful of nuts, then when none were forthcoming grunted in disappointment and shambled off along the perimeter of the lodge. They lost sight of it behind the trees, and the evening shadows.

Even though they had spent every prior night squeezed together in the tent, sleeping in what remained of the lodge's bedrooms had brought back a forgotten propriety. They'd decided without discussion that Hannah and Hiroko would sleep head to toe in Zach's bed, while Seb and Adrien did the same in the spare one. Neither mattress had survived the arrival of the trees unpunctured, but each was far comfier than a camp mat on a forest floor.

The others seemed to relax after discovering a pig, and not a gunman, outside of the lodge, but Adrien found he could not do so. He lay on his back in the pitch dark and kept rubbing the tips of his thumbs together, no matter how hard he willed himself to stop. At some deep hour a barn owl took to hooting, and he swore he could hear the onrush of feathers sweeping back and forth above the roof. Then came a taut hiss that he hoped was just a tabby cat, and a brief thrashing of branches and a dead silence before the night creatures started moving again. He begged sleep to take him. He was so damned sick of the worry that beset his every hour of consciousness.

In the dawn light he woke with a start to a pig nuzzling his face. He sat bolt upright in alarm, then realised it was a pig from a dream and that the thing prodding his cheek was Seb's foot. The boy still slept soundly, the lucky devil, but Adrien knew his own full bladder would not let him do the same. He dragged himself out of bed, tugged on his jeans, socks and boots, then creaked down the stairs pulling on his coat and wiping dust from his eyes. Outside, the spiders were breakfasting on what moths and gnats they had caught overnight, and the branches of the trees were stretching with timber yawns as a dawn light danced westward through the canopy. Adrien chose a tree some distance from the house and unzipped his fly, puffing with relief as he urinated against the trunk. The birds carolled in the treetops and a breeze fluted through the wood. 'Maybe,' Adrien thought out loud, 'today is the day to head home.'

He had been thinking on and off about the journey back, and he did not relish the idea of it. Just as he had anticipated finding

Zach alive and well and strapping, he had presumed to see certain other things on his way here. He had thought he would witness the army at work, or places where bulldozers were in action ripping down the forest. Somewhere, he had assumed, *something* would be getting back to normal, but instead there had only been woodland, and the roads all lost and scrambled, and of course those little wooden monsters that he was trying his best not to consider.

With a sorry groan, he finished urinating and turned back for the lodge. He was still zipping up his fly when something cracked behind him.

Adrien froze. Shadows swayed across the forest floor. The boughs above him groaned in their every fibre.

When, at last, he found the courage to turn around, he had readied himself for a figure made from sticks and leaves, or a wolf, or a beast like a kirin supposed dead since the Ice Age. What he had not expected was a man with a gun.

'Don't move another muscle,' said the man.

Adrien did as he was told, motionless except for the muscles of his throat, which were yo-yoing up and down in his neck. The gunman was younger than Adrien, but bespectacled like him. His blonde hair and beard looked like they'd been neatly cropped a fortnight before. Dressed in a pair of torn suit trousers and a stained office shirt, he was a handsome man with the kind of face that could command a room, although the only thing that transfixed Adrien was the gun, which the man kept trained on him.

'Please,' Adrien said, 'don't shoot me.'

The man blinked. He had the clenching blink of an insomniac, and when he spoke his words were crisply enunciated. 'What are you doing here?'

Adrien could feel the sweat beginning on his back. 'Come . . . oh God . . . come to find Zach.' His eyes darted back and forth from the face of the man to the gun barrel's empty mouth.

'Make some sense,' said the man.

Adrien tried to find a way to be calm, but the gun's muzzle was such a tiny circle of dead space. And how could he make sense?

Make sense of what? Of what he was doing here? 'I only hoped,' he began, 'to come and learn something about woodcraft from Zach. Then I was going home. I was never really going to go to Ireland.'

The man didn't lower his weapon. 'What does all that mean?'

'Please don't shoot me.'

'Why would I want to shoot you? I've only just met you.'

'I . . . I thought . . .' Did he dare to believe that the man was but an armed traveller, as wary of strangers as he? The man didn't sound like a thug, and the linens of his shirt and trousers looked as if they had once hung on an expensive tailor's rails.

'I have, though,' said the man. 'Shot people, that is. No use in pretending otherwise.'

Screws turned in Adrien's throat. 'You have?' he wheezed. 'Are you the one who shot Zach?'

'I've never known any Zach. I didn't know any of their names.'

'Are you going to shoot me too?'

The man sucked his bottom lip. 'You aren't very brave, are you?'

'Am I supposed to be?'

The man lifted the gun to look along its sights. 'Some people are.'

A branch swung horizontally and crashed into the man's arm, knocking the weapon at once from his hands and following through hard into his gut. He doubled over with a grunt, but then Hiroko followed up with the branch gripped tight in both hands, cudgelling his bowed head. The man dropped into the loam and lay there prone, blood leaking out of his scalp and into his hair.

Adrien, likewise, flopped onto the floor. 'Thank you,' he wheezed to Hiroko. 'Thank God for you.' She grabbed his arm and tried to help him up, but no sooner did he try to stand than he felt the relief whoosh to his head, and the woods turned white and he teetered sideways into unconsciousness.

5

Unicorn

Hannah lay face down on the bed, struggling all over again to accept what had happened to Zach. She had barely slept a wink, and she knew she had kept Hiroko awake too, for at some early hour the girl had stood up and pulled on her clothes and slipped out of the bedroom door.

The trees brushed and clattered against the walls of the lodge, and Hannah wished they would be silent. Since Zach's death she had begun to think of them as a dumb flock of creatures, standing idly by while their shepherd was lost. Then it seemed to her that the soil that nourished the trees was not worthy of housing Zach's body. She tried not to think of what would be happening to him, down there in the roots' realm.

She had always pictured Zach working himself grey, growing ever more into himself with age. Then, one dappled afternoon in the silver-haired and liver-spotted years of his life, he would sit down in the shade of his favourite oak and lower his chin to his chest for the last time. He deserved that ending, not for his final expression to be one of disbelief and disappointment. Hannah could barely even acknowledge that he had been shot, and that somewhere out there was the person who had done it. It was just as it had been with their mother, although this time she had no brother to support her, and not even a vacant and heartbroken father.

Hannah pressed her face against her pillow, which was damp from intermittent tears. Now and then she held her breath and listened, half-expecting some great shout from the soil as Zach's grave rent open and he clawed his way out. She only ever heard the chatter of the leaves.

'Mum?' It was Seb, poking his head around the door. 'Mum, are you awake?'

'I don't think I've slept all night.'

There was an urgency to his voice. 'You have to come downstairs.' Hannah didn't move a muscle.

He came over and tugged at her foot. 'You have to, Mum.'

She sat up, rubbing her arms and trying to smile at him. 'Everything alright, Seb?'

'They've caught him. Hiroko and Adrien have. He's tied to a chair in the sitting room.'

She stared at her son, almost wishing he were joking. '*Him?*' she said, feigning that she hadn't a clue.

Seb tugged again at her foot. 'Yes. Him.'

Her immediate thought was that she was not ready. She was too woozy with grief for this confrontation, but already Seb was helping her out of bed and holding her hand as he led her step-by-step towards it.

Halfway down the stairs she grabbed the banister and dug her heels in. 'I don't feel good this morning,' she whispered. 'I haven't slept. I don't know if I can cope with this right now.'

'But he's downstairs, Mum,' said Seb, not without concern. 'A gunman. We've got no choice.'

She wished it were otherwise, but she supposed it was the truth.

Hiroko had tied the gunman to the chair Zach used to sit on. That in itself was almost too much for Hannah. Of course the girl couldn't know that Zach's chairs, all mismatched antiques, had a strict hierarchy of favourites. Hannah took a deep breath and looked anywhere but at the gunman, but they were all waiting on her to do so and at last she looked. He had blood in his hair and his head was bowed. When he looked up his glasses were smeared with grease. His eyes were crisp behind them.

'Which one are you?' he asked her.

She could only stare back at him, still rubbing her arms. 'Zach's sister,' she said.

'Sister . . .' He nodded. 'Please can I get a glass of water? My tongue is very dry.'

'No,' said Seb immediately.

The man raised an eyebrow. 'I didn't ask you. I asked the sister.' He looked back from Seb to Hannah. 'Would *you* get me a glass of water?'

Hannah found herself moving towards the bucket of rainwater, but Seb seized her arm. Even that made her unsteady on her feet, and she had to grab hold of him for support.

'If I give you a glass of water,' she said, 'you have to promise to tell me everything that happened.'

'Of course,' said the man.

'He won't,' said Seb.

'You . . . you will, right?' asked Hannah, as she headed for the bucket.

'I said I would, and I'm the one tied up. You don't have to plead with me.'

Hannah paused, leaning over the bucket, and looked at her reflection wavering in the water. *Sister* . . . She was the one who needed a cold drink, and she filled a glass and downed it in one. She turned around and everyone was watching her, but she just patted her hips, took a deep breath, then rushed out of the room.

Seb found her sitting on the bottom step of the stairs. She was doing all she could to picture Zach's lodge in better days. Zach coming out of the kitchen door in a paper hat, carrying a birthday cake alight with candles, so anxious not to drop it that every muscle of his face was clenched in concentration. Zach coming home in the evening from a day's work in the woods, tired but content with his lot, bits of twig or moss caught in his hair or the fabric of his jacket.

'Wouldn't it be nice,' she whispered to Seb, 'if picturing it hard enough made it real again?'

Her son sat on the step alongside her. 'What do you want to do, Mum?'

She didn't reply.

'Just don't be beaten by this,' he said, in almost a whisper.

She patted his knee and rose to her feet. She strode briskly back into the room and stared at the gunman. 'You're going to tell us, do you understand? If it *wasn't* you who shot him, you'd have just said so by now. So you're going to tell us what happened.'

The gunman didn't bat an eyelid. He only looked up at her with no malice and no compassion either. At once she was light-headed again. 'You're going to tell us,' she repeated, but the volume fell out of her voice.

'I wouldn't know where to begin,' he said.

Again Hannah left the room.

'This isn't working,' said Seb, after he had followed her.

'How can it? What do you expect me to say to him? Zach's dead, and nothing can change that. And that man . . . that man in there probably . . .'

'Let's go outside. You were right. I'm sorry. We don't need to do this right now, and neither do we all need to watch him at once. You need space to work out what you want to say and do.'

He took her by the arm and led her outdoors, into the rising warmth of the morning. When he sat her down on the step she felt as fragile as the dew. 'Wait here,' said Seb, with a gentle squeeze of her hand. 'I'll have a chat with Hiroko and Adrien.'

He returned inside. Hannah waited, tapping her fingernails against the step.

'Here's the plan,' said Seb, upon returning. 'Adrien's going to keep an eye on him. The guy's tied up. He can't do anything. Hiroko and I will try to find some food. I'll look for all the edible plants you taught me. That means you're free to just go for a walk, Mum. Get your head straight. Only . . . don't stay *here*, not anywhere near the lodge or Zach's grave.' He touched her elbow. 'Fresh air will do you good. That's what you always told me.'

She nodded as bravely as she could and stood up. She felt slightly firmer on her feet, knowing that Seb was looking out for her.

So it was that Hannah wandered uphill through the forest, and for the first time in memory had no heart for it. Seb was wrong if he thought she could get away from what had happened by walking. She was as familiar with this stretch of woodland as she had been with Zach's lodge. Although it appeared wild and free, every acre had been lovingly managed by him. Wherever she looked there were traces of her brother: the bird and bat boxes he had affixed high up in the tree trunks; the steel crutch added to a sapling to support its straight growth; the ivy cut back and parched to rescue the trees from its strangulations.

'Was even that too much for you?' she asked of the woods, glaring up at the canopy. 'You would let him die for as small a thing as that?'

There was some blight up here, some vegetable disease that had hollowed several of the trunks until haunted creaks rose from their cavities. She watched two crimson millipedes pursue each other through tunnels in a rotten log.

'He would have tried to fix this for you,' she muttered. 'Done all he could to make you well again.'

She rubbed her eyes. She had to pause and hold on to a branch when the lightness went through her, but after a minute she was steady enough to hike onward again. Of course she knew that it had been a gun, probably that very man's gun, and not the woods that had killed Zach. 'But you didn't do anything to prevent it,' she snapped. 'After he devoted his life to you.'

Pausing at the sight of something turquoise in the undergrowth, she found it to be a speckled segment of eggshell, underneath one of Zach's bird boxes. Nearby, with its head resting on the pillow of a wood anemone, lay a shrivelled chick, grey and rotting. Pushed, no doubt. Hannah had always hated that they pushed one another, and that it delighted their mothers, and she folded her arms and stalked onward through the forest.

Now she arrived at a spot her brother had taken her to countless times, where a dependable branch protruded over steeply sloping ground. From it Zach had lashed a swing made from half the varnished plank of a garden bench, and Hannah had an urge to sit on it one more time. Both rope and wood creaked as she climbed aboard. They had used to arc here. If you built enough momentum, the swing would carry you out above the slope and grant you a view across the treetops below. Instead she only scuffed it into motion, letting it sway her.

'Is he the one who killed you?' she whispered to wherever Zach was.

The only answer came from the creaking rope, for which she was the pendulum.

She remembered trudging through these woods with Zach, inhaling the scents of May's blossom. They had come up here and he had pushed her until she swung the highest she could go. She remembered being a little girl on their garden swing, and he had pushed her just the same. They were celebrating the day he left home for agricultural college, when even their reticent father laughed and was merry. They were celebrating his graduation. They were grown-ups, pulping berries to make one of his wines, and she could smell the juice as they mashed it in a pan.

She clenched her fists around the rope and pushed off with her legs. The swing lifted backwards and then swooped out, over the slope, and she leaned her body to make it buck higher.

Perhaps it was being in motion that shook loose her mind, but as she swung she recalled other, less pleasant memories. The day their father packed their mother's clothes away. The smell of the house after he'd been drinking. Night after night of falling asleep to the sounds of his piano-playing, outpourings of notes looping long into the small hours. She and Zach had got through it together, and his heart was beating in every recollection.

The swing launched out above the roof of the woodland. The treetops bristled as far as the eye could see, with only a half-collapsed pylon a reminder of what the world had been like before.

Hannah swept backwards and then out again, heaving the rope to go higher. She rose, rose with the creak of the swing, and fell back.

It was during her next forward rush that she saw the foliage shaking below. She had to wait for another forward swing to be sure, but yes, there it was, a thrashing patch of leaves and branches at the foot of the slope. Then came a long bellow, half lost behind the groaning of the rope at her ear and the whooshing of the air. She pushed down her feet and scuffed to a halt.

When the bellow came again another followed, deeper in pitch than the first. Hannah jumped off the swing and headed towards it, cautiously at first, then letting the downhill momentum of the slope carry her. Only when she arrived at the place where she'd seen the greenery shaking did she pull up sharp.

In front of her were two bull kirins, and they were fighting.

Judging by the animals' injuries, the duel had been a close-fought affair, now reaching its climax. The bulls faced one another for their final clash. They were massive animals with brown fur and scarred and leathery shoulders, each labouring to breathe against its wounds. Each clenched its eyes when it blinked, as if to reopen them was as hard a task as lifting the great spiked horn atop its skull. They stamped their feet and snorted with breath so hot it blurred the air. One was bleeding profusely from a dozen wounds across its neck and head. The other had fewer cuts, but one deep gouge in its throat. Blood flowed from it with every exhalation, dribbling to clot in its dewlap.

The kirins stamped the earth, lowered their heads and brayed. With instant acceleration they broke into a charge, and when they met they jarred the very air. Horns clashed and locked like sabres, neck muscles bunched with all the power they could muster, feet danced unnervingly quick, and they pissed as they fought and moaned sometimes the way that trees moan. Then their horns came unlocked, and each slid home. The first sliced deep through the leathery hump of its foe bull's shoulder. The second found the throat wound it had already made. This it ripped wider, and blood slapped from the opening like water shed from a branch. That bull's forelegs buckled. It went to ground half kneeling, half collapsed. The victor stood still for a moment, staring blankly around it. Its eyes passed over Hannah as it did so, and she had no idea whether or not it had noticed her. Then it harrumphed and turned away, departing with a wheeze in its belly.

The defeated bull watched it go. Then, with a resigned huff, it lowered its head to the earth. Hannah could see the scores and chips taken out of its horn, the ivory exposed in white lines, some of which were coloured in red. Its shoulders swelled and sagged as its lungs tried to cope, but breathing was difficult when each inhalation escaped through the hole in its neck. It huffed and laid its head to the side, to try to ease the weight of its enormous horn. Its eyelashes were thick and golden, half closed over exhausted eyes.

Hannah approached with her hands clasped in front of her mouth. It was going to die now, she supposed. What a waste. She thought of black rhinos impaling their young, of tigers mauling their own litters. She bit her lip, and the kirin watched her. Clear droplets welled on its eyelashes. They were only sweat, she supposed, as she sat down on a log at a respectful distance, but they looked like heavy tears. She pressed her hands together between her knees. Each breath the kirin took flowed out slower than the last, and after each she was surprised to hear it attempt to draw breath again.

There had been nothing but dying, since the trees came. This kirin, Diane, her beloved Zach. Hannah choked on the grief welling up in her. She got up and swished at a fly descending on the kirin's wounds. It buzzed around her arm and landed in the blood all the same.

Hannah swatted at the fly again, and again it took off and again tried to land. 'Have a bit of heart,' she hissed. 'It's not even dead yet.'

She crouched at the kirin's side and, very gently, reached out to touch it. Its coat was warm from the heat of its exhaustion, and it didn't seem to notice when she slid her hands through its fur. As its eyeballs began to roll upwards, Hannah saw that its irises were flecked with silver, and that on the underside of the animal's chin there was a flash of diamond-white fur.

The fly hummed but waited to land. Grey daylight shone between the leaves. A bird was singing in its nest. The kirin stopped breathing.

Hannah screamed. She screwed up her fists so tight that her fingernails cut into her palms. All of her anger surged out in a bellow, as loud as the clashing of the bulls.

6

Murderers

At first, when Adrien found himself alone again with the gunman, they did not talk. Adrien was satisfied to just slouch in one of Zach's armchairs and nurse his throbbing forehead. Meanwhile the gunman watched him in studied silence. They had gagged him but, after a time, the gag had slipped down around his chin. Still he did not speak.

Adrien wondered if it would matter if he took a brief nap. Whether the gunman's bonds were secure enough or whether he might find a way to murder him in his sleep. He sighed and pinched the bridge of his nose.

'You can gag me again,' said the gunman eventually, 'if it will help you feel more comfortable.'

'Why would I want to gag you, if you're not even speaking?'

'I just thought it might help you to relax around me.'

'I'm about as relaxed as I can be, thank you very much.'

The man laughed. 'This is an awkward situation, isn't it? It's going to be a pain in the arse for everyone, if you keep me like this.'

'Better than you shooting us.'

'Yes, yes I suppose that's true. But it might be better still if you shoot me.'

'Don't get ahead of yourself. That might just happen.'

'I think we both know that it won't.' The gunman took a deep breath, then let it out slowly, savouring it. 'I would have done it, you know. Shot you, if I had to. I've killed three people since the trees came.'

Adrien studied him for a moment. His keen eyes. His crisp speech. Whether to believe him or not. He wasn't used to discussing death threats so casually. 'I preferred it,' he said eventually, 'when we were sitting in silence.'

The gunman nodded. 'Just one last thing. Can you clean my head up? It feels strange where your friend clubbed me. Cold. Dirty. I don't want to get an infection.'

They looked at each other for an unguarded moment, and then Adrien laughed shrilly. 'I'm not your nurse. Why are you even asking me?'

The man smiled. 'Alright,' he said, 'your point is made.'

It was quiet in the lodge without the others around. The trees kept still against the walls, and the birds were too busy gathering the day's grubs to call to one another.

'Okay,' Adrien said, getting up. 'But this is only because I'm better than you. This is the sodding Geneva convention.'

He found an old dish-washing sponge and wet it in one of the buckets they had used to collect rainwater. The gunman made an appreciative noise when Adrien dabbed at the congealing blood in his hair. 'Is it very bad?' he asked. 'It hurts like hell.'

Some of the blonde had dyed red, but the wounds themselves were not deep. 'You'll live,' said Adrien. 'It's just swollen up and cut in a few places. Look on the bright side. At least you still have all your hair.'

The gunman laughed as if they were friends, and Adrien grimaced and lifted the bucket of rainwater. They had caught plenty, so he had no worries about wasting it.

'Thank you, by the way,' said the gunman. 'You're kind.'

'My pleasure. Now all I have to do is wash you clean.'

He sloshed the cold water across the gunman's scalp, drenching his head and neck and face, soaking his clothes. Droplets streamed off his nose and he screwed up his eyes and spluttered and sneezed. 'I suppose you think,' he said, when the water had drained clear, 'that I deserved that.'

'You deserve a whole lot more,' said Adrien, returning to his chair, 'if what you say you've done is true.'

Adrien sat down and looked upon his bedraggled handiwork, and was at once frustrated to feel guilty. How ridiculous to feel sympathy for someone like this. The gunman was poking his tongue out, trying to lap up the last drips of water.

After a few more minutes, Adrien got up with a harrumph and filled a glass. 'Drink it,' he said, holding it to his lips. The gunman glugged greedily, and drew a long pleasured breath when he had finished. 'Thank you. Thank you very much.'

Adrien sat down again. 'You're fortunate you got me. If you got the girl watching over you, you'd be lucky to get through the morning with all of your teeth still in place.'

The man chuckled. 'But now you see the problem, don't you? You can't keep me like this for ever. I need to drink, eat. At some point I'll need to relieve myself.'

Adrien held up a finger. 'One thing at a time. I'm hoping we can be reasonable. Work things out.'

'That can't happen. I'm afraid it's just one of those things. Opposing forces coming to a head. You and I are like two stags smashing antlers.'

'Not really. I've got you tied up. Your antlers have already been smashed. All I've done is wash the blood away.'

'Yes, yes I suppose that's true. Except . . .' But he didn't finish the sentence.

Adrien knew he was waiting to be asked to continue. He resisted for a long thirty seconds, during which his headache renewed its throb behind his forehead. Then he huffed, 'Go on, just say it, whatever it is. Except for what?'

'Except you can't let me walk off into the forest like you would a defeated stag. You can't trust me if you let me go.'

'Is that a supposition or a statement of intent?'

The gunman smiled. 'There are no policemen. There are no judges now.'

'There will be. When things get back to normal you'll be straight into a jail cell.'

'Be serious. I can tell you know better.'

Adrien tried to sound defiant, but his voice wavered. 'You can't tell anything about me.'

'I'm good at telling things about people. And I'll tell you something else, for free. Things *are* back to normal. In the woods is how we're supposed to be.'

Adrien stood up and took a few paces towards him. 'I think I'm going to do as you suggested now.'

'What? Shoot me?' For half a second only, the gunman looked panicked.

'Gag you, of course.'

The gunman nodded (was that a flicker of relief?). 'What do you think I did for a living?'

Adrien waved a hand dismissively. 'I don't care.'

'I was a solicitor. Four weeks ago I was a defence lawyer.'

'Four weeks ago I was the president of the United States.'

He laughed. 'Good one. But, seriously, you were as you are now. Of course you were. You believed in the same authorities you still believe in today. Eventually you will have to confront their disappearance, just like I did. You will either decide that you are your own authority or imagine a new one. For my part, I had a head start. I have spent years of my life defending men whose crimes were indefensible. When the trees came, I knew how things would play out. I had long ago lost all faith in systems. In proxy authorities. Superficialities, all of them. What's your name?'

Adrien opened his mouth to give it, then for some reason decided to hold back. 'I'm not telling you.'

'Then I'll just have to call you Mr President. Here are your new policies, Mr President. Now that things are back to normal, there isn't fairness. There isn't compromise. There is only the coming together of force against force. Stags locking antlers. Men have always been this way, but some spent a little while fooling

167

themselves otherwise. When push comes to shove, justice is only ever the deferral of force onto some other man's shoulders.'

'I have no idea what you're talking about.'

'I'm telling you that if you shoot me, nobody will come after you. Nobody will care. The only consequence will be that you'll no longer have to keep me captive. And yet . . . you'll no longer be able to defer the burden of having shot me onto someone else. Some anonymous judge or lawyer such as I was. But neither will you have to feed me, or keep my ropes secure, or accompany me while I urinate.'

'You make a compelling case.'

'You won't do it, though. I think you'll try to talk your way out. Even your feisty little friend who hit me, she won't do it either. You'll try to reason with me, and I'll present you over and over with the plain truth of the way Mother Nature made us, and it will exacerbate you, and at last you will turn me loose, and then I will have won.'

'And what,' asked Adrien with something of a snarl, 'do you imagine your prize will be?'

But before the man could answer, Adrien yanked the gag into his mouth, and tied it very tight around the back of his head.

The gunman's gag held, after that, so no more words were exchanged. Adrien slouched in the armchair and wished that ice still existed, so he could pack some against his forehead. He supposed there would be none until winter, although his headache felt like it would last until then. Whenever he looked up, the eyes of the gunman met his, and he looked away again.

After a long hour, Hannah returned looking dishevelled. There were twigs in her hair and her lips looked grey and drawn. She stared briefly at the gunman, then at Adrien and asked, 'Is Seb back?'

'Not yet.'

'Good. I wouldn't want him here for this, nor Hiroko. I *saw*, Adrien. Near the hill where Zach and I used to swing.'

Adrien got up from the armchair. 'Saw what? Are you alright? You look—'

'Kirins. And everything, actually. I saw everything very clearly.'

Adrien couldn't tell precisely what, but something was different about Hannah. Something in the way she held herself. 'Hannah, maybe you should have a lie-down . . .'

She turned her attention to the gunman and yanked the gag out of his mouth. 'I want to start again,' she said.

'Okay,' he said. 'Cleared your head now, *sister*?'

'Something like that.'

'I've been talking with the president, over there. Explaining to him the dilemma that you have. I'll need to eat before long. Need the bathroom. You can't keep me tied up for ever.'

'I know. Believe me I do. I'm going to ask you one more time what I asked you before. And then I'm going to change tack and it will be worse for you. Do you want to confess? Perhaps that will change my mind about things, although I can't guarantee it. If you didn't shoot Zach, you'd at least have tried to prove it by now.'

The gunman tried to sit forward against his bonds, but the knots were still tight. 'I have shot three,' he said.

That checked some of Hannah's momentum. 'Three what? Three people?'

He sucked his lip and looked past her, into thin air. 'The first one had a gun pointed back at me. Can you imagine? Two days after the trees came and we were in the wild west. I didn't know him. We had both discovered, at the same moment and quite incidentally, a crate of wine, and we were both armed. I don't think either of us even raised his gun the first. I think we mirrored each other, and both thought ourselves acting in defence. At least, that's how I remember it. How ridiculous to be squaring off like that, over something so meaningless as a crate of wine.'

'Do you expect me to pity you?'

The man smiled. 'I just started to wonder, what if I actually did it? Nothing would happen. There would be no investigation, no detectives. And I do not believe in God, or hell or any of that

169

rubbish. And all it would take would be the slightest movement of my finger against the trigger.'

He blinked hard. He looked like he had missed a lot of sleep. 'The second one,' he said, 'I did just to forget about the first. I was not . . . prepared for how it would stick. I believe there are some who never develop the revulsion that comes with a killing. They are your typical psychopaths, if you'll permit a generalisation. There have been studies, etcetera. I am not one of those. And how strange it was, that I cared so little for that man when he was alive that I could shoot him, but that after he died I wanted to know every last detail of his life. Not just his name and occupation, but the faces of his loved ones. His childhood. What the touch of his wife meant to him. What were the thoughts that woke him in the small hours of the night. What bored him. I wanted to know the very stuff of his mind, which I had put an end to. It was . . . relentless. Do you know there are tribes in remote places who believe that, when you take another person's life, you absorb their very soul into your own? And so you must learn all you can of your enemies while they are still alive, not merely to study their weaknesses but to know what you must coexist with, should you defeat them. We have lost all this wisdom. We'll need to relearn it.'

'Zach wasn't your enemy. He was nobody's enemy.'

'After that first one wouldn't get out of my head, I had the idea – not my finest ever, I must confess'– he laughed and shook his head – 'that I could only put a stop to it by doing another.' He sighed. 'It was an old woman and she took me in and cooked me a bowl of revolting porridge and made me a cheese sandwich to take with me on my travels. She wouldn't have known anything about it, I can assure you of that. I was behind her and too close to miss. After that I started to think about her life too, muddled up, in a way, with the first's.'

Hannah stood very stiffly over him and asked, in a brittle voice, 'What about the third? Who was the last person that you killed?'

He smiled. 'None of them were personal, that's what I'm trying to explain.'

'Did you shoot Zach?'

'Who was Zach?'

'I damned well told you already.'

'If I say I did it, what then? Does it make it easier for you to decide what to do with me?'

The gunman leaned back his head and looked at the ceiling. Hannah was about to press for an answer when Adrien interjected. 'Maybe that's enough. Hannah, you're looking . . . shattered. Let's wait until the kids are back. If this guy pisses himself he pisses himself.'

'He did it, Adrien,' Hannah scowled, 'I'm sure it was him.'

The gunman licked his lips. 'Are you his one and only sibling, Hannah, or are there more of you?'

'Don't fuck with me. And *don't* use my name. You think this is some sort of challenge?'

'It's like I told the president. This is how the world works now. We square off against one another. Stags locking—'

'Give me a straightforward answer. I . . . I *will* get one, do you understand?'

'And if I don't? What will you dare to do, exactly? I thought you said you were going to change tack.'

Hannah turned away from him abruptly. She brushed past Adrien and out of the door. He heard her stamping up the stairs.

There was a lengthy silence. A cricket was somewhere in the room with them, winding its clock.

'If you have any decency,' said Adrien, 'you'll give her the answers she needs.'

'Don't you get it? There is no decency in the forest. Her needs and my own are at odds.'

'Is that why you shot him? Because you needed something of his? His food? A roof over your head? You didn't consider that you could have just asked him for help?'

'Listen, Mr President. You're not at all brave enough for the world you find yourself in.'

'So you have said.'

Hannah was thumping back down the stairs. When she strode back into the room, she had the jacket she had found in Zach's bedroom folded over her arm.

'Is this yours?'

The gunman fixed his eyes on it. 'Yeah. I was wondering where I'd left that.'

Hannah flung it aside. Underneath it she held the man's rifle, pointed towards him. 'You shot my brother, you piece of shit.'

'Hannah . . .' Adrien raised his hands in a gesture of calm.

She trained the weapon clumsily on the gunman, who eyed it back with care.

'Is this,' she asked, her voice quaking, 'the thing you used to shoot him?'

The gunman nodded towards Adrien. 'I was just explaining to your friend here that we live by a new set of—'

She kicked him so hard that the chair clattered sideways and he wheezed as the breath went out of him. The chair fell at the wall, and the gunman's head clunked against it and he landed on his side blinking with pain. Hannah stamped on his bound fingers and the veins bulged in his throat when he yelled.

'Tell me,' she hissed, crouching next to him, 'why you killed him.'

'Hannah!' squealed Adrien, wringing his hands, but she ignored him. The gunman was forced to jostle his head up cramped against the wall, just to look back at her. 'Now we come to it,' he said, then spat phlegm onto the floor. 'Perhaps at last you really want to go through with it.'

'I think we should stop this now,' said Adrien.

'What I really want,' growled Hannah, 'I can't have any more. Because you took it from me. All I have left is to know what it was like for him, in those last few moments.'

'It was raining. I needed a place to stay dry.'

'He would have let you shelter from the rain,' she said. 'He was a good man.'

'There are no good men and there are no bad. Good and bad are just ideas, made up by priests and the power-mad. There is just earth and appetite, nothing more. Surely you can see that. These are not rules I made.'

A crow rasped outside and Adrien looked out just in time to see it sweeping upwards past the window, wings spread like a pair of strangling hands, up and out of sight to where the branches leaned above Zach's grave. 'Hannah,' said Adrien as softly as he could manage. 'I think you've made your point.'

'No,' she said. 'Not yet I haven't.'

The gunman glared up at her when she aimed the rifle. 'If you think that the gun will resolve matters then you're mistaken. And if you really do decide to use it, at least ask me my name first. Ask me who I am and where I came from. Who my mother was. My adorable father. If you don't ask me now then you'll never get the chance.'

'I don't want to know anything about you. I want you to feel what it was like for him. Sitting against the wall. Looking down this barrel.'

'But the difference is,' the man said with a contented smile, 'your brother knew I was going to shoot him. Whereas in your case it is all a bluff.'

There was a brief violent bark as the bullet fired, and the weapon jumped in Hannah's hands like a sleeper startled awake. The gunman was dead, a piece of his cheekbone indented and his glasses tipped vertical on the bridge of his nose. The wall was flecked where it had been plain before. Hannah turned to Adrien but he just stood there gaping at her with his hands shaking in front of him. She shrieked and flung the gun across the room, but it made no difference. She was as white as salt, and the gunman was dead.

7

The Grave

In dapple-lit glades, along the banks of streams whose shimmering surfaces reflected the trees that lined them, and through a swaying undergrowth as high as her waist, Hannah searched for wildflowers. After an hour or two she had chosen an armful: white wood orchids with their butterflied petals, peals of indigo bellflowers and a cottony binding of meadowsweet from along the riverside. The wiriest ground ivy was her final ingredient, which she stripped of its leaves and knotted into a wreath to better thread to it all the other blooms.

Zach's rectangle of earth had no headstone, so the ring of flowers she laid there was its only monument. To this she added herself, sitting cross-legged at the foot of the grave. The trees stood lofty and broad-shouldered, every branch beginning high up its trunk and reaching sunward, as if disdainful of the soil beneath. Zach had kept that soil good with grit and bonemeal until he himself had been laid in it.

Hannah bunched her fists and drummed them against her forehead. When she closed her eyes, the sight of what she had done was never far away. The bullet wound in the gunman's head drew all of her thoughts towards it like a black hole.

When Seb found her there, she wanted to get up and go indoors. She did not want to hold the conversation she had been putting off having with her son. Apart from when he'd told her that, along with Hiroko, he'd rolled the gunman's body in a sheet and dragged it into the woods, they had not yet spoken about what she had done. They had hardly talked at all. She wondered what lonely glade they had left it in, and how long before the worms came up and the crows flapped down.

'Hello, Sebastian,' she said meekly, when he sat cross-legged beside her. He had brought flowers of his own, pink hellebores that she did not tell him were poisonous.

He laid the flowers next to her wreath. 'Hello, Mum.'

The forefinger of her right hand began to twitch. That kept happening. She wrapped her other hand around it and squeezed hard until it stopped. Seb watched without comment.

Part of her, she realised, wanted her son to say he hated her now. If Seb would only be shocked and appalled, and call her the murderer that she was, she might begin to come to terms with herself. When she closed her eyes the sight of what she'd done was never far away, and her thoughts kept returning to the bullet hole she'd opened in the side of the gunman's head. She could still hear the shot ringing out in her ears, and feel the energy of the rifle's recoil in her elbows. Worse than either was her anger, which she would have expected to die with the gunman. It had stayed on in her belly, and now she did not know which was worse: that she had killed a man, or that despite her disgust at doing so she was *pleased* that he was dead.

'What kind of monster am I?' she asked, unable to look at Seb. 'What must you think?'

Seb pulled up blades of grass, piling the thin leaves into a green heap. 'Mum . . . I've got a story to tell you. Will you listen?'

She nodded.

'Okay, here goes. One autumn, when I was a kid, me and Zach went out for a walk in the woods here, just the two of us. I had that blue mobile phone, do you remember it? My first phone. I took it along on that walk with Zach and it really annoyed him. More than I could understand at the time. Why, he asked me, was I glued to its screen? Why was I missing all the birds and dragonflies and the leaves turning red? I said it was for signal. I had no signal in the lodge, let alone in the forest. If I got half a second of signal it would make my day. I bloody loved that phone.' Seb sighed. 'Anyway, I told Zach that my phone was more interesting than any tree or leaf he could ever show me, and you can imagine how he took that. He said . . . he said in that annoying rhetorical way of his, *What's the point of being alive if all you do is look at a screen?* Hah. I was, what, eleven? I couldn't explain, but I knew what the point was. I remember I put the phone in my pocket, after that, and we kept walking without saying a thing. Then, after a bit, I wondered again if the phone had got a signal. But it wasn't in my pocket.'

'You'd lost it?'

'Yeah. And at first Zach was all, like, that's just as well. But I went crazy. I started looking in the dirt and rummaging in the leaves. I don't know how long it was before he said he'd lead me back through the woods for it. I don't think he hoped to under-stand why it was important to me, but he was willing to concede that if *I* was at all important to him then, well, maybe the things I thought were important mattered too. Even when it made no sense to him and never would. Like I said, it was autumn. Leaves up to our ankles. We crawled on our hands and knees, back along the path we'd taken, digging up the mush with our fingers. We didn't find the phone, but after a while of crawling about together it didn't matter so much. It just . . . stopped mattering. We were laughing at each other and covered in leaves. And . . . and the reason why I'm telling you this is that I'd forgotten about it until today. I didn't want to come and live here with Zach because I'd only remembered the uncle who didn't give a shit about the stuff I did. But Zach was on his hands and knees, hunting for my phone among the leaves. What happened to him here didn't have to. It was done to him, Mum, by a man who was nothing like him. You mustn't forget that.'

She let out a deep breath. 'You're kind, Seb.'

He smiled at her. 'I don't think we should stay here.'

'We can't go home. Not after all this.'

'No. But I don't think Zach would have wanted us to stay.'

Hannah frowned. 'He would. This place was his dream. He'd be grateful to us for keeping it going.'

'But we can't keep it going, can we? Nothing can keep it going without him. Zach would understand. It's going to twist you up to be here. I already can't bear it.'

'But . . . what would you have us do instead?'

'Help Adrien.'

She looked at him as if he was kidding, but Seb was serious. An adult's seriousness, for which she was simultaneously grateful and saddened. 'Seb, I don't even know if Adrien—'

'He's going to Ireland.'

'I'm not so sure he really is.'

'He is. Believe me.'

She shook her head, unsure. Yet already relief was dripping into her. Not because of what Seb had suggested doing, nor even where he had suggested going, but because it seemed he was offering to guide her.

Later that day, Hannah sat at the window of Zach's bedroom, leaning her elbows on the sill and looking out at the woods that had filled his garden.

'Hey,' said Adrien, stepping gingerly into the bedroom. 'I just wanted to check how you were doing.'

She waved a hand airily. 'Oh, you know.'

'No, I don't. I've no idea. Look . . . I wanted to tell you that, if you wanted to, um . . . God, I don't know . . . talk. About what happened. Then . . . you know, you're welcome to, uhh . . . talk to me. Because . . . although I don't know if I think it was necessarily the right thing for *you*, to do what you did, and it was . . .' He wiped his forehead. 'It was a *horrible* thing to have to witness, I don't . . . I don't . . . I don't think differently of you, for doing it. It wasn't the same as what that man did to your brother. It's important to remember that. I'm worried that you're sitting there trying to convince yourself you're a bad person, when you just . . . you did something . . . something anyone might have to do.'

Hannah pressed her fingertips against the windowpane, which by some small miracle had survived the coming of the trees. 'How strange,' she said softly. 'That's what I keep saying to myself. I should be hearing sirens. Someone should come for me and then . . . then that bastard wouldn't be right. He said there's nobody out there who'll make me pay for what I've done. He said . . . he said . . .'

'I think you should forget about everything he said. And I think you're going to make *yourself* pay. I can see it already. Maybe that's one difference it would be good to remember.'

She closed her eyes and leaned her head against the cool surface of the window. The blood had come out like the quick sweep of a matador's flag, and then it had been over and done.

'Listen,' said Adrien, after a minute. 'When I watched you do what you did . . . after the initial shock of it . . . I felt . . . relieved.'

Hannah opened her eyes.

'If that makes me a cold bastard,' he said, 'then so be it. I suppose it does. That man said I wasn't at all prepared for the way the world is now, and maybe I'm not, not yet, but I'm a bit more prepared than I was before he said it. If you'd told me I'd react this way a month ago I might have protested. But not now.'

'I didn't plan to do it,' she said. 'I mean, it's almost as if I did it with my hand, not my head. No, that's not right. With a gut reaction. No thinking at all. I did it with my anger. I was just so stunned by how little that man cared.'

'Hannah . . . if I were brave enough, and that man had killed my brother, I might have shot him too.'

Hannah swallowed. 'Thank you, Adrien.'

Adrien blushed. 'Now then . . . why don't you get some rest? Try not to dwell on things. I'll leave you in peace.'

He had already shuffled halfway out of the door when she called out his name very quietly.

'There's something I have to ask,' she said.

'Oh, yes? What's that?'

'I wondered if we might come with you.'

Adrien frowned. 'Come with me where?'

'To Ireland.'

He gaped at her. All he could say was, 'Ireland . . .'

'It's unexpected, I know, but you see I've had a change of heart. I can't stay here, not with all that's happened. I need to, you know, head towards something, and I don't have anything else to head to now that Zach's . . . now that . . . that. I need some sort of momentum, Adrien, and maybe . . . maybe when you think about it, you could use a helping hand.'

'Right,' he said, 'you want to go to Ireland.'

She looked away. 'I thought it would be this way. You're not going, are you? Seb said you were, but you're not.'

'Of course I'm going,' said Adrien, in a twisting pitch, 'but the thing is . . . the thing is, er . . .'

Hannah returned her head to its resting place against the window.

'Oh fuck it,' said Adrien.

She looked up.

'Hannah,' he said, 'I never much fancied the idea of carrying on alone. It would be my pleasure to have you come with me. To Ireland.'

8

Fox

They left the lodge the following morning, for just as when they'd departed their own houses, they could only pack and prepare what they could carry on their backs. Hannah spent an hour alone at her brother's grave, and then they were away, passing quickly through the centuries-old forest that Zach had tended, then into land that had been forest for barely three weeks. There the trees were bigger, the bark craggier, the roots running in great ridges through the soil.

They came to a small town in the evening, but did not enter and made camp on its outskirts. Rain fell overnight and pattered off the tent roof, and the ground was moist come morning. They pushed on through the town and found it to be almost entirely abandoned, fit only for weeds and the first germinating saplings. Broken roofs had let the rainwater in, to pool in whatever was left of the rooms beneath. Mould had flowered, and insects had hatched in their millions to gnaw the fixtures and wallpaper. Wherever there was mud or soft soil, there were also trails of angular footprints, left by countless vermin. Sometimes there were also fresh human tracks, but what people they encountered were always sorry sights, poking through the rubble or staring vacantly into the canopy.

Beyond the town the land grew hillier, although it was hard at first to notice beneath the trees. It fell, as if by default, to Hiroko to decide when they should rest and when they should push on. Hannah had none of the energy that had propelled them to Zach's

180

lodge, and sometimes it was all she could do to put one foot in front of another.

Stones began to rear out of the hills, alongside the tree trunks. Some looked dirty enough to have been ejected from the soil when the forest came, while others were sun and wind-worn, as if they had stood there when the land was bare. For three days they hiked through such wilder places, and Hiroko called them to an early halt on each, in order to have daylight left for hunting and foraging. Hannah, however, found she had hardly any appetite, and the prospect of scrounging for mushrooms no longer appealed to either her head or her stomach.

'Why don't I do it?' Seb suggested. 'You've taught me all the basics, and you can check what I bring back for anything that's poisonous.'

Hannah was only too glad to let him do so, and he took her foraging knapsack when he walked off alongside Hiroko. They notched the tree trunks with their knives as they went, to mark a path to follow back to the tent.

Five days after leaving Zach's lodge, they came upon a group of some thirty or forty people, camping on a stretch of dual carriage-way. They had constructed rudimentary shelters beneath a flyover, and were erecting fences using sawn wood. The instant Hiroko led the others into view, somebody from atop the flyover whistled, and several young men hurried down to meet them.

'You can't stop here,' said the first man.

'We don't want to,' said Hiroko, folding her arms.

The men glanced at each other. 'Okay. That's okay, then. It's just that we've had trouble, and most people who find us are looking to get out of the woods.'

'This isn't out of the woods,' said Adrien.

'It will be, when we're done.'

Hannah looked past the men, to the place they were building. It was nothing special, just a few acres of concrete with unfounded huts sitting atop it. There were also stumps, some two dozen of them, where the settlers had cleared space by felling trees.

'What have you got to eat?' asked Hannah. 'Have you got any livestock? Have you planted anything?'

'We get by from scavenging, mostly. There's still food to be found, here and there.'

Hannah shook her head. 'You'll need a reserve, if you're going to stay in one place. In the winter you're going to starve. Don't think that nature will do you any favours.'

'Steady on, Mum,' said Seb.

'I'm telling them for their own good.' Hannah raised a finger towards the group's spokesman. 'Even if you knew everything there was to know about the woods, nature wouldn't help you when you needed it to.'

'Listen,' said the man, 'we know it won't be easy, but we've made up our minds. Those who wanted to do things differently have already left. We had a big bust-up just this morning, in fact, and they set off for somewhere else.' Now he too folded his arms. 'I think it's probably best if you don't hang around here either.'

Hannah didn't object, and they passed by the flyover and heard a baby wailing somewhere behind a wooden wall. As they left the place behind them, they saw the many shallow footprints of the group of dissenters who the man had described, and they led in the same direction as themselves.

'The ones who left had the right idea,' Hannah muttered as they went. 'You can't live off a strip of broken tarmac.'

'People want homes,' said Adrien. 'And I can't say I blame them.'

They continued west, and the crowd's many footprints preceded them. The land began to rise again, and the stones showing out of it were the biggest they'd yet seen. Then Hiroko held up a hand and they all stopped as still as they could. They'd grown used to that command, which she gave whenever she spotted prey in sling-shot range. This time, however, her weapon stayed holstered. She pointed instead to the forest floor.

'What is it?' asked Hannah.

The soil beneath their feet was moist and dark, with fallen leaves wilting into it here and there.

'They've gone,' said Hiroko.

'What have?'

Hiroko turned and pointed at the ground they had just covered. Their footsteps traced back through the soil, pressed into those of the crowd they had been following.

'Oh,' said Adrien. 'Oh dear.'

The footsteps of the crowd vanished a few yards behind them, as suddenly as if the woods had erased the tracks. Past that point, only their own remained.

As the days that followed passed by, and if ever the land dropped suddenly, the four travellers were sometimes offered a view due north, where a mountainous horizon jutted beneath purple clouds. Sometimes gushing rivers crossed their path, too deep to wade. Then they had to walk a half-day or more along tree-lined banks to find a place where they could cross. Some of the smaller villages and hamlets they came upon were, like the flyover, busy with efforts at reconstruction. In others, nothing survived worth repairing. The people in each place seemed unduly territorial, and attached to their broken architecture as if it were the only dry land in an ocean.

Between the villages the land heaped and sloped too many times to count. Seb suggested that, for a game, they try to point out faces in the stones and boulders. Many had great noses of rock, or furrowed foreheads, and still more had beards and eyebrows of bright green moss. Adrien proved especially good at spotting the chiselled likenesses of celebrities and politicians who none of them had even once thought of since the trees came. To Hannah especially, such figures seemed like distant history now, although she did not say as much, just as she did not take part in the game. Whenever she thought about playing, she looked and saw the same face repeated in every stone, and there always seemed to be a pockmark of erosion where the bullet had gone in.

The compass told them they were drifting west by north-west, and on the next hillside, playing the boulder game again, they found an entire ring of tall stones. Hannah traced her fingers across one's cold surface. 'These aren't boulders,' she said, 'they're menhirs. This was a henge of some sort.'

Each menhir in the circle stood five or six feet tall, arranged in a geometry forgotten with its arrangers. The stones pointed up like giant thumbs, mercifully free of anything like faces. Some had cavities chiselled at shoulder height, which might once have socketed other stones now half sunk into the earth or lost. The dipping sunlight banded the earth with the shadows of plants and rocks alike, and Hannah wondered whether there had once been a certain hour, on a day long before the trees came, when it would have shone meaning into the henge's pattern.

'There was a stone like this near Handel's Wood,' she told the others. 'Not as big as these or as elegant, but I used to sit on it when I wanted a quiet place to think. I sometimes wondered if it was put there just for that purpose. Not for any complicated religious reasons or for any kind of time-keeping or calendar, but just as a place to stop and think. And I used to wonder, if that were true, what all those ancient people thought about when they sat there.'

She looked sideways at Seb. After she had found she was pregnant, after Callum had turned the community against her, she'd gone to that standing stone most every night, trying to picture the person her baby might grow up to be. Now that baby was nearly grown into a man, and with the light striking him side-on, she looked for something of Zach's reflection in him. To her disappointment, all she could see was Callum's.

The stone circle seemed as good a place as any to make camp, and the adults got the fire going while the teenagers set out hunting. When they returned they did so hauling a dead sheep, and Hannah looked away. It was only a ewe with a mouthful of long yellow teeth, but its eyes stared out of its upturned head with a calm surety never found in living members of its species. For the first time in her life, Hannah was grateful to crows for seizing up eyeballs. It seemed like an act of guardianship.

184

'We saw a whole flock of these,' said Hiroko, 'chewing their way through the woodland. They're leaving hardly anything green to eat, but we can at least eat *them*.'

Hannah opened their sack of supplies, to distract herself. The few shrivelling mushrooms left inside would be her evening meal, but that didn't matter. The act of chewing, of hearing the wet movements of her tongue against the roof of her mouth, made her feel too close to what she had done at Zach's lodge. To her alarm, the gunman's death was getting harder to deal with every day. Even to drink water could sometimes be too painful, even to sneeze. The hole in the side of his head had opened up as easily as a mouth.

'Sorry I found nothing better for you, Mum,' said Seb. 'I wish I'd found something green myself.'

Hannah's smile, the one that was supposed to tell him it was all okay, would not come.

The flames that night burned tall and dancing. The flickering light turned the menhirs a ruddy orange, and revealed the grooves carved into their surfaces, worn almost flat by time but pronounced again by fire. Whether they were the lines of old runes or simply decorative patterns, Hannah did not know. Seb and Adrien were talking, but she didn't listen. She only watched Hiroko slump the sheep over a flat rock and start cutting out its guts. It was unceremonious butchery, but in that orange glow, on a stone that might once have been part of the circle, Hannah could not help but think it resembled some ritual of old. Blood and flesh and sacrifice. That was the way of the world.

'Hey,' said Seb, 'what was that?'

Adrien let out a long, nasal yawn. 'What was what?'

'Shh!' hissed the boy, springing to his feet. Hiroko joined him, stringing her slingshot, and Hannah tilted her head and did her best to listen.

'I can't hear anything,' whispered Hiroko.

'What kind of noise are we listening for?' asked Adrien, beginning to sound nervous.

'*Shh!*'

Something yelped. A tiny gruff yap from somewhere nearby. Hannah stood up. 'There,' she said, pointing.

It stepped into view as if materialising out of the firelight. A fox kit, staring up at them frightened and innocent. Its eyes were as green as the edges of a lemon rind. Its nose was a wet point.

'Is it alone?' asked Seb. 'I'd have thought it would be with its mother.'

'It's alone,' said Hiroko, crouching to be closer to its level.

'You don't know that,' said Hannah, peering into the darkness for the vixen.

'Of course it's alone,' said Hiroko. 'It wouldn't come out of its den unless it lost its mother.'

'It might have followed her.'

'Not a kit this small. I know about foxes.'

Hannah frowned. 'So do I. And if it's lost its mother, then that's a terrible shame because it means it's going to die. It's going to die and it might even have been abandoned. Vixens do that, if their kits are born too late in the year. They just abandon them, let them die of the cold.'

Hiroko was staring at her. 'This one won't be abandoned.'

'It already *has been*.'

Hiroko glowered at her briefly, then said, 'You're wrong,' and returned her attention to the fox.

Hannah was surprised by how resolute, even how shrill, her own voice sounded. She took a deep breath and tried to sound kinder. 'All I'm saying is that I think it's best if you leave it be.'

'You're still wrong,' said Hiroko. She held out her hand, and the kit watched her and flicked its tail.

'It will give you a nasty bite,' said Hannah.

The fox kit approached Hiroko in stops and starts. When the girl touched its nose, it bit her finger, and Hannah was surprised at herself for feeling pleased to have been proven right. Yet the baby fox did not sink its teeth in. It pricked out four beads of blood, and Hiroko squealed with delight. At that Hannah took an uncomfortable step backwards. What kind of girl was this, who enjoyed being bitten by foxes?

'It likes you,' said Seb.

Hiroko reached out her other hand and scratched the fur between the fox kit's ears. The tiny animal purred, then coyly lapped up the blood it had drawn from her fingers.

'I like it, too,' said Hiroko.

'It doesn't *like* you,' puffed Hannah. 'It doesn't think in that way. It's a wild animal, for heaven's sake.'

Hiroko picked it up.

'Put it down,' insisted Hannah.

'What's got into you?' scowled Hiroko. 'It's like you want me to leave it to die.'

I do, thought Hannah, but didn't say so. She was suddenly embarrassed, and felt her cheeks turning red. But yes, she wanted it to die. Death was what happened to fox kits abandoned by their mothers.

Hiroko cooed over the kit and it nestled into the crook of her elbow, as might the tiniest child. When, for a few seconds, it turned and fixed Hannah with its yellow-green eyes, she knew at once what it felt like to be a hypnotised rabbit. Its black lip was a calligrapher's stroke. Its smile was a secret kept.

The baby fox tracked a passing moth with its gaze. 'I'm going to call him Yasuo,' said Hiroko. 'My grandfather's name.'

Hannah wanted to knock Yasuo out of Hiroko's arms. She wanted to chase him away into the night, and strike him if he returned. She folded her arms and returned to the warmth of the campfire. If Hiroko said so, she supposed, then the fox was coming with them. But as far as Hannah was concerned, nothing in nature could be trusted any more.

9

First Blood

It was not only roads that had been pulled out of shape by the coming of the trees. Rivers had been diverted and dammed, or had burst out of banks undone by roots. Flash floods had carved out new routes to the coast, and the recent rainfall on the mountains had seen cold racing rapids swerve through the forest, sweeping away wildflowers and small mammals without mercy.

Ten days after leaving Zach's lodge, and by their reckoning a full month since the trees came, Hiroko led the travellers to the edge of a town that had been hit by such flooding. Water had flushed rot and dust up from under the dereliction but, finding its onward passage dammed by swathes of wreckage, had swirled back on itself and half submerged the town. The trees that stood in the streets looked engorged and drunk, their leaves dripping now and then into the water. Blanched branches floated on an opaque surface, and when Hiroko shot a duck she did not keep it, for its feathers were bubbled with noxious suds. Moribund herons stood knee-deep amid flotsam, watching dead fish float past on aimless currents, while a pack of filthy rats scratched and nipped each other in their bath of river scum.

The water was too deep to wade through, so they made camp upland of the town and hoped they'd figure out a way to cross. Once the tent was pitched, Hiroko and Seb set off uphill to hunt less polluted prey, and Hiroko carried Yasuo the fox kit with her.

'Sorry about the way my mum's been lately,' said Seb, as they walked. 'She's having a rough time coping.'

'I'm sorry, too,' said Hiroko, and hoped Seb had some idea of how hard she found it to apologise for anything in life. 'It's obvious she's finding it hard. I guess I could have been more understanding.'

'That's okay. I think you were right to adopt Yasuo. I'm already quite fond of the little guy. You'll make a good fox mum.'

Hiroko thought momentarily of her own mother, and had to close her eyes. 'I don't think I could ever be an actual parent,' she said. 'I'd just be so scared of fucking it up.'

'Me too. I'm definitely never having any kids.'

In Hiroko's hood, which was where she had been keeping him, Yasuo shifted in his fur and buried his snout against her neck.

'Is that because of your dad?' she asked Seb.

'You've guessed it.'

'What happened with him?'

Seb shrugged. 'Nothing, basically. He's never taken any responsibility whatsoever. Oh sure, every blue moon he'll telephone me. Then he always says he wants to reignite our relationship, or something like that, as if we ever had one in the first place. It really upsets Mum, when he calls like that. And it pisses me off too. I don't even talk to him any more. I just put the phone down. Sometimes I hope he'll actually show up and say that stuff to my face, just so I can punch him in his.'

Hiroko paused for a moment, unused to such vitriol from Seb, but she supposed she might become just as angry, should she dare talk about her father.

'I'm sorry to hear it,' she said.

'It's okay. The way I see it is . . . he's just like one half of the spark plugs that started me. Nothing more. Certainly not a parent.'

They walked for a few more minutes without speaking, then Hiroko said, 'With mine it was Saori.'

Seb looked surprised that she'd volunteered any information at all about her family.

Hiroko blushed.

'What's Saori?' Seb asked.

'A name,' she said, then strode off ahead of him, stiff with embarrassment. They had been meandering their way back up the slopes on the eastern side of the flooded town, but having gained some height they had now veered back around to the west. 'Look!' Hiroko called back, relieved for the distraction of some stone feature up ahead. At first she had thought it a lone menhir, but as they drew closer it proved to be the start of a thing much larger.

'A viaduct!' gasped Seb, catching up.

The viaduct was still intact, arch after arch. The trees had twisted themselves around its pillars but brought none of them down.

'*This* is how we'll get across,' declared Hiroko, for the viaduct bridged their side of the valley to the other.

'To think,' said Seb, 'this was towering over us the whole time.'

'There were too many trees to see it.'

'I know, but . . . it makes you wonder what else we could be missing.'

No sooner had they stepped out onto the viaduct's straight stone path than the wind turned wilder. Hiroko braced herself as her hair flapped and Yasuo's claws clung on through her top. It was the first time since the coming of the trees that she had been able to see such a distance as this. From up here she and Seb could look up the valley at the mountains in the northern distance, straggled with trees. As the land turned more craggy the plants grew shorter, stubborn and sprawling, whereas to the south there was a sea of dense green, parted by a cleft where the valley bottom and the river ran. The sunlight found the flooded floor of the town, and it was as if there were a broken copy of the sky reflected amid the ruins.

'Are you okay?' asked Seb, watching her.

'Yeah, of course,' lied Hiroko, surprised that the distance had so hurt her. She could see so far, yet the distance to the horizon was barely even an inch compared with the distance between her and Japan.

'You're homesick,' said Seb.

'No I'm not.'

'If it makes you feel any better, and I know it's not the same . . . I miss my home too. I miss my bedroom. I miss electricity.'

Hiroko watched two dots in the sky grow into birds. A pair of kestrels winging their way up the valley. At the last they dipped their flight and sped under one of the stone arches of the viaduct. Then they were away, shooting for the mountains with two high shrieks unstrung on the wind.

'You told me you were from a place called . . . Iwate,' said Seb, getting the pronunciation wrong.

Hiroko leaned on the viaduct wall and pressed her palms flat against the wind-cooled stone. 'Ee-wha-teh,' she corrected him, 'and I told you I didn't want to talk about it.'

'Then why tell me about it in the first place?'

'I don't know. Because you're really insistent, I suppose.'

'Talk to me about something you *do* want to, then. Talk to me about Carter.'

Hiroko hung her head and closed her eyes, to try to demonstrate just how limited her patience was for where this conversation was going. But Carter loomed in the dark of her mind as large as he had done in the forested sierras of California, loping along and delighting in his own skill with a slingshot. He could have brought down both those kestrels in a flash. Carter could hit the eye of an ant blindfolded.

'What I don't understand,' Seb persisted, 'is why, if you're from . . . Iwate, you were hanging out with a trapper in California.'

She sighed. 'My dad's firm moved us there.'

Seb frowned. 'His firm? Oh. I assumed your dad was like Carter.'

'No. He was just another salaryman. But he . . . had dreams of something different. When he was my age, his family moved to a place in the woods in Iwate Prefecture. That was where he met my mother, and they became childhood sweethearts. The woods there meant a lot to them.'

'Whereabouts are these woods?'

'Does it even matter now?'

'Of course.'

191

'North-east Japan. In the middle of nowhere. You wouldn't have seen them in any tourist stuff.'

Seb leaned against the wall alongside her. Far below, the heads of weeping willows swayed and stirred the water. 'But you moved back,' he said. 'You said you came to England from Japan, not America.'

Hiroko gripped the viaduct wall. 'We didn't move back. My father said we were going to, but we didn't.'

'But you told me you came from Japan . . .'

'We didn't move back to *Iwate*. We moved to Tokyo.'

'Oh. Why? His firm took him there, too?'

'No. He left that firm. He said it was time for a new chapter in our lives. We were supposed to go and live in the forest house.'

'What's the forest house?'

The wall in her grasp was as hard as the mountains to her back. It hurt her fingernails when she dug them into it, but she dug all the same. How excited she'd been on that hot Californian night when her father had sat her down and said, *I have a surprise for you, Hiroko, and I think you're going to like it. We're moving back to Japan.* She had whooped and stood up with her hands shaking in front of her mouth as if she were some stupid high school prom queen. *We're going to go and live in a forest house, like the ones your mother and I grew up in. We're going to do it at last.*

'This is it, isn't it?' asked Seb in a low voice. 'This is what your dad did wrong.'

We're going to make that forest house ours, Hiroko. It'll be just like the one your grandparents live in. It'll be just the two of us, living off the land.

'My whole life,' Hiroko spat, 'he raised me . . . he fucking *trained* me, do you understand? Trained me to be like my ancestors. A forest soul.'

'But he took you to Tokyo instead?'

'Because of Saori.'

'And she . . . let me guess. Girlfriend?'

Hiroko nodded. Then suddenly she punched the wall so hard that the pain rang all the way up through her elbow and filled her shoulder with an instant ache.

192

'Hiroko . . . I didn't mean to upset you.'

'Yes,' she said. 'Yes you did.'

'No I didn't. That's not true.'

'Then *why* did you make me talk about it?'

She pressed her hands to her eyes and growled at her own heart to try to stop it hurting. Yasuo yelped at her sudden aggression, and twisted with fear in her hood. 'Sorry,' she whispered as she reached up to stroke him. 'Sorry, Yasuo.'

'*I'm* sorry, too,' said Seb. 'I pushed it too far. But hey, listen . . . I've got something for you. I was saving it for . . . I don't know what. Now it can be my apology.'

Hiroko only raised an eyebrow, but Seb grinned, reached into his pocket and pulled out a chocolate bar.

It was still in its bright red wrapper, and despite herself Hiroko laughed when he handed it to her. Its packaging crackled enticingly in her grip, until she tore it open and broke the bar in two. When she gave Seb one half back their fingers touched, and he blushed. He ate his first mouthful very quickly, but she chewed hers slowly, trying to savour every morsel. She pushed the block of it against the roof of her mouth, pressing it there with her tongue until it melted into luxury.

'Hey,' said Seb when she had finished, and pointed at his lips.

At first Hiroko thought he was asking her to kiss him, and she didn't know what to do. Carter had said that the worst kind of noose trap was the one that your heart made for you.

Seb was still pointing at his mouth. 'You've got chocolate all over your lips,' he explained, and she looked away down the valley.

There had been boys, in the past, but the ones in America had either fancied her for all the wrong reasons or mocked her. Two or three she had kissed, but there had been no thrill in it, and afterwards they always seemed to expect to hang out, to go to the movies or go bowling or sit around indoors listening to their indoors thoughts. And as for Seb, surely Seb was as indoors as they came. Even now he was giving her that strange, lopsided look, as if she were a code he could decipher on a screen.

193

'It's alright, you know,' he said.

'What is?'

'Feeling homesick. It's nothing to be embarrassed about.'

She turned away, wishing he hadn't said that. Some feelings you buried for a reason, just as you buried a carcass to stop diseases from spreading.

'I mean . . . it might help to talk about it. Doesn't have to be now. I'm just saying that I know what it's like to lose all respect for your father. It's something I've done.'

'Don't push it, Seb,' she said. 'I've had enough family talk for one day.'

'But, Hiroko . . . I don't see the same reaction in you, when you talk about your dad. I actually wonder if the two of you—'

'*Please* . . .'

Seb was in full flow now. '—could have made things work again. He let you down, I can see that, but I think perhaps you miss him, too. You haven't said where you left things with him, when you got on the plane. Were you at each other's throats? And you haven't even mentioned your mo—'

She swung around and punched him. She didn't mean to, but the decision was in her knuckles, not her mind. The blow cracked squarely on his nose and floored him onto the stone. He squealed at once and grabbed at his face, gasping for air, and she knew from the bubbling sound of his breath that she had just broken his nose.

'Oh, fuck,' she said. 'Seb? Seb, I'm sorry.'

Seb tried to say something but blood was coursing over his top lip. It had already painted a red line down his T-shirt, and when he attempted to stand he swayed so dramatically that Hiroko feared he would stagger off the viaduct. She grabbed and steadied him by holding his shoulders. Meanwhile Yasuo skittered down to the floor, and stared with wide-eyed excitement at the drip-drip-drip of Seb's bright blood.

'I am *so* sorry,' Hiroko whispered, holding Seb upright.

He spat out red saliva. His head swayed and his eyes glazed over and came back again. Hiroko pulled off the hoodie he had given her and scrunched it up so he could use it to stem the bleeding.

'I'm going to have to set it for you,' she said.

For a moment he looked terrified, but then he nodded and she was impressed by his bravery. She steadied herself, pinched hold of his nose (his chest heaved at the touch), then snapped it back into position.

He screeched, so loud and sharp that the noise swept back and forth off the valley's hillsides and Yasuo sprang away to hide behind Hiroko. Seb's hands flailed out and gripped the first things they could, which were Hiroko's arms. He let go and swooned but she caught him again, and drew him tight so he could nod against her shoulder.

'That's the worst of it,' she said, as the first part of his pain subsided. 'That's the worst, I promise.'

When eventually Seb spoke, he sounded like he had the flu. 'Huv you ever haghd your noze broken?'

'No.'

'So hoe the hell wuhd you know?'

Then he made a strange, deep gurgle that panicked her and made her wonder whether she had damaged more than just his nose. After a minute she realised it was laughter. 'Hurrg . . . hurrg . . . hurrg . . .' he croaked. 'I s'pose I deserved thaght.'

She realised that at some point she had taken hold of his hands, and was clasping them in hers. 'No,' she whispered, 'of course you didn't. You just wanted to get to know me better.'

Seb laughed again, but Hiroko still felt awful. Apologies were nothing but words. Deeds were what mattered, and she had just broken his nose.

And so, never much daunted by a trickle of blood, she kissed him.

10

Whisperers

The sea, thought Adrien, as over the next few days the valleys smoothed out into flatter country, would decide everything. He was glad to have given Hannah some sort of direction but he worried, whenever he watched her struggling to place one foot in front of the other, that in truth it was only a postponement. The water, in all likelihood, would be a dead end. It was inconceivable that there would still be ferries running, and they had nothing valuable to trade for passage on a smaller boat. Adrien had imagined, in a fanciful moment, them all building a raft out of wood, but he could barely swim the length of a heated pool and would no doubt drown when the first hefty wave sloshed him overboard. No, the sea would decide everything. And what it would decide was that their journey had come to a crunching halt, and that Adrien had no choice but to put on a brave face and turn back for home, and when he got there dust the leaves from his armchair and await Michelle's return. That, after all, had been his first plan and the most sensible. Michelle would never expect him to make his way to Ireland, and if anyone could contrive to cross in the other direction it would be her. Adrien would wait for her, and if she did not come he would assume she'd given up on him and set up with Roland, and he would not hold that against her. When he put himself in Michelle's shoes, and thought of the self-pitying oaf of a husband who she'd left on the sofa when she'd departed that day, he was all too happy to jettison Adrien Thomas out of his life.

Adrien shifted the weight of his rucksack and trudged on through the forest. Hannah kept falling behind, whereupon he would drop back alongside her and smile, and she would try to smile in return. The teenagers, meanwhile, picked them a path using the compass and Hiroko's instincts. What they hoped to get out of this journey was beyond Adrien. He could tell, however, what was going on between *them*. They had shown no mushy signs of affection (he supposed Hiroko wasn't the sort), but ever since they'd returned from the viaduct, something had been different. Seb had said he'd broken his nose by falling off a boulder. He was actually a competent liar, but all his fine acting had been spoiled by his accomplice. Hiroko had been unable to stop staring at her boots, scraping the heel of one at the toes of the other. As for Yasuo, he'd made a noise like a laugh while Seb told the story, and looked with eager mirth from his mistress to the boy.

The next day brought rain. The first sign of it was a fat drop that hit Adrien in the eye, and soon after the woods began to rattle with water. It was hard at first to know how heavy it fell, for the canopy provided an initial defence against the downpour. Then came the boom of thunder, and the leaves shivered en masse as if they were the storm cloud itself. Soon the foliage bowed under the weight of all its caught water. Chutes of it tipped through the branches without warning, and it always seemed to Adrien that he was the one beneath it who got soaked.

To his relief, the compass eventually brought them to a country church, the rain hammering off its lead roof and a first stroke of sheet lightning silhouetting it against the treetops. 'Hannah,' shouted Adrien above the thunder, pointing to a bristled tree that arced its back like a cat against the church's wall, 'isn't that the same kind as the one in the churchyard where we met?'

Hannah bent her neck to look up at it. 'Yeah,' she said flatly, 'a yew.'

The yew shivered in the rain, its fronds combed by stormwater. 'Come on,' said Adrien, shaking himself. 'It's only going to piss it down even harder out here. Let's get inside.'

'You three go in,' said Hannah, her voice almost washed away on the air. 'I've always felt . . . uncomfortable . . . in churches. I'll stay out here.'

'Mum,' said Seb, 'you can't. You'll catch a chill.'

'I'll huddle in the porch. No point worrying about me.'

Adrien flapped his hands about, as if that would sway her. 'But it's tipping it down!'

She shook her head.

'Okay,' he conceded, then turned to the teenagers. 'What about you two?'

Hannah replied before Seb could. 'Please don't wait out here with me, Seb. I'll be fine, honestly. There's only room in this porch for one, and I've stood through worse rain than this. Go in, all three of you.'

Adrien looked from the hissing rain to the solid church door, to the insubstantial porch where Hannah would be sheltering. 'Right,' he said, 'what we'll do . . . what we'll do is see if there's anything inside that will help keep you sheltered. We'll dress you in a vicar's robe, if we have to.'

Again she tried to smile for him, then he swung open the door and led the other two through it.

Inside, they were stunned for a moment to discover a generator whirring behind a large halogen lamp, a bright nucleus like ball lightning. Around this crowded nine or ten people, some standing, some seated, all looking up at the newcomers. There were several frightened-looking men wearing flat caps, and a handful of women in cagoules, scarves and jumpers. The lamp flung Gothic shadows at the ceiling, and made the carved saints and grotesques up there pull tortured faces.

The architectural tricks of churches had never really impressed any sense of sanctity onto Adrien. He had been to some truly vast cathedrals in his time, but had only ever been left cold by the shadow of so much stone. If he was ever trapped there for too long (say, for the length of a church service) he always began to feel that he had been buried alive. In this church, however, there was a new architecture. What they had seen of the yew from outside proved now to be not much more than an offshoot, for in here its true glory was revealed. It had congregated the pews with its boughs and shattered the slabbed monuments. It had pulled out the font like a plug chain. Its fingers had sunk through cracks in the flagstones and its trunk, as it groped up the insides of the tower, had forced loose the bell. For a moment Adrien could ignore the people around the lamp, imagining instead that bell tolling and clanging its final peals when it crashed down to the floor, where it now lay a quarter buried in stone. He thought of his own wedding bells, ringing out dimly through the intervening years. He had checked his watch. He had been on the church green sweating in the sunshine, smiling and nattering to guests and feeling sick from his top to his tails. Then there had been Michelle, gliding into the church in her wedding dress, bright in the shady aisle like a moonbeam through the night.

He gulped. Everyone was looking at him, even Hiroko and Seb, as if he were for some reason their spokesman. 'Um, good afternoon,' he said.

'Afternoon,' said a man among those gathered at the lamp. 'If it's shelter you want then welcome. If it's trouble, then know we won't stand for it.'

Adrien held up his hands. 'Trouble is the last thing on our minds. We just want to wait out the storm.'

'Then make yourselves at home,' said someone else. It was the vicar, a barrel-necked man in a leather jacket and dog collar. 'Do you want a cup of tea?'

Adrien laughed, delighted at the very idea, and watched with pleasure the steam hooting out of the kettle, anticipating the hot liquid that would take his mind off his clothes, which were stuck damply to his flesh. 'Would it be impolite to ask for a fourth cup?' he said. 'We've a friend who's decided to wait outside.'

'Out in the storm?'

'Yes. Well, she's squeezed in the doorway. She, er . . . she doesn't like churches.'

199

While the water poured and the teabag was stirred, Adrien looked up at the church's ceiling. Sculpted into the beams that crossed it were devils and angels and stranger faces still. It took him a moment to realise that some of those faces were made out of leaves, albeit wood-carved ones. Their mouths hung open either to spew out more foliage or swallow it up. One puckish face had oak leaves for eyebrows and a chin of ivy. Another had cheekbones of holly and flat, stemmed lips. There was one with forget-me-not eyes and flowering whiskers. There was another with a hooked nose and ivy for a mane. Every one of them was different, but all were chiselled by the bold, crude skill of a country carpenter. They adorned every level as high as Adrien could see, but he could tell there were more on the edge of the light. Sometimes, when the lamp flickered, they looked like they were moving, and he didn't like what they reminded him of. Adrien didn't remember any such monsters in the Bible, although he had only ever got as far as the bit with the chariots.

The vicar, having poured the tea, cast around to find an umbrella.

'I'll take it out to her,' said Adrien, still feeling uneasy about the carvings. He received the first steaming mug and the umbrella from the vicar, then tried clumsily to tuck the latter under his armpit while reaching for the second cup.

'Let me help you,' laughed the vicar, patting one of his pockets to find a pack of cigarettes. 'I could use a smoke anyway.'

Leaving Seb and Hiroko to dry out indoors, and Yasuo to shake his red fur and peer suspiciously at the halogen lamp, the pair of them headed outside.

Hannah was clearly pleased to see them, having squeezed herself against the door to try to avoid a seam of droplets coming through the cracked porch roof.

'Hey,' said the vicar, handing her one of the cups of tea, 'we come bearing gifts.'

She took it gratefully and when, after that, the vicar pulled from his jacket the pack of cigarettes and offered one to them both, Adrien was surprised by how hungrily she accepted.

'I never took you for a smoker,' Adrien said, as he took a cigarette of his own from the vicar.

'I haven't touched one since I was a student.'

'There's no need to feel guilty about having one now,' said the vicar. 'Unless you stumble upon a cigarette factory on your travels, you're never going to get the chance to pick up the habit.'

They leaned in with their cigarettes between their lips, and the vicar struck the lighter and the flame danced in front of their faces. The priest's hands looked older than the rest of him. Adrien found himself weirdly reassured by their proximity, sucking in on the cigarette and watching the tip of it glow red.

'So,' asked the vicar of Hannah, when they were all set, 'why are you insisting on getting soaked out here?'

'It's nothing,' said Hannah, blushing. 'And I'm very grateful that you came out here with tea and smokes.'

'Religion, right? You don't have much truck with it.'

'Something like that, yeah.'

The vicar laughed grimly into his mug of tea. 'We're a nicer bunch these days, I promise, or at least some of us are. Not so many wars and burnings at the stake around these parts. But don't worry, it's nice to see someone sticking to their principles.'

'Um, if you must know, it's not specifically those things that put me off. It's just the thing about the garden.'

'Eden?'

Hannah nodded. 'Just, you know, that idea that the world is supposed to be our garden.'

The vicar mulled it over. 'Hmm. Most people pick something else to object to. I'd never even thought of that one before. I suppose I'd once have told you that Eden was only ever a story, to try to help us understand why the world always seems to *hurt* so much. Now, I don't know. I don't know what I believe any more.' He sipped his tea.

'Sometimes I wish I was a vicar,' piped up Adrien. 'I've always thought there must be a lot of comfort to be had from believing in God, and all his angels and stuff. Especially after a disaster like this.'

'I don't, though,' said the vicar. 'Don't believe. I lost my faith years ago, and disasters have only made it harder.'

Adrien didn't know what to say. There would have been a time when he might have taken a certain perverse glee in hearing what the vicar had just told him. It would have been an intellectual victory of a sort, for an unbeliever such as himself. Today, to his surprise, he realised he was sorry to hear it.

'Do you mind me asking why?'

The vicar shrugged. The branches dripped behind him. 'Long story. I converted my wife. Took me fifteen years to do so, and in that time a lot of tragedies and funerals and disappointments and all the other things that normally tip people towards God. I was pleased about it for maybe a day or two, but some new converts become really zealous and, as it turned out, Celia was one of them. All of a sudden she had such concrete opinions. She took it a step beyond anything I'd ever thought . . . kept making grandiose statements about how this thing was godly and this ungodly, this person good and that bad. I listened to her and I had a kind of counter-epiphany. Realised I'd long been drifting, and that my only real faith was in . . . was in . . . I suppose you could say it was in surprises.'

'There are bad people, though,' said Hannah, as if seeking affirmation. 'There are good people and there are bad. Your wife is right about that.'

'Was,' flinched the vicar. 'You mean my wife *was* right . . .'

'Oh. Oh, I'm so sorry.'

'No need to be. How were you supposed to know? But a tree came up through the vicarage and pulled the roof down on her. She had got up to pour me a glass of water because I was thirsty in bed and too lazy to do anything about it. Now she is the one in heaven and I am the heathen bound for hell, if I'm not there already.'

'That's so sad,' said Hannah tenderly. 'I've . . . lost my brother. And . . . too many have died.'

'Yes. That they have.'

'Too many,' she said again, staring at the ground.

Adrien stepped in. 'So,' he asked the vicar, 'why are you still wearing a dog collar, if you've come over to the side of the Philistines?'

The vicar laughed. 'I never told my congregation about my dilemma. Still haven't. I don't think they'd understand. And anyway, old churches like this one are about much more than belief. Some of the old folks inside had great-grandparents who used to come here every Sunday. Some of them had great-*great*-grandparents, and some even greater greats than that. There's one or two here reckon they're descended from the carpenters who made this place what it is . . . or what it was.'

'I saw the carvings inside,' said Adrien.

The vicar smiled, then said to Hannah, 'It's a shame you won't come in. We're lucky. We've got — we've *still* got, miraculously — some of the finest examples of medieval carpentry in the country. Mine's a biased opinion of course, but if you won't come inside, at least look at this one above the door . . .' He stepped out into the open rain and at once it began to splatter his hair and gem his eyelashes. Hannah and Adrien joined him, and they stood in a huddle with the brolly too small to stop the falling water from striking, and they looked at the carving atop the porch.

It was a flat gargoyle with a face made of leaves and arms made from branches. Its tongue was a long veined frond, from the end of which wiggled drop after drop, as if the tongue itself were salivating. Adrien shuddered at the sight of it. When he looked back down, the vicar was watching him closely, and he tried to pretend he'd shuddered because of the rain.

'This is something you recognise,' said the vicar.

'Umm . . .' said Adrien with a glance at Hannah, who was still lost in the carving. 'Sort of.'

'You wouldn't be the first.'

Adrien immediately dropped all pretence. 'What do you mean by that?'

'A fair few travellers have stopped here since the trees came, some of them in need of directions, some with a compass like you have. One time there was a whole busload, hungry as horses, and we had a bit of a standoff. Regardless, I've shown all of them these carvings . . . and watched their reactions.'

Now Hannah looked confused. 'What exactly are you two talking about?'

'A few other people,' continued the vicar, 'have told me they've seen them. The rest, of course, haven't a clue what I mean. Don't ask me why one person sees and most don't. Maybe it's a matter of faith. Maybe it depends on whether the creatures *want* to be seen.'

'Hang on a minute,' said Hannah, looking from one man to the other. 'You're still talking about these carvings, right?'

'Whisperers, I call them,' said the vicar. 'Because of the noise they make. Three times I've seen one. Each time it's been sitting on the church roof looking down at me. One of them had ears as big as a rabbit's, and I could have sworn they were made out of leaves. They were angled at the sun, if you know what I mean, the way leaves always are. Anyway, each time I blinked and it had vanished. Gone, just like that.'

Hannah gaped from the vicar to Adrien. 'Have *you* seen this, Adrien?'

'Hannah,' he began awkwardly. 'If I'd had the chance I'd have told you about them. But it was . . . hard to know how to begin.'

'Are you kidding me? How long have you been seeing them for?'

'Since not long after the trees came. I suppose it's a bit like how you saw a kirin. And I saw these . . . these . . .'

'Whisperers,' suggested the vicar.

Adrien nodded. The name was right for them. 'I don't suppose,' he asked, 'that you, or anyone else you asked, ever saw them running towards something? As if they . . . almost as if they wanted you to follow?'

The vicar frowned. 'Running towards what?'

'Er . . . a tree.'

'A tree?' asked the vicar and Hannah at once.

Adrien spread out his arms. 'Like this. With two big arms, almost like a seat. Huge and . . . and . . . dark and . . .' He lowered his arms again. 'You haven't seen it, have you?'

The vicar shook his head. 'Sorry. Nobody I've spoken to has mentioned that.'

'Okay,' said Adrien, worried and disappointed in equal measure as the rain slapped down around them.

'I'm still really confused,' said Hannah. 'What exactly are they?'

'I wish I knew,' said the vicar. 'There's a sweet old lady inside who I confided all this to, and she keeps telling me they're a sign from the Almighty. Why shouldn't she think that, when they look so much like these faces carved all over her church? I don't argue with her, but there are devils carved in churches, too.'

'Is that what you think they are?' asked Adrien anxiously. 'Devils?'

The vicar shrugged again. 'They could be angels, for all I know. They could be anything. There's nothing like them anywhere in scripture.'

Hannah looked back up at the sculpture jutting out from the porch. 'Then what are these . . . *whisperers* . . . doing all over a church?'

'Not just this one,' said the vicar. 'You'll find them in many old churches, not only in this country but in mainland Europe, too. I did some research on the carvings a few years back. Nothing very scholarly, you have to understand, just stuff for the parish news-letter. Turns out that nobody really knows what they're doing here. The carpenters and stonemasons who made them never recorded why or where they got their ideas from.'

'Then . . . they're an old thing?'

'This one's as old as the church rafters, which are seven hundred years and counting.'

'There would have been forests everywhere back then,' mused Hannah. 'The people here would have lived their whole lives in the woods.'

The rain wetted the foliate gargoyle's lips, and seemed to make them salivate. Its eyes, livened by the moisture, stared keenly down.

For a moment Adrien felt as if they were searching him, although what they hoped to find he could not guess. All he knew was that they made his skin prickle, and he had to look away.

Once the rain had stopped falling, the four travellers bade their thank yous and farewells to the vicar and tried to cover a few more miles before sundown. That evening and night remained dry, but the days that followed brought more thunderous showers, from which they had scarce luck finding shelter. They camped twice in wild places and once in someone's sitting room, where they took it in turns to slouch in an armchair that had survived the trees' coming. The land rose and fell as they travelled, sometimes so steeply that they had to use branches for handholds. Other times they crossed trenches that the roots had crowbarred open, and in one saw a glimmering mineral seam polished bright by the rain.

Adrien found it had become second nature to plug the poles of their tent together and drag the canvas over the frame. Setting up camp remained his responsibility, while Hiroko and Seb continued to seek out food. He had begun to pride himself on his knack with Hiroko's tinderbox, but he knew that his real task was to look out for Hannah. Some nights she seemed almost to have come to terms with what she had done to the gunman, and the two of them would laugh and swap stories. Other nights she was monosyllabic and had to hold her forefinger still to stop it from twitching. Always she seemed exhausted, and Adrien wished she would try to get more sleep. Yet every morning she was awake the first of them, and every night she lay wide awake long after the others had dozed off.

Adrien was pleased, therefore, when on one such evening, nearly a week after leaving the church, while the teenagers were out hunting and the fire already brought to life, and while he was in the middle of telling Hannah an old staffroom tale he thought she might find amusing, he heard her start to snore. He didn't care if he had bored her to sleep, in fact he was delighted if he'd done so. He crept around the fire and laid his jacket across her, then returned to his post and smiled to hear her mumbling into dreams.

The hour was growing late and the woods were fading into a drowsy evening murk, but Adrien made sure to stay alert for Hiroko and Seb's return. He didn't want them to come back loudly and wake Hannah, so when he heard something like a footfall, he looked up and said, '*Shh*,' with a finger to his lips.

Sshhhh, came the reply from the forest, and Adrien spun around in alarm. It was not, after all, the teenagers returning.

It was a whisperer.

Its head was so crooked it was almost at a right angle, and its back arched up behind it like a cat's. It stalked slowly towards Adrien on all fours, with a ridge of thorns protruding from its wooden spine.

Adrien sprang to his feet, hissing Hannah's name across the fire. She did not wake.

There was no breeze, and the campfire's smoke rose straight and true. Nevertheless the leaves stirred, and when Adrien followed the sound up into the branches he saw three more whisperers crouched in a line, as motionless as sleeping owls.

'Hannah!' he said, and would have hurried around the fire to wake her, had not the first whisperer already crept so close. Now, in every direction Adrien looked, he noticed more and more of the things. One had a face of gilled fungus, and was hanging off the underside of a branch. Another was a graceless knot of briars, seeming to possess no head at all.

'Hannah!' yelled Adrien. 'Please! Hannah, wake up!'

Hannah only slept. The flicker of a smile crossed her face.

The whisperers began to come down from the branches. They sprang and scrambled and flopped to the forest floor, and several Adrien had not yet spotted reared up out of the weeds and leaf mush, raising whatever ears, ruffs and craggy shackles they possessed.

Adrien's breath caught in his throat. He feared they were going to swarm him, but instead they all just turned and ran. They teetered away at zigzag pace with their arms held aloft and their misshapen heads bobbing, and Adrien might have been relieved had he not looked up and seen what they were running towards. There it stood, in the place before the limit of sight, just as he had known it would when he looked. It was the darkest part of the evening, the tree shaped something like a chair, with its two lower boughs stretching to right and left. Its higher branches spread out symmetrically, much further up its mighty trunk.

A groan came out of the tree, as if some invisible giant was shifting its weight on its seat. Now that Adrien stared harder he could see that there *was* movement on it, but all of it was small. The whisperers were crawling on its bark, hurrying over its trunk like ants on a hive.

Suddenly the fire went out.

It died with a hiss of smoke, which rose and dispersed in a grey-blue cloud. Adrien squealed and held his hands to his collar. The logs fumed as if they had been put out by the ensuing darkness. Gloom doused the woods, washing the half-light of the evening from every branch.

'Hannah!' shouted Adrien, and was about to rush to her and shake her awake when something sighed in the smouldering remains of the fire. The burned sticks lifted, pushed themselves off the ground, and were a pair of arms and a rack of ribs. An ashen whisperer climbed to its feet, its legs wonky struts, its head a burn-blister of log. It stared at Adrien for a moment, and a dozen beats of his heart pounded by. Then it limped away, after the others of its kind, towards the massive tree. It paused and looked back after a dozen paces, as if to ensure that Adrien was still watching, then continued on its path.

The great tree groaned, as if calling the whisperer home. Its wooden creak seemed to take a hundred years to fade away, and through all that time Adrien stood transfixed and listening to its long note. The loss of the light had turned it to a vast silhouette whose many upper branches were arranged against the canopy like a crown of antlers. Then, just as Adrien was coming back to his senses, one of them moved. It straightened out and bent back into shape.

208

With a yawn, Hannah rolled over and woke up. At once Adrien dashed to her side and yanked her to her feet, yelling, 'Come on! No time!' She spluttered and protested, but he began to drag her away. They had gone only a few paces before she dug her heels in. 'Adrien! What's going on?'

He turned to point to the tree, but it was gone. The whisperers were gone too, even that last one who had risen from the ash. There was only what remained of the fire, a fizzled pile of sticks in the dark.

'It was . . . it was . . .' said Adrien, blinking and staring around him.

'What's going on? Why did you put the fire out?'

'I didn't! It was . . . was . . .'

Hannah rubbed her eyes. 'Jesus, I must have been sleeping really deeply. My body feels so heavy . . .'

'There was a moving branch!'

'What do you mean? What's spooked you, Adrien? Hang on a minute, did you see those things again?'

But before Adrien could elaborate, Seb called faintly out of the distance. 'Mum? Adrien? Where are you guys?'

'Over here!' yelled Hannah, then looked back to Adrien. 'Tell me what just happened. Was it the whisperers?'

Adrien nodded. 'Yes,' he said, taking deep breaths and smoothing out his jacket. 'Yes, it was them. But it was something else, too.'

III

I

The Coast

Adrien Thomas had feared many things in his life, but when seabirds shrieked overhead at the end of another week's walking, he felt a jolt of terror so sharp that he had to sit down on a log with a hand over his heart.

A change had come over the forest that week, just as the dusks had come incrementally earlier each night. A yellow tint had fringed the leaves, while those trees that had arrived thinking it summer or spring had grown harder to spot among the ones who'd thought it autumn. Villages came and went, obstacles of brick and glass. Unframed doors led to nowhere. Drainpipes collected the water of afternoon rain showers and ran it aimlessly from branch to branch. One time, after heavy rain had fallen and the travellers had emerged from a ruined village hall, they looked up through thinning foliage and saw many blocks of cloud levitating above the streets, like the ghosts of the buildings that had once stood there.

Then came the day they heard the seabirds. A shriek and then another, and then a squabbling overhead. Adrien looked up from his seat on the log to see black and white feathers raking the canopy. It was gulls mobbing a crow, and at the sight of them a strong north-westerly blew up out of nowhere and put salt in his nostrils.

'Are you alright?' asked Seb, sitting down alongside Adrien.

'Oh, of course,' he said, and knew how unconvincing it sounded. 'I don't know what got into me. Those gulls . . . they startled me, that's all.'

'Maybe you're nervous. It's understandable.'

'And what would I be nervous about?'

'Reaching the coast. There being no way to cross.'

Adrien puffed out his cheeks. 'Maybe,' he said, 'maybe you're right.'

But once he'd forced himself back to his feet and motioned for them all to start walking again, and heard the yawks of the seagulls fade into the western distance, Adrien wondered if it were not the opposite. Perhaps it was not the sea's expected dead end that he was afraid of; perhaps it was finding a means to get to Ireland, after all.

The next town they entered made them all feel sure that the coast was imminent. Perhaps it was the predominance of blue and white paint on crumbled walls, perhaps the several premises of fishmongers each gutted and reeking. They saw more people than they had in any town since the first days of their journey, although none of them appeared to be residents. They were all travellers such as themselves, dispossessed and hungry-looking. Just like them, they were headed for the water.

After a winding downhill street of broken shops and hotels, the trees quite suddenly parted. Ahead of them spread a harbour, the surface of the water grey as lead. The harbour wall was bouldered with the smashed edifices of seafront cottages, some of which had been hurled by the trees into the water. What boats had been moored to it were scuppered beyond repair, with shallow waves skulking through their broken hulls and masts.

Here, at last, were the kinds of crowds the woods had seemed to swallow. People were everywhere, milling along the harbour front or sitting on protrusions of the wall, dangling fishing lines into the water. On a patched-up jetty, people had stripped down to their underwear to wash themselves in dirty water.

'None of these boats are going anywhere,' said Hiroko, looking at the shipwrecks. 'Especially not those.'

She pointed to more boats, floating further back from the harbour wall. These had not been smashed by debris, but they were black and charred and the water surrounding them was iridescent with oil.

'What happened to them?' wondered Seb.

'Sabotaged,' said someone behind them.

They turned to see an old man guarding a half-eaten fish, flakes of which were trapped in his whiskers. 'They sabotaged them,' he said, and took another bite.

'Who?' asked Seb. 'Who sabotaged them?'

'Just people. Didn't see. But my boat was one, and it was my dad's before me. It's down there on the bottom now.'

'We're here,' said Hiroko, 'to find one that's still floating.'

'Ha! You'll be lucky. If you had a boat, why would you keep it here, where people would try to take it from you? Whatever boats are left are far away, looking for places without trees.'

'I thought as much,' mumbled Adrien, too quietly for the others to hear.

They left the old man to his fish and followed the harbour line towards its narrow mouth. When the sea opened out before them it made the harbour look like nothing but a droplet. The coastline stretched north and south, bulging with cliffs and rocky outcrops, challenging their eyes to follow. The sea went on even further, as flat and grey as the end of everything.

Cawing seabirds wheeled in the sky, and highest among them was a giant bird of prey with a white tail and a bright yellow beak. 'What bird is that, Mum?' asked Seb, and Hannah frowned and peered up at it. It sickled through the air, folded its wings and dived, hitting the sea in a rake of spray. When, a few seconds later, it headed skyward again with a fish flapping in its claws, she said, 'A sea eagle, I think. Although they haven't lived this far south in centuries.'

Away to their left, a manmade breakwater sheared off a long and pebbly beach. The space between that and the forest behind it was crowded with even more people than at the harbour. Tents had been erected in line after line. Fires burned everywhere, their smoke dispersing the smell of cooked fish.

'God knows why they've all camped so exposed,' said Hiroko. 'If they only went into the woods a short distance, they'd have way better protection from the sea.'

'They're frightened of the trees,' suggested Seb. 'They'd probably rather freeze here than go back to being underneath them.'

Adrien gazed back at the treeline and felt as if the woods, too, were an ocean, between which and the water this open ground was but an exposed spar. Even as he looked, another rabble of travellers emerged from the forest and came to a halt, dazzled by the size of the sea.

He took off his glasses and pinched the bridge of his nose. Just as he'd expected, there was no way to cross to Ireland. Yet none of his pessimism had prepared him for the cold and heavy sensation that now filled up his gut. He felt as if he were two hundred feet further forward, and had opened his mouth and swallowed gallons of salt water and seaweed. It didn't make sense. He had wanted this failure, this excuse to turn back, but now that it was upon him he found that he did not want it at all.

Work out what you really want from life, Michelle had tasked him, and he'd sat in his armchair just as he'd hoped to go home and sit in it again. Adrien stared out at the peaks of the waves coming in, and each was a knife slid in between his ribs. What did it mean to have been so cowardly? Wasn't it as certain as the sea was vast that any lover worthy of that name would have striven every day to be reunited with his love? Yet he had been content to hide away, and to wish Michelle all the best with another man.

Seb put a hand on his shoulder. Adrien would have reached up to grab it, were it not for the impropriety of doing so.

'You'd better not be giving up,' said Seb.

'Why shouldn't I? It's high time I did. There are no boats. I'll just have to take it on the chin and go home.'

'Not yet. We don't know what we might find yet. We just have to hope for surprises.'

And as the boy said that, and much to his own confusion, Adrien felt as if some small chunk of driftwood had bobbed to the surface of all the swallowed waters inside of himself. He clung on to it with all the small resolve he possessed.

216

That afternoon, while Hannah got the camp set up and Hiroko and Yasuo disappeared to shoot gulls, Seb spent the rest of the day towing Adrien between the campers on the coast, asking whether they'd seen any boats. All those they met were escapees from the woods, who covered their possessions with blankets when the newcomers approached, or watched their cuffs as if at any moment a blade might spring out of one. Some of those who had been there longest admitted they had seen one or two boats but added that, should a vessel make anchor, there would always be a crowd of others trying to board it. What made Adrien and Seb so special, they demanded to know, that they thought they could take precedence over those who had been camped there far longer? When, that night, man and boy returned to the tent, Adrien at once retired to his sleeping bag and zipped himself in tight. The sea gushed and snorted, while outside the tent Seb repeated all they had heard to Hannah. Hiroko had still not returned, so when Seb left to find her and Hannah fell silent, Adrien had only the distant hubbub of countless strangers to distract him from the vastness of the water, along with an ever-so-faint whisper, coming from the trees.

2

Slingshot

Adrien wasn't the only one made pensive by arriving at the coast. At first, Hiroko had tried to ignore the lump that had formed in her throat as soon as she'd set eyes on the water. She had coolly strode off to hunt seagulls, and for every bird she brought down Yasuo had cheered her on with a hungry yip. She had shot four, but only two of those had been dead upon landing. The other two had some life left, which she'd squeezed out with her boot. At first she hadn't understood why she'd found it troubling to do so. She'd ignored the uncomfortable feeling and cut out a piece of breast for Yasuo, then tied the gulls' feet together and hung them over her shoulder. Yet she had not returned at once to her companions. Instead, she'd found a rocky outcrop some distance from the clustered campfires, far enough from their warmth to be deserted by the people of the beaches, and was sitting there still as the sun set over the water, her hood raised and her eyes fixed on the violet gradient of the evening sky.

Eventually, she managed to work out why the gulls' deaths had troubled her. It was the stilling of their wings, the loss of flight. It was the reminder of her own permanent grounding.

Yasuo lay curled on her lap, pointing his nose upward at whatever angle Hiroko directed her gaze. They were not looking for the first timid stars, so many more of which were visible these days, nor for the hairline moon. They were looking for a red blinking tail-light that Hiroko knew she'd never see. In the woods it had sometimes seemed impossible that human beings had ever taken flight in great vessels of aluminium, let alone that she had been just such a traveller only a few weeks before. To think, when she had boarded her plane back in Tokyo, she'd fantasised about never returning there.

She stroked the fur of Yasuo's scruff. The kit nipped her fingers as she did so, and she felt his affectionate teeth pricking out the blood. The skin of her hands had become traced all over with bite-lines and tiny scabs. A dot-to-dot of nips and scratch marks, some of which would scar. She liked it. As if it were a tribal marking.

A fox can be almost human, her grandmother had once told her, and her elderly *sobo* should be the one to know. She had lived her whole life in her house in Iwate Prefecture's beech forests, where foxes came and went all day and night.

They are animals that remind us of ourselves. Opportunistic. Quick-witted. Will eat anything under the sun. Beautiful some days, mangy on others. Can hypnotise you with their eyes.

Her grandmother knew all about foxes. Her garden was an orchard, and at the foot of the orchard lay a cleared space that she said was a no-man's-land, separating the apple trees from those of the wildwood beyond. In the wildwood was a shrine, which her grandmother tended. Little more than a stone house the size of a beehive, it had a low torii arch that marked both the start and the finish of the path that led to it. It had been built in centuries past to honour Inari, whose messengers were foxes, but Hiroko's grandmother told of how, in bygone days when there were no bullet trains and hardly any roads reaching into the forests of Iwate Prefecture, the local people had taken to honouring the messengers over the god. The shrine had become covered in foxes. Hundreds of them, all cut from wood or stone with varying skill, some of them detailed with chipped paint and ribbons, some so poorly carved that you'd never know what they were supposed to represent, were there not so many more to compare them with. The shrine had once been a busy place, but now hardly anyone paid their respects. Sometimes a grey-haired villager would make the journey, but if they found Hiroko's grandmother cleaning it up with her broom they would turn and scurry home without looking back. 'They say I am a *majyo*,' Hiroko's grandmother had once confided with a grin, 'and that I make my spells there.'

Hiroko closed her eyes to prevent the tears from welling. Her childhood visits to those beech woods were among her most treasured memories. Always her *sobo* would be waiting, when she and her father arrived, and would present to her an apple bright as amber, and tell her fox stories until the sun turned red.

Boots crunched on sand. Yasuo barked and lifted his nose, then barked again enthusiastically.

Hiroko blinked the moisture from her eyes and remembered where she was: on the beach beneath a violet sky and its absence of aeroplane trails. Seb approached her cautiously, with the collar of his jacket turned up against the sea breeze.

'Hey,' he said. 'I came to look for you.'

She shrugged. That was self-explanatory.

He stood awkwardly over her, with his hands in his pockets. His nose was healing slowly, although a v-shaped purple line still marked the break. He would look different, once the bruising subsided. The gristle would set in a lopsided bulge, and he would appear older than he was, and perhaps tougher too. She reckoned she preferred it. She dug out a smile for him, then looked back up at the moon and stars.

A sudden light appeared in the sky, leaping down it like a spark struck by a flint. Her breath caught in her throat.

'Look!' exclaimed Seb. 'A shooting star!'

But her breath had caught because, for a deluded instant, she'd thought it was a tail-light.

'What's wrong?' asked Seb, after a minute. 'Are you feeling homesick again?'

Hiroko folded her arms. 'I'd have thought you'd have been put off saying that.'

Seb touched his fingers to his nose. 'I thought this was because I asked about your mother.'

She laughed. 'And now you've brought *that* up again too!'

He sat alongside her on the rocks, close enough for their shoulders to brush. She was grateful at once for that smallest contact, and Yasuo was evidently pleased to see Seb too, clambering off her lap to stand on his knees. Seb scratched him between his ears, and the kit nuzzled closer to enjoy the attention.

Seb had been careful, Hiroko knew, not to push for anything more since kissing her. He had let her be the one to initiate things, no doubt wary of getting punched again. Hiroko had only tried to kiss him one more time, and neither that nor their first kiss had been prolonged or powerful. That was not through lack of enthusiasm, but because both of their breaths were stale, and their lips chafed from the chillier nights. What meant more was closing their arms tight around one another, was to run their fingers gently through each other's hair, to slip their hands beneath their shirts and feel the heat from the smalls of their backs.

And all the time Seb had been picking away at her defences with these damned questions of his, asking her again and again to untie some further part of the knot that was herself.

'I found you something,' he said, showing her a wad of blank postcards. 'I found them in a trashed-out tourist shop. I thought maybe you could write them.'

She hesitated, then took them uncertainly. Yasuo lost interest at once. He settled down and laid his chin on his paws, his tail snaking back and forth against Seb's thigh.

The postcards were pictures of the ocean before them and the seafront town in more colourful repair. 'Why would I want to write these? There isn't any post any more.'

'Of course there isn't. That's the good thing about them. Nobody will ever read what you have to say. I thought you could write them to your father. To your grandmother. Even an angry one to Saori. Anything that helps.'

Hiroko drew in a long breath. 'If you haven't got something nice to say, you shouldn't say anything at all.'

'Bullshit. I used to post pages on my website that no hyperlinks led to, and no search engines registered. You'd have to type the exact addresses to find them, and you couldn't do that if you didn't know what to type. But they still existed, do you see? They were still out there. Each page was like a letter, one for Callum, one for Mum, one for Zach . . . you get the idea. I changed what I'd put there whenever I felt like it, but you're the first person I've ever told of their existence. I don't think anybody ever read them, but the point was they'd been written.'

Suddenly Hiroko burst into tears. Seb gaped at her, too surprised to act. Then she pulled herself back together with a growl. 'I'm sorry you had to see that,' she said stonily. 'Please forget it ever happened.'

'Hiroko, I'm sorry if I—'

'It wasn't you.'

'I didn't mean to—'

'I said forget it.'

He fell silent for a minute. In the gloom she saw a crab moving, tiptoeing sideways over the stones. She bit her lip. Yes, alright, she would admit it. She was homesick. She missed her grandmother walking in her orchard. She missed her grandfather sitting on the deck of the house, waiting silently for night to fall.

She missed her father.

'Have you got a pen?' she asked.

Seb handed one to her.

Hiroko cycled through the cards. Here was a photo of the seaside on a day of blue skies and ice creams. Here was a balmy afternoon and dolphins swimming in the bay. Here were fireworks blossoming over the water. She turned that card over and faced the blank reverse, gripping the pen so tight that her fist was shaking. She didn't expect to be able to write anything, but when the nib touched the card something strange happened. The words sprang out of her without thought or decision, as if the kanji were all contained in the ink. Before she knew it she had written out the symbols for Grandmother, and, *What am I supposed to do? It's all too far away and too much. I need you to say a prayer for me, at the fox shrine. I need you to say a prayer for my father. I need* – but then she was out of space, having written too large and uncontrolled. She tapped the pen against her chin.

'This is a bad idea,' she said.

'Why? You looked like you had something to say.'

She shook her head. 'It feels like . . . pulling out a plug.'

'That's how it's supposed to feel.'

'You do one.'

'Me?'

She chose a picture of the harbour, full of boats. On the reverse she wrote *Callum*, and held it out to him along with the pen. 'Write it.'

He didn't take the postcard. 'I don't know . . .'

'See. Not so easy now, is it?'

'You wrote yours in Japanese. You'll be able to read what I write on mine.'

'Who cares? But I won't look, if it makes you happier. Or maybe you could write it in computerspeak, or something.'

'It doesn't really work like that. And anyway . . . look how peacefully Yasuo is sleeping. I think it's better if I stay nice and still.'

At once, Yasuo's eyes snapped open. He stood up with a yawn and a stretch, then prowled off Seb's lap to rejoin Hiroko.

'Ha!' she said, scooping up the fox and placing him back in her hood. Then she forced the postcard into Seb's hand.

Seb toyed with the pen for a moment, without speaking. 'Okay,' he said eventually, and touched the nib to the card as if it were a match to tinder.

A minute later he had filled the card with angrily scribbled sentences, and his fists were shaking.

'Told you,' said Hiroko.

Seb took a deep breath and pressed his hands together. Then he looked calm again. 'Point taken,' he said, 'but I think it was worth it.'

Hiroko sighed. 'Okay.' She took the pen back off him. She chose another card, and wrote the kanji for *Otosan* in the top corner. That was Nihongo for *Father*.

Seb watched her. Hiroko waited for anger to move her pen.

It didn't come.

She started to cry again. After a moment, Seb put an arm around her. She could feel Yasuo's heartbeat through the fur against her neck.

I miss you, she wrote. That was all.

In the other half of the postcard she had to do the hardest part: her father's Tokyo address. That horrible, sky-high apartment he'd asked her to think of as home. A place she had spent the last month and a half determined not to think of at all, telling herself it was because she hated it so. Hated the urbanity of it, the white paint, the right angles, the tidiness.

She clamped her teeth around the end of the pen. Suddenly she was hoping like crazy that the apartment hadn't fallen down. She knew there was a picture of that happening, somewhere in the back of her mind, and she had been trying desperately to lock it up there. 'See,' she whispered to Seb, 'you should keep this stuff shut away.'

If Tokyo had crumbled, falling into a sudden forest, and if her father had fallen with it, what had he thought of as it happened? What had crossed his mind while the floor trembled and gave way? His own impending death? Saori, who perhaps he held in his arms? Or had it been Hiroko's mother, in the time when they'd been together, before their daughter was born?

'Perhaps he's thinking about you,' said Seb. 'Right now.'

The salt breeze rippled Hiroko's hair. Yasuo pressed himself urgently against her ear.

'I doubt it,' she said.

'Do you want to write any more?'

'Do *you*?'

'No. So . . . what shall we do?'

Hiroko removed her boots and socks.

'What are you doing?'

She plucked Yasuo out of her hood and laid him on the rocks. She thought the fox might object, but he just sat calmly on his haunches and began to preen his fur. Then Hiroko jumped down into the shallows, ignoring the cold that at once lapped her ankles. She waved the postcards at Seb. 'I'm posting these,' she said. 'What about you?'

Seb looked out towards the horizon and then laughed and removed his own footwear. He joined her with a splash. The tide inched back and forth around their rolled-up trouser legs.

They threw the postcards as far as they could, but a white breaker brought them back to shore. They fished them up again.

'We have to go deeper,' decided Hiroko. She pulled off her hoodie and returned to the rocks to put it there beside Yasuo. 'Look after this,' she instructed the fox, who immediately snuggled into it to make the most of its warmth. Hiroko undressed out of her top and her jeans and gave those to him too.

'Er . . .' said Seb, staring at her.

There she stood in nothing but her bra and knickers, feeling the goosebumps rising all along her thighs and arms.

'What?' she asked defiantly.

The sun was gone now entirely, and the night was full of the galaxy. Another shooting star scratched the heavens, then another and another.

'Do yours,' she said.

Seb nodded and undressed with sudden fearful determination. Clearly he felt the cold more keenly than she, trying in vain to wrap his arms around all of his body at once. She pulled them apart and pushed her own flesh against his, and slid her fingers through his hair to grasp his scalp. They didn't kiss. They pushed their foreheads hard against one another's, locking eyes point-blank in the dark.

'Now swim,' Hiroko commanded, and showed the way.

They front-crawled out through the white spume of the breakers, to where the sea was as black as the space the stars shot through. They trod water in the deep and the cold, and let go of the postcards there. The tide was gentle, but the chill bit so hard they could feel every drop of blood in their bodies. Despite that they laughed and pressed foreheads again, even though the water sloshed salt into their nostrils.

3

Gunman

Hannah could hardly believe that she'd used to find the sea so unlovable. As a little girl she had hated it, considering it the definition of monotony. Now, when she woke within earshot, its noise alone made her feel no bigger than a pebble washed up on its shores. Desiring more of that feeling of smallness, and though it was early in the morning, she left the others asleep in the tent and wandered down to the place where the breakers slid ashore.

She removed her boots and socks, rolled up her jeans and waded out. She flinched at first from the cold but pressed on enraptured, only having to paddle a short distance before the beach fell out of sight and she could pretend that all the world was empty sea under an empty sky. Standing there, submerged up to her knees, she thought she would have preferred some biblical flood to have swept the world, rather than the forest. It would have been cleaner, easier to comprehend.

When eventually she paddled back to the beach, she realised that the sea had another surprise in store for her. It had returned her appetite, and she was suddenly the hungriest she'd been since finding Zach. It seemed a fitting tribute to both her brother and the water to go coastal foraging, so she set out to scrounge through rock pools and thatches of seaweed. Yet, to her disappointment, all these were already picked bare. Anything that remained had been pulped by many boots, and even at that early hour several other people were already wading in those places, and their bored scampering children hunting for dribbles of kelp. Someone informed her that there had been a genocide of crabs and winkles, and poisonings and even deaths from badly cooked shellfish, and that such instances were increasing in frequency as more and more people emerged onto the beaches. Hannah sighed, and supposed she would have to venture back into the woods for food.

Everything fell very quiet when she stepped beneath the silent boughs of the forest. The trees here were shaggy with moss, so that even though the leaves were ageing the daylight caught in the tangles above. The undergrowth was dank and perfect for mushrooms, but within fifteen minutes Hannah had also found wild parsnips, horseradishes and long purple carrots. It made no sense to her that so many of the people on the beaches looked so hungry.

'Isn't it obvious?' said the only other person she met under the branches. 'Most of them have seen things in the woods they wish they could forget, and the rest are too terrified by the stories that the first lot tell. They'll start to cut the trees down soon, once they're brave enough, but for now they only want to keep away from them.'

Hannah kept on foraging, with nicks in her fingers from the thorns she searched through, and hands stained purple from the berries she picked. Small fussy birds hopped and croaked around her, and darted forth to snatch up anything she worked loose but did not gather. Squirrels with twitching noses raced her jealously when she gathered up hazelnuts. Flies whirred after the sugar of crab apples. Whether they had arrived thinking it spring or high summer, most trees were beginning to agree that it was early autumn: the first week of October, by Hannah's reckoning. As she foraged she remembered, as if it were some deeply buried childhood memory, that she had used to love this time of year. Loved brisk autumn walks and the first chance to wear gloves and cosy scarves, loved conkers on strings and bonfire smoke on the air. She was just beginning to feel like something of her old self, when she saw the gunman.

He was, he had to be, a figment of her imagination. The real gunman was dead, left to rot in some unmarked ditch near Zach's lodge. Yet there he stood, in the middle distance in the woods, and his spectacles were upturned on his forehead and the sunlight twinkled on the exit wound that Hannah had put there. She spun away, heading at once for the sea, but stopped when she heard him groan behind her.

'You're dead,' Hannah whispered. 'There's no way you're here.'

But he groaned again, as if he had somehow clung to life and staggered all the way to the sea behind her. She took another pace away from him but found she could go no further. She remembered what the gunman had done to Zach, remembered the noise of the flies when they exited her brother's chest.

'You're dead,' she said again, this time with a growl. Then all of a sudden she was marching back towards him, her foraging knife held tight in her fist.

'You're dead!' she yelled before realising, after a few more fierce paces, that the gunman was nothing but a stump the size of a person, with two branches shaped a bit like arms and a moist red fungus feeding on the bark at head height. Hannah drew to a halt beside it, and the decaying timber creaked in the breeze.

She stabbed her knife in. She pulled it out and stabbed again, then again and again until the blade wedged. She let go with a scream and flung herself down on the leaf litter. That it had all been a trick of the light was no relief. The gunman *had* been real, once upon a time, and it had been for long enough to ruin her life. She stood up and kicked away her foraging with a shout. Mushrooms and vegetables spun through the forest and rattled into the undergrowth, into which the squabbling birds and squirrels at once descended. Hannah yanked her knife free and stalked away, but only once she'd burst out of the woods and crossed the beach and splashed down into the shallows, into the vast cold sea that soaked her walking boots and jeans up to her knees, did she stop. The waves foamed and collapsed. Gulls shrieked in harsh voices.

Hannah could hardly believe that she'd used to find the woods so lovable.

That evening, Hannah found Adrien alone at the furthest end of the beach. Here it was easy to escape the crowds, for nobody wished to venture far from their campfires after sundown. She took a seat on the shingle alongside Adrien, both of them sitting cross-legged in the last of the light. 'Has it been a bad day?' she asked.

'Something like that. I'm still trying to find out about boats. Asking everyone I can about them.'

'Doesn't sound like you got very far.'

Adrien sighed and leaned back to better face Hannah. 'Nowhere at all. I didn't think I'd want one this badly, but . . . things go strangely, don't they? Or maybe it's just me. I never really know what I want until I'm faced with not having it.'

'Of course you wanted a boat. It makes perfect sense.'

'Yeah . . .' he said, and poked at the shingle. 'But what about you? You don't look too chirpy, either, if you don't mind me saying so.'

'I thought I saw the gunman. So I'm not doing too well, either.'

'Oh. Shit. Where?'

She told him what had happened and, although she didn't mean to, described in forensic detail the piece of fungus she'd mistaken for his head wound.

'Hannah, listen,' said Adrien when she'd finished. 'You're exhausted, and your mind is playing tricks on you. That's all. I'm sure it's not uncommon, among people who—'

'Who have killed someone?'

'That's not what I was going to say. I meant you should try to forget about it, that's all.'

Hannah smiled ruefully. 'The funny thing is that I'd done just that. The moment before I saw him, I was enjoying the sea and feeling the best I have done since I shot him.'

'You didn't *see* him. Remember that. You saw a tree.'

She rubbed her eyes. 'Do you think this is something that will keep happening? Because I don't know if I have the strength for that. Didn't he say something about this himself? That murderers can't stop thinking about the people who they've killed.'

Adrien looked pained. 'You're not a murderer, Hannah.'

'Aren't I? What other word is there for me?'

'Not that one. That's the word we use for him.'

'I did the same thing he did.'

Adrien looked frustrated. Eventually, he shook his head and said, 'I just hate watching you torture yourself.'

Hannah looked out at the sea. The eddies of the surf spread out in white, then drained away leaving darkened sand in their wake. 'It's not much fun to watch you do it, either. Adrien . . . I think you might be looking too hard for this boat. And too close. Take a step back and you might see the bigger picture.'

Adrien swept a hand across the line of the horizon. 'This is already a bloody big picture. Miles and miles of water and no way to get to Ireland.'

'I can't blame you for feeling frustrated. I know how much it means to you to find her.'

'Uhh . . . yeah.' He cleared his throat. 'Yeah, I hope.'

'You hope? What does that mean?'

'I never much meant to go through with this. You must have known that all along. I thought I'd turn around and head home long before we got this far. It was supposed to be only a matter of time before people fixed everything, before I felt safe enough to sit back and wait for Michelle. But now that we've come all this way, things feel even more broken than they did at the start.'

Hannah could see he wasn't finished. She waited for him to continue.

'I actually expected to be satisfied with this,' he said after a minute. 'That the sea would save me my blushes. I could *look* like I was brave enough to cross, but never get the chance to. I thought there would be no shame in being defeated that way, and I think I could accept that Michelle might not want to rescue things.

Sometimes I ask myself if *I* really want to. Wouldn't I be braver, if I did? But . . . if my marriage is at an end . . . I want a proper finish. To tell her it's alright. I don't want it to just ebb out.'

'Adrien . . . it hasn't ebbed out.'

The moonlight showed the moisture on his eyelids. 'I wouldn't blame Michelle if she wanted it to have done. I wouldn't blame her if she'd shacked up with Roland. I might do the same, if I was in her shoes. He's handsome, he's dignified . . . he still has all the hair on his bloody head. He has this soft, deep Irish accent, like rolling in caramel. I can't help but think that, if some catastrophe trapped me with Roland and left my useless husband on the other side of the sea, I might roll around in caramel and thank my lucky stars for it.'

'But you're not in her shoes,' said Hannah. 'You're in your own.'

Adrien took a long, composing breath. 'And you,' he said, with a touch of touché, 'aren't in the gunman's.'

Hannah watched waves burst against the end of the breakwater. Above them the stars were shining, and the cliffs showed their backs to the moon.

'We're a pair of disasters, aren't we?' she said.

Adrien laughed.

'But thank you, Adrien.'

'For what?'

'Having some belief in me.'

He looked surprised to be thanked for anything, but she was truly grateful for it.

'You and I both need to face our demons,' she said.

'I wouldn't know where to start.'

'I might. For you, at least, not me.'

'That wouldn't be a favour I could promise to return.'

'Doesn't matter. What matters is to fix things.'

Adrien eyed her cautiously. 'You've got something in mind, haven't you?'

'You won't enjoy it,' she said with a nod. 'You'll hate it, in fact. But that's the nature of it, I suppose.'

In the morning, Hannah zigzagged between the beach's many camps and chalets, summoning Adrien's demons. The morning itself was no infernal one, for the sun shone unobstructed, warming her bare arms and glittering across the sea from headland to headland. In that light even the destruction along the shore looked picturesque. Weeks of wind had sprinkled the ruined seafront with sand, and the sunshine winked off granules of shell amid the grit. Still Hannah was nervous. After she had organised everything and all that was required was Adrien's presence, she hesitated in sight of their tent, where he sat in the shade sipping thistle tea.

She approached, and tried to sound jovial. 'Are you ready, Adrien? Because it's time.'

Adrien looked surprised, as if he had forgotten ever having agreed to this. Reluctantly, he rose and followed her to the edge of the beach, where she had arranged a grid of twenty deckchairs. In each sat a child, some very young, some nearly as old as Seb and Hiroko, the two of whom reclined in the back row like the bad kids in a class. Gathered to one side were several parents, waiting expectantly.

'No,' Adrien spat at once, sounding betrayed. 'No, no, no! Hannah, how could you?'

She grabbed him to stop him from turning away.

'Please, Adrien! These kids have got nothing here. They run around the beaches all day, frightened of the trees and frightened of wolves and frightened of their own imaginations. But at my merest suggestion that we should do this, they lit up! Their parents too! You'll never have an easier class than this. *Give* them something.'

'This is the last thing in the world,' Adrien growled, 'that I would have expected from somebody trying to help me.'

Hannah was no good at talking to audiences, but she knew she had to say something public now, to bind this one to Adrien. She hoped he'd forgive her eventually. 'H–hello children,' she announced, while Adrien went into a cower. 'This is Mr Thomas, who's kindly offered to teach you some . . . things. And, um, over to you, Mr Thomas.'

She stepped back and stood at his shoulder. Adrien said nothing, as tense as if he expected her to crack a whip off his back. The children began to fidget and stare into space. The parents muttered to one another. At the back of the class, Yasuo propped himself up on Hiroko's shoulder, and was interested in everything on the beach except Adrien.

Adrien took a deep breath. 'Mr Thomas,' he said, almost inaudibly. One of his hands pawed up to his throat, and stayed there in substitution for a collar and tie.

'Mr Thomas,' he said again. 'That's . . . that's my name.'

The children's murmurs subsided for a moment, and Hannah held her breath. Adrien had thirty seconds, at best, to win them over.

'Well,' he said, then coughed and started again. 'Well, er . . . I've been asked to teach. Um, but, umm . . . teaching is hard when you're all so many ages and you haven't got exercise books or reading books or even a board and pen. You're going to have to suffer with just the sound of my voice. Anyone who doesn't like that idea is welcome to leave.'

He gave them ample time, but no one took up his offer.

'Well. I am an English teacher. Who here likes English?'

Adrien waited. No hands went up, and he gave a brittle nod as if that was just what he'd expected. Then several children raised their arms, and after that the shyer ones began to raise theirs too. 'Oh,' said Adrien, and Hannah smiled at how genuinely surprised he sounded.

More hands went up. 'Wow,' said Adrien, 'that's . . . that's good. But I haven't got any books to show you. I'm just going to have to describe them to you. Could some of you . . . could some of you perhaps tell me what your favourite books are?'

Again the hands were slow to come, and before the first one went up Adrien wrinkled his nose as if he had been duped by false enthusiasm. Then one by one the fingers rose, some of them straining to outdo the rest.

233

When he asked them to speak in turn, their answers ranged through stories of all styles and sizes, and made Hannah feel very badly read. One girl talked about Jacobean poetry like a miniature professor.

'Right,' said Adrien, rolling up his sleeves. 'Alright. You like a lot of different things, but I'll try to think of a book that has something for everyone. How about . . . how about a book that was never really meant to be a book at all? Does anybody know what kind of book that might be?'

A freckled girl raised her arm. Adrien gestured to her to speak and she licked her lips and then asked in a quiet voice strained by the pushing sea, 'A play?'

'Yes! Good God, yes! Does anyone know who William Shakespeare was?'

They all nodded, but Hannah chewed her thumbnail and worried he was going to lose them with something too highbrow.

'Stupid question, I suppose. Would anybody be so good as to tell me about him, all the same?'

He pointed to a bespectacled boy near the back, who Hannah thought looked like a much younger Adrien.

'He was, um,' said the boy, 'the greatest playwright, um, who ever lived. Um. He lived, um, in the Elizabethan times. He wrote *Romeo and*, um-um-um, *Juliet* and . . . and . . .'

'Good, good, that's right,' swept in Adrien. '*Romeo and Juliet*, perhaps the greatest love story ever told. Who here would like to know more about *Romeo and Juliet*?'

Several girls nodded but the boys shook their heads. 'Alright, alright, how about another of Shakespeare's greats? Perhaps the greatest. How about a story that's a love story *and* a thriller, that's romance and battles and treachery?'

They all nodded, and he began to recount the events of *Hamlet*. Hannah was surprised by how vividly he did it, dwelling on the gory bits and the romantic bits and quoting whole passages in a dramatic voice that she had never known was in him. These rhymed snippets in particular enchanted the children, mesmerised them, and Hannah reckoned that although it might not be Shakespeare's spell, it was a magic nevertheless, cast by schooling itself. What upheaval and trauma these children must have been through since the trees came, but here in their deckchair classroom they were able to return for a time to their most familiar of activities. More make-believe than education, a game of pupils and teacher, it helped them forget their fears for a short and precious hour.

When the lesson ended and the children left their seats, chatting to their parents about books, Adrien turned to Hannah and could not stop hopping with enthusiasm. He had already promised the kids another lesson the next day, and at that they had cheered. 'They bloody cheered!' he exclaimed. 'Did you hear that? That wasn't a sarcastic cheer, was it? Oh bugger, was that a sarcastic cheer? Do they actually want to come back tomorrow?'

Hannah grinned. 'Kids like learning. It's what kids do.'

'How?' he gasped. 'How did you do it? I mean . . . at first I could have killed you for arranging this, but it's precisely the security these children need. This is really something. Really something. Even if they misbehave tomorrow, I shan't mind. It'll just mean they feel safe to do so.' And he threw his arms around her and hugged her tight, rocking her from side to side. Then he remembered himself, and although she was laughing he let go of her and took a step away, patting down his pockets with embarrassment.

'I didn't do anything,' Hannah chuckled. 'Only borrowed some deckchairs and brought them a teacher.'

'Thank you,' said Adrien, still awkward. They hugged again and, although it was a far more timid embrace, they held each other with genuine affection.

4

Captain

The next day and the next, Adrien taught the beach's children. Hannah didn't stay for all the lessons, but sometimes looked down the beach and smiled at the deckchairs in formation, and all of their bright-eyed incumbents listening to Mr Thomas. For her own part she paid heed to the sea, and its rhythms felt like a lesson all her own. She was able to picture Zach clearer if she stared into the waves. The salt air never muddled his death with the gunman's.

Hiroko and Seb came and went, and sometimes returned out of the forest late at night with scratches on their skin and bits of twig and leaf caught up in their hair. Hannah smiled at this too, for it was the first time in her life that her son had brought back memories of her own youth. She felt closer to him then than she had done in years, even if she hardly ever saw or spoke to him.

At the end of the fourth afternoon since arriving at the coast, when Seb and Hiroko were away and Hannah was sitting with Adrien on the beachfront with the late sunlight sparkling off the foam atop the waves, Adrien laughed and said to her, 'Do you know something? Today I almost thought I had the answer.'

'To the crossing?'

He nodded. 'But it turned out to be nothing.'

'Tell me anyway,' said Hannah.

Adrien only stared out to sea. There was an orange fishing buoy still floating a long way offshore, although now and then it sank beneath the swell.

'Tell me,' Hannah insisted.

'There's this girl,' he said slowly, 'a little scampish blonde thing at the deckchair classroom, who can't be more than seven. Nora is her name. An Irish girl, who wants to get home. And anyway . . . I was teaching Homer to the class. Sirens and sharp rocks, you know. Kids love that stuff if you put the adventure into it. We started talking about real boats, specifically all those smashed ones in the harbour. One of the boys said it was good that they were smashed, and that sailors were the bad guys because they never came to help any of us on the beaches. He said if he saw a sailor today he'd sing his boat onto the rocks just like a siren, and that would teach the sailor a lesson.'

Hannah chuckled. 'That's kids.'

'Yeah, well no sooner had that boy said it than little Nora leaned over from next to him and stabbed him with a pencil.'

'Ouch.'

Now it was Adrien's turn to chuckle. 'Only in his arm. Just a sting. But she told him in no uncertain terms that sailors aren't the bad guys because *her daddy is a sailor and he's the best man in the world.*'

Hannah considered this news for a moment. 'A sailor might have a better idea how to—'

'Exactly! That's what I thought. So I went to see him as soon as the class had finished. He's building a boat.'

'Building one? Are you serious?'

Adrien smiled ruefully. 'Yeah. He said he hoped to have it finished by midsummer.'

Hannah frowned. 'It's past midsummer already . . .'

'Midsummer next year.'

'Oh.'

'Yeah. And he said he had a kind of waiting list of people who want to sail with him, when it's done.'

Hannah mulled it over, and watched as a slew of big waves again submerged the fishing buoy. 'It's a start, though, Adrien. Did he say anything else?'

'What else was there to say? If that's the best an actual sailor can manage, what hope is there for the rest of us?'

237

'I don't know. I thought he might be able to offer some advice . . .'

Adrien only shrugged. The fishing buoy resurfaced, and Hannah could agree that its tiny dab of colour only made the sea look larger. Still, Adrien's news was the best they had to go on since coming out of the woods, and it warranted a little further investigation.

The sailor was not there when Hannah arrived at his camp beside the forest's edge, but she knew the tent adjoining it was his from a long blue tarpaulin weighed down with stones. Beneath it was a shallow mound that she guessed was his boat, and despite Adrien's forewarnings its size still disappointed her. She supposed there was still a lot of work to be done.

A few minutes later, the sailor emerged out of the woods with his little girl Nora chattering at his side. Nora noticed Hannah first, coming to a halt and squinting up at her. Then she said something Hannah didn't hear, and her father looked at Hannah with one eyebrow raised. He was tall, with curly hair softened from black to brown by sunlight, and a short ragged beard that followed his jawline. His jeans were rolled up and he stood barefoot on the stones of the beach, wearing a white vest that exposed the top part of a tattoo covering his back. 'You're here about the boat, I assume?' he asked in a wary Irish accent.

Hannah nodded. 'I just wanted to introduce myself.'

He laughed. 'And put yourself on my waiting list, is that it?'

'Something like that. I'm Hannah, by the way.'

'Eoin,' said the sailor, watching her with eyes as keen as a seabird's. He looked a year or two her elder, too young for all of the lines branching down his cheeks, even though they suited him well, when all of a sudden he smiled. 'Wait . . . you're Mr Thomas's friend!'

'That's right. Although I think he prefers Adrien.'

'That's what he told me,' chuckled Eoin, then looked serious again. 'Shame I couldn't do more for him. I appreciate what he's doing for Nora, and for the rest of the kids here. But he really wanted to get to Ireland.'

'Ireland is where his wife is.'

'And what about you? You're his . . .'

'Just his friend.'

'Ah.' Eoin whistled to Nora, and gestured towards the sea. 'You can run and play now,' he said to the girl. 'Daddy's going to do some talking.'

Nora rolled her eyes and sped away over the pebbles, charging into the shallows with a whoop. Eoin watched her for a moment with unconcealed admiration, then turned back to Hannah. 'So . . . you have family in Ireland, too?'

'All I want is to keep moving. That's enough for me for now.'

Eoin nodded carefully. 'You've something you want to get away from.'

'No,' Hannah said quickly.

For a moment he seemed to study her, then he strode forward and pulled the tarpaulin aside. 'Here she is! My boat, or what will become her, one of these days.'

The revealed boat was even more disappointing than Hannah had imagined it would be. Nothing much more than a rowing bench, and the rail that would fit around the top of the hull.

'I took this bit of gunwale from the harbour,' Eoin said, gesturing to the rail. 'Everything is cracked and damaged, so this was a lucky find. It's been a lot of work, tidying things up and getting the rowing bench comfy.'

Hannah stared at the sparse arrangement of wood before her, and understood why Adrien had been made so dejected by the sight of it. 'I suppose I just hoped . . .' she began.

'There was more of it?' laughed Eoin. 'There was a way to do it faster? That's what everybody says. But do you know very much about boat-building?'

Hannah shook her head. 'I don't even know a thing about the sea. I admit I was never very interested in it until we came here, out of the woods. Even when I was a girl the sea always seemed so harsh. So . . . inhospitable.'

'And here? I bet you're sick of trees now, right?'

239

Not just the trees, she thought, but it was better not to elaborate. She dreaded to think how Eoin would react if she told him that she'd learned to love the sea's great emptiness because somewhere in the endless tangles of the forest behind them lay the body of a man she had shot in the head.

'The sea's inhospitality has grown on me,' she said, 'let's put it that way. It doesn't pretend to be anything it's not.'

Again Eoin raised an eyebrow. 'You sound like a proper old salt. And you're right, you know. The sea can be a mean old bitch, but she makes no bones about it. A shark is a shark, my old captain used to say.'

'A shark is a shark. I like that.'

'Most of the things my old captain said were about rugby and liquor, but he got that one right.'

Hannah nodded. 'It's not the same in the woods. Even something like a wolf, it . . . it disguises what it really is. Makes you think it's beautiful. Even the trees starve each other of the light. I've always called myself a person who loves nature, but I suppose what I've thought of as nature has always been trees, mammals, flowers . . . so much life you can distract yourself from the death.'

Eoin was watching her with a curious expression, but Hannah was in full flow now and her fists were clenched. 'I think,' she said, 'that the sea might be the truer face of nature. It's where everything came from, after all. The sea never hides what it can do to you, how deep it goes or how far. And every shell on the beach is a reminder . . . is like a bit of bone from something the sea has already killed. The sea is more honest than the woods.'

Eoin laughed. Hannah blushed and looked away at the water, which hissed and withdrew foaming, then cupped a wave out of itself and lapsed it onto the sand.

'What a speech,' Hannah said. 'That's what you're thinking. You're laughing at me.'

'No.' Eoin held up his hands. 'Quite the opposite, in fact. I was thinking *Amen*. It sounds to me like you know the sea very well.'

He began to walk away from her, down the slope of the beach towards the water's edge. She followed him, and the pebbles gave way to a spread of dark sand. There Eoin slipped off his shoes and padded into the shallows.

'Everything you just said is true,' he said, watching the waves coming in, 'and when you know people who have drowned, or not come back to port after a storm, you feel it all the more cruelly. It took me a long time to learn to actually love the sea. Back when I was a boy, becoming a sailor seemed to me the only way out of the village where I grew up. But I was very seasick to begin with. I'm glad, now. My first captain would only apprentice those who had no sea legs. He said that all there was to learn about life could be learned by hanging your head overboard and throwing up into ocean water.'

Hannah crouched down and took off her shoes and socks. Then she stepped into the shallows alongside Eoin. 'Was this the same captain who said the thing about the shark?'

'No,' grinned Eoin. 'A different one. We're all gasbags, us sailors.'

'So did you?' she asked, already feeling comfortable enough in Eoin's company to do so teasingly. 'When you hung your head overboard, did you learn all there was to know about life?'

He laughed. 'Sailors are also prone to exaggeration. But I learned one or two things.'

The water was cold and restless at Hannah's ankles. That didn't seem to put off Nora, who was kicking it up into white explosions nearby.

'Why do you really want to cross this water, Hannah?'

'I told you. I just want to keep moving.'

'Because you've got a secret.'

She stared resolutely at the horizon. 'I never said that.'

'Maybe you've seen something. A lot of people have. Something horrible that you can't bear to talk about.'

She thought of the gunman pressed awkwardly against the wall. The way, when the bullet had entered, his body had jerked as if at the end of a leash.

'Or you've seen something stranger. People say that the paths have tricked them, or even that there are little figures walking in the woods.'

241

Hannah thought about the two bull kirins, battling on the slopes above Zach's lodge. They reminded her of what had followed, and she didn't much want to talk about those either. 'Adrien's your man for little figures,' she said, trying to deflect Eoin's interest. 'He's seen some of them. Whisperers, he calls them, but . . .' She stopped herself. 'Actually, he might be embarrassed that I've told you.'

'It's okay,' said Eoin. 'I believe him.'

'Have *you* seen them, too?'

'Hang on a minute . . . Nora, everything alright?'

Nora had stopped splashing and was standing within earshot, listening to their talk.

'Everything's fine,' she said at once, and immediately scampered away, bending to collect shells from out of the sand.

Eoin lowered his voice. 'I try not to spook her with this kind of talk, but I've seen other things, in my time.'

'What sort of things?'

'It was years ago, now. Sailors have been seeing strange sights ever since they first put out to sea. People have thrown themselves overboard and drowned for weird sights, swimming in the water. Deserts are the same. You know, making mirages and dust devils when people are surrounded by sand. And I once met a pilot who saw a flock of yellow lights in the sky. People called him crazy, said he was daydreaming about UFOs, but you could see the fear and the certainty in his eyes. He didn't want that to have happened to him. So why shouldn't there be strange sights in the forest? It's when we stay indoors that we stop believing in things.'

Hannah remembered the look on Adrien's face, in the moments after the campfire had put itself out. His eyes had looked just like Eoin had described the pilot's. 'I don't think,' she said, 'that Adrien would call what he's seen a mirage.'

'Oh no. Don't get me wrong, I'm not calling anything a trick of the light. Like I said, I've seen things too.' He nodded towards the beach, where Nora had gathered a handful of shells. 'I saw her mother once, swimming in the distance. Afterwards, I told myself it was just a dolphin, or driftwood reflecting the sun, but I didn't believe it. She was so real, when I saw her, that if it weren't for Nora I'd have jumped in and drowned myself just for the chance to catch up with her.'

'I'm sorry to hear that, Eoin. Nora's mother . . . did she . . . die at sea?'

Eoin bit his lip. 'Ah-ah,' he said, with a shake of his head. 'In a hospital, where she'd been a long time. Cancer, you know? Some years ago.'

'Oh. That's awful. It's what happened to my dad, but I can't imagine . . .'

Eoin sighed. 'You can imagine some of it, then. And I'm sorry to hear about your dad.' He smiled at her as he pointed back to the pieces of his boat. 'We're going to sail that thing to her family's old house, on the south coast, past Dungarvan. And who knows, Nora's granny and granda might still be there to help her grow up. That girl needs more than just her daddy around. She needs better role models, for one thing! But *that's* why I felt bad for your friend Adrien when I let him down about the boat. I'm grateful to him for taking Nora's mind off the woods. And, you know, it would be nice to help him find his wife. People should be together, while they still can.'

'Yes,' said Hannah, folding her arms and thinking at once about Zach. 'They should be, if they can.'

'And what about you? Your family? Your boy is here with you, right? But what about his . . .'

'I don't care where his father is. Callum left us and we let ourselves forget him.'

They looked at each other for a moment.

'It's hard being the only parent,' Eoin said.

'Yeah. It is.' It was an obvious statement to make, but she was grateful to him all the same, since it came from honest experience, not supposition. At once she looked down at the surf, feeling guilty for finding Eoin attractive. *There are no good men and there are no bad*, the gunman had said, and she had pulled the trigger and his life had stopped there at her feet.

'Well, Hannah,' said Eoin. 'If you're not going to tell me your secret, I'm not going to tell you mine.'

'I . . . don't have one.'

Eoin laughed, a jovial challenge to come clean, but he had underestimated her secret and his smile was too pleasant to extinguish with the truth of it. 'If I told you,' she began, 'you wouldn't want to carry on this conversation.'

Still he was smiling. 'Is that a clue? Then maybe I'll give you one in return.' He leaned forward a little, and his bearded face came close to her ear, and she could smell the sea and old sweat on him. 'If a shipwright,' he whispered, 'ever found himself boat-building in a place without boats, and if half of the people living round him all wanted a way to get across the ocean, might he not be wise to make his boat *look* a lot less finished than it really was?'

'What are you saying?' Hannah whispered back, searching his expression for confirmation. 'You've just shown me your boat. It really *isn't* finished.'

Eoin stood up straight and stepped away from her. 'That's all the clues that you're getting for now. Come back and see me again soon, Hannah. You're the first person I've met since I washed up here who talks about the sea like she knows what's in it.'

5

Heart of the Forest

'Hey! Mr Thomas!'

Adrien had just finished another day of teaching and was heading back towards the tent, when Nora skipped alongside him and tugged at his sleeve.

'What is it?' he asked, stifling a yawn. He hadn't slept well during the night, having dreamed of giant, chairlike trees with beckoning branches. He wasn't sure he had enough energy to keep up with Nora right now.

'I've got a secret,' she declared.

'Good. Better not tell me, then. You have to keep secrets. That's the whole point of having them.'

Nora folded her arms and her skip turned into a strut. 'That's really boring. Especially when this secret is about *you*.'

'Me?'

'To do with you.'

'Is that so?'

He had heard this kind of thing before, and considered it a good sign now. Playgrounds were rumour mills and children believed all kinds of stories. In his time he had been an ex-spy, a bomb-maker on the run from the cops and, perhaps most disconcerting, a former cardinal. If the kids from the deckchair classroom were making up tall tales, it only served to show how comfortable they were becoming in their makeshift school.

'So?' demanded Nora.

'So what?'

'Don't you want to know my secret?'

'Like I said, if you tell me it won't be a secret any more.'

She folded her arms. 'There's a mad lady living on the beach.'

Adrien frowned. He wasn't sure what that had to do with him. 'It's not nice to call people mad, Nora.'

'But that's what she is. All the kids say so.'

'Kids say a lot of things, believe me.'

Nora looked suddenly infuriated. She kicked at a shell, and it scudded away over the pebbles. '*This* mad lady has seen the same little people you have.'

'Hang on a minute,' said Adrien, suddenly all ears. 'Hang on . . . what exactly are you talking about?'

'The ones made out of sticks.'

'How . . . how on earth do you know about them?'

'I overheard Hannah telling it to my daddy.' Nora blushed, but the blush left her as quick as it came. '*Well?* Will you let me take you to her, or won't you?'

Nora's mad lady lived in a camper van, at the farthest reach of the bay. It was parked facing the sea, beside the high-tide line where the shingle dropped steep as a kerb. If it drove just a few more yards it would be carried away when the waves came in. The afternoon was dull, and the beach brought only beige to the grey sea and sky. Even the paint on the camper van's chassis, which must once have been olive or tan, had long since faded out of colour. Its curtains were drawn shut behind closed windows, but beside it stood a young woman with a hoe, the blade of which clattered and jumped when she tugged it through the shingle.

'Is that her?' whispered Adrien, giving Nora a nudge.

'Don't think so. Everybody says she's much older.'

'Hello!' called Adrien as they approached. 'Good afternoon!'

The young woman was tall and thin, with dark hair as straight as the tool she was using. She propped the hoe vertically and leaned her weight against it. She looked bone-tired, and watched them with suspicious eyes.

'Good afternoon,' said Adrien again, unsure of how else to begin. 'Um . . . everything alright here?'

The woman shrugged. 'What does it look like? Things have been better.'

'Why are you hoeing the beach?'

She tapped the tool against the stones. 'On a hiding to nothing. I'm trying to clear every last bit of seaweed from this patch. I know it sounds crazy but, since her accident, Mum won't set foot outside if she sees any.'

'That's why we're here,' said Nora confidently. 'Because of your crazy mum.'

The woman narrowed her eyes. 'Is that so?'

Nora nodded readily. 'Mr Thomas can help her. And so we've come.'

The woman looked from Nora to Adrien. 'And what are you, Mr Thomas? A doctor? A psychologist?'

'He's a teacher,' said Nora, as if that made him an authority on everything.

Adrien gave as open a smile as he could muster. 'Just call me Adrien,' he said.

The woman looked ready to tell him to leave, then stopped herself. 'Oh . . . actually, I think I've heard about you. That's a good thing you're doing for those kids.' She regarded him thoughtfully for a moment, tapping her fingers along the handle of the hoe. 'I'm Clara. And my *crazy mum* is better known as Gweneth.'

Adrien smiled. 'Nora's just trying to help. She's a good kid.'

'And why on earth would you think you can help my mum?'

Adrien had no idea, and if Nora had not told him what she had about the whisperers he would already have apologised and made an exit. Instead he said, 'I don't know what good I can be, but I heard that your mum has . . . seen things in the woods.'

'She has. God knows what, though. It's all but destroying her.'

'It . . . must be awful. I'm sorry.'

'You've no idea.'

Adrien stood up straighter. 'I think I've seen something too.'

Clara didn't look impressed. She reached into her pocket and pulled out a key, which she jangled from its chain. 'I've locked her in. I've locked all the windows as well. Mum hardly moves a muscle these days, she only sits there reading her magazines, but . . . twice now she's made a dash for it. No doubt you've heard the stories.'

Adrien shook his head. 'I'm still quite new here.'

'Well . . . you wouldn't think it, from the way Mum is in there, but she's quick when she wants to be. Both times she burst out of the door and started swimming for the horizon. Didn't even kick off her shoes or anything. She was never much of a swimmer, and I only just managed to catch her before she went under. Both times she turned blank on me as soon as we were back ashore. She wouldn't even dry herself down. So, you see, I can't afford to let her out of my sight. I have to lock her in if I go anywhere.'

'How long has this been going on for?' asked Adrien.

'Three weeks, or something like that. We didn't live far from here, before the trees came, so we were some of the first to come out of the woods. It hit Mum hard, losing everything, but I found this van whose owners . . . weren't going to need it any more, and I thought things might slowly look up for us. We were parked over by the treeline when Mum had her accident. I mean, I call it an accident because that's what it feels like. It feels like something went horribly wrong that day.'

'And what . . . what happened?'

Clara shrugged. 'She saw something. She said she'd been seeing things in the woods since the trees came, but I put it down to shock and exhaustion. Like I say, Mum had always been . . . easily overcome by things. Even when I was a girl, she used to have really bad days, and nothing we could do could lift her out of them.'

'What did she see?'

Clara didn't look inclined to say. '*How* exactly are you offering to help my mother, again?'

'He's seen them too,' announced Nora. 'The little people made of sticks.'

248

Clara seemed caught between suspicion and surprise. Adrien cleared his throat, itched his collar and tried to squash away his embarrassment. 'And a tree,' he said. 'A very big tree that vanishes just as quickly as the other ones came.'

'If you've really seen *that*,' said Clara, after mulling it over for a moment, 'then you've survived it better than my mum.'

'Do you mind if I talk to her?'

She sighed. 'What harm can it do? Just don't expect to get anything sensible out of her in return.'

After she had leaned the hoe against the side of the camper van, Clara unlocked the door and stepped inside. Adrien and Nora followed, into a stuffy interior that smelled of recently dried paint. All of the fittings had been redecorated in a sickly magnolia, but the coat was uneven and dribbles and splatters had dried to the linoleum floor.

'I had to paint everything after Mum's accident,' explained Clara, tapping a cupboard. 'The vinyl on the furniture had a woodgrain effect. She went berserk to see it.'

Adrien tried not to look uneasy, but he wished that Clara had not closed the door behind them. The camper van felt even smaller than it really was, thanks largely to piles of clothes, bedding and salvage stacked in whatever spaces Clara had been able to find. Only the table at the far end remained bare, and at this Gweneth was sitting.

Whereas her daughter was tall and long-haired, Gweneth was a diminutive woman with hair cropped very short. Her lips were drawn and her eyelids as grey and pronounced as puffballs: she looked as if she had neither left that table nor breathed fresh air since the trees came. Likewise she had not looked up at Adrien and Nora since they'd entered, and had barely stirred except to turn the pages of a glossy magazine that lay opened before her. It was a de luxe catalogue of housekeeping and gardening ideas, its corners dog-eared from too much reading.

'That's all she does now,' muttered Clara. 'Just sits there reading.'

Nora remained by the door but, after a nod of assent from Clara, Adrien took a seat at the table. He cleared his throat but Gweneth paid him no heed, only carried on leafing through her magazine.

'Um . . . hello, Gweneth. My name is Adrien Thomas. Your daughter tells me that you've seen things.'

The woman turned a page and smoothed it flat. Then she traced her fingernails lightly over the photograph. The image showed a bathroom with a free-standing bath and brass taps, and an indoor tree potted in one corner. 'Water,' said Gweneth, running her finger up the tree's trunk. Then she turned to the next page and smoothed it out just as she had the one before.

'I've come here to talk to you,' said Adrien, 'about what you saw.'

Gweneth tapped the magazine. The new page showed an immaculate lawn, with a Grecian fountain flowing into a pond.

'Moles,' she said. 'Worms.'

Adrien glanced to Nora, who was shifting her weight from foot to foot, clearly having second thoughts about coming here. 'Is this what you meant?' he asked Clara. 'Is this the kind of thing she always says?'

'More or less. Apart from on her swimming trips. Then she screams all sorts of craziness.'

'Roots,' whispered Gweneth, and turned the page.

Adrien laid his hands flat on the table. 'I've seen them, too.' He leaned forward. 'Little figures, walking about or crawling on all fours. I call them whisperers.'

Gweneth pursed her lips and gave a dead whistle.

'Yes,' said Adrien. 'Yes, that's exactly the noise they make. And . . . and I've seen a tree. *Their* tree, I think.'

Still she didn't look at him, only turned to the next page of her magazine. It revealed a shampoo advertisement, which Gweneth's fingers traced as if searching for something. They made their way along the tanned jawline of the model, then down her long neck and throat. 'Nothing,' she muttered, and reached to turn the page.

'How many have you seen?' asked Adrien. 'How many whisperers?'

Gweneth's hand paused with the paper half-lifted. Her cheeks twitched. Her throat bobbed as she swallowed. 'Hundreds,' she said.

Adrien looked back to the others. Nora had hold of the door handle now, while Clara had folded her arms and pulled back a curtain to glower out at the grey pouring waves.

'Hundreds,' repeated Adrien carefully. 'I . . . I certainly haven't seen that many.'

'You have,' said Gweneth, and smoothed out her page. 'If you've seen their tree.'

Adrien licked his lips. 'You . . . you mean a big tree, one with branches like this?' He spread out his arms to indicate a pair of massive boughs, and at that moment a gust of wind rang off the wall of the camper van, then passed beneath it humming. For a second Adrien felt as if he were at last in a boat, but a tin one in danger of capsizing.

'Look.' Gweneth tapped one finger against the photo on her newest page. It showed a chair, standing in the drawing room of some luxuriant palace or country estate. Tapestries adorned the walls and chandeliers hung from the ceiling. Everything was gilded and fine, especially the chair itself. Its legs and arms were finely carved to look like animal paws, and its padded backrest was embroidered with a creamy pattern of thorns and ivy.

'Yes,' gulped Adrien. 'I thought it looked a bit like a chair, too.'

Gweneth stroked the seat's golden arms. 'Not a chair,' she said.

'Not a chair?' frowned Adrien, peering closer. There was no doubt the photo showed a chair.

'A *throne.*'

At once Adrien felt uneasy. It was a loose wet feeling that slipped into his belly, as if he had swallowed a ball of cold algae. But she was right. That was a far better word for a tree as big as the one he had seen. No mere chair was that immense, that sprawling.

'It's where it sits,' said Gweneth.

'What . . . it's where what sits? I didn't see anything sitting.'

Adrien pictured the tree, the *throne* tree as she would have it, and found that his unease had kept the memory fresh. He had seen whisperers crawling on it, for sure, but nothing he would describe as seated. Unless . . .

He remembered the branch that had reached out and stretched like the leg of a spider.

'Don't go near,' said Gweneth.

Adrien checked on Nora, who was chewing on a strand of her hair. He tried to keep his voice calm for her sake. 'And if I did,' he asked, 'what would I see?'

For the first time, Adrien felt as if Gweneth was actually address-ing him. 'A test,' she said, looking him in the eye.

'That . . . doesn't sound so bad.'

She raised a hand to her temple, and its fingers were trembling. 'Don't look,' she said, and her eyes glazed and became distant again. 'Don't go near! It has a mouth. A hollow. Don't look in! A worm. A mole. A hawk. A chick. All the mouths. Mouth after mouth.' She pressed her hand across her eyes, but it jittered out of place. 'I don't want to see any more! I . . . I give up, don't you hear? I give up I give up I give up. Just let me go, and don't show me any more . . .'

Adrien leaned back, unnerved, then shuffled out from the table and stood up. 'I'm terribly sorry,' he said to Clara. 'I thought I might be able to help. I didn't mean to make her do this . . .'

'I give up!' cried Gweneth, pushing the butts of her wrists against her eyes.

'I thought I might be able to help,' blurted Adrien again, as Clara shoved past him to comfort her mother. But immediately Gweneth lurched to her feet. She had turned as white as foam, and as her daughter grabbed her and forced her back into her chair she shouted, 'Don't show me any more!' and then collapsed sobbing in the younger woman's grip. Adrien grabbed Nora's hand and fumbled with the latch on the camper-van door. As soon as he had it open he ushered the girl out, then sprang down to the beach after her. Nora was already running, and together they raced away across the shingle as fast as the little girl's legs could cope with.

They did not stop until the van was long out of sight. Then they drew to a halt, facing each other and panting.

'I'm so sorry, Mr Thomas,' gasped Nora, tears forming in her eyes. 'I'm so so sorry I took us in there.'

'Don't be,' said Adrien, trying to sound as reassuring as he could. 'No harm done. We're both in one piece, aren't we?'

'I was scared. She *was* mad, wasn't she?'

Adrien looked towards the forest's edge, at all the green shadows and clawed branches extended for the sun. There was no comfort to be had in that direction, but when he reached on instinct for the memory of his armchair and a cold glass of beer, and for Stetsons and spurs and saloon-bar brawls, he felt even sicker than he had before. He did not want to return to those days, even if he didn't know what he wanted in their place.

'Yes, Nora,' he gulped. 'Gweneth was mad as a hatter, and you'll be fine. You've no need to worry about a single word that she said.'

6

Captain

Hannah dreamed of the gunman.

The two of them lay on the beach, and he was asleep alongside her. She could tell he was alive because he was snoring, but there was a hole in his skull that kept filling up with red and then emptying, just as a hole dug in the sand loses water.

In the dream she sat up and was holding the gun again, and it felt as familiar as a household appliance. She pointed it at the gunman's head, deciding whether or not to shoot. His lips made a bubbling noise like waves fizzling out against the shingle. A hint of a smile turned up the corners of his mouth.

When she fired, the gunshot was so loud that it woke her. She launched herself to her feet and out of her sleeping bag, then staggered out of the tent. Her eardrums were ringing as if the sound had really happened, and she crouched with her hands over her head until calm returned to her heart.

The morning hid beneath a cool sea mist, under whose cover the trees swayed like giant stalks on the ocean bottom. Wide awake now, Hannah walked along the seafront and listened to the waves crashing invisibly, then picked her way down to the shingle and followed the bay's long curve. Every now and then the mist parted and enfolded her again, and in one such pocket of visibility she saw a starfish inching through a rock pool, and could not believe that such a sight would visit her now when she had never seen such a thing before in all her life. Other times she spotted opalescent shells, and held them up and regarded them for long minutes, wondering how oozing and shapeless sea creatures could grow such fanned or coiled structures from the slime of their backs. Inspecting one peculiarly wizened specimen, she jumped in alarm to see a sudden unfolding of needle legs from its opening, and a head moustached with pink mandibles that peered its black eyes into hers before vanishing back into its shelter. She placed it in the secrecy of another rock pool, but thought of its stalked blank gaze each time she closed her eyes.

The best shells she found Hannah kept, with a plan to string them together as a present for Nora. She hoped that Eoin had some sort of small drill among his shipwright's tools, one she could use to fashion the shells into a necklace. It would be a nice gift for the girl, and a good excuse to talk to Eoin again. Hannah had been thinking, lately, that the silver lining of staying here until midsummer would be staying near the sailor. Staying, and learning more about the sea.

The morning mist was a million perfect prisms, each reflecting white with every colour of the light. Sometimes Hannah fancied she could make out those pinprick droplets marching off the sea and into the woods. This close to the water, the trees were bleached out entirely by the weather. They should not enjoy growing so close to salt water, but from their direction Hannah could hear their eager creaks and groans, as if they were straining to put forth roots even into the shingle. Something snagged her ankle and she had to crouch just to see it was a noose of seaweed. Then, as she unhooped it, she heard heavy, rhythmic splashes coming through the shallows.

She remained in a crouch, thinking at once of the gunman. She told herself not to be stupid, for why would he be splashing through the water, but some of the fright of her earlier dream still lingered. *Splash . . . splash . . .* came the noise in the shallows. A chill tingled across her flesh and her trigger finger began to twitch. She screwed shut her eyes and saw the gunman's glasses turned vertical against his forehead, and a rim of bone visible where the bullet had entered.

The splashes drew closer, closer, and then stopped. Whatever had made them remained hidden behind sparkling white.

Crunch . . . crunch . . . Now it was making its way onto the beach.

The mists thickened, then formed up around the grey silhouette of a man. He stooped to lift something off the sand and, convinced it was a gun, Hannah cried out.

The man shouted back at her, but it was with shock and not malice. A moment later he was breaking through the mist towards her, and she realised that it wasn't a gun he'd picked up but a towel, and that the man had been swimming naked and alone.

'*Hannah?*' he asked.

It was Eoin.

At once all of Hannah's fear swooned into embarrassment. Terror dissolved in a hot blood rush. She collapsed onto her backside with a hard thump.

'Hannah,' Eoin said again, coming towards her with the towel wrapped around his waist. 'You scared me half to death.'

'I'm so sorry,' she spluttered, 'I had no idea you were, you were . . .'

He looked confused. 'Swimming?'

'Yes!'

He laughed and shook his head, and tied a knot in the towel to secure it from slipping. 'There's no reason to apologise. This is the sea, not a private pool.'

Hannah prayed that the mist was powdering her blushes. She felt so stupid now. 'Of course. Sorry. You just surprised me, that's all.'

He drew closer. Water had darkened his hair to black, and tumbled in drips from his beard. His torso was thin brawn like deck rope, and there were droplets caught and shining in the hair of his chest.

'Let me grab my clothes,' he said, and turned back to where he'd left them. As he did so she saw, for the first time fully, the tattoo that filled up his back.

It was a capricorn, with great curling horns and hoofed fore-legs, then finned lower quarters that spread into a fish's tail. It covered Eoin's back as a crest covers a heraldic shield, and the horns reached all the way to his shoulders. His wet skin made the tattoo look as blue as fresh ink, and Hannah was still staring at it when he looked back at her.

'Er . . . uhh . . .' she said, 'aren't you cold?'

He pulled his shirt over his head. 'You learn to forget the cold when you're a sailor.' He put on his underwear beneath the towel. 'On land you've always got a hope of shelter. But at sea you can never be sure of it.' He grinned and tossed aside the towel, then stepped into his jeans. 'It's early. Are you having trouble sleeping, Hannah?'

'Um, yes. Yes, I am.'

'Me too. It's the trees, I think. I'll be so glad when the boat is finished. What about you? What's keeping you awake?'

Hannah shrugged. 'I've always woken up early.'

A wave clapped hard against a rock and threw spray into the air. There was something about the sound and the sudden flicker of liquid that made Hannah flinch, but she quickly pulled herself back together and hoped Eoin had not noticed.

'It's the secret that you have,' he said, 'isn't it?'

She folded her arms. 'I already told you there isn't any secret.'

He nodded. 'And I thought I made it clear that I didn't believe you.'

'Eoin . . . if you knew . . . you wouldn't want to know *me* any more.'

'Am I allowed to be the judge of that?'

'No,' she said quietly. 'No, you're not.'

'I trust you, Hannah,' he said.

'You hardly even know me.'

'But we have the sea in common. So I'm going to tell you the secret that I have, in the hope that some day soon you'll tell me yours.'

The mist was lifting into thick cloud, its undersides pearly white. The sea stretched far beneath it, all the way to Ireland, all the way to all the coastlines of the world.

'My boat is nearly finished,' Eoin said.

Hannah didn't know how to react. 'No it isn't,' she said eventually. 'I mean . . . you showed me what you've done so far, and it's hardly even started . . .'

'I showed you some of the gunwale and a rowing bench, but those parts are just a kind of decoy. I polish them and sand them down from time to time and I keep them covered with a tarpaulin, and people come and ask me how long till I set sail and I show them those parts and send them away disappointed. Then, at night sometimes when no one can see, I drag what I've done on the beach into the woods, and bring back some other half-made part to stash under the covers. My real work I've done in the forest. I've fished up a lot more from the harbour than I let people know, and I found more parts and tools in a lifeboat house down the coast. I have a hull, Hannah, and she's keeled and made watertight. With a few pairs of helping hands – four pairs should be just about right – she'll be seaworthy in a few weeks' time. I'm sorry to have tricked you, Hannah, but I had to decide whether I could trust you.'

So it was that, come nightfall, Eoin led them all into the forest and showed them his boat. It was built upwards from the hull of an existing craft, which he had repaired and repanelled. He had stripped much of the old frame bare, but the replacement wood was finely worked and curved quite beautifully towards the hull. The vessel's crown jewel was a small diesel motor, to which Adrien and Seb were able to contribute the bottles of fuel they'd taken from the petrol station.

'On the night we set sail,' Eoin explained, 'we'll carry her in parts down to the water. That's when I'll fix her together entirely, and as soon as that's done we can leave. And we will, by the way, have to set sail at night. Otherwise we'll have half the people on these beaches jumping aboard with us.'

During the days that followed, Adrien taught the children of the deckchair classroom while Hannah, Hiroko and Seb took it in turns to seek out food and sneak into the woods with Eoin to help him finish his boat. The sailor directed them as best he could, but much of the work needed a precision only he could provide. To Hannah's surprise, Seb was the best of them at matching it. They moved their tent next to Eoin's and sometimes, when they had finished for the day and were all exhausted, shipwright and boy would sit up late, discussing the technicalities and dimensions of the vessel's design. Eventually, such conversations would always turn to stories of the sea, and of tropical oceans and typhoons from Eoin's youth. If Hannah couldn't sleep, she would curl up and listen, and try to imagine all that power of water.

Then, one morning when the boat was nearing completion, a seething rainstorm hit the shoreline and filled the air with salt. By the time noon arrived, the sky was so overcast it was like midnight. The first intonations of thunder sounded, and the wind screeched over the beach and into the woods, twanging their tents' guy ropes. Hannah crouched beneath the canvas with the others and watched the wind fling sand into the forest. The waves gnashed like they meant to follow.

'Come on,' Hiroko whispered to Seb.

Then, to Hannah's astonishment, the girl dashed out into the rain and stood straight-backed and staring upward at the clouds above the beach. Yasuo sped after her, to run orange circles around her ankles and yap at the weather. Then Seb rushed out too, and all three of them stamped about in the beating water hooting and howling. White fire scored the sky, as if scratching runes into its surface. When a thunderclap came, Hiroko flung her hands high and hollered back, and Seb's delighted laughter carried on the rumbling wind, and Yasuo gave a shriek as piercing as an icicle. Hannah looked to Adrien, wondering if he would also turn wild and throw shapes in time with the lightning, but he was looking into the woods, not out to sea, and looked so preoccupied as to have hardly noticed the teenagers dancing.

Eventually the wind picked up into a gale and put stings in the raindrops, and only then did Hiroko and Seb crouch back into the tent, shivering and grinning. The spray painted white the flex and warp of the air, and great gusts boomed into the forest from the direction of the beach. Then, as the storm peaked, the wind gushed full circle, into the trees and back again, clattering out leaves and twigs which swept overhead like bats and were lost in the darkness far from shore.

When at last the water calmed, it was full of statues. At first Hannah thought that the storm had blown the cargo of some ship of mannequins onto the beach, but when they all trod down to the water to inspect them further, she saw that they were hunks of driftwood. Eoin and Nora appeared shortly after that, and the sailor led them in salvaging the wood. Only Adrien hung back on the shingle, neither joining in nor watching them. He just kept looking back at the forest, and stuffing his hands into his pockets and bunching his shoulders up towards his ears. Hannah was about to go and talk to him when Eoin announced a competition. Whoever could find the shapeliest piece of driftwood would see it bolted to the prow of their boat as a figurehead, and they all laughed and compared ideas of what each weathered lump most looked like. Nora wanted to know whether Hannah thought this one was a horse, or this one a tigress, and by the time Hannah had finished offering opinions on the matter, and headed back up the beach to speak with Adrien, he was gone. He must have scuffed away unnoticed, while they were busy with the driftwood.

7

Heart of the Forest

There were two winds blowing on the shore that afternoon, as Adrien wandered it lost in thought. The first was a salty shade of the earlier storm, hissing with the tide, ghosting off each land-bound push of the waves. The second was its reply from the woods, coming sometimes like a horn blast and sometimes like a whisper. If the two met they spun the air into a bluster, flapping Adrien's hair and chilling his bald spot. He took to covering it pre-emptively with his hand, as if it were a small mammal in need of protection.

'I love you, you know,' Michelle had once said, after she had ruffled what was left of his hair. 'No matter if every last bit falls out. You should remember that. Besides, it happens to all men.'

But it didn't. Not like this. He looked like some bloody ridiculous monk, these days. And other men his age had long locks of it or rock-star hair or were those bastards who shaved it even to the point of baldness, despite every follicle still functioning intact.

He wondered if Michelle remembered that moment, and whether she did so with any of the patience she had shown back then. She had lost faith in him so gradually that at first he'd hardly even noticed. He doubted she had any faith at all left now.

Adrien had used to walk home to Michelle, at the end of every day at the school, in a kind of stupor. She'd tried to make him see the funny side, before she changed tack and bought him his year to make sense of himself. 'You take it all too seriously,' she'd said on one of those earlier occasions. 'It's just a game the kids are playing.

And remember that the rules of the game let you bollock them. You just need to make use of that authority.'

But it had not seemed like a game, at the end of each of those days, and Adrien hadn't felt like an authority on anything. His pupils had been older than those of the deckchair classroom, and shared none of those children's desire for the normality of school life. They had sniffed out Adrien's low self-esteem like dogs sniffing out fear. They had pranked him and harried him, and he had been locked out of his classroom and locked into store cupboards. After teaching particular classes, he'd often trudged to the staff toilets, taken off his jacket and laid it neatly alongside the sink. It would be covered in what the schoolboys called *lace*, which meant long strings of saliva flicked from finger and thumb. Adrien had dabbed them away with a sponge kept in his jacket pocket for that very purpose and felt, quite eerily, just as he had done during his own school years. Bullied by just such boys.

It wasn't the spit itself that had upset him. It was that there existed the same sorts of boys today as had existed in his own youth, and that on parents' evenings there had come fathers who were man-shaped versions of the same. 'Boys will be boys,' Michelle had told him, 'and let's face it, it could be something worse,' but Adrien had walked home and the world had looked grey and hard and masculine, even the sky and the clouds and the clipped verges. Even his house seemed all concrete, and the carpets all concrete and the furniture all concrete. Was this the world he was supposed to assume some authority over? He had felt utterly petrified by the idea.

On occasions such as those, it would always take Michelle an hour or two to make things right, softening the concrete world with the lightness of her touch, or the brush of her hair against his cheek when she hugged him, or her caress on the small of his back. 'I love you for worrying so much,' she'd said. 'For wanting everything to be so impossibly perfect.'

Adrien sighed, and scuffed his feet along the sand. Back then he might have been unhappy twenty-three hours out of twenty-four, but those hours of relief when Michelle had rescued him were some of the finest hours he'd ever known.

'And what,' he asked himself, 'did you repay her with?'

Time passed. The afternoon dribbled away. Adrien was still meandering on the beach come the evening. Staring up now and then at the emerging Pole Star, that tiny naked light, and wondering why he'd ever given up his childhood hobby of stargazing. It had been his relief from the bullies, and he had loved the strangely cultish feeling of gathering on a hilltop to stare at the heavens. As a boy, stargazing had made him feel like there was something awe-inspiring about his own insignificance. It had let him be satisfied with smallness, instead of lacking for it. He had used to imagine himself neither as a space captain nor an intergalactic hero but as a comet, a nugget of cold rock whirling long orbits round a brilliant star.

The sea sifted. The trees creaked and shivered. Adrien closed his eyes and tried to pretend what he had not pretended since childhood. Cold to the bone and streaming out a wake of ice. Hurtling unimpeded through the simplicity of nothingness. It brought a fraction of a smile to his otherwise troubled face. Outer space was no more complicated than an elaborate machine. There was nothing up there to eat you, nothing small and creeping to haunt you with its dead wooden stare, nothing to fall in or out of love with. Down on the Earth everything was so much more imperfect, and the most imperfect thing of all was Adrien Thomas.

The two winds kept blowing, back and forth between woods and waves, but after a time it was the water's wind that quietened, as if its attention had fluttered away on the tide. Adrien was just beginning to think he should head back to the tent, when something moaned in the forest.

It was a sound so forlorn that, for half a second, Adrien assumed it was a noise from inside himself. Then it came again, a drawn-out timber whine, and he realised it had sounded behind him. He looked over his shoulder and saw the whisperers' tree, the one that poor broken Gweneth had called a throne.

At once he looked left and right for help, but he had wandered far from the town and was all alone on this stretch of beach. It was just him and the great plant, which stood on the near fringe of the forest rearing high above all the other trees. Dark and leafless, it looked like some hardy survivor of the cruellest winter ever to bite the world. Its two lower boughs ended as bluntly as screwed-up fists, but the creaking noise that Adrien had heard had not come from them. It sounded again now, from higher up the trunk where the branches fanned out like the prongs of a crown, and its noise was like a deep hymn sung from the back of the throat. Adrien drew in a long breath of his own and tried to stay calm. He told himself it was only a tree, a plant, a plain vegetable. It could not touch him down here by the water.

With a rustle, a whisperer stood up where the undergrowth met the beach. It was the thinnest Adrien had yet seen, its body as fragile and decorative as a fern. Near it rose another with a doleful face and stumpy legs. Then there was a third, a fourth and fifth, and two conjoined like grafted wood. When Adrien looked back to the throne tree he could see them crawling all over its branches, and up and down the sombre bark of its trunk.

Something twitched in the sand at Adrien's feet. He looked down to see a crab paused there, mid-shuffle, its stalk eyes trained on the forest's edge. Over there was another, and here and there lugworms pumping their bodies out of the sand, only to stiffen upon surfacing, their featureless heads pointing at the throne. A cormorant landed with a hurried beating of wings, then stood up just as motionless as the worms, its beak angled in the same direction. Adrien gulped and looked too, but felt like he could see only half of what the animals did. He wondered what it was about the tree that so transfixed them.

There was still some light left in the sky, but the throne tree was almost as dark as a silhouette. Its upper branches creaked as they swayed in the breeze. Then, with a deep and tortured squeal, one of the highest swung against another and scraped bark along bark.

For a moment the two looked just like the itching legs of some colossal insect.

Adrien's throat made a strangled noise. Those were not branches. None of those higher growths were branches.

They were the legs of something sitting on the throne tree.

Now that he had seen it, Adrien felt as if his eyes had come uncrossed. The thing up there was all legs, like some grandmother tarantula flexing her limbs atop her den. The evening was too murky to count all those appendages, but each of them branched at every joint. Elbows split into forearms, forearms into multiple wrists, wrists fanned out into innumerable crooked digits. The creature didn't even have a body to speak of, only a wooden knot from which all of its protrusions emerged. Even as Adrien watched, three of those legs stretched out and at once retracted. The creature groaned as it tested them, and the noise stuck like a stitch in Adrien's belly.

This thing, Adrien realised, was the reason for the whisperers' bustling. They clambered up and down the tree trunk to attend it, or to whisper in its presence. Sometimes the creature moaned as if calling out from a long slumber, and the whisperers would scurry about this way and that, and all of the leaves of the forest would shiver with an echo.

'What are you?' mumbled Adrien, but the wide open air between him and the woodfringe stole all the volume from his words.

In a sudden spasm, the thing flung wide its legs and wailed. Adrien staggered backwards even as its exhalation gushed over the sand, a choking rush of earth smells and nectar and the sugar of sap and the excretions of worms, all borne on moist air and a rattling confetti of leaves. Gagging on the sweetness and the rottenness of it, Adrien turned away and shielded his mouth and nose, but even his own breath in that gust seemed too sickly to inhale. His stomach bucked and his vision swirled into brightness and he thought he was passing out. He teetered in some halfway state between fainting and consciousness, and everything turned a dazzling greenish-white, and his vision broke up like light falling through treetops. For a few untethered seconds he thought he heard the beating pinions of a crow and the cantering hooves of a deer. He thought he felt a woodpecker rattling his ear, and a squirrel's tail whisking over his cheek. Leaves whirled around him. He tripped on his own feet and the sand rushed up to greet him, everything plunging into pitch dark and cold, and he thought he felt wriggling grubs all over his flesh.

He grunted as he hit the ground, but somehow he did not pass out. His delirium faded along with the noise of the creature's cry, and after a few seconds he was able to prop himself back up and spit out a mouthful of grit. The beach, the woods and the sea all settled back into their rightful places.

The throne tree had vanished from the forest's edge. So had the thing that had lurked atop it, along with all of its attendant whisperers bar one. That stood as upright as a bulrush and, although Adrien couldn't even tell if it had eyes, he knew that it was watching him.

The whisperer made a short, hissing noise like a snake's, then turned and fled into the forest.

Adrien puffed out the breath he had been holding. He wiped his arm across his forehead and tried to make sense of what had just happened. There was a taste like uncooked meat on his tongue and there was a ringing in his ear. His left cheek tingled, and when he touched his fingers to it he half-expected to find strands of squirrel fur stuck to his skin. There was nothing, of course, just as in the forest there were only ordinary trees, stirring innocuously in the wind.

8

Fox

'I've got something for you,' said Hiroko. 'To say thank you for the postcards.'

Seb looked at the two strips of leather she was holding up. 'Belts?' he asked, confused. 'But . . . I've already got one.'

'These aren't belts, stupid. They're holding straps. To stop luggage sliding around on a boat.'

'Er, right . . . Thanks, I suppose. But what do we need these for? Strapping down the tent when we cross?'

'*No.* Come with me.'

'Where are we going?'

But Hiroko didn't explain. Instead, with Yasuo purring on her shoulder, she led him along the coast. North of the town she took him, where the stratas of the cliffs jutted in and out like stacks of different-sized books. Wildflowers grew on some ledges, as well as scrawny trees not much bigger than bonsais.

'How far are we going?' asked Seb, when they had been walking for almost half an hour.

'Further yet,' said Hiroko, and smiled to herself.

Another half-hour passed before she spotted their destination up ahead. Someone from the beach camps had told her about it the day before, although in her imagination it had been taller. It was a lighthouse, standing at the end of a headland. The trees had taken it apart as easily as a child's tower of blocks, but they had not cast the pieces down into the frothing waters at the bottom of the cliffs.

267

Instead they had separated them, spacing them between their branches and trunks, so that the pieces became a vertical sequence of tree houses. Broad stripes of blue paint were still visible on some of their crumbling sections, but the topmost parts were invisible among the treetops.

'Up there,' said Hiroko, pointing. 'People say it's where a pair of them are nesting.'

'Where what—' began Seb, but at once a sea eagle took flight from out of the lighthouse, its wings broad and rippling as it swept for the ocean.

'Come on,' laughed Hiroko, and started walking again.

It took them another twenty minutes to reach the foot of the lighthouse. Yasuo ran ahead of them all the way, sometimes pausing to turn over a shell with his nose, but he wanted to be picked up again when the beach ended and the path up the cliff began.

The little fox was growing every day and Hiroko sometimes found it hard to carry him in her hood. On the other hand, she was getting stronger and Yasuo was learning to perch his forepaws on her shoulder for support. When he pulled himself upright like that, and she saw him sideways out of the corner of her eye, his figure struck her as almost human, albeit only a foot tall and with ears as big as leaves. She was glad he had stayed with her, despite Hannah's warnings that he might abandon her at a moment's notice. She was glad, too, that she had named him after her grandfather. Every time she said Yasuo's name she thought fondly of her elderly *sobo* and *sofu*, and fox stories told to her as a girl, and of her grandfather's silent vigil in a rocking chair, whittling wood while she walked with her grandmother in the orchard.

She let out an involuntary sigh.

'What's up?' asked Seb, at once picking up on her sadness.

'It's nothing,' said Hiroko, although she knew Seb wouldn't believe her.

Among the many fox magics her *sobo* had delighted in describing, the one that had most captured her imagination was the power to alter form. The most eldritch among foxes could turn (or so her grandmother would claim in that musical croak that was her story-telling voice) into human beings. Then they would creep into the lives of lonely and impressionable souls and offer them long-sought affection. 'They say there have been marriages,' her grandmother had once told her, 'and babies born who look human, but are neither truly one thing nor the other.'

'How would you tell?' Hiroko had asked her once. 'How would you know if you were one of those children?'

'You would seek out your reflection in running water. If you saw yourself red and whiskered, well . . . then you'd know.'

Yasuo barked to regain Hiroko's attention, and barked again, and she crouched down and lifted him up, holding him under the armpits like a baby. Many times, even in recent years, she had looked for her reflection in running water. Normally it was hard to find, for brooks babbled and streams surged. If she ever managed to see it she was disappointed. It never looked anything like the animal she now helped onto her shoulder. It was just another human girl.

The cliff face here was scored with diagonal crags, as if all of its weight were slumping sideways into the sea. The path up it was nothing more than a series of such ledges, with a scramble some-times needed to climb from one to the other. Finding handholds in such weathered rocks was not difficult, but Hiroko stopped halfway up the first stretch to offer Seb some assistance. To her surprise, he was right behind her.

'What?' he laughed, upon seeing her surprise. 'Stop looking so shocked. Mum taught me how to climb when I was small.'

'Good,' said Hiroko, after a moment. 'Then let's go faster.'

A few minutes later, they were up, and the broken lighthouse rose before them.

'Now what?' asked Seb.

'In,' she said, and led the way.

It was still possible to enter through the lighthouse's doorway, even though the door itself was gone and the rest of the bricks surrounding its frame had been torn upwards. Patches of the ground floor had survived the arrival of three particularly massive trees, but the levels above had been destroyed. Only intermittent stretches of a staircase remained, connecting the floors of the lighthouse like a contorted spine.

'What do you think?' asked Hiroko, looking up. The tiers above were still whirlpools of brick and brown leaf.

'I think we can get up,' said Seb, 'but I can't tell why you want us to.'

Hiroko grinned and set foot on the first step of the staircase. The wood was damp from rainwater and creaked beneath her boots, but it was firm enough to support her weight. A dozen steps up, the stairs came to their first abrupt end, but there was a low bough she could step on and sidle along until she reached the next run. Seb kept up competently, just as he had on the cliff, and as they climbed higher only Yasuo seemed troubled by vertigo. The further up they got, the more evidence they saw of the sea eagles. Fragments of an old egg lay smashed in one place against bricks streaked white by droppings. Threads of dropped fish meat had hardened to the bricks and soon, when peering upward, Hiroko began to see the nest itself, and above that the grey of the sky. Neither of the birds were currently at home, but the smell of them certainly was. It was brine and blood and something more brisk, like the wind blowing ten thousand feet above the sea.

The final stretch of staircase came to an end and the branches grew too narrow to trust. Hiroko and Seb were as high as they could go, but it was enough. Here were a few square yards of floor intact, and walls on three sides. To the west, the branches opened wide, and there was a spectacular view of the ocean. The sun was coming down and growing fat, and against the backdrop of its light the two eagles circled like the hands of some delicate clockwork.

Hiroko might have stopped and admired them, had not there been something else too distracting, which they could not have seen from below.

It was the lighthouse's lamp. It had fallen from its original height, but had then been caught in the branches. Once a giant, many-panelled device of lenses and filaments, it had fractured as it fell and cracked in every facet. It was now an orb of frosted glass and splintered prisms, and a handful of its broken surfaces faced the sun directly, and were lit up like the sparkles in quartz.

'That's pretty,' said Seb eventually. 'Is that what you wanted to show me?'

'No,' said Hiroko. 'I didn't even know it was still here.'

She crouched and picked something up off the floor. '*This* is what we're here for.'

She brandished a wing feather, chocolate brown and flecked with white like the sea spray that flecks the beach. When she tickled Seb with it he laughed but clung to the wall.

'Bloody hell, Hiroko! There are a lot of ways to fall from here!'

'Crybaby,' she said. 'Come on.'

Quickly she began to search the place for more feathers, finding them here and there among the leaves. Seb helped, and when they had gathered a dozen or more, Hiroko said, 'Figured it out yet?'

'I've figured out nothing. I'm just following your lead.'

She shook her head in disbelief, then untied from around her waist the two leather straps she'd shown him earlier. She unsheathed her knife and took out thread from her pocket, then sat cross-legged to cut holes along the leather. After a moment she paused and looked to Seb again. 'Understand now?'

'Maybe,' he said, sitting beside her. He chose one of the eagle feathers and fed its quill through the first of the holes she'd cut in the strap.

Hiroko secured it in place with the thread. 'Carter had a friend who was a shaman,' Hiroko said. 'He used to stop by to eat jerky with us in the woods. I think they'd been to war together, although neither would say. Anyway, one time this guy told me that to wear part of an animal was to ask its spirit to watch over you.'

Yasuo, in her hood, yawned and closed his eyes against her neck.

They got to work on the other feathers. It was slow and careful work, and the sun moved an inch down the sky and its light shone orange in more and more facets of the shattered lamp. Then, when they'd almost finished the headdresses, one of the eagles returned to its roost. Hiroko and Seb seized each other's hands as it whooshed in through the open wall and then up, its outstretched wingspan rippling in the air. In its talons was a mighty fish, glittering and thrashing and dripping beads of water.

The eagle touched down in the nest above them with a scream. Hiroko grabbed Seb's biceps and squeezed. They were doing things like that now, instead of kissing. Just grabbing each other whenever the moment felt right. There was a thrill in such spontaneous intimacy, but to Hiroko's frustration it never lasted. She'd feel Seb tensing with that same desire she had inside her, that sensation not unlike dread in her stomach. And then they would let go of one another and let their arms drop uselessly to their sides, just as they did now. He would not push for anything since the breaking of his nose. She wanted to push for it but had once again become caught in the snare of her own emotions, so much harder to break free of than a real pit trap or wire noose.

It was too difficult a thing to discuss, so Hiroko could only guess what Seb thought of her. Did he think she was experienced? The truth was that she felt she ought to be. Sex just seemed the kind of thing a girl should have done before she'd killed too many things to keep count of. One boy in Japan had offered it to her, almost as casually as if it were chewing gum, and she'd followed her instincts and issued dire threats about just what she'd do to him with a knife if he ever asked again. Not long after that, though, she'd wished she'd taken him up on the offer. Just to see what it was like. By then, of course, it had been impossible. He had believed her every word and was too terrified to even come near.

Something floated through the air between her and Seb. One more eagle feather, oscillating in the glimmering lamplight. Grateful for the distraction, they both tried to grab it at once. Seb's hand clasped around Hiroko's even as she caught hold of the feather.

'Um,' he said and let go, blushing.

'This is the last one we need,' said Hiroko, staring resolutely at the feather.

'The finishing touch.'

She fastened it into her headdress, but found she was unable to look up at Seb. 'They're ready to wear now,' she said.

'Yep.'

'So what are we waiting for?'

'I don't know,' he said. 'I suppose I was waiting for you to say when.'

'Okay.' She turned the headdress in her hands. 'Okay . . . One, two, three . . .'

They put their headdresses on their heads. She supposed she had no choice but to look at him now, but moving her neck to do so was like bending straight a lead pipe. She winced after she'd done it, as if it had hurt her. Then she laughed.

She couldn't help herself, because Seb looked so ridiculous. He laughed too, and she supposed she looked just as stupid, and their laughter danced up through the ruins above them and caused the eagle there to screech and thump its wings. At this they gasped and laughed harder, for the bird's cry was so savage and free. It made Hiroko's insides feel like they were carefree, soaring through the air on the back of the wind and then, and then . . .

'What's wrong?' asked Seb.

'I don't know,' she said, pulling off the headdress. 'It's like I can't . . . can't ever . . .' But she didn't know how to express it. She glowered out at the sea, where with the late hour of the afternoon the sun was dropping fast. Behind her the lamp was a sponge for the light.

'We were having fun,' said Seb, 'and then—'

'I was an idiot,' she said. 'I remembered what Carter's friend said and I thought that a headdress . . . I thought that feathers . . .'

Now Seb looked as sad as she did. 'You thought an eagle spirit might help you feel closer to home.'

Hiroko covered her face with her hands. 'Like something a little girl would think.'

'But I can understand why you'd—'

'*No,*' she spat. 'You can't understand!'

He took off his own headdress. 'I'm sorry, Hiroko. I just hate to see you being so hard on yourself. I wasn't pretending I know what it's like.'

'What am I doing here?' she asked, in a tiny voice.

'What do you mean? You wanted us to come up here.'

She stared west at the sun. Even that seemed nearer than her father, her *sobo* and *sofu*. And as for her mother, *she* felt the farthest of all.

'They're so many miles behind me,' she said.

'Oh. Oh, Hiroko . . . I'm so sorry. You know I wish there was something I could do.'

'I'm sorry, too,' she said eventually. 'And you *do* understand a bit of what it's like.'

'What do you mean?'

'How far away does your uncle feel?'

Seb looked down at the floor. 'Different distances on different days.'

'But never close.'

He shook his head.

'And I'm sorry I broke your nose when you asked about my mother. It's almost impossible just to think about her, let alone talk.'

'You mustn't feel you have to tell me anything if you don't—'

'I killed her, Seb.'

His lips stiffened, parted in the shape of his next word. Hiroko folded her arms and looked away.

'You . . . you . . .' he struggled. 'What do you mean?'

'I killed her, and that's the reason for everything. Why my dad took the job in America. Why he wanted to be miles from home.'

'When did this happen?' croaked Seb.

'When I was small.'

'It was . . . an accident?'

She shrugged. 'Does it matter?'

'I don't know. Maybe.'

'How it happened doesn't change that I did it.'

'Hiroko . . . please tell me.'

'I *don't remember*,' she whispered, 'and Dad hates to talk about it. He just says that life isn't kind enough, and we should leave it at that. But I . . . I managed to find out from my grandmother. She said the hospital did all they could, but there were just too many complications. She said they had to cut me out of my *obasaan*'s stomach, and she never even got to meet me.'

Seb threw his arms around her so hard that he knocked the breath out of her. He didn't let go, only held her body close against his. 'You don't have to be this tough,' he said, loud, in her ear. 'And listen to me, Hiroko. Eagle feathers might not fix things, and it might seem like stuff is only getting harder. But I'm going to do everything possible to help you. And I won't let anyone stop me, yourself included.'

She let Seb hold on to her. Beside them the great lamp shimmered with reflected light, and was their private moon in an eyrie of their own. Then, with fumbling fingers, she reached for the buttons of his shirt.

9

Crossing

The next evening, Eoin announced that the boat was finished. As long as the weather obliged, they would set sail the following night. Adrien and his companions all gathered round and gave three cheers, and Hannah opened with a fizz a bottle of tonic she had found in a buried house. She'd pressed some forest fruits into a syrup, and now mixed them with the tonic. Everyone touched cups and pledged a toast to the crossing, and Nora's face screwed up from the tartness of the drink.

The girl fell asleep first, then Seb and Hiroko. Yasuo yawned and settled in among the teenagers' hair, and Eoin was out cold as soon as his eyes closed. Hannah didn't look like she'd ever sleep again, but Adrien began to nod off with an expression of troubled concentration fixed on his face. He hadn't told the others about the thing he had seen on the throne tree. He wouldn't have even known how to begin, but his sleep when it came was as thick as the soil, and his dreams were full of earthworms and roots.

Come late afternoon the next day, the water lay flat and metallic. Eoin swam out a good distance, diving under the surface to test the currents, then waded back to the beach and clapped Seb on the shoulder. They all knew they would be leaving that night.

As soon as darkness fell they disassembled their tents, not saying a word as they did so. Their luggage was already packed, and Adrien and Nora stood guard over it while the others slipped into the woods to drag the boat to the beach. Once they had done so, the others kept watch as Eoin and Seb secured the final fittings, then all together they pushed it out until the tide took over, and one by one pulled each other onboard. Eoin wanted to conserve the motor's fuel until it was most sorely needed, so they took up oars and rowed as they had practised in between stints restoring the vessel.

Under the lights of the many stars, the coast shrank from something that had seemed so firm and large underfoot to something slight and receding, a thinning wedge between the darkness of the water and the enormous sparkling sky. Here and there along the shore guttered the final glows of campfires, but the people on the beaches were asleep and their dim red lights dwindled quick as embers. Then the land faded and was gone.

The water slurped the oars. The waves swelled large but never steep. After an hour, on Eoin's instruction, they paused and breakfasted on fresh water and food from their packs. In the meantime the shipwright unravelled a small sail that they had cut out of canvas, and tested it to see what power he could coax out of the wind. The breeze offered up some gentle momentum, which meant they could row in shifts for the next couple of hours until at last, when the sun began to rise, the wind dropped and Eoin tugged the motor's cord. The blades began to chop a frothy V into the water behind them, and they all loafed back on their benches, stretching their arms and staring around them at a dawn view identical in all directions. Sea that might have been endless. Sky blank as an unfinished map. In the woods they had often felt a green claustrophobia, but as day broke here they faced its exact opposite, and eventually they stopped looking to the plain horizons and preferred the details of the boat and their own selves and rucksacks crammed into it. At sea, it seemed, there was only the distance.

Adrien listened to the gurgle of the water parting for the boat. He kept thinking about his encounter on the beach, although he still did not know what to make of it other than to resolve that, should he ever see the throne tree again, he would run screaming in the opposite direction. He told himself he was an expert at putting off thinking about things, and should do so now, but every time he managed a reminder sprang from an unexpected source. Even here, out to sea, he could be prompted. The woodgrain on the boat's timber cladding became like the wrinkles in some ancient hide. The polished knots in the deck became like the hollow eyes of the whisperers.

Adrien hung his head overboard to avoid looking at the timber. The others nodded knowingly at one another, and he knew they mistook him for seasick.

The waves, in the end, gave Adrien a much-needed distraction. Out to sea they grew bigger, and swelled up a memory of simpler times. Five nights' holiday that he and Michelle had taken along France's Côte de Granit Rose. In the final light of those summer days, the cliffs had softened to a pink so delicate that they had lost all hardness and looked more like marshmallow than granite. Adrien and Michelle had spent that week simply wandering the Côte, losing themselves in whatever suited them. In the evenings they ate fish so fresh they half expected it to flip off their plates, drank much wine and slept heavily. Then they woke in the early afternoons to do it all over again.

Adrien had meant to pose the question on the first of those days. Courage, however, came harder than intention, and it took him until the fourth attempt to grasp the opportunity. It was an evening in which the sun balanced red on the horizon and lingered late, as if it had seen the far side of the world and deemed it less interesting than that of Michelle and Adrien. The couple bought an inflatable dinghy, which they splashed out to an islet of rocks where the stones stood up in fairytale parapets, warm and salmon-coloured in the sunset. When they reclined on them they found the firm surfaces perfectly eroded to fit the shapes of their bodies. Adrien did his best not to stare at Michelle's legs, bared by her swimsuit. For his part he wore only waterproof shorts, the beginnings of his flabby tummy protruding over their elastic.

He had been proud of his foresight when purchasing those shorts. They had a pocket in their lining kept shut by a zip and a strap of Velcro. A perfect hiding place for a ring. But when it came to the moment, the fabric of the pocket was drenched and his fingers jiggled madly to try to get in. Michelle watched him fumbling in his loins, her bemused expression turning Adrien redder than the sun.

'Um,' he had said eventually, poking around his nether regions until they at last produced the ring, 'Um?'

She had flung herself at him and wrapped her arms around his neck, and they had embraced and stood together flesh against flesh, and she had whispered her *Yes* as hot as a kiss in his ear, and he had been happier than he could ever remember. The proposal thus surmounted, it had seemed to him that the hard work was over, and that all that remained was to live out their lives in wedded bliss. They would let love, Adrien had thought so contentedly, be both their anchor and the wind in their sails. Everything would work out for the best.

The sun had crossed the better part of the sky by the time the Irish coast grew from a thread to a long array of sandy beaches. The sun and the sand's reflection turned the sea bone-coloured in the bays and inlets, and urgent gulls shot overhead without calling. As their boat drew closer to shore, the travellers could see further inland. It was forested as far as the eye could see.

'Were there always woods here?' asked Adrien of Eoin.

The shipwright shook his head. 'Not this time last year.'

'That settles that, then,' said Adrien.

Suddenly the motor gave a noise like a sigh of relief, then stopped chopping when the fuel ran out. Although everyone was exhausted, they all took up oars for the final stretch, buoyed by the sight of land and eager for a beach where they could drop anchor. In the south-west distance, they thought they could discern the shapes of people moving about on the sand, and coloured shapes behind them that might have been tents. They turned north and rowed along the coast in the other direction.

Turning into one of several wide and deserted bays, they saw columns of trees snaking out towards the beach, wherever there was soil enough to support them. Some had grown too tall, with roots too shallow, to stand up to the ocean's gales. They were knocked over and half-buried in blown sand, their leafless branches reaching back for the denser woods like desperate arms. Those inland trees were browning fast, and here and there had already rusted for the coming autumn.

They put the boat ashore, and disembarked with wobbly legs. After they had built their campfire, Seb volunteered to scrounge nearby for supplies. When he set off to do so, Hiroko went at his side.

Eoin looked back out to sea. 'Dusk's coming. Would you mind stoking the fire, Adrien? I've a mind to set some lines out on some rocks I thought I saw north of here. If we get lucky we might have fish for breakfast.'

'Go ahead,' said Adrien, licking his lips. 'We'll get it nice and hot for you.'

'Stay here, Nora,' said Eoin, grabbing his pack. 'And make sure to keep warm.' Then he headed back towards the water.

Nora needed no excuse to take off her boots and socks and warm her toes near the gathering flames. Hannah looked at her, then at Adrien, and then without a word followed Eoin.

'Oh,' said Adrien, finding himself alone with the child. 'That's how it is, is it?'

Nora grinned toothily up at him, but Adrien found he did not mind being babysitter. He was going to miss the girl, when she sailed away with Eoin in the morning. 'You must be glad,' said Nora, wriggling her toes in the firelight.

'Glad about what?'

'Getting away from those little people you saw.'

Adrien poked at the campfire with a branch. The salt air had dried the branches into perfect tinder, and the flames crackled and stood up tall.

'Do you know what a pessimist is, Nora?'

'No.'

280

'A pessimist is me.'

'I don't understand.'

Adrien sighed. 'I mean . . . I'm not so sure I'll be rid of those things that easily.'

'But they're on the other side of the sea now. I'm glad we got away from them. I'm glad we got away from that scary lady in the camper van. She gave me nightmares.'

'She, at least, won't be troubling you here. I don't think there's any reason to be worried about her.'

'But you do think . . . what? That the little stick people will swim after you, all the way to Ireland?'

'No.' Adrien looked over his shoulder at the sombre expanse of the Irish forest. 'I don't think it's going to work like that. Not with the trees having appeared here too. Just call it a hunch.'

'Is that was a pessimist means? Someone who does things with a hunch?'

'Kind of.'

'I don't think I'm going to be a pessimist when I grow up.'

He chuckled. 'I never thought I was going to be one either, when I was your age.'

Nora yawned indifferently. 'Do you know any bedtime stories, Mr Thomas?'

Adrien flinched. 'You don't have to call me that any more. Just Adrien is fine.'

'It would feel . . . funny to call you Adrien. I mean, Mr Thomas is your name.'

'Not any more it isn't.'

Nora looked puzzled. 'Isn't it?'

'No. The school is over, isn't it?'

'I know how to do Monsieur Thomas, if you want. I can do both!'

'I'm not Monsieur Thomas and I'm not Herr Thomas and I'm not Signor Thomas and I'm not bloody Thomas-sensei like Hiroko bloody taught you. I have no surname. I want to be Adrien again now, and no more.'

Nora was silent for half a minute. The logs spat and the embers leapt.

'What about your wife?'

Adrien stoked the fire with his branch. 'What about her?'

'Isn't she Mrs Thomas?'

'No.'

'Madame Thomas, then?'

'No.

'Then *what's* her name?'

'Michelle.'

'I know that.'

He sighed. 'Why ask me, if you know it already?'

Silence again. Wood broke in the flames with a satisfying hiss.

'I just don't understand what she is, if she isn't Mrs Thomas.'

Bits of bark glowed ruby red while others papered into ash. 'This is the very last thing I'm going to teach you,' said Adrien quietly.

'What is?'

'*This*. You don't know the answers to everything, when you grow up.'

'But you're a teacher.'

'An English teacher. All I know is stories.'

'That's good,' she said, 'since you never answered my question.'

'What question was that?'

'I asked you if you knew any bedtime stories.'

'Not really. Just big books and plays.'

Her bare toes squirmed expectantly. 'A fairy story, though. You must know one of those.'

'Fairy stories are all about wolves and bears and hags in the woods. I'd rather not think about any of that stuff.'

'What about that one you told us in the classroom?'

He racked his brains, but he was certain he'd taught no fairy tales on the beach. 'You must be getting sleepy, Nora. We didn't do any of those.'

'Don't you remember? The one about the fairy queen?'

He scratched his head. 'Oh. You don't mean a fairy story. You mean a play. That was *A Midsummer Night's Dream*.'

'Whatever,' she said. 'Hang on a second.' Then she flopped back onto the earth and covered herself in one of Eoin's jumpers, which he had left her for a blanket. 'Right,' she said, 'comfy.'

'Lucky you.'

'That means I'm ready.'

'Ready for what?'

'My story, of course.'

Adrien sighed. 'Don't you remember it?'

'Yes.'

'Then close your eyes and picture it as hard as you can.'

Nora snorted with derision. 'That's stupid. You're not a storyteller.'

'I never claimed to be.'

'Daddy says that all teaching is storytelling.'

'Adrien says that all sailing is talking out of your arse.'

She giggled. 'Daddy won't like that.'

'Please don't tell him I said it.'

'You swear more than the others.'

'Someone's got to swear the most.'

'But why is it you?'

Adrien stabbed at the blazing logs. They rolled and fountained sparks, and the smoke hissed and fumed towards the woodland. 'I swear,' said Adrien, meaning it, 'because I must.'

'You don't *must* anything.'

'That's what you think. You wait until you're my age.'

She screwed up her nose. 'I can't even imagine it.'

'Good.'

'If you want,' she said, 'it could just be a real-life story. You *have* to know one of those.'

And, quick as crackling wood, a story came to him. 'You really want one of those, huh?'

'Yes I do.'

'You know the endings are different in real-life stories?'

'Of course I know that.'

'Well, then, it goes like this . . . It was the evening of our third wedding anniversary. Michelle had cooked me coq au vin, which is my favourite, and after we had eaten it she pushed a present towards me across the table.'

'How had she wrapped it?'

'I . . . I don't remember. Red paper, maybe. Or maybe it was silver.'

'Bow or no bow?'

'No bow. How am I supposed to remember that? I tend to open presents quickly.'

'I tend to do it very slowly. Carry on.'

'*For you*, Michelle said. *To say thank you for these three wonderful years. And may there be many more.* I could tell from the shape and weight of the present that it was a book, but I hadn't expected anything. I hadn't even bought her a present.'

'Shame on you.'

'Thanks, Nora. Anyway, Michelle was very excited about giving it to me. *Be careful when you unwrap it*, she said. *Don't just tear in blindly. You don't want to damage it.* So . . . I peeled back the paper.' Adrien sat up straight, the firelight playing across his face. 'Yes! Yes, it did have a ribbon! It was in green paper with a golden bow! I don't know how I'd forgotten.'

Nora wriggled her feet.

'When I pulled the book out of its wrappings it was very old. A faded brown cover and pages dry as sandpaper. But age had made it beautiful, I thought. Michelle was grinning from ear to ear. *It's what we watched on our honeymoon*, she said, as if I needed a reminder.'

He remembered tracing his fingers over the cover illustration. The antiquity of the binding had been so pleasant to the touch.

'Carry on,' said Nora, stifling a yawn.

'It was *A Midsummer Night's Dream*. That was the book, the script of the play. I asked her how old it was, and where did she find it? *One hundred years*, she said. And *in Edinburgh*.'

The cover had shown, in Art Nouveau's pure winding lines, Titania the fairy queen caressing the cheek of Bottom the weaver, whose head had been transformed to that of an ass. In the queen's hair and gown were leaves and twigs and flowers, so artfully incorporated that in places she seemed made out of the very forest itself. And as for Bottom, even though his expression was that of a stubborn beast, he looked very much in love.

'A hundred years,' said Nora softly, and the *years* turned into another yawn.

'That's right. A hundred years. And she'd gone all the way to Edinburgh to collect it.'

'Edinburgh,' she half-repeated, half-yawned.

'Edinburgh. I asked her, *When*? She said *Last weekend, when I told you I was away with work*. She'd driven up there on Saturday and back on Sunday morning. Apparently the dealer refused flat out to post it, in case it got damaged.'

The light was fading quickly now, and Nora breathed her first wispy snore. Adrien looked at her and smiled, then carried on regardless.

'I opened the book,' he said, 'and turned one by one through the pages. I remember every delicious rustle. I remember the smell . . . Now and then there was a plate, with an illustration as beautiful as the cover's. Michelle said *Isn't it perfect?* And it was. All of it was. The present, the meal, the occasion.'

He scowled at himself. Everything had been perfect except for one thing.

Michelle had looked at him across the table and said, 'You're going to tell me there's an except.'

'No,' he'd said, 'it's nothing.'

'But there is. There always is, these days.'

How wounded she had sounded, and rightfully so. He'd become suddenly nervous of bringing her to tears on their special day.

'No. Honestly. Really it's nothing.'

'It's something.'

Then he'd pointed, timidly and with trembling finger, to the source of his consternation.

'The candle? Are you serious?'

It had been burning all through the meal and he had done his very best to ignore it. But although it was a small thing it begged his attention and he could no more put it out of his mind than he could a leech sucking on his vein. 'You know I've always had trouble with candles,' he said feebly. 'They're terribly unsafe.'

She folded her arms. 'You're not going to blow it out.'

'What?'

'I'm not going to let you blow it out. It will do you good to keep it burning.'

'But it's so dangerous! It could burn the house down.'

She held her hands to her head. 'Great! That's exactly what I want to happen.'

'Are you crazy? If you're proposing some sort of insurance stunt I really don't think—'

'Jesus, Adrien, it was a metaphor. I thought those were your thing.'

He stared at her blankly.

'When I met you,' she said, gasping back tears, 'I was sure we could make just the biggest inferno. But every time I get even so much as a candle burning, you suffer it for a while in silence and then . . . and then you lean right down and you puff it out.'

Adrien groaned and flopped onto his back, watching the smoke of the campfire swarm into the darkening sky. Before crossing the water, his plan to go home and wait for Michelle had excused him from fearing what he most feared now. If his marriage was a bay of candles, he could remember days when they had all shone brightly with a steady amber light. How many had he snuffed out since then? Tonight his marriage seemed all shadows, but if Michelle had found her way back to him in England it would have proved that at least one was still burning. Were he to find her stopped here in Ireland, wouldn't that prove just the opposite? Wouldn't that mean that there was no light left to draw her home? Then what an unwanted arrival he would be.

Adrien shut his eyes and held himself very tight. Not far inland the trees creaked and strained. He dreaded stepping back under them, in part because of wolves and whisperers and the creature he'd seen on the beach, in part because of what he'd have to face up to if he ever found Michelle.

10

Unicorn

Hannah walked alongside Eoin, who followed the curve of the bay to look for rocks to hang his fishing lines from. Drifts of black cloud stretched out above the water, and a quavering light on the horizon was all that was left of their sailing day.

'Here,' said Eoin, 'before I forget.' He handed her a piece of paper, drawn with flowing lines, circled milestones and the names of landmarks. 'That's as best a map as I can draw. Do you know about this place you're headed to? This Caisleán Hotel?'

'Not really. I suppose it's just a conference hotel like any other.'

He shook his head. 'Mrs Thomas has a very generous employer, to send her and her colleagues there. It's almost a castle, that place. That's what caisleán means. It's not as old as a real castle, mind you, but it's all towers and balconies and so on. It was built by some English lord or other with big ideas about himself, and when he went bust he sold it to become a hotel. It's very overblown. Very fancy.'

She was surprised. 'You've been there?'

'Been past it. You can't really miss it. It's a bit of a local land-mark. Or an eyesore.'

'From the way Adrien described it, I thought it was just some place beside a motorway.'

Eoin laughed. 'Even he thought so until he told me the name. He said he'd never asked Michelle much about it. He told me it makes him jealous to think of his wife abroad, because of some fella who's there with her . . . I forget his name.'

'Roland. He's worried Michelle is having an affair.'

'Is that true?'

'I haven't the faintest idea. I've never met her. But I suspect . . . I *know* Adrien has a tendency to expect the worst in everything.'

'That's too true. For my part, I hope he finds her. I hope they can work things out.'

Hannah tried to catch Eoin's eye, but he was still scanning the coast for a fishing spot. 'Me too,' she said. 'People should try to work things out.'

She rolled up the map he had drawn her and held it between both hands like a precious scroll. 'Thanks for camping with us tonight,' she said.

'Nothing to thank me for. I couldn't row another stroke this evening.'

'I suppose I just imagined that we'd go our separate ways as soon as we came ashore . . .'

Eoin quickened his steps. The sea tossed and turned, rolling in its crumpled sheets. And now there were smooth rocks up ahead, a long chain of them running flat-topped into the shallows.

'Those are just the sort we're looking for,' he said.

'What I'm trying to tell you,' said Hannah, speeding up to match his turn of pace, 'is that I think it's such a shame that we're going in different directions.'

'Aye,' he said, 'that it is.'

'I wish we had a bit more time.'

He stopped and turned to look at her. The sand and the black sea framed him tall against them. 'We have a bit more time now.'

'Do we? I mean, you'll be gone in the morning.'

He started walking again, and when he reached the rocks bounded onto them and began unravelling his fishing lines, not once looking back down to where she stood on the sand.

'Eoin,' began Hannah. 'Have I said something wrong?'

The sailor sighed. 'I only wish you'd been able to tell me. Then we might have found a way past it together.'

He moved along the rock to wedge another line in, and Hannah's forefinger began to tap of its own accord. 'You don't understand,' she said.

At last Eoin looked at her. 'It's eating away at you. You need to open up about it.'

'If you knew what I'd done you'd—'

'Seb told me. A few nights ago while the rest of you were asleep.'

Hannah's jaw dropped open, but Eoin raised a hand. 'Don't blame him. And I didn't ask him to tell me, by the way. He's worried about you. Same goes for me. But, just like him, I don't blame you for doing it.'

'You . . . you . . . Seb *told* you?'

Eoin extended a hand to her, offering to help her up onto the stones. After a pause Hannah accepted it, and his arm was as strong as a spring, hauling her up alongside him.

'Why didn't you say that you knew?' she asked.

'I wanted you to be the one to bring it up.'

'That's a hell of a thing to expect of someone. We've only known each other for a couple of weeks.'

'I might have been able to help.'

Hannah shook her head tearfully. 'Have you ever shot someone, Eoin?'

'No.'

'Then there's not much helping you can do.'

'If you think like that, then you'll never find help. Unless it's from another man like him. Is that what you want?'

She didn't answer.

'He isn't with you any more, Hannah. There's a sea between you and him now.'

'I know that. I know.' But she did not quite believe it. It didn't matter where the gunman's body lay. He would have decomposed by now, far quicker than Zach or properly buried things. He would have broken up in a matter of days, dragged apart by beasts, his flesh becoming theirs. What was left of him would be immersed in the soil, drunk by roots and turned to seeds and fruits. The wind would disperse them. The flights of the birds would wing him far and wide.

'You've already helped me,' said Hannah quietly. 'By giving me an escape from him. I never knew how beautiful the sea was, until I met you.'

Eoin smiled, but Hannah wasn't sure he really understood. 'A shark is a shark,' he said. 'Remember that.'

She wiped her face and looked away from him, at the sea spread out beyond them, night-black and endless.

'It feels too late to open up about this now.'

'If you say it is, then I suppose that's true.'

'I shot him in the head,' she gasped. 'I tied him up and kicked him to the ground and I killed him. I did to him what he'd done to Zach, and I wish like crazy that I hadn't, and then, and then . . .' She thought of the stump she had mistaken for the gunman, and the ferocity with which she'd marched on it to ensure that he was dead. She wiped her eyes. 'Other times,' she said, 'I wouldn't have it any other way.'

Eoin stepped closer to her, as if all of that could be shut out, as if they could make the forest vanish and be alone on a pared-back shore.

'Things can be simpler,' he said, 'if you let them be.'

She lifted her hand and touched her trigger-finger to his cheek. To begin with it jittered faintly against the coarse hairs of his beard, but he didn't move a muscle and, after a minute, it stilled. She shuffled closer. Their bodies were touching. Eoin smelled of salt and rockpools.

If Hannah closed her eyes, even if she blinked, the memory of what she'd done was a fly buzzing around in her mind. She tried not to close them. When they kissed, she watched the sailor's grey irises until she was nearly dizzy, and only then did she let her eyelids slip. Then she concentrated solely on the movements of his lips, the brine of his saliva. His breathing was the breaking of the waves.

'Come with me,' said Eoin, resting his forehead against hers when the kiss was over. 'It's not so far from here to Michelle's hotel, and Adrien will find his way sure enough. You've done so much for him already. Come with me. We can sail towards Dungarvan together.'

Her heart jumped into her throat. 'Are you serious?'

'Of course.'

She held him tighter. 'I'd . . . I'd love that.'

'If that man is in the soil, put the soil behind you. You don't need it any more. Come with me. I'll teach you watercraft.'

'But there's Seb to think of. Hiroko, too, I suppose.'

'They can come with us. We can build a place together. It's beautiful along this coast.'

He stroked her cheekbone. She rested her fingertips against his jaw. She could picture herself gazing out to sea every morning and night, held in Eoin's arms like this. Letting the waves silence all thought of the gunman. Away to her left the forest looked like the silhouette of some vast, serrated blade, sawing away at the stars and the open night. A vixen called out in the wood, and something else screeched as it died, and the branches shook as if elated by such sounds. The forest was all tangled shadow and treachery, while to the other side of her the sea was a steady pouring rhythm. It might be salt-harsh and deep cold, but you could have faith in that.

'I'll have to talk to Seb.'

'Of course you will.'

'But, Eoin . . . I want to stay with you.'

'And me with you.'

Her face filled with gratitude. 'Thank you,' she whispered.

'It'll be my pleasure.'

She laid her head against his collar and breathed deep of the air against his chest. His heartbeat was as strong and steady as a rowing song.

Something bellowed in the woods.

'What the hell was that?' asked Eoin, drawing away and stepping forward protectively.

The near part of the woodfringe shook. Sticks cracked and leaves crunched. Hannah tensed and wished she'd brought her foraging knife with her. Then a branch reached out from the forest. It was a twigless and leafless spar, ending in a sharpened point. When a snout followed it, then a cumbersome head, Hannah realised it was no branch, but a horn.

The moonlight glinted off the mucus in the kirin's wide nostrils, and picked out its eyes beneath their leathery lids. It was another bull, barging out of the undergrowth to plod onto the sand, its fur chestnut and missing in patches where fighting scars had rent it. Its mouth hung open wide, grunting with every breath. It plodded towards Hannah and Eoin on huge flat feet, and every footstep threw up a dust cloud of sand.

'Back off the rocks and into the shallows,' urged Eoin, holding an arm out to shield Hannah. 'If we have to we can swim for safety.'

Hannah began to back away, but as soon as she'd scrambled down onto the damp sand the kirin shook its head and she saw something that froze her. The foam of the breakers tugged at her ankles, but she did not retreat alongside it. The kirin raised its nose and snorted, and there was a flash of diamond-white fur beneath its chin.

'That can't be . . .' said Hannah, but now she recognised the lattice of scars across its nose, and the two chips notched out of the tip of its horn.

'Oh my God,' she said, covering her mouth.

'Come on, Hannah,' urged Eoin, pulling at her arm.

She brushed his hand aside and began to walk forward, up the beach. The breakers hissed and foamed and when, out of the corner of her eye, she saw Eoin about to grab her, she was too quick for him. She ducked away and skipped forward, coming to a halt not an arm's length from the kirin.

It watched her down the length of its massive horn, in a fashion that might have been adorably cross-eyed had the beast not possessed the brute strength to break bones with a shrug. 'You can't be . . .' she whispered, but there were the silver flecks in its irises, there the golden eyelashes she had watched blink their last on the slopes above Zach's lodge.

Very slowly, she reached out to touch. The kirin snorted, and whipped its head to the side, so that Hannah snatched back her hand in alarm. But it was only turning, plodding back towards the forest. She watched it go, and for a moment from the treeline it stared back at her, its eye an expressionless ball. Then with a bray like a blast from a tuba, it muscled between the trunks and was gone.

'Now I've seen everything,' said Eoin, behind her.

Hannah held her breath, for to hold it seemed like the only thing keeping her together. She could feel a hot line through her heart, as if the kirin's horn had sliced it clean in two.

'Talk to me, Hannah,' said Eoin. 'It was almost as if you—'

'Recognised it. Yes.'

She turned to him and laid her hand on his chest, but it was with reservation now, rather than desire. 'I can't. I'm sorry, Eoin. I wish I could, but I can't.'

He frowned. 'I don't understand.'

'I have to go back into the woods. Zach's whole life . . . *my* whole life has been about the forest . . . If I let myself hate it I'll have . . . I'll have let the gunman do something even more awful to us both. I shot him in the woods. I feel like he's in there still. But if that's where he is, that's where I have to go if I ever want to defeat him.'

In the morning they stood on the shore in an awkward circle, waiting for somebody to initiate their parting. Neither Hannah nor Eoin could bear to do so, and in the end Hiroko stepped forward and hugged Nora first and then her father. Eoin shook hands with Adrien and called him his shipmate, then shook Seb's and told him he would make a fine shipwright. Nora flung her arms around Hannah's waist and pressed her whole body tightly against her legs. 'I want you to have something,' the girl said in a hurry, her face red with emotion. Then she offered Hannah with both hands a seashell, a fold of white enamel like a ceramic ear. Hannah turned it over to trace its ridged exterior, flecked with dots of pink and brown.

'Are you sure, Nora? This is very kind of you.'

She nodded vigorously, biting her front teeth into her bottom lip.

Hannah slipped it carefully into her bag. Then she took a deep breath and looked up at Eoin. For the first time since she'd known him he looked like an old and storm-battered mariner loath to once more strike out to sea.

She held out her arms and they embraced far more rigidly than either intended. It felt ridiculous, as if they were two battling crabs, and not parting friends who had not much hope of ever seeing one another again. He had drawn her another map, to complement the one of Michelle's hotel. It was the way to find him by the sea, he said, if ever the woods betrayed her again.

They all helped push out the boat, and Eoin lifted Nora in, then climbed aboard. As he reached for the oars his body seemed to strain like a vessel on the utmost sway of the tide. He looked back at Hannah so full of regret it was as if he had a different face, then he gazed out to sea for a moment. When next he looked back he wore a pretence. 'Safe journey, my friends.' He saluted them with one oar then began to row, sploshing steadily away, and after a few minutes had passed they watched him disappear around the headland.

Hannah felt as if she had watched the waves go out, never to come in again. She stared at the vacant water for a full minute, while the others waited for her in silence. Then she turned and walked with them over the soft beach to the woods.

They stepped into the forest and left behind them the mantras of the sea. Soon their noses were overwhelmed not with brine but with the pickled smells of dying flowers and the musts of stacked fungi. They trod a path of fallen leaves and scattered light, heading north-west this time, into a forest descending into autumn.

II

Fox

After their long stay on the shore, Hiroko felt strangely out of place in the forest. It had become such a damp and yellow realm, and was so heavy with water that the boughs all seemed to sag. Many of the leaves had turned limp and blotted with black, sometimes dropping to a moist floor that burped and squelched underfoot.

Hiroko led them using the compass and the map Eoin had drawn, but for Adrien's sake did not voice her reservations about either. Ireland had been devastated just like Wales and England, and Hiroko doubted they would find Michelle's hotel still standing, could they even find it at all. Just as maps and magnetism had only been able to lead them to the vague vicinity of Zach's lodge, they were going to need a kirin or a lucky break to cover the final distance.

The days that followed ran into each other. In the mornings grey bands of mist rose out of the forest floor, as if this were the place where the rain slept the nights. They followed the compass needle and tried to stay stoic about the drenched undergrowth that soaked their trouser legs and shoes. Sometimes the rain showers would pour out of the sky so suddenly that they had to fling themselves against the biggest tree trunks they could find, since these had the thickest branches under which to shelter. Only at night did the skies become clearer. Then the decaying canopy turned to a moth-eaten gauze, above which the stars shone keen and bright.

They passed through many villages, whose smashed wooden houses now served as nourishment for huge rinds of fungus. A few of these Hannah said were edible, even if they tasted like chalk and stained their fingers orange when they picked them. Other houses had been rebuilt into hamlets of sheds and lean-tos, with ceilings of tarpaulin and amateurish wicker. The inhabitants of such places looked, for the most part, dishevelled and hungry. Some had chopped down trees in between their dwellings, although it had clearly proved hard to dispose of all they'd felled. Severed trunks leaned on the living, and both had turned black with rot. Huge logs lay piled against one another, or heaped into bonfires so wet they had failed to burn.

Not everyone they met was losing their battle to survive in the woods. Four nights after leaving the coast, the travellers enjoyed the hospitality of an extended family of twenty-one, who had abandoned their various old homes to build a new one on the edge of a small lake. They had in common an ancient grandmother, whose sage bearing was a painful reminder of Hiroko's own, and freckles, of which between them they owned several thousands.

There were fish to be caught in the lake, but the family were wary of killing too many and having none left to eat in the future. They had instead made a snail farm out of three old bath tubs, bedding them with leaves on which the snails grew fat. From these the family selected the very largest, to skewer on sticks and toast like marshmallows over their fire.

One of the young mothers there, a slight and sharp-eyed woman called Ruth, had constructed frog traps surrounding the house. In exchange for as many hunting techniques as Hiroko could impart, she taught the girl how to build them. Hiroko considered the frog traps a stroke of genius, even if they were not much more than a bucket buried up to its rim in the ground. To turn it into a trap, the handle was lifted and fixed in place to form an arch from which a worm could be hung. Then the pit of the bucket was covered with a false lid, which in most cases Ruth had made from a plastic dinner plate. Each plate was slightly smaller than its bucket's rim and was hung, just like the worm, by a thread from the upright handle. Dangling like that, and disguised by a handful of fallen leaves, the plate balanced horizontally and looked as stable as any other ground. Yet it perfectly hid the bucket beneath and, as soon as a frog hopped aboard, gave way like a trapdoor. The luckless amphibian never got its hoped-for taste of wormflesh, tumbling instead into a hole too deep to leap out of.

'I used to fix a small lamp on one, too,' Ruth explained to Hiroko. 'The moths loved it and flew all around, and the frogs loved the moths and fell in dozens at a time.' Then she frowned. 'Some bastard stole that lamp on his way through here, not a week ago, so I had to come up with a new kind of superbait.'

Ruth reached into the bucket and scooped out the bait in question. 'This is the only frog who doesn't get eaten. But with *her* sitting in the bucket, all of the boy frogs come flocking. I call her Cleopatra.'

Cleopatra was the greenest, most bulbous frog Hiroko had ever set eyes on, her flippers long and horny and her eyes swirled like two polluted crystal balls. She seemed nonplussed by the fates of her admirers, who Hiroko enjoyed learning how to cook that evening. She made sure to feed one to Yasuo, confident that foxes ate frogs in the wild, but after one bite he spat the meat on the ground. He grumbled for the next fifteen minutes, like a disgruntled customer let down by a favourite restaurant.

The next morning, Ruth led Hiroko between the frog traps she had dug and the rabbit snares Hiroko had taught her to lay. Ruth had her baby boy strapped to her body by a sling, while Hiroko carried Yasuo at times on her shoulder and at times let him down to gambol ahead through the undergrowth, the white tip of his tail weaving back and forth like the flight of a moth.

'Have you not,' Ruth asked Hiroko as they collected their spoils, 'been tempted to settle down in a place like this?'

'No,' replied Hiroko immediately. 'Never.'

'But you and Seb would make such a—'

'We won't, though. We can't.'

Ruth looked surprised, but Hiroko was too busy biting her lip to elaborate. She had never really had any place she thought of as home, unless it was her grandparents' house tucked beneath the beeches. She and her father had moved two or three times between rented properties in San Francisco, and none of those had felt like home either. Home was the forest house her father had promised her. Home was somewhere in a future that could never happen now.

'What about after you find the hotel?' Ruth asked. 'What will you do after that?'

'We might never find it. Compasses can only take you so far.'

'You make it sound like you don't want to . . .'

'I *do* want to,' said Hiroko hurriedly, 'but I don't want to stop. I never want to stop. Not anywhere.'

Later that day, the travellers bade farewell to Ruth and her assembled family. With no little ceremony, the elderly grandmother presented them with a plastic ice-cream tub, filled with hard smoked frog meat. Hiroko grinned at Ruth when she cracked it open to peek inside and see the strips of amphibian jerky, which smelled of bonfires and marsh salt, but Ruth only looked tearful, trying to smile at Hiroko while simultaneously stroking the fine hair on her baby boy's head.

'This is for you,' said the grandmother in her cracked voice, and after a moment Hiroko realised that she was talking to her. 'Ruth said you might like it.'

The gift the old woman was offering was a rectangular pouch of faded red silk, tied shut by a knot of gold thread. It was smaller and thinner than a purse, and Hiroko stared from it to the grandmother and then back. It was an *omamori* charm. It couldn't be anything else.

'Where did you get this?' Hiroko demanded after a minute.

'Hachimantai. Long before you were born.'

'Hachimantai? In Japan? Are you serious?'

'It was many, many years ago. And this luck charm has served me well since then, as you can see.' The old woman gestured to her offspring and their partners and their children, gathered close around her.

'I can't accept this,' said Hiroko.

'You will,' said the old woman with certainty.

Hiroko did, and with that they left the family behind them. For a while they were able to follow the banks of a crystal-clear spring that was headed for Ruth's lake, but when its course turned south towards its origins they had to vault it and carry on north-west. Insects whined in the damp at all hours, and every now and then Hiroko felt the itch of a new bite. All the while, she kept the silk pouch pressed tight against the palm of her hand.

'This is for you,' her father had said, offering her a blue *omamori* tied shut by white thread. 'I got them for luck. That we might move to our forest house soon.'

They'd already been back in Japan for three weeks when he'd said that, staying with Hiroko's grandparents. On most of those days her father had disappeared to go house-hunting, leaving Hiroko to help her elderly *sobo* in the orchard. Each time he'd returned later than the last, explaining that the perfect house was an elusive beast, one that needed to be stalked before it could be found. Hiroko could understand that, despite her impatience, but the blue *omamori* bemused her. Her father had never been a superstitious man, even when it came to something as innocuous as a temple luck charm. She knew it was a commonplace gesture to buy them as gifts, and that nowadays fewer and fewer people really believed there was genuinely luck to be had from them, but it was not the *omamori*'s purchase that was so out of character. It was that her father had actually chosen to visit a temple. '*Arigatou . . .*' she'd said, accepting it from him.

'What's in it?' asked Seb, walking just behind her through the woods.

Hiroko shook herself, then looked down at the little red pouch from Ruth's grandmother. 'Don't know,' she said.

'Aren't you going to open it?'

'It's an *omamori*. You don't open it. It'll have a sutra inside, or the name of the shrine it was bought from. It's supposed to bring good fortune, but if you take it out of the pouch it becomes just words on paper.'

Seb looked confused. 'So . . . what is it when it's in the pouch?'

'It's *not* in the pouch. It's in some other place. Don't you get it?'

He still looked confused, but Hiroko was feeling too on edge to have patience with him. 'It's in the spirit world or something,' she said, then immediately felt stupid for sounding like she believed in all that stuff. 'Oh for fuck's sake, Seb, it's just some bit of junk from a temple stall.'

That was her own grandmother's view of *omamori*. 'Plastic rubbish,' she'd often pronounced, 'attracts plastic spirits.'

Hiroko couldn't think of anyone who'd dare to argue with her *sobo*, even if an *omamori* wasn't made from plastic. On the day after her father had given her the blue one, after he'd disappeared again to look at houses, the old woman had noticed it hanging from a hook in Hiroko's room. 'Where did you get that?' she'd asked, narrowing her eyes.

'My *otosan* gave it to me.'

'Hmph. Open it.'

Hiroko frowned. 'You're not supposed to. It brings—'

'Bad luck?' wheezed her grandmother, her grin showing off her crooked teeth. 'Do you think bad luck would *dare* to come in here?'

Hiroko nodded obediently and unpicked the *omamori*'s seal. The thread unfastened with ease. Inside was a strip of inscribed paper.

'I . . . I don't know what these words mean,' she said, puzzling over them.

'Hand it to me.' Her grandmother held out her fingers. Hiroko did as she asked, whereupon she gave the inscription a cursory glance and then enclosed it in her fist.

'Aren't you going to tell me what it said?' asked Hiroko after a minute, when all the old woman had done was stare at her.

'It's the name of the temple your father bought it from.'

'Oh. From the way you reacted, I thought that—'

'It's in Tokyo.'

'What?'

'I suspected as much. He has been careless. I found some of his train tickets.'

'Train tickets?'

'Most days, perhaps *every* day since you came here, he has run away to Tokyo.'

'No he hasn't.' Hiroko didn't want to believe it. 'Why would he do that?'

Her *sobo* sighed and looked out of the window, beyond which the yellow depths of the beech forest rustled. The old woman's tongue made a dry click as it wetted her lips. 'One day,' she said at last, 'I will show you the cuts your parents made in the orchard.'

But Hiroko could hardly bear to listen. Tokyo? Her father had actually been going to Tokyo? Why hadn't he told her?

'They cut them into the apple trees. When they were just starting out. Two teenage sweethearts. I never thought it would last.'

Tokyo was *miles* away. Miles from the forests her father had always promised her. What had he been doing there?

'They carved their names, mainly. Cut hearts around them. Your mother engraved bad poetry.'

Hiroko began to feel light-headed, hot in her chest and cold in her belly, and dizzy and rigid at once. *Run away* to Tokyo? Run away from what? How would they find the forest house if her father wasn't even looking?

'The bark has grown over most of the cuts, since those days. The kanji they wrote in the tree trunks are sealed away. But, if you know where to look, you can still see certain signs of them. That is how trees remember, after all, and how they remind you.' The old woman shook her head solemnly. 'Your father, Hiroko, can't bear such reminders.'

'Hiroko . . .'

Hiroko mopped her eyes dry with the sleeves of her hoodie. Yasuo licked her cheek, and she scowled and recalled the miles between everything.

'Hiroko . . .' said Seb.

With a grunt, she let go of the red *omamori*. It drifted to the floor like a leaf, but she didn't even pause to watch it fall.

'Hey,' said Seb, surprised, 'you can't just leave it here . . .'

But Hiroko was already striding away, and didn't even look back when Yasuo tensed against the flesh of her neck.

Seb, however, stopped walking at once.

Half a minute later he caught up with her, saying nothing further, only tucking something red into the pocket of his shirt.

12

Heart of the Forest

The next night the temperature plunged, and their tent and sleeping bags seemed far too thin to warm them. They found a looted lorry just before sundown, so huddled together in the back of it to sleep, their bodies with scant heat to share. They ended up lying just as Hiroko and Seb had done on recent nights: in each other's arms. Adrien felt terribly embarrassed about it, despite the urgent cold hardening his nose and the rims of his ears. They had to negotiate each other's comfort to settle into a sort of four-way embrace, in which he was acutely aware that his body was the most cushioned and his exposed skin the most clammy. He cleared his throat awkwardly when Hannah nodded off against his collar, yet he was also aware of how much thinner her body was than it looked; and the unexpected boniness of Hiroko's under her baggy hoodie; and how broad and warm Seb had become. Through the joint effort of their shivering and the rattling lullaby of their teeth, they trembled and chattered each other to sleep.

When, after what seemed like endless hours of waking and dozing, waking and dozing, the sunlight crept into the woods, every leaf and blade of grass looked rimed with the cold morning air.

'If this is how it's going to be from now on,' said Seb, as they put on their rucksacks and set out, 'I think we should take shifts to keep a fire going all night.'

'That won't help on rainy nights,' said Adrien, still feeling cold to his bone marrow. 'God knows how we'll cope in the winter.'

'There'll be a few more warm days yet,' said Hannah, 'so it's not all doom and gloom. But that's a good idea about the fire, Seb. I never thought we'd still be travelling at this time of year. I thought we'd be safely sheltering in Zach's lodge.'

'I know you did, Mum . . . and who knows? Maybe we can shelter a few nights in Michelle's hotel. What do you think about that, Adrien?'

'I don't think we should get ahead of ourselves.'

'But we—'

Adrien held up a hand. 'I don't think we should get ahead of ourselves.'

In the meantime, at least, it was better to be exhausted than frozen, better to ache than to shiver, so all that day they pressed on as fast as their tired legs could carry them. Although the land rose in a gradual ascent, they walked with the stumbling gait of those going downhill. When at last, in the mid-afternoon, Adrien flopped down the first from tiredness, the others dropped around him almost immediately. They sat in a sorry circle, the descending sun nothing but a blinding light to their tired eyes. Then Hannah sprang up and pointed to a heap of something.

'Look!' she exclaimed. 'Dung!'

She rushed to it and crouched to inspect it at once, poking it open with a twig. Adrien watched with disgust as she exposed gooey rolls of the stuff, moist and rich and still steaming. For a moment he panicked that this was some new and extreme form of foraging, and that Hannah would pluck something out of the faeces and call it their dinner.

'I can only think of one animal that could produce something this heavy,' Hannah said with a grin. 'Well? Aren't we going to carry on? We can't be that far behind it.'

The others didn't share her resurgent energy but, amid grumbling from Adrien, they got to their feet and followed. Soon they found more clues of the kirin's passing, be they fur scraps caught on a thorn or sometimes a steady row of prints in mud. The animal itself, however, seemed perpetually just ahead of them, like a name forgotten on the tip of the tongue.

Not long before dusk, the ground turned to cement. Within a dozen paces they were in the forecourt of a truck depot, where the trees towered so high that they dwarfed the lorries rusting in their branches. For once it was a relief to reach a town, for even ruined walls could offer better shelter from the wind than could the bare woods. There was also something surprisingly clean about the place. Two months had passed since the trees came, enough time for the bodies to be tidied away and for thunderstorms to scour the concrete of leaked sewage and feculence. The buildings had been reroofed by a thatch of autumn leaves, and it seemed that people had moved back into one or two houses, although more often than not they were armed and only scowled back grimly when the travellers hailed them. They steered well wide, and in a street full of oaks saw two boys gathering the green spiked shells of conkers. Upon seeing them, the boys sprang up and fled as if their lives depended on it, their footfalls pounding off the damp tarmac underneath the leaf litter.

All four of them kept their eyes peeled for a place to spend the night, somewhere that would be both unclaimed and a shelter from the cold. They had just come to an intersection of several streets, looking for this, when they finally saw the kirin.

It stood where the roads met, beside a fountain carved with angels. The basin was full of rainwater and the golden leaves of the sycamores that leaned above it. From this the kirin was drinking with pleasured slurps. Its horn looked like a sheet of flint, clinking against the stone of the fountain, longer than its neck and head combined. Its woolly fur was tangled here and there with bits of leaf. When it had finished drinking it lifted its head and stared at them down the blade of its horn. Droplets of water caught in the wrinkles of its muzzle. It harrumphed at them, and they saw its breath cloud the cool air, and then it turned to depart. From the side it looked colossal and squat, but from behind it looked equine. It plodded away with sycamore seeds spinning in its wake.

They followed it for half an hour, until at last they had to let it get away from them so that they could find their place to sleep. They chose the remains of a café, and used broken tables to build a makeshift windbreak in its doorway. Sleep was once again an elusive pleasure, and come morning all of their eyes and limbs were heavy. It was just as they were removing their barricade from the door that Adrien dropped the piece he was moving and climbed past it into the street.

'What is it?' asked Seb, the nearest to him.

'Right there,' said Adrien. 'Across the road from us, all this time.'

They all peered out at the building opposite.

'Is that a theatre,' asked Seb, 'or an arts centre or something?'

'Yes! But look at what they were showing!'

Blowing above the theatre's doorway was a tattered banner, advertising its final production.

'*A Midsummer Night's Dream*,' read Seb. 'Why is that so special?'

'It's . . . it's personal.'

Adrien crossed the road to stand in the theatre's entrance. The doors had been flung wide by long, ushering boughs. In the lobby, the carpet was buried under brown and amber leaves.

'Would any of you mind if I took a look inside?'

They all shrugged that it was fine by them, so Adrien led them, footsteps crunching, into the theatre proper. The auditorium's roof had been torn away and replaced by the beams of the canopy, from which hung heaps of foliage. Chandeliers would once have glittered there, but only clusters of their glass remained, dangling like catkins.

A new audience had filled up the seats. Trees sprawled among the rows, loafing their boughs like rude feet on the chairs in front of them. Down at the stage, the curtains had been thumbed back and starched into place by sap. Now a bowed wooden cast trod the boards, some striking poses with their branches, others draped in costumes, for behind them the sets had been demolished and the contents of the prop rails flung left, right and centre. There were many-coloured gowns and garlands, and great pairs of glimmering fabric wings, and fake swords and a broken lyre, and everywhere fluttering pages of the script, and a crown of antlers and a suit of furred trousers made to resemble the hind legs of a goat.

Adrien toyed with the thin hairs on the back of his head. On honeymoon in Paris, he and Michelle had watched *Le Songe d'une nuit d'été*. He had worried that *A Midsummer Night's Dream* translated into another language might bore her, but she had loved it even more than him. She had always possessed, he supposed, an uncanny ability to enjoy things just the way they were.

'What is it?' asked Seb, stepping alongside him. 'Are you okay?'

'Don't know yet,' he croaked.

'You don't look so good. Do you think you should sit down?'

Adrien nodded. 'Good idea.' And where had they sat? They had not been very near the front, nor far to one side. Somewhere in the middle, and Adrien sidled from seat to seat and row to row, clambering sometimes over the trees, until he found a spot that seemed to match that in his memory. There he sat with his hands crushed together between his knees. The others hovered nearby, unsure whether to disturb him or to leave him to his reverie.

'Would you three mind,' he asked with a swallow, 'if I had ten minutes alone in here?'

For a moment he thought they would refuse. He could tell that they were worried about him.

'I'll be alright,' he promised. 'I just need a bit of thinking space.'

Hannah nodded reluctantly. 'Okay. We'll wait for you in the café where we camped. But . . . please be careful.'

She smiled encouragingly and then, along with the teenagers, left through the stall doors.

Adrien took a deep breath and leaned his head back against the seat cushion. The theatre seemed very quiet, now that he was alone in it.

After the curtains had closed and the applause had faded, they'd walked arm-in-arm out of the theatre. They were like first-time drunks and lovers both, still snorting with laughter at Bottom the idiot, with his head turned to a donkey's by fairy magic. Truth be told, both Adrien and Michelle had been tipsy even after their interval drinks, and when one of the actors had intoned in a deep, loud voice, '*Dieu te bénisse, Bottom! Tu es traduit . . .*' Adrien had leaned on Michelle's shoulder and repeated it in English. 'Bless you, Bottom! Thou art translated!' At that Michelle had snorted with laughter, and when the people in the row in front had turned around to glower at her, she'd wiggled her tongue out at them (and he had loved her all the more for it).

What had happened next? They had been happy; back to the hotel; more wine; breakfast by the river; day trip; restaurant meal. It was easy to be happy on honeymoon, when you took the lead role in your own life. It was when you got home and you felt like an extra delivering the same few lines every night that happiness became elusive.

Adrien skipped forwards through time, on through the acts of their marriage. Their story played out just as he knew it would, with no great villainy (indeed, the real disasters and the losses had always brought them closer together) but a multitude of small affronts, all of them his. All of their arguments, when it came down to it, had started because of him. He had seen the world too fearfully, he could acknowledge that now, although he did not know if he could ever break that habit. 'Sometimes it seems,' Michelle had once said, 'that unless things work out perfectly, all you want to do is hide away from them. Then you hate yourself for not being braver, and it's like you eat yourself alive.'

The wind dipped through the exposed roof of the theatre, and the leaves that frilled the proscenium arch hissed for silence. Adrien got up and walked down the ramp, and at the bottom of it heaved himself onto the stage. He stood at its centre, looking back out at the auditorium. It would rot away into tatters. It would never again fill up with a human audience. Still he felt a strange scrutiny on him, as if he were indeed a performer and all of the trees harsh critics itching to pass judgment on him. He had never been comfortable as the centre of attention, even in classrooms.

He looked at the props and the costumes. Dangling from a nearby branch was a donkey's head. It was a full-fitting mask for the actor playing Bottom to wear, once the fairies had made an ass out of him. '*Tu es traduit,*' Adrien whispered, taking it down from the branch.

He turned it around in his hands. Bottom, the prize idiot from a rabble of idiots. Adrien traced his fingers down its donkey nose, as if it were a real animal leaning over a fence. Its ears were wired straight, and the long face and muzzle had been sculpted from something like papier mâché. The lips were parted wide and the teeth covered in a reflective fabric that would catch the spotlights and make the mouth space seem darker, for out through the mouth the eyes of the actor would peer.

Adrien punched it. The delicately crafted eye burst inward, and when he tore the hole wider the mask ripped along its seams as easily as a paper bag. He yanked out the wire and flung it aside and shredded what was left of the mask and threw it on the floor and had glitter all over his fingernails.

He clasped his hands to the top of his head, and to touch his bald spot was to remember just how long he'd been destroying himself. His baldness was his diary, his rings in the bark. He wondered if he would have gone bald so quickly were he a better man, a man like Roland, who was sure of himself and his place in the world. Had he as good as torn his hair out, just by being the man he was? Michelle had tried to save him from it, but he had never shared the faith she'd had in him. Self-loathing was a diffi-cult thing for those who had none of their own to understand. It had its own seasons. It could trick you into thinking it had lifted, only to come cycling around again. You attacked yourself in the same ways you always had. You flung the same accusations. Perhaps you could no more rid yourself of self-loathing than you could rid the world of winter. What was certain was that, like winter, in its wake it left you bare. That was what it had done to

Adrien's marriage. It had blown out all the candles and left only the cold.

'Help me,' he said, although he did not know to who. It was the same abject plea he had uttered a hundred times before in his life, the same he had made on the night the trees came, after he had crawled into bed fat with processed chicken and discounted beer. He held out little hope of an answer. If someone as good as Michelle could not help him, he doubted whether anyone could.

The branches swayed against the circle of the missing ceiling. The wind raked the clouds. Adrien hung his head and groaned.

Ten seconds later, his groan was still echoing in the theatre. Then he saw movement out of the corner of his eye.

Adrien stiffened, like an actor succumbing to stage fright. When finally he looked, it was just in time to spot a whisperer loping along a rafter. Then came another, running over a branch like an acrobat before a jump. And there, among the rows and rows of seating in the middle of the auditorium, was the throne tree.

That it had appeared in the blink of an eye, without so much as a sound or a waft of displaced air, was not even the most alarming thing about it. This time it had only its lower branches, that pair of them that grew horizontally like the arms of a gigantic chair. Above them its trunk came to an end as abruptly as any broken stump. All of its higher branches were missing.

The throne was empty.

A whisperer with teeth of thorns crawled onto the stage. Another sidled along a branch of a tree where the pages of the prompter's script hung scattered, and its tiny footsteps dislodged some of the sheets so that they floated down to the boards below. Now a full audience of the little monsters was appearing throughout the theatre, climbing onto the tops of the seats or finding perches on low-hanging boughs. Over there was one that seemed all head and no body, with dock leaves for ears. In another place was one plated and horned by bark, as a stag beetle is by its shell. The noise they made was a ceaseless hiss, filling up the auditorium like the hubbub before a performance.

'But where . . .' murmured Adrien, his gaze pulled back towards the empty throne tree.

Something in the rafters creaked.

One by one, the whisperers looked up, but for a minute all Adrien could do was stand very still, trying to compose himself. At last he looked too, and the creature he had seen on the beach was hanging where the theatre's roof should have been.

All of Adrien's breath wheezed out of him at the sight of it. It looked like the crown of a tree come loose of its trunk, a dark outline against the sky above. Its countless forking limbs were so enmeshed with the branches of the theatre that it was hard to tell where the creature stopped and the trees began, except when one of its legs swayed free of any anchoring trunk and took a step through the canopy. It took another step after that, and another simultaneously. It moved with the slowness of a crab, but its destination was clear. The creature was coming down towards Adrien.

At first Adrien could find no strength to flee. Even when the creature had descended near enough for him to smell it on the air, a whiff like mouldering leaves and rancid fruit, he couldn't do much more than gape. Its great long legs, clad in bark and haired by twigs, moved with a groping motion as if it were blind. When finally Adrien came to his senses, it had clambered so near he could see a kind of opening in the hub of shoulders that was all it had for a body. In the middle of that wooden knot from which all its limbs grew, was a mouth. It was a dark hollow gleaming with sap, seams of which had crystallised like an amber saliva on its lips.

Adrien ran.

He had gone only a few strides before a whisperer blocked his path. Its slack jaws were full of woodworm grubs, which dripped out of tunnel-holes in its cheeks as well as from its fibrous tongue. Adrien spun around to go another way, but found a second whisperer waiting there on all fours. Neither of them was looking at him. They both had their necks arched to gaze at the descending

312

creature, but when Adrien tried to run in a third direction there was another blocking that way too, and another after that, and more and more of them piling onto the stage, each with its eyes bent upwards and a dry noise flowing out of its throat.

They were whispering to the creature, Adrien realised. And in response it groaned, and its many limbs swayed like those of a sea anemone reaching out in its pool. As it lurched ever closer, the smell of it doubled. Its stench was rot and must and growth in the damp, so potent it made Adrien's mind bob against his skull. The creature only moaned all the deeper, and one leg scraped and itched its body as it moved, dislodging pieces of dank and dead bark.

Don't go near, Gweneth had said, in her camper van on the beach. *Don't look in*. Adrien needed no convincing, yet when he glanced upwards there was something about the shape of the creature that transfixed him. Its limbs were a symmetrical question, like the lines of a psychiatrist's blot test. When they creaked it was the noise of a whole corridor of long-unopened doors, and there was something haunting about that sound that resonated in Adrien's gut. His eyes became lost in the joints and kinks of its arms. Every limb bent and branched backwards towards that rot-black mouth at the heart of it.

Without warning, the whisperers around him changed their chant. They turned it to a lisping falsetto and, as if goaded along, the creature made an effort to hurry towards them. It moved with a doddery gait, twisting and unbending its array of claws and knees, the twigs at the end of each leg clinging to less animate sticks for support. Limb followed limb, and at last the thing weighed its heavy frame down onto the stage.

The stink of the creature was the air itself now, filling Adrien's mouth and tingling on his tongue. He remained too petrified to move. He could see the creases and the wrinkles in the monstrosity's bark, see lacerations gleaming with sap where its hide had split open. For all its strangeness and horror it seemed pained somehow, like a waterlogged spider waiting to either dry out or perish.

Adrien's eyes were drawn back to the centre of it, and there were strands of resiny mucus dangling from its maw.

A moment later, it wailed. With the noise came a wave of shrill breath so nauseating that Adrien clutched his hands to his throat. His nostrils flared and contracted as if trying to flap out the stink, but it had filled his lungs already, and blood rushed to his head and he staggered backwards, feeling like he was going to faint. He tried to fix his eyes on something, anything at all to stay conscious, but the only thing he could find was the creature's open mouth.

It was a black hole. So dark he couldn't look away. With a dizzy grunt he slouched forward, and the creature shrieked again and its breath overflowed him, seemed to sweep under him and hoist him up. Briefly he managed to fight it. He pulled himself backwards, but its hollow mouth drew his gaze in like gravity, and even as he tried to resist, he lost his balance and teetered.

He fell. It was as if his head flopped one way and his thoughts another. His consciousness was blown away like a veneer of dust. Everything turned to pitch black.

Time might have passed. Adrien did not know. He did not know if he was alive or dead, out cold on the stage or swallowed whole by the creature. He did not know anything, for however long he did not know . . .

Then, after a long or short while, he knew there was a worm.

The wriggle of its jelly body confirmed it. Where it was headed and where *he* was he could not tell, but a moment later a paddling of fur and claws followed it. The darkness dislodged into more of the same, and a mole caught the worm and curled up velvet as it ate. Then it tunnelled on, and for more immeasurable moments there was nothing.

Adrien waited. He waited. He waited. Waiting was what he was. He was a sparkle concealed in the unlit world, and he remembered out of nowhere that he was biding his time for a luck of heat and rainfall. Then, suddenly, that time was upon him. He would have said he knew it in his bones, but he had no bones. He had only a kernel to know it with.

He put forth shoots. He clambered straight and pure green into the light, feeling for the very first time its scorching brightness on his outstretched palms. His body was as thin as a thread, but all around him stood the trees that were his elders, and he could hardly believe he might reach their height some day.

Something snorted. There was a grunt and a snaffle and the next instant he was back in darkness. The tusks of the forest hog closed around him as they dug him out of the ground, and he was crushed against molars and swallowed into acid but he did not pass away.

He passed on.

He swaggered through the forest with his curling tail swishing behind him, and he shoved his snout into the mud and loved the damp mush of it point-blank against his nostrils. If he found an acorn he crunched it between his teeth and trotted on, humming an oinking song in the deep of his throat. He jaunted down tracks he had long ago trampled into place, daydreaming of truffles and musing about pignuts, until a howl pricked up his ears.

The pack were on him in a second. A weight on his back and the reek of canine piss, and he rolled over squealing and thrashing his trotters but there were too many of them. Too many biting jaws to block them all, and the wolves' fangs found their way through his throat and belly and they tore him open and were swallowing mouthfuls of his innards, even as he felt the blood still flowing within.

He passed on. Running with the pack through the dappled light of the forest smacking his tongue against his lips to taste the salt pig blood and the wind of his running. When he came upon the scent of a stag it wrenched him after it and his brothers and sisters understood and they ran with their ears flat against their necks. The speed at which they ran was so great that before he knew it he had already passed on all over again. He had hooves galloping through the leaf litter, and his antlers were raking the branches and his ears swivelled and tracked every chasing wolf and he knew he could outpace them all. Then before he had time to make sense of it he was bounding over a branch with his bushy tail flicking out behind him, and he leapt into the air and suddenly had black feathers for fingers and he was ascending, up and up with the rest of his murder through the leaves of the canopy. Beneath him was the roof of the forest crisping to brown, and his thoughts whirled above it like the leaves thrown up by the crows' passing, and then the birds flew on while his thoughts drifted down, down, down towards the trees.

His hair came in many shapes and hues of green. In patches it was tinted orange or to a copper that rustled not just for the flights of crows but for every bird that combed it with its wings. Caterpillars itched him like head lice, and sometimes a cow or a horse or a kirin would reach up with blunt teeth and yank out a mouthful of his locks. That did not trouble him. He would need no hair in the coming days of winter. In readiness for the cold he bastioned himself in upright trunks. He armoured his fingers in gauntlets of twisted twigs. He bunched his toes up underground.

He was a hundred-branched oak, straddling the forest, lightning-scarred and full of crags. He was a canny old yew, polishing his poison berries. He was a sapling thin as a ribbon. He was a bulb, back in the soil, and one moment later he was a vole prospecting the bulb. He was the owl that plunged from on high, and he wailed a shrill rodent death-wail even as his beak tore triangles out of himself, and he savoured the meat he was stripping from under his fur and he spat his bones back out in a pellet. He was a fly, drunk on the leftovers, boggled by the prism world seen through his thousand-faceted eyes. He was a millipede tapdancing beneath the damp of a rock. Down into the dirt and up again. He was a white moth taking off on its lightning flight, and a bat chasing the thunderclaps of the moth's wingbeats. He was more things than he could think of at once. He was a snail corkscrewing backwards into his shell, a bee in drunken love with nectar, an ant marching after an ant into an egg chamber where his queen lay in never-ending labour. Down into the dirt and up again. He was every mosquito in the swarm that hatched above the river, and he buzzed into the forest to go dipping for blood. He bit a rat: he was a rat scurrying into the warren mouth. He raced through the tunnels and he was a flea on the rat's back and he ricocheted from hide to hide. At the bottom of a burrow, far underground where they had a hundred squeaking words for darkness, he became the mother rat who had long forgotten the number of her offspring, and beneath her fur and muscle he became each half-formed life growing in her womb. His cells doubled and redoubled until he was seventeen foetuses, each reclining in the heat of his mother's belly as one might in a hot bath, and he waited with sealed-up eyes for his lives to begin. When the time was right, he kicked himself free and knew only to seek out his mother's teats in the pitch, and he was again that mother rat who had long lain in childbirth, and how ravenous he was. And look, the seventeenth among his babies was a runt, who could never struggle hard enough to survive. He drew it in close, in the tenderest embrace, and he was that blind runt too, glad of the sudden maternal warmth. His incisors slit through his own newborn ratflesh like scissors through silk, and he put himself back in the belly from whence he had come.

Down. Down into the dirt.

And up again.

Adrien cried out and flung himself to his feet. He stood upright, on trembling legs, in the theatre, and the creature was gone. The throne tree had vanished too, and all of the whisperers save one. That was a malformed thing, hung with foxgloves as a leper is by bells, and it hissed at him with a rasping tongue and then turned, and limped away.

A minute passed before Adrien could even think about moving. His hair and shirt were sweated to his skin and each of his muscles ached in its own fashion. When he finally tried to take a step, his thighs and calves cramped at once, and he had to sit down gasping and feeling rigid as wood. Strange afterthoughts flitted through his mind. Feathers. Fur. Soil against his tongue. He crammed his fist into his mouth to stop himself from vomiting.

'What the hell just happened?' he muttered, a minute later.

But he was alone with the trees, and they offered no answer.

317

13

Direction

Hannah could guess that something had happened as soon as she saw Adrien staggering back across the road towards the café. His hair was stuck down by sweat and his skin was blotchy all over. He moved as if he'd forgotten how to properly use his legs, so she hurried out to meet him. Without saying a word, she wrapped her arms around him and at once he mumbled, 'Thank you,' and leaned against her. She guided him back to the café and lowered him onto a stool, while Seb fetched his rucksack and rummaged for spare clothes.

'Was it the whisperers?' asked Hannah.

'Yes,' croaked Adrien. 'And . . . and . . .' He buried his face in his hands.

Hannah didn't let go of him, but they all stood around in silence, unsure how best to help. It was some five minutes before Adrien tried to speak again, and then only in half a voice.

'There was something else. I looked into its mouth, and . . . and . . .'

'Take your time,' advised Hannah, while Adrien looked back fearfully towards the theatre. 'Don't talk if you don't want to.'

At that he looked grateful, and accepted her offer of silence. It took him an hour to be ready to set out, and although he kept pace with them he also kept his eyes lowered and his lips sealed. Hannah did not press him on what he'd seen, hoping he'd find a way to describe it in due course. They followed the compass north by north-west, coming out of the town and into flat land filled with thick trunks. Some of the trees the lightning had stricken, and turned skeletal despite their girth and grandeur. Others were as orange as fireworks, and sometimes their leaves drifted free like fizzing sparks.

Hannah kept Adrien company while Hiroko picked them a path. Now and then he flinched at something in the woods, but never at the things that had always used to terrify him. The eerie creaks of branches and the sudden screeches of birds he ignored, whereas at smaller sights he often lurched away and covered his mouth with his fist, or unashamedly reached out to grab hold of Hannah's arm.

The sun was huge and sinking, and sending sideways beams of light through the forest, when Adrien tried again to talk about what had happened. The land had begun to slope and they were trudging uphill past an isolated industrial building that might have been some sort of factory, when suddenly he covered his face. He groaned and sank into a crouch, and Hannah whistled to Hiroko and Seb to slow up. Then she knelt beside him and slipped her arms around his shoulders.

'Adrien, what's wrong? What can I do to help?'

He cleared his throat and pointed to the factory's wall. 'It's the lichen,' he whispered, and she looked and saw ochre circles of the stuff all over the bricks, and more made from tiny plates of pewter green.

'Jesus,' he said, taking off his glasses and wiping his eyes. 'I keep remembering stuff. You must think I've gone crazy.'

'No. Just . . . help me understand.'

He gestured again at the wall, although he obviously couldn't bear to look at it. 'It's not one thing, is it? A lichen, I mean. It's a fungus and an algae living mixed together. *You'd* know about a thing like that.'

Hannah nodded. 'But I don't see why—'

'Would *I*? Would I know about it? So how come I do?' He covered his mouth and held his breath for a minute, then nodded and carried on in a whisper. 'It's because I can *remember* it, Hannah. As if I was lying on a hard stone bed, as if my arms and legs were all tangled up with somebody else's. Only I wasn't on a bed, was I? And I wasn't with *somebody* else. I saw so much, Hannah, and I keep remembering more.'

'I . . . I don't understand. Adrien . . . please try to tell me what happened in that theatre.'

He bit his lip. There were tears in his eyes. 'The whisperers came. And another thing.'

'Another whisperer?'

'Maybe. But a hell of a lot bigger. A hell of a lot more frightening, too.'

Hannah reached out a hand and helped him get back to his feet. 'Listen carefully,' she said, not letting go. 'Whatever's happened . . . all three of us are going to help you to face it.'

The next day the going became harder, up and down furrows full of ever bigger stones. On the steepest land the trees leaned sideways out of the soil for a chance to cheat the sunlight, and it was in the shade of one such slope that they came upon a set of narrow rail tracks. They were the kind used by mine carts of old, and they headed north-west along with their path. Eventually they plunged into the mouth of a tunnel.

The travellers rested for a half-hour in the opening, although the pause was chiefly for Adrien's benefit. He had slept fitfully all night, waking them often with sudden cries or the thrashing of his arms. In the morning he had seemed more composed, but spoke only rarely and remained easily startled by sights and sounds from the undergrowth.

Eventually, he signalled that he was ready to proceed, and they stepped into the tunnel. Hiroko, however, stopped them at once. She had spotted something on the arch of the entrance.

'Look,' she said, tracing a finger over score-marks in the brick. 'And here and here. As if somebody's sharpened a giant knife against it.'

'Or a horn,' said Seb.

'The kirin came through here, then,' said Hannah, clapping her hands. 'It's going ahead of us. Showing the way.'

She grinned at them all, but Hiroko and Seb had never seemed much moved by the kirin and Adrien was in no fit state to smile at anything. Hannah sighed and reserved her delight for herself. For an innocent moment she looked forward to telling Zach about it. Then the pain of her grief swallowed her happiness just as the tunnel swallowed the light when they entered.

The passage ran far longer than any of them had envisaged, curving subtly on its course so that they could see no exit and all vision dimmed away. There was no choice but to tread on blindly, cold vegetable tendrils brushing through their hair. When Hannah raised a hand she could feel stalactites of root hanging from the ceiling, but underneath the cement was weirdly smooth, untouched by the trees.

They were midway through the passage, their footsteps ringing muted echoes off the walls, when a gunshot sounded. Hannah jumped and gasped, but the sound of her own breath was much louder than the shot had been. It had come from far off, beyond the tunnel's exit.

'It's alright, Mum,' said Seb, somewhere nearby in the dark. 'I think it was a long way away.'

'I'm okay,' she said. 'I'm okay.' But she reached into her pocket and gripped tight the thing that came to hand, which was the seashell Nora had given her.

Seb took her other hand and squeezed it, and Hannah let out all of the breath she had been holding since the shot. Then Seb said something to Hiroko ahead of her, and she realised it had not been his hand that had squeezed hers. It was Adrien's, and she smiled gratefully in what she hoped was his direction.

At last a navy smudge emerged ahead of them. Gradually it brightened, and their first glimpse of the tunnel exit appeared like a hairline moon, waxing fuller as they progressed, until they had to pause and shield their eyes before they could look again. They began to see each other's faces once more, and Hannah realised they were all looking at her with concern. She tried to smile for them, but she was unsure what expression she managed to make. She touched Nora's seashell to her ear and the sound of the ocean was at least some reassurance.

They continued along the cart tracks, past a derelict factory whose chimney stood dwarfed among fir trees. 'Here,' said Hiroko, pointing at the earth. And there were the kirin's footprints, clear and fresh, and Hannah tried to fix her mind on them and forget about the gunshot.

Beyond the factory the land built gently through a series of uphill ridges. When they reached the crest, Hannah expected to find an amenable downhill on the other side. What they found instead was a pit. It was a vast scar left by some mining operation, slopes of grit on three sides and the telltale dust of coal on the air. The trees had struggled to find purchase and only grew in scrawny bunches, many of which had lost their hold and tumbled head-over-heels into the pit. It was the first time Hannah had seen the forest so beaten by what had gone before it. Nothing grew at the bottom, for it was a graveyard of ash-rolled logs, but into it the cart tracks wriggled, heading for various tunnel entrances all boarded up. It was a sight so sweeping and empty of life that it took Hannah a moment to notice the kirin.

It lay on its side in the deep middle of the pit. A man was crouching over it with his back to them, pulling things out of its body. By his side stood an eager Alsatian, transfixed by its master's butchery. Hannah covered her mouth, for although they were too far away to see the bullet wound, the opening the man had cut into the animal's belly was a smile, bright and red.

322

IV

I

The Night the Trees Came

With its headlamps beaming and its engines sucking at the rain-streaked night, the jumbo jet thundered over the runway. At full speed its nose peaked into the air, its wheels lifted and it had left the earth. It roared into the sky with the noise of its flight echoing behind it, and in its wake the runway staff in fluorescent jackets drove into place beneath the floodlights. A transit buggy skated along a sidetrack, turned and steered towards the terminal building. Its tyres squirted up rainwater as they went, and nearly crushed a whisperer also making its way, at a much more laboured pace, in the direction of the terminal.

The buggy's driver was talking into her radio mouthpiece and the darkness was thick and filthy wet. Even had the driver spotted the whisperer through all of that, she would have mistaken it for just another collection of windblown twigs. The whisperer, however, seemed untroubled by the weather. It hobbled along with steady purpose, its long arms trailing the ground like a gibbon's. From its forehead grew two budding sprigs of leaves, and these it directed ahead of itself like antennae. When it reached the parkway for the newly arrived flights it paused and stood a while, observing the cabin crews. They were bringing out sacks of litter from a plane, while luggage trucks parked beside the hold to receive suitcases. The long-armed whisperer watched and remained silent. It had been silent for a long, long time.

With an awkward tilt of its neck, the whisperer gazed upwards at the windows of the nearby terminal. Up there was another of its kind, clinging to the frame to peer in through the glass. That one was tiny, its arms and legs just stems bending out of an ivy body. It too went unnoticed, the hour being that when an airport's incumbents are all either sleep-deprived or shuffling their time zones, but after a short while it let go of its hold on the window frame. The wind took it at once, ruffling the leaves of its body as it tossed and looped it through the air, sweeping it back and forth until, at last, it laid it on the tarmac not far from where the first whisperer stood. At once it got up, on wire-thin feet, and together the pair loped and hopped across two runways and a stretch of grass drenched flat by the rain.

Eventually they came to a roundabout on which grew a dozen stunted lime trees. Beneath one of these a fissure had opened in the earth, several feet long. *This* was the sort of thing the airport staff might notice, had any passed to inspect it, but the fissure looked so freshly made that it was as if it had just that moment torn open. In its mouth another whisperer waited, a bloated and haggard thing with a mane of curling white roots. It squatted in the crack as if it were holding it open, albeit with limbs that looked more like tentacles than arms. Towards it, from another direction, hobbled a fourth whisperer, then a fifth and sixth. Each brushed into the fissure and found its way into a tunnel leading down from there into the earth. Once the last had entered, the root-haired gatekeeper followed, and the fissure closed behind it and was sealed shut by the mushing of the rain.

Down in single file the whisperers went, moving as purposefully in the blind dark as they had beneath the floodlights of the airport. Down in silence. Down and down the tunnel that bent and wound like a riddle. Along their way they passed the openings of other passages, out of which more whisperers limped and tiptoed to join their trooping line. Things became damp. Things became chill. The tunnel roof dripped with mineral liquor, although none of the marching figures paid it any heed. Deep through their earthen corridors they waddled and lurched, deeper and deeper, and although it was possible they remained beneath the airport, there were tunnel mouths down here from which warmer air blew, and others from which a breeze rasped that was bitingly cold. A whisperer with limbs of spined cactus joined the procession, moving on all fours with the slow strokes of a reptile. Another arrived with a proud and shaggy coat of evergreen needles, and there were crystals of ice still melting between its spines. Down they all went. Down together, until at last they reached the end of their path.

They had come to a chamber, a cavernous space, and although it was possible that it lay beneath the airport its ceiling was hung with roots of all bends and thicknesses, and the air was stirred with both the scent of pine and the bitterness of myrrh. Other tunnels opened into the chamber, and from these more whisperers poured, clambering up the earthen walls and crawling in lines along ledges. Still they made no sound, moving as silently as spiders, but from the heart of the cavern there came now and then a slow and dormant creak. Growing there in the darkness was some kind of tree, some underground species of plant with no need for the daylight. Had any shone that far below the earth it might have illuminated a singular pair of great branches, each sweeping sideways like the arms of an enormous chair, and a high trunk with many smaller, crooked branches splaying out from its top. It was from this tree, or something on it, that the creaks kept sounding.

Some time passed before the final whisperer arrived and took its place in the assembly, but none of those already gathered made so much as a hiss as they waited. The only sounds were the slow echoes from the tree, along with the occasional plinks and plonks of water droplets tumbling from the cavern roof. Then, when the final whisperer had at last taken its place in the chamber, every tiny mouth creaked open. Every tongue tested its stretch.

As one, they all began to whisper.

2

Gunman

For a minute, none of them moved. The wind circled the dead slopes of the coal pit. Then Hannah began to shake her head. 'No . . .' she whispered, 'no, no he can't have done . . .'

The man at the bottom of the pit pulled out more of the kirin's innards and spooled them alongside him on the ground. Hannah felt as if her own insides were being scooped out just the same.

'Hannah, are you alright?' asked Adrien gravely.

'But he can't . . .' she said.

Hiroko stood up straighter than the rest of them. 'He has.'

Hannah wanted to charge down the slope and put the animal back together. Its blood was so fresh that it was as if it were some new, truer colour of red. 'It can't be dead,' she protested. 'The kirin is . . . it's supposed to be . . .'

Her mind filled up, unbidden, with images of Zach as they had found him. As they had buried him. Memory painted his chest as bright a red as this, and she turned to her companions with tear-blurred eyes. 'Why would he do this? Why would anyone do this?'

'I'm going to ask him,' said Hiroko, clenching her fists. She set off briskly down the slope, and the others followed less boldly.

They were halfway towards the man when the Alsatian's head snapped round to stare at them. It barked once, twice, and the man turned his head and looked sideways over his shoulder, much as a hawk does. Then he returned to his work. His chest was bare, his lower body clad in soldier's fatigues and jackboots. When they reached him he remained busy with the carcass, and it was only the eyes of the dog and the dead kirin that greeted them at the bottom of the pit. Hannah could hardly bear to look, but she felt that she owed it to the kirin to do so. Blood had spattered its horn, and all the iridescence of the enamel was lost beneath the overbearing colour.

'Shitty place for an afternoon walk,' said the man, without turning.

The four travellers glanced at each other. Hiroko's hand brushed the hilt of her slingshot. 'We were following this animal,' she said.

The man paused. He dropped, with a slap, the kirin's liver onto the crimson pile beside him, and the noise hit Hannah like a blow to the belly. He didn't even want the ivory, she realised. This was only about meat.

The man raised himself onto his haunches and jabbed his knife into the corpse to sheathe it. He wiped his hands, palms then backs, on the kirin's pelt, then stood up.

Hannah had been so fixated on the kirin that only now did she notice the man's rifle. She stumbled backwards at the sight of it, fast as she could, her legs acting of their own volition. She tripped and fell with the wind knocked out of her and coal dust swirling up from the ground she'd hit.

'Mum?' Seb crouched over her and tried to help her up.

'Are you alright?' asked the man. He didn't speak with an Irish accent but with the Queen's English, cold as industry. 'I've got a bottle of water over there,' he said. 'Have some if you want.'

With Seb's assistance, Hannah got back to her feet. She made sure not to look at the gun, only at its bearer. He was tall and broad, muscled like a primate. His skin had the same weathered complexion as her own, and his hair was a similar shade of blonde. He wore a pair of thin-framed glasses, and in the corner of one lens was a fleck of something pink.

'I think it's your rifle,' Seb tried to explain. 'Mum . . . had a bad run-in with a gun.'

'Lots of run-ins with guns end badly,' smirked the man, then jabbed his thumb in the direction of the kirin. 'Just ask that thing.'

He laughed at his own joke, then let it fade when he saw Hannah's scowl. The Alsatian, a flea-bitten cur with one torn ear, growled at her distrustingly. 'You did this,' said Hiroko, pointing at the carcass.

'Of course I did,' conceded the man. 'What of it?'

'It was unnecessary!'

'Says who?'

'We all do,' said Hiroko, and Hannah was grateful for the steel in the girl's voice. The Alsatian turned and sniffed at Hiroko, and when it took a hungry step towards her the man had to reach down and grip its collar to restrain it. Yasuo poked his head out from Hiroko's hood, and hissed at both man and dog. At the sight of the fox the Alsatian lunged on instinct, and the man grunted with the sudden effort of holding it back. The dog bared its teeth and barked until its master silenced it with a whisper of something into its ear and a heavy pat of its neck. Then it whined and stopped struggling, although it did not take its eyes off Yasuo.

'What kind of girl are you,' asked the man, unamused, 'carrying a fox about in your hood?'

'What kind of man are you,' retorted Hiroko at once, 'shooting a kirin?'

'Is that what you call one of these?' He stared dispassionately at his kill. 'I wouldn't have called it that.'

'It wouldn't have threatened you,' said Hiroko. 'It was a herbivore.'

'You think I can't see that? But why should I care? I have mouths to feed.'

'You . . . you have family?' asked Hannah, finding the idea strangely painful.

'Why is that so hard to believe?' The man reached out and scratched the Alsatian's skull. 'But . . . no. Not any more. What I have is orders. I was sent out to find food.'

'Sent out?' Hannah looked again at his fatigues and his military boots. 'Are you a soldier?'

'No. I just got these clothes off an army man. I'd make a terrible soldier.' The man glared again at Hiroko. 'I don't like being told what to do.'

'What . . . what are you, then?'

'I don't have a job any more, if that's what you mean. But my name's Leonard, if you want to know it. Are you going to tell me yours? You're some sort of family?'

'She's my mum,' explained Seb, stepping in when it became clear that Hannah wouldn't answer. 'I'm Seb, and she's Hannah. And these are Hiroko and Adrien.'

Leonard pointed from Hannah to Adrien. 'Brother and sister, right?'

Hannah flinched. 'My brother was killed. Adrien and I are friends.'

Leonard looked back at her and pouted. 'A lot of shitty things have happened, haven't they? Now, if you'll excuse me . . .' He turned around, crouched, then tugged his knife back out of the kirin's hide.

'What are you going to do with the rest of it?' demanded Hiroko. 'That's too much meat for you to carry anywhere on your own.'

'Stash it somewhere. Come back for it soon.'

'Where are you taking it?

'A lot of questions.' Leonard lifted the animal's belly fat and worked his blade in. 'But if you must know, I've shacked up with a sort of community, about four days' walk from here. We're set up in an old hotel.'

Adrien gasped.

'Now *you* look like you need some water,' said Leonard.

'A what?' whispered Adrien, looking petrified.

'A hotel,' repeated Leonard, 'although you couldn't really call it that any more. It *was* the Caisleán Hotel. Grand old place. Not so grand now.'

Adrien didn't move a muscle. The breeze drifted down the slopes of the pit and raised ghosts from the coal dust.

'The Caisleán Hotel is where we're headed,' said Seb.

Leonard looked at each of them in turn. 'You're joking, right? Did you hear about us?'

'We were following the kirin,' said Hannah in a queasy voice.

'We've come all the way from England,' added Seb. 'Crossed the sea. Walked every step of the way, just to find that place.'

At that Leonard looked stupefied. He laughed, then stopped laughing again abruptly. 'To find *our* place? You'd better not have set your hopes too high.'

'Actually, it was, um,' said Adrien, in a high pitch, 'it was . . .'

Leonard was still laughing. 'You've got a room reservation, or something? You think you're going on a holiday?'

'It was to find my wife.'

Leonard frowned. 'Is that so?'

There was silence for half a minute, then Leonard tapped the flat of his knife against his thigh. 'So . . . ? Has your wife got a name?'

Adrien took a deep breath, then didn't say anything. Hannah could almost see the words stuck on his tongue, bunging up his mouth with the fear of speaking them. This awful man with kirin blood all up his arms had just revealed that he had the power to bring their whole journey to a deflated end. Right here in this pit, Leonard could tell them whether or not Michelle was at the Caislean Hotel, whether she had lived or died, whether their journey had come to its end. 'Mish . . .' croaked Adrien. 'Mish . . . Her name is Michelle Thomas.'

All four of them tensed for Leonard's answer. His lips pursed. His eyes narrowed.

'You'd better come with me,' he said.

'What?' spluttered Adrien. 'What do you mean? Is she okay? Is she there?'

After what seemed like an age, Leonard smiled. *A shark is a shark*, Eoin had said.

'I'll lead you there,' said Leonard, 'if you carry your share of my meat for me.'

'But . . . but . . .' Adrien protested. 'You have to at least tell me whether she's alive!'

'I don't have to do anything,' said Leonard. 'I happen to think it's none of my business. Better if you wait and see. So . . . enough talk. I've got meat to chop, and you four can either help me or get lost.'

He turned and ran the knife back into the kirin.

It seemed they had little choice but to accept Leonard's offer, and each of them shoulder a portion of kirin meat. Leonard cut a polythene sack into squares, then tied each around a fleshy bundle, its jelly and its juices glistening inside the transparent plastic. Seb tried to carry Hannah's bundle for her, but she insisted that she take her share, and indeed felt like part of some strange cortège when they left the coal pit behind them.

The meat was an awkward load to carry, not so much because of the weight but because it was hard to grip the packaging. Blood and air bubbles flowed against the plastic as if seeking an escape, and Hannah imagined opening the bag like a magician's sack and a living kirin springing forth to trample Leonard. Several times, as they walked, Adrien pressed their new guide for information about Michelle. Several times Leonard took delight in evading an answer. There was something about the way he did so that reminded Hannah of how he'd pulled the innards from the kirin, and with each rebuff Adrien looked more miserable than before.

The rest of the time, Leonard seemed disinclined towards conversation, only speaking to issue commands to his Alsatian, who kept pace at his side and occasionally stole hungry looks at Yasuo. That night, however, he built them a fire, and Hannah had to admit she was grateful for it. Then Leonard began to place kirin meat over the flames.

'Um,' said Adrien, 'do you mind?'

'Do I mind what?' asked Leonard.

'We were following this animal.'

'So? You don't want anything to eat, is that it?'

'We were . . . we were . . .' Adrien glanced at Hannah. 'Don't you see? We were following it.'

333

'And lo and behold you've found it,' said Leonard, and threw another thick slab on the fire. 'What did you expect would happen next?'

'We expected it to be alive!' spat Hannah, and Leonard looked up at her as if surprised. The meat sizzled in the flames, and gasped when one fatty seam burst.

Hannah stood up and stalked away. She found a cold log to sit on, with her arms folded and tears streaming freely down her cheeks. Adrien joined her, not a minute later. Seb and Hiroko came right after that.

Leonard didn't have a tent, but nor did he ask them for a place in theirs. Neither did they offer, since he seemed happy to curl up outside it with his dog, his long fingers still stroking the animal even while he slept. As usual, Hannah woke first in the morning, and gently lifted Adrien's arm aside to leave the tent and stretch her spine in the beginning dawn. She watched Leonard's ribs heave in time with his dog's, then looked at his rifle lying beside him. The gun made her feel different inside. As cold and unbending as its barrel. What would it be like, she wondered, to take it up and point it at Leonard, and have revenge for killing the kirin?

She stepped away hurriedly. She knew the answer to that question, knew just what it would be like. She was surprised by her willingness to ask it.

3

Pharmacy

Travelling with Leonard made Adrien feel just like he had on his first day on the road, when he had laboured under the weight of his holdall and rucksack full to bursting. Today he had only a bag of kirin meat on top of what he was used to carrying, but Leonard's company was a burden all its own. For the first time, Adrien truly appreciated how good he'd had things when it was just the four of them, and how conscientious Hiroko had been as their pace-setter. Now the girl had no time to object when Leonard forced them along at a march. She had to be constantly on her guard against the Alsatian, who never stopped watching Yasuo in her hood or on her shoulder.

Adrien did his best to be terrified of what might happen when they reached the hotel. That at least was a familiar apprehension, far preferable to the many smaller frights in the woods. He tried to focus on it, but seemingly innocuous sights kept tripping his memory. When he saw an ant carrying a flake of leaf, he could at once remember straddling along on six legs. He could remember lugging a giant sheet of green down into a tunnel, taking it as a gift to the chamber of his bloated queen.

He shuddered, and did his best to be terrified of finding the hotel.

Towards evening, Leonard halted them on the edge of a village. It was not for a rest stop or a break for sustenance, but a warning. 'A lot of bones in this one,' said Leonard. 'I came through it on my way. My guess is that people fought each other here, but don't

335

worry. It must have been a while ago, and all the blood and guts are gone now. It's just the bones that are left.'

Once, it would have been a sleepy village, all narrow roads and quaint cottages. The skeletons Leonard had warned of were strewn across its main street, although at first they were easy to miss. Beasts and birds had stripped and scattered them, and not a joint remained attached. They crossed what had been the village green in sombre silence, until Leonard gave a gnashed command to his Alsatian and it bounded away as if unleashed. It trotted around among the bones and chose a shoulder blade to pick up and carry in its jaws.

Adrien grimaced at the animal's behaviour, then was at first relieved to see it drop the bone. Its mouth opened wider and its tongue lolled out as it turned its head sideways, training its nose on something. With a ripple of muscle and fur, it padded in through the empty doorframe of a shop, and Leonard readied his rifle and waited to find out what it had caught scent of. A few seconds later, the Alsatian sent back a vicious bark, followed by a man's startled shriek. Leonard dashed after his dog, and the others followed suit.

The shop had been the village pharmacy, and the green plastic cross of its signage dangled over its ruin. Amid the rubble knelt an emaciated man in a torn and open shirt, boxer shorts without trousers, and shoes without socks. In a world deprived of wash-basins he was nevertheless exceptionally filthy, and his smell stood out above the chemical reek of spilled medicine. It was not the Alsatian that had made him shriek, for he was clawing through the piles of chipped plaster and glass as if he had not even noticed the animal. Neither did he look up at any of them when they entered, only pushed his filthy fingers against the sides of his head and sobbed.

With a sharp whistle from its master, the Alsatian came to heel. 'Come on,' said Leonard, and turned to leave the pharmacy.

'Where are you going?' asked Hannah.

'Same place I was a minute ago. The place I was taking you, last time I checked.'

336

'Aren't we going to help him?'

'Who? This one? He's far beyond help.' Leonard pulled his rifle off his shoulder and offered it to Hannah. 'Unless you want to put him out of his misery.'

Hannah recoiled, but at the same time the kneeling man began to weep, and the tear trails down his cheeks were the only clean parts of his body. Each grimace served better than the last to highlight how hollow his cheeks were, and how sunken his eyes.

Seb raised his voice as he approached. 'Hello? Hello . . . what are you looking for in here?'

The man's stare was a loose thing that floated over Seb's shoulder. 'Pain-killers.'

'You're hurt?'

'In here,' the man said, tapping the side of his head. As he did so, his shirt swayed open and showed how pronounced his ribs were.

'You need to eat something,' said Seb.

'Eat and eat,' said the man.

Leonard rolled his eyes. 'No time for this, kid. Leave the poor bastard to his digging.'

'There *is* time,' protested Seb. 'He needs help.'

'Of course he does. But it's not the kind any of us can give.' Leonard pointed to the sky, which was visible in dim rectangles between the rafters. 'In the meantime, we've got at least an hour's walking left today.'

Adrien cleared his throat and planted his feet. When he spoke up, his voice didn't sound as unequivocal as he'd have liked, but there was something too pitiful about the man to simply abandon him here. 'No, Leonard. Walking is over for today. We're making camp.'

Leonard's eyes met his for a moment, and were as searching as the thin man's were vacant. Then he flapped a hand as if tossing something aside. 'You're the one who's desperate to find your wife. If you want to waste your time here, it's no skin off my nose.' Then, as he turned to leave the pharmacy, he added over his shoulder, 'I'll start

337

a fire, but that man is done for. He'll be dead before morning, mark my words. Don't think you're wasting any of my meat on him.'

It took Adrien and the others some time to convince the man to sit with them. When they had done so, and when the flames began to crackle and come forth from the logs Leonard had piled up, the awful truth became clear that Leonard was right. Something worse than malnutrition was ebbing the man's strength away, something irreparably broken in his spirit. They gave him one coat to wear and another to blanket his legs, and Seb buttoned up his shirt for him and poured him water, yet even in the fire's strong light he looked as thin as black ice. For the second night running, Leonard opened his bag of meat and threw some on the flames, but the others had only a few leaves and mushrooms to share. Some of these they placed in the man's cupped hands, where he regarded them for a while in silence. Then he brought them to his mouth as if they were communion and reached out his tongue to taste them, or so Adrien thought. Instead he retched, a pathetic spray of bile that drizzled his food. After that he simply let the things they'd given him fall between his fingers, and Adrien and his friends shared pitiful expressions. Then Leonard, whose meat had cooked now to his liking, forked it out of the fire and began to gnaw at the hot flesh with a smacking of lips. He tossed another cut to the Alsatian, and when they were both done they licked the grease out of beard and fur alike.

The man cleared his throat and began to speak. 'They don't like the fire,' he said, pronouncing each word as if he were addressing a hall full of people, 'but they're jealous of the meat you have.'

Leonard chuckled, and picked a piece of kirin gristle from between his teeth. 'Told you he was beyond our help.'

The man paid him no heed. 'The fire is too bright. Night eyes aren't made for this.'

Leonard waggled a bit of bone at the man. 'And are these your imaginary friends, that you're talking about?'

'No.'

338

'Then who?' asked Seb, with far more concern.

'Badgers,' said the man. 'Stoats. Rooks. Rats. Weasels. Owls. *That* . . .' He pointed upwards, at the branches, and for a few brief seconds Adrien saw something moving there. His heart skipped a beat because he thought it might be a whisperer, but then the Alsatian sprang to its feet and growled, and the firelight showed the long glossy fur of an animal of some kind.

'What was that?' asked Seb, when it had retreated into shadow.

'A pine marten, I think,' said Hannah. 'That's a rare sight.'

The Alsatian huffed and sat back down. Meanwhile the man had bowed his head, and his forehead shone with beads of firelit sweat. 'Meat,' he said, and licked his lips. His shoulders heaved and sloped forwards. 'Meat is all they see.'

'Do they now?' chuckled Leonard.

'Better not to cook it. Better to get your teeth in deep, while the blood's still hot.'

'If this is a funny way of asking for some of my steak,' said Leonard, 'then bad luck and get your own.'

The man wasn't listening. 'It's gone to find the eggs from the nest. The tastiest eggs with the chicks inside.'

'Are you talking about the pine marten, now?' asked Hannah.

'In the egg it's so sweet. You float in the slime, and when your mother sits in the nest you get so warm.' The man wrapped his arms around himself, a weak smile passing over his face. 'You grow, then. Do all the growing you can in the heat. It makes you want to break out and yell for worms, and you don't know any better and you don't know how cruel things are on the outside.' He shook his head sorrowfully. 'But when you're the mother bird, that's when you know.'

'You're a crackpot,' said Leonard, and yawned.

The man covered his face with his hands, but stared out wide-eyed between his fingers. 'You can hardly bear to watch,' he hissed, 'but how can you look away? You sat on those eggs day after day and you felt those little ones nudging in their shells.'

339

'Someone find him a chick to cuddle up to,' laughed Leonard, 'if that will only shut him up.'

The man stared into the fire, but not even the flames' roaring yellow could colour his face. He rubbed at his stomach, and looked even more hungry than before. 'And then you watch the marten climb the branches, all dark and slippery as oil, and it eats those eggs you tended, without a care in the world. There's blood running red out of the shells, and all you can do is watch and sing.'

'Things die,' said Leonard. 'Deal with it. If you can't you're good as dead yourself.'

'But they taste so *good*!' said the man, again clutching his belly. 'They taste *divine*! Little balls of meat with a kick in them, and if you get there just after the mother bird's been sitting you can drink the syrup warm and sticky.'

Leonard stood up and swept his foot into the burning logs of the fire. A cloud of sparks and smoke erupted at the sick man, and he squealed and flapped at the air. Ash and embers spun around him, and Seb sprang to his feet and shouted, 'Leonard!' with unconcealed fury.

'Relax,' said Leonard, sitting back down. The ash dispersed and the embers blinked out, and the man was left sweating and rubbing fire dust from his eyes. Nevertheless he had stopped his rambling. 'Thank you,' he said, after a minute.

'Pleasure,' said Leonard.

Meanwhile, Adrien had been listening with a horrible sense of familiarity. 'Are you going to be okay?' he asked quietly, to which the man did not respond. He seemed lost, too deep, in his own broken thoughts.

The night arrived swiftly, assisted by a pall of cloud that deepened the sunset's purple to a velvety black. Leonard lay down and slept, his arm around the neck of his dog and its whiskers nuzzling his jaw. Hiroko, Seb and Hannah nodded off one by one, but the man from the pharmacy didn't seem to tire, sitting upright and deathly still while the firelight stretched his clammy skin ever tighter across his bones.

When the others were all sleeping, Adrien sidled around the fire and sat down beside him. 'That stuff you said about the chicks, the meat, the mother bird . . . all that stuff . . . you said it like . . . like you knew it.'

The man didn't answer, only stared into the flames.

Adrien lowered his voice. 'You said it like you'd *been* it.'

The fire spat and shot up orange, but still the man did not stir.

'I saw,' said Adrien carefully, 'a tree shaped like a throne, standing in the forest where there'd been only ordinary trees before. Something was sitting on it, some kind of creature with many legs. And surrounding it there were . . . whisperers, I call them, hundreds of little things made out of twigs and leaves. And then, the next time I saw it, the creature had left the throne, and it was in the canopy, and it . . .'

Suddenly the man began to talk. 'It came down through the branches towards me, step by step, and I couldn't move. It had a mouth in the middle of it, like an octopus's mouth. I didn't want to look but I couldn't help it, and then . . . I don't know if I passed out. I don't know if I stayed awake. I looked inside and saw . . .'

'. . . the forest,' said Adrien. 'You saw a vision of the forest.'

For the first time, the man's eyes lost some of their glaze. They finally met Adrien's own. 'I didn't ask for it.'

'Me neither,' said Adrien. 'I have no idea why it showed itself to me.'

'I think the vision is a test,' said the man.

'A test? What do you mean?'

'A question.' The man looked back into the fire, although his eyes wouldn't stay still. Their pupils danced like flies newly hatched over water. 'I said *I give up*, there's your answer. I said *I fail it*.'

'What was the test?' asked Adrien, fearing he would lose him again. 'What was the question?'

The man's hand shot out and grabbed Adrien's. Its fingers were ice-cold, and at first all Adrien wanted to do was snatch back his own from its clutches.

'Can I keep you?' asked the man. Then, without letting go of Adrien's hand, he began to sob. Adrien let him cling on, even though he could tell that the man's mind was already slipping back into its delirious state. 'It's okay,' whispered Adrien, and although he wished he could get more answers, he hadn't the heart to unsettle him further. 'It's going to be okay.'

The man wept and stared into the flames. The fire sent up sparks. He and Adrien held hands in silence for a long time, until at last the man reached into his pocket and showed Adrien a piece of paper. On the paper was a photograph of a woman. 'My wife,' said the man, almost inaudibly.

'Is she . . . gone?'

The man didn't reply.

Adrien reached into his pocket and retrieved his photo of Michelle. Looking at her wedding day smile brought a hint of happiness to the man's own face. 'Good,' he whispered, and closed his eyes.

An hour or so later, having held Adrien's hand all that time, the man died. The fire had lowered, the clouds had sealed the night, and when the man's hand slipped out from his grip, Adrien thought at first that he'd nodded off. His head bowed and came to rest on Adrien's shoulder, but only once Adrien had lifted it and lowered him onto his back did he realise that he was not breathing.

Adrien froze, full of sudden fear. The man's borrowed coats, and even his own shirt, looked many sizes too big for him. Adrien tried to steady his shaking arms by folding them tight, but he only managed to press his heartbeat into double time. He looked to his slumbering companions and noticed that Yasuo's eyes were open. The fox's tail flicked to one side and stroked Hiroko's cheek, and she sat up slowly as if rising to sleepwalk.

'Are you alright?' she asked Adrien.

Adrien gestured to the dead man's face, the fire's half harrowed and the other half blotted out by the night. 'He . . . he just died. I mean . . . just like that.'

Hiroko's eyes were glazed from dreaming, and she seemed undaunted by the man's lifeless body. 'He'd seen the same things you have,' she suggested.

'Maybe.'

'I heard you talking before I fell asleep.'

'It certainly sounded like he had.'

She nodded. 'Are you going to end up like him?'

Adrien folded his arms around himself. 'No idea. Watch this space.'

Hiroko chuckled, and although it was only a brief sound it was so musical and carefree that it made Adrien flinch.

'I hardly think,' he said, 'that now is an appropriate time for laughter. This poor man has just *died*.'

Hiroko was unrepentant. 'You aren't going to end up like him.'

'Says who?'

Yasuo purred and hooked his claws into the fabric of Hiroko's hoodie. She helped him up onto her shoulder, where he licked her jaw and then turned his gaze back on Adrien. Above them the thinning leaves whispered, like a chant for the recently departed. Adrien looked up for a sight of some creeping or waddling whisperer, but there were only sticks and brown fronds.

'It's what I like about you,' said Hiroko.

He looked back at her and the firelight painted her almost as orange as Yasuo. 'Whatever can you mean?'

'You're a survivor.'

Adrien couldn't help but smile at that ridiculous compliment. 'I'm not. Really I'm not. God knows how you've come to that conclusion, when you've spent all this time with me.'

'I've watched you change. You're stronger now. Not so fat.'

'*Thanks.*'

'But what I really mean is inside,' she said, touching one grubby forefinger to her breastbone. 'That's where you survive. You go down really easily, but when you hit the bottom you somehow cope. After a while, you find a way back up again.'

'Is that how you define a survivor? Some kind of bottom feeder?'

'It's one kind,' shrugged Hiroko.

'I wish I was . . . I don't know, the other kind. The big and strong kind.'

'Stop wishing that. Carter used to say it's survival of the fittest, not the strongest or the biggest. He called it survival of the *apt*.'

Adrien was about to retort that he'd never felt much aptitude for anything, when one of the logs burst in the fire. As the sparks whirled out of the timber the light stretched and warped the shape of the glade they were in. The mud in Hiroko's hair and the dirt trails along her arms and neck looked crimson in that light. Adrien supposed there might be blood in those stains as much as old soil, and not for the first time the girl seemed strange and bestial to him. He tried to imagine her mentor Carter, but when he pictured the woodsman it was Zach who he saw, dead as they'd found him. Then he remembered all the other non-survivors: his neighbour Mrs Howell; Diane eaten by wolves; this poor man beside him. He feared it would not be long before he too would be counted among them.

4

Hotel

In the morning Leonard told them that, if they put on a good march, they would be at the hotel by late afternoon the next day. They did their best to match his pace, under swaying giants already turned to their brownest colours, and through other patches of the forest that were even further ahead with their changing. Stretches of orange and burgundy rustled overhead and underfoot, and when Adrien caught a falling leaf it felt as dry as snakeskin. He turned it over in his hand and, for a confused moment, could remember having skin as papery as the leaf's.

They ate lunch beside a small pond, whose water was opaque and lifeless and whose surface was stickered with faded lilypads, then pressed on. In some rare places, green islets remained among the trees, while in others winter's bareness had arrived early, punching gaps in the foliage through which the sky looked murky and near. What leaves were yet to fall rubbed together like cold palms, and reminded Adrien of the frosts and snows to come.

'Stop,' said Leonard, and whistled his dog to a halt. They all obeyed his command, and Adrien held his breath and waited to find out what had stopped the big man in his tracks.

'All of you should look at this,' he said, striding forward and squatting down to point to something in the leaf litter. They gathered around expectantly, Adrien preparing to see something horrible, some human bone or piece of meat that had tickled Leonard's fancy.

'Hang on a minute . . .' said Hannah, crouching opposite Leonard and staring at the same thing he was.

'It looks like a pinkgill,' said Leonard, stroking his beard, 'but I don't think I've ever . . .'

'Seen one quite like this,' said Hannah. 'Me neither. Not first-hand, at least.'

'I'm right, then. This is a rare one.'

'Zach,' began Hannah, eyes still locked on what they'd found, 'took me on holiday to France. A long time ago, before Seb was born. The rare ones were what we went looking for. There are some so scarce they haven't even got names.'

'This is one of those,' said Leonard. 'I'm certain of it.'

It was a mushroom, a single slender stalk with a blue-grey cap. There was nothing flamboyant about it, but there was some-thing enchanting about its colour. It was the hue of a still pool at dusk, or a bluebell fading into mist. As if on the same sudden impulse, both Hannah and Leonard reached out to touch it. Then, each seeing the other's hand moving, they drew their own back.

'After you,' said Leonard.

Hannah carefully tilted the mushroom to see its underside. The gills were pronounced, their shadows a deeper tint of that alluring blue, but the spores that speckled the ground in its shade were a fine and dusty pink.

'I know it sounds crazy,' said Hannah, 'after everything that's happened. But I'm actually kind of stunned to see this.'

She and Leonard looked up at each other and simultaneously beamed with childish glee. Then Hannah's face fell, and she folded her arms.

Now it was Leonard's turn to touch the mushroom. He moved it from side to side between finger and thumb. 'Do you want to pick it, or can I?'

Hannah's intake of breath was so loud it made Adrien jump. 'You're not serious.'

'Of course I am.'

'We just agreed . . . this is so rare it doesn't even have a name.'

'Doesn't that make you all the more tempted?'

'To *pick* it? No!'

He watched her for a moment. 'It's a mushroom. It will be gone by itself in no time'

'No reason to hurry it along.'

'You must have picked a thousand mushrooms in your life.'

Hannah shrugged tightly.

'I get it,' said Leonard, lowering his voice. 'You're the only one who gets to decide. If you say it's special, we all have to agree or be damned. It's just like with that big dumb animal I shot. But you should try taking something as a trophy some time.'

Hannah looked too red-hot with anger to respond, so Leonard only laughed and reached to pick the mushroom.

There was the sound of rubber straining.

'Don't touch it,' said Hiroko, aiming her slingshot at Leonard.

The big man's face darkened. A growl began in his Alsatian's throat. 'Or what? You're going to shoot me? Over a mushroom?' He jostled the rifle on his shoulder. 'I'm not exactly outgunned.'

'Don't fuck with me,' said Hiroko.

Leonard smiled sweetly at her, and the Alsatian squared off and stared with hungry eyes. 'Don't fuck with *me*,' he said, and made again to pick.

The stone struck his hand and he leapt back with a howl. A red mark like lipstick showed on his knuckle, and he sucked it as he rounded on Hiroko. His Alsatian bounded forward eagerly, and was barking at once, and Yasuo hissed back from Hiroko's hood.

'You little bitch!' roared Leonard. 'How dare you?'

Hiroko stood her ground, another stone readied in an instant. 'I can hurt you a lot more if I actually *try*.'

With a growl, Leonard pulled his dog to heel. He shook his hand as if the pain were drops of water. 'Enough!' he spat, and turned away, leaving the pretty blue mushroom untouched behind him.

The next day, just as the afternoon was stretching thin and it looked as if they might need to make one more night's camp before arriving at the hotel, Leonard's Alsatian rushed off ahead of them, barking as it ran. The big man smiled and led them up a hill, but it was not long before the forest floor plateaued out in front of them. A minute later, the ground dropped away again, and then they stepped out of the woods.

They stood looking down into a broad-bottomed valley. They could see all the way across to its far slopes, because almost all of the trees that had grown in it had been felled.

Leonard spread his arms. 'You've arrived,' he proclaimed. 'Down there is the Caisleán Hotel.'

Adrien held his breath. After the claustrophobia of the woods, the deforested land seemed as wide open as a desert. The earth was stump-stubbled and scorched black by burnings. Weeds grew here and there, but they were bedraggled explorers lost in an expanse. A shrill wind dashed up and down the slopes, and high up in the exposed sky, trails of cloud hurried east to west.

'Is that really it?' asked Adrien at last.

At the bottom of the valley stood the Caisleán Hotel. Once upon a time, it must have been as imposing as a French chateau, but now, like every building they had seen on their journey, it had been demolished by trees. Despite that, it was the greenest thing in the valley. The trees that had destroyed it were the only ones that had not been chopped down, and that was no doubt because their trunks had fused with the building itself. Their crowns were entwined with the chimney stacks and eaves, and with the decorative turrets they had snapped from the roof. Their branches wove in and out of the walls and the dainty ornamented balconies. They held up the remains of windows to the light, and the glass shone like gold foil.

'We don't know what to do with the place,' said Leonard. 'One of these days, it will all just fall down.'

Even as he spoke, a handful of bricks came loose from one wall of the hotel and showered to the ground, trailing dust.

'Like I said,' continued Leonard, 'no five-star bedrooms for you.' He pointed to a different part of the valley bottom, one at a safe distance from the hotel. '*That* little shithole is the place where we're heading.'

It was a settlement of sorts, thirty or forty crude shelters constructed along a grid of muddy tracks. Mud, in fact, floored the entirety of the valley and glistened in the sunlight.

'Wow,' said Seb, puffing out his cheeks. 'You've turned this whole valley into a wasteland.'

'Disappointed?' chuckled Leonard, as he led them downhill towards the settlement. 'I told you not to get your hopes up.'

Adrien kept silent as they followed, wondering what lay in wait for him ahead. He had hoped, in the early days of their journey, that somehow the very act of travelling might solve him, and that he would arrive a new proposition, a better man than the one Michelle had left grouchy on the sofa that morning. He had hoped to learn to live in the woods as had Zach, to grow strong and carry an axe like some hero forester in a fairy story. He had hoped to become charismatic like Eoin, to spellbind his many admirers with tales of his derring-do. He would have liked to learn some predatory toughness from Hiroko, or to have faith in things like Hannah did. He would have settled, even, for some of Seb's level-headed perceptiveness, but the truth was that he was the same tormented Adrien Thomas that he'd been when he'd left his house in England.

The charred slopes crunched underfoot like a beach, releasing smells of ash and tar and the burned sugars of incinerated resin. Further downhill the mud began, swamping the stumps in brown. Occasionally some grimy and bedraggled weed raised a flag of green above the filth, but more commonly the only other colour was of flesh, for there were earthworms aplenty dragging themselves about on the slopes. For an ugly moment Adrien could recall being stretched and oozing, and having no sight and craving the best leaves, dragging them below ground along with himself to massage his body between papery sheets.

He shuddered, and hoped his mind was not bound for the same fate as that of the man they had found in the pharmacy.

Already they were close enough to see some thirty or forty people busying themselves around the settlement, and the shelters looked like they could house at least twice that many. Heaps of logs were everywhere, the surplus from chopping down so many trees. Some had been cut into a heavy-set fence, used to demarcate a field of sorts, although that was even muddier than the ground surrounding it. Five emaciated cattle stood in the enclosure, their snouts smattered with mud and their ribs pronounced along their flanks. Chickens roamed around their hooves, beaks plunging in and out of the dirt. At the scent of them, Yasuo sat up with a purr, and almost immediately Leonard's Alsatian reappeared, bounding towards them with its ears back and its tongue flapping out of its jaws. Hiroko held her fox tight, and whisked him safely into the hood of her top.

They reached the first of the shelters and stepped on to a path of planks that had been laid between them, this too sticky with mud. Still they followed it, turning past a wide yard full of scrap. Every conceivable detritus had been heaped up there: pieces of car, pieces of engine, posts and plinths and gutters, chairs, tables, microwaves and fridge-freezers. A team of people were dragging even more salvage down from the woods, to dump it on a mountainous pile. Other folk crawled over this with spanners, pliers or simple crowbars made from branches, dismantling it and dividing it into smaller collections of useful parts. A smell of spoiled fuel and left-over bins hung over the place, despite the wind that raced back and forth as fast as the Alsatian. Likewise a gang of children were stomping through the scrapheap, filthy and laughing, and elsewhere a trio of elderly women watched them play, nattering to each other in their frail old murmurs.

Adrien supposed that all of them were so grateful to have left the woods that they were prepared to tolerate the lifelessness of such a place as this. He, however, could not so easily stomach it. The sheer barrenness of the valley made every tiny flash of life seem bright. Among the buildings and the paths the countless stumps lay forgotten and taken for dead, but if Adrien stooped closer and reached out a hand (he wished he had not done so, even as he did), he could see the cracks in the bark and the new growth mustering within. Despite losing their trunks, the roots would remain, and their appetites along with them. He wondered how deep they sank. He had to take off his glasses for a moment and press his wrists against his eyes, to try to silence his sudden under-ground thoughts. How thirsty life was, down there! He remembered forcing himself in, through the soil, and spreading out and sucking all the water into himself . . .

Seb crouched and put his arms around him. 'It's okay, Adrien. I can't imagine how nervous you must be, but just remember . , . whatever happens with Michelle, the three of us will be behind you.'

Adrien's tongue felt too parched to reply, but he stood up with the boy's help. Michelle. Of course. He tried to worry solely about Michelle.

Seb held on to him as they followed Leonard the final distance, towards the biggest of the wooden buildings. It was a sort of head-quarters, with people coming and going through its several entrances. 'This,' announced Leonard, when they had nearly reached it, 'is where our man in charge will be. This is where you'll get your answers.'

Seb let go of Adrien then, but Hannah reached out and squeezed his hand, and her fingers were as rough and warm as they'd been on the day he'd first met her. 'Good luck,' she said.

Adrien nodded, sucked in all the air his lungs could carry, and went with them all into the big building.

It was a simple structure, a long hall full of more stored timber and several huddles of people. Adrien didn't know whether he was more relieved or upset to see no Michelle among any of them. Some gazed up with disinterest at the newcomers, but they clearly all recognised Leonard as someone to be wary of, and made sure not to be found in his path when he led Adrien and the others across the room.

At the far end of the hall were a table and chairs that looked like they'd been rescued from the hotel, since they were incongruously antique. Sitting in the largest and finest of them, issuing instruc-tions to those seated in the others, was a handsome man who had somehow managed to stay shaved, groomed and scrubbed. He had dark eyes, dark hair, and a bass voice that he accompanied with smiles and sweeping gestures. The expensive shirt he wore bore none of the rips and blemishes that all other clothes had suffered. Likewise his trousers were clean chinos, without grass stains or holes in the knees.

'Wait for him to finish,' Leonard whispered, holding out an arm to keep Adrien and the others at a respectful distance. The people in the smaller chairs surrounding the man nodded and listened intently, and one even noted down the things he was saying. Then the man clapped his hands and they all pushed back their chairs and stood. He shared a few brief jokes with some of them, before they each went on their way.

Alone now, the man turned to Leonard and flashed him a brotherly grin. He strode down from his chair and the two of them shook hands firmly, after which Leonard held high his bag of kirin meat.

'Wonderful!' exclaimed the man, rubbing his hands. 'You always come back trumps, Leonard, but this is really excelling yourself.'

He turned to the others, as if noticing them for the first time. His smile was bright and sweeping as a searchlight. 'And I don't believe we've met . . . You must be newcomers, and you're all very much welcome, so long as you're happy to chip in. Welcome, welcome, welll . . .'

In an instant his charm and confidence staled. His lips curled.

He had become as inert, in fact, as Adrien had been ever since he'd set eyes on him.

'How on earth . . .' said the man.

'Hello, Roland,' said Adrien.

5

Michelle

'*Adrien?*'

Nothing was ever so cruelly surprising as real life. Since arriving in Ireland, Adrien had imagined all manner of disastrous endings to their journey, many of which featured Roland prominently. Yet he had never gone so far as to picture this: Roland the king of a castle, issuing orders to his countless subjects.

Of the two men, Roland was of course the quickest to recover his cool. 'It *is* you, Adrien. Well, well, well.'

'Yes . . . me,' said Adrien, who didn't suppose he'd had any cool to recover in the first place. He couldn't stop staring at Roland. He had always felt a resentful sort of admiration for men like him, men who radiated such self-assuredness, but today Roland seemed doubly bright. Every stranger in the hall seemed to admire him, too. Even Leonard stood alongside him with the same satisfied air as the Alsatian did at his own side.

Roland shook his head and laughed. 'As tongue-tied as ever, Adrien? You're not going to tell me what on earth you're doing here?'

Adrien opened his mouth to reply, but could not find the words to do so. He felt as if he had been pushed out in front of a class again, although this time it was full of all the bullies of his childhood, grown up tougher and surer of themselves than ever before.

Roland raised one eyebrow. 'Perhaps it's obvious,' he mused. 'Although I fear it may have been a fool's errand.'

'They say they walked all the way from England,' Leonard said, 'and took a boat across the sea. But when I heard they were looking for Michelle, I thought it best to save them for you.'

Again Roland laughed. It was a rich laugh, a fireside laugh, and as hard as a stone hearth. 'You really came all this way to find her?'

'Yes,' replied Adrien in a strangled voice.

'Isn't it a bit late for grand gestures?'

Adrien looked down at his toes and tried not to listen to his own incredulous mind, which was leaping to agree with Roland. 'Maybe,' he said. 'I don't know.'

But *yes*. Hadn't it felt like a fool's errand, right from the start? To have got here at all was such a great achievement, for someone like Adrien Thomas. He should be satisfied with that, and hold his head high, and get the hell out of here and let Roland continue whatever important business he was conducting. Could he even say, for certain, that he had come here because of Michelle? Or had he simply arrived by accident, blown here by the needs of Hannah and the others like some puffed-up carrier bag flapped by the wind?

'Enough,' announced Hiroko. 'You tell him whether Michelle's here or not. Stop being such an asshole about it.'

'Watch out for this one,' advised Leonard. 'She thinks she's bloody Tarzan.'

The girl and her fox stepped forward and stood at Adrien's shoulder, and no sooner had she done so than it seemed to Adrien as if the air had changed in the hall and he was able to stand up straighter. It might have been more like a sapling's straightness than the strength of a full-grown trunk, but it was enough to look up at Roland again.

'Is this a friend of yours, Adrien?' asked Roland. 'And is she always so rude? What about these others? Aren't you going to introduce us?'

'These are my friends,' said Adrien, and it felt good to say so. 'This is Inoue Hiroko, and Yasuo, and Hannah and Sebastian Tate. My friends.'

A turn of Roland's lips showed his displeasure, even if they were quickly smiling again. 'And have they all come to find their former wives and husbands, too?'

'Stop this, Roland,' said Seb. 'He's here to speak with Michelle, not you.'

Two perfect rows of teeth lined Roland's smile. 'You're a charming bunch, aren't you?'

'I . . . I mean I do, insist,' said Adrien, even though he found it hard to breathe while being so bold. 'I *do* insist that you, uhh . . . tell me where Michelle is. And if you don't, then I'll . . . I'll . . .'

'You'll what?' chuckled Leonard.

'He'll find out from someone else,' said Hannah. 'Simple.'

'Wow.' Roland shook his head. 'Wow, Adrien, this is more than a little awkward, you know.' He let the silence hang for a moment, then motioned to Leonard with his hand. 'Go and fetch her, then. We might as well put him out of his misery.'

Leonard nodded, but for a moment did not move. He had his eyes half-closed and was smiling, as if basking in the sun. *He had known*, Adrien realised. He had known all along that he was leading them to wherever this was going. Perhaps he had even relished it.

Leonard turned and stalked out of the hall. His Alsatian took one last hungry look at Yasuo, then followed its master.

They were all quiet for a minute, during which time the smile never entirely left Roland's face. Then he shook his head with a show of disbelief and said to Adrien, 'I think you'd appreciate some space for this reunion. Aren't I right?' He raised his voice to address everyone in the hall. 'Excuse me, people! We need to give this poor man some breathing room. Why don't we all wait outside?'

'We're not going anywhere,' said Hiroko.

'I'd imagine,' said Roland, 'that Adrien might prefer it if you did. He won't want to be any more embarrassed than he already is.'

'He isn't embarrassed,' said Hiroko defiantly, and Yasuo yapped as if in agreement. Then they both looked to Adrien for confirmation.

Adrien didn't know if it was embarrassment, dread or failure that he felt crammed full of inside. All he knew was that at least one part of him would be grateful if the floorboards opened up and swallowed him whole. Another part wished he had stayed on the beach with his deckchair classroom, and another was the told-you-so part that had rubbished coming here from the start. But just then a wolf spider glided diagonally down from the ceiling on an invisible thread, and Adrien recalled out of the blue what it felt like to abseil so weightlessly, to shimmy with eight long legs. He gasped and clutched his stomach, remembering silk glands inside himself tight as balls of twine.

'I can provide you with a bucket,' said Roland, watching him with barely concealed amusement.

Adrien shook his head and waited for the feeling to pass. Then he stood up straight again, trying to ignore the feeling of phantom spinnerets. 'No thank you,' he said quietly. 'That wasn't what you think it was.'

'Nonsense,' said Roland. 'I know a nervous man when I see one.'

'You wouldn't know the first thing about it.'

At that Roland looked surprised, but Adrien continued before he could say anything. 'You know what, Roland? You're right that I'd like my friends to wait outside. If . . . if this is going to be in any way difficult for Michelle, then I don't want to make it any harder for her.'

Roland snorted. 'How incredibly noble of you. Come on then, everyone, let's do as Adrien bids us.'

Hiroko looked unwilling to move, but Seb pulled her away. The girl accompanied the others reluctantly, and as Roland led them outside he ushered the various strangers out of the hall with them. Adrien was left all alone, with not even a tree for company.

He didn't watch them go, only stood facing Roland's table, as he had stood in the past in a church, facing an altar draped in cloth. He remembered the scent of Michelle's hair that day, an aroma that had been cruelly stirred up for him by some note in Roland's lingering scent. He wondered, as he heard everybody's footsteps fade and the hall fall silent, whether he were really alone now, or whether his wife was already standing back there in the doorway, observing him. He had turned at the altar and seen her stepping dressed in white, her bouquet in her grasp, her skin radiant even in the church's stone shadows. With every step of that walk her eyes had been fixed on him. Whatever had she seen in him? He wondered it still, and pressed his hands to his collar.

Something moved on the table. The wolf spider again, which halted its gallop halfway across the wooden surface. Adrien thought at once of the thing from the theatre, then shuddered and folded his arms tight. The spider raced away and disappeared over the edge of the table.

'Adrien.'

All of a sudden, Michelle was right there behind him. Now, after all this time, near enough to feel her breath trace his neck.

'Adrien,' she said. 'Oh, Adrien. I can't believe you've done this.'

He turned around.

Michelle was beautiful. Adrien still thought that. Yet she also looked a different woman to the one he had harrumphed at when she left for the airport. It had been, what? Ten weeks? Eleven? Time passed as it pleased in the woods. He did not remember those one or two grey hairs running among the brunette ones, nor that she had quite so many freckles, nor that her irises were quite that shade of brown. Maybe it was because she was without eye shadow, or any other makeup. Maybe (he thought it the more likely) he had not paid enough attention. Not in a long time.

'I never expected this, Adrien. Never in a million years. I mean, it's . . . it's . . .' and Michelle laughed. The sound was hollow. At last she said, 'It's daring, that's what it is.'

'Not daring,' he said, 'Not really, Michelle. I don't think any of the courage was mine.'

She nodded, as if she could well believe that. 'Those people you came with, waiting outside. Who are they? Where did they come from?'

'They're . . . my friends. I met them.'

Michelle looked suspicious. 'I remember, not a few months ago . . . you said you hated having friends. You said all they did was waste your free time, and cost you money at Christmas.'

'That sounds just like something I would have said.'

They stared at each other for a minute.

'Oh, Adrien . . .' she said, with a faint shake of her head.

He didn't know what to say in return, other than, 'Michelle . . .'

'That woman you came here with. You're not . . .'

'No.'

Michelle puffed out her cheeks. 'Maybe that's a shame. Maybe that would have made this easier. So . . . why are they with you?'

'It's complicated.'

'Everything always was, with you.'

He grimaced. He supposed the happier days of their marriage felt as long ago to Michelle as they did to him.

She looked away to her side, where there was nothing to see but the wall. 'Can we be frank with each other, Adrien?'

'You have every right to it. We can be however frank you need.'

'Thank you.' She puffed out her cheeks. 'You . . . you go first.'

'Go first?'

'Yes. I need a moment. I mean . . . these last months I've thought of a million things I'd love to say to you, but this is such a surprise. I need a moment to put things into words. You go first. I'll go second.'

'Okay. Sure.' Adrien chewed his lip, and looked inside himself for the right kinds of words. She wasn't wrong, he'd had plenty of time to rehearse this. Yet he'd never got as far, in any of his rehearsals, as actually having to say anything to her. In his imagined versions of this moment all of the talking had been done by her, either berating him or eulogising Roland. He had just stood there, nodding along and attacking himself in time with her.

'Michelle . . .' he began, and willed his tongue to come up with something. 'This is . . . this is a pleasure.'

She frowned. 'It's a pleasure?'

'Yes . . .'

'What do you mean?'

'Uhh . . . There's more.' He tapped his thumbs together. 'Look, Michelle, I never thought we'd get to have this conversation.'

'You didn't think you'd find me here?'

'I assumed that if you were here, it was because you'd decided to stay.'

Michelle nodded.

'And that . . . you wouldn't want to hear from me . . .'

She waited for him to continue. Just as he had remembered her with browner hair and smoother skin, he had remembered her more certain of everything than this.

'But I . . . I do want to say that I'm sorry. I know it went wrong because of me. I was the one who soured everything. I can see that very clearly now.'

She folded her arms. 'Do you love me, Adrien? Did you come here because you love me?'

His throat made a pitiful gurgling noise that seemed to go on for ever, despite his desire to silence it. *Had* that been why he had come? *Did* he love her? He had the awful feeling that, if either of those things had been the case, he would have answered her now without hesitation.

'Because I think . . . I think, Adrien, that when we first met you were so overwhelmed that somebody had started to love you that you didn't ever stop to check whether you felt the same thing in return. You just felt like you had to go ahead and marry me. You didn't love me, even then, not deep down. You just never had the courage to *look* deep down. Maybe you still never have.' Tears began to streak down Michelle's cheeks. 'I mean, have you ever, ever, stopped and searched to the heart of yourself, Adrien? Because that's all I asked you to do. I gave you a year! All I wanted you to do was look one day, just on one single day . . . was *stop* for a moment and dig through all your awkwardness and self-loathing and look at what you wanted. And then, I suppose, I wanted you to tell me whether or not you really loved me.' She swallowed a deep breath. 'There,' she said. 'That's one of the things I've been wanting to say to you.'

'Michelle . . .' began Adrien, and even saying her name felt like scraping the bottom of his lungs. 'It wasn't like that. I did . . . I did love you.'

'You did love me,' she repeated flatly.

'Yes.'

'What did I do, then, to lose it?'

'Nothing.'

'I must have done something.'

He shook his head. 'It was all me. That's obvious now. All of our problems stemmed from me.'

She sighed. She pulled two of the chairs away from the table, and placed them side-by-side looking down the length of the hall. 'Sit,' she said, taking one of them.

He did so. He wanted to say that he had not realised that love could wither, that it was a leaf that would shrivel without water and light. No one had ever explained that.

'I thought that love,' Michelle said, with a sad shake of her head, 'was supposed to overcome. I wanted our love to be the thing that fixed you.'

To his shame, Adrien couldn't bear to look at her. 'It . . . it . . .'

'You were unfixable, though, weren't you, Adrien?'

He couldn't reply.

'It's as simple as love and hate,' she said, 'and you hated yourself too much to have any room left for love. I tried to help you, but it wasn't enough.'

There was silence for a minute. Eventually, Adrien said, 'It was never as easy as that. It sounds easy, looking back on it, but it was never easy at the time.'

'All you had to do was stop hating yourself.'

'I couldn't. I was . . . lost to it. Maybe I still am.'

'But I sometimes felt like you *loved* to hate yourself.'

'I . . . maybe I did.'

'Why, though? Why would you choose that over happiness? When Leonard said you'd showed up here, I thought . . . I thought a lot of things. I thought maybe you were going to tell me that the trees had been the catalyst, and you'd worked yourself out, and that you really did love me, and then . . . then maybe things would have to be different right now. But why have you come, Adrien, if it wasn't for that?'

'I . . . I walked . . . I came all this way . . .' He trailed off. It would give him too much credit to say he'd always meant to get here, or that he'd have carried on without Hannah's need to be heading towards something. The most truthful answer was that he had been afraid, and hadn't wanted to be alone, and that a kirin had led them.

'I don't want to get back together,' Michelle said, miserably. 'Just in case you were going to suggest something like that. You know it's over between us, I think, and that it was over before the trees came. People talk about love like it's the be-all and the end-all. I don't know about that, any more. What good is being in love with a person, if it only binds you to a thousand quiet disappointments, and new problems for every one that you fix? And now, like you say, you've travelled all this way to see me, and I'm waiting for you to tell me that you've worked out what you really want, and you haven't actually got anything to say.'

Adrien winced. 'I want . . . I want . . . Look, Michelle, I suppose I just thought that, if you were still here, you and Roland would be . . .'

Michelle looked down at her palms. 'Yes,' she said, wearily, 'of course. I guess we will have to talk about Roland.'

'How long have you two . . . ?'

She cringed. 'How long has it been since the trees came?'

'What? I mean . . . you weren't *before*?'

She began, gently, to cry. 'Jesus, Adrien. Of course not! What do you take me for? I was married, Adrien. Oh, sure, he made his moves, but I was married. I mean, I know technically I still am, but . . . but . . . what you have to understand is . . . I was so frightened. On that night, when the trees arrived. People died horribly here. When the hotel caved in, people were crushed and we couldn't get them out. Some of them kept screaming for days. But despite everything, that wasn't what I was frightened about. I was just so terrified that something had happened to you. That the roof had come down on you while you slept. I felt so alone, Adrien. I started looking for something, anything, to cling to of my life before. I mean . . . of *before* before. I wanted to believe you were alive, and I wanted to believe you'd come looking for me, and that when you found me you'd be . . . you'd be fixed. But, as it turned out, I couldn't believe that. That was too difficult to believe in. So I looked for something else.'

'And you found Roland.'

She hung her head.

'Michelle, listen . . . you don't owe me anything.'

'I do,' she whispered. 'I made promises to you. To love and to cherish, have and to hold. I did my best to keep them, Adrien, for as long as I could. But you made it so hard for me.'

He conceded that with a nod. 'Does . . . does Roland . . . does he look after you alright?'

'Oh, sure. Of course.'

'Good,' muttered Adrien, 'good.'

Michelle dried her eyes, but he knew her make-the-best-of-it voice when he heard it. 'He's always *looked after* me. And he's really imposed himself on this place. Some stuff here is already just like it was before the trees came. He's, you know, preparing us for winter, and doing all the other things that are necessary. People trust him, put faith in him.'

'Good. That's . . . good.'

'Stop saying that.' She drummed her fists against her knees. 'How can you sit there and say that it's good?'

'Because I want you to be happy.'

'And are you so damned certain I could never be happy with you that you'd walk all the way here from England, just to tell me that it's *good* that I'm with Roland? Aren't you even going to fight for what we had?'

'Are you?' he asked meekly.

'What do you think this is? What do you think I'm doing right now?'

'You said it was over between us. That it had been before the trees came.'

362

'It *is*! I just don't want it to have all been worth nothing.'

Adrien didn't know what to say.

'What was it like,' asked Michelle, almost in a whisper, 'when the trees hit our house?'

This, at least, he knew how to tell her. 'Messy. Our bedroom door got blocked entirely. I had to climb out of the window. You remember how I used to lie in bed so many nights, trying to figure out how many sheets I'd need to tie to make a rope?'

She nodded. 'I remember.'

'I'm afraid the garden was ruined. And . . . and Mrs Howell, well, she didn't make it. And about the only thing that survived was my dad's old grandfather clock that you couldn't stand.'

She gave a short gasp of laughter. 'I hated that thing.'

'Well it's still there. Still chiming. Unless it's been stolen.'

'By a thief with very poor taste,' she said with half a smile.

Adrien smiled too. 'You couldn't break that thing if you hit it with a sledgehammer.'

They were both silent for a minute.

'I can hardly believe that you're sitting here next to me,' said Michelle. 'And all of this has happened around us. So *much* has happened, but I suppose you and I are in the same place we were when we left things.'

Adrien looked down at the space between his feet. There was a knot in the timber there, a dark oval shape, and he rubbed his shoulder as he looked at it, for upon seeing it an ache had begun to pain him in the bone. He thought of dead branches dropped from the trunks that had borne them, and the year-on-year thickening of bark as it grew over the lumps they'd left behind.

'Things have changed,' he said. 'Maybe just not in the way that either of us would have hoped.'

Michelle wiped her eyes.

He ran a hand back through what remained of his hair. 'Michelle, I . . . I took and took from you, I know. I owe you so much more than I can ever offer back.'

'It was given. All of it was. It never had a price.'

He pursed his lips. Stared at the knot in the timber.

Michelle took a deep breath and held it in for a moment, then nodded and exhaled and said, 'I don't think I love you any more, either. I don't think either of us loves the other. But I still wish you could be happy.'

All of a sudden Adrien longed with all his heart for those honeymoon days on the Côte de Granit Rose, or their earliest weeks when he'd lied to her night after night about art. Things had seemed more open, then. There had been time in their future, and he supposed he had expected time to smooth over the cracks in himself. Now he felt a kind of postponed grief, as if he had heard certain news of the demise of some long-lost friend, the hope for whom had slowly dwindled over the years.

'I suppose,' said Michelle, after a pause, 'I still just can't understand why, if it wasn't to save our marriage, you came all this way.'

'I think I was made to,' said Adrien, although he knew that wouldn't satisfy her. He had never been able to explain that he was not like her or Roland. He could not just decide on a thing and impose it. Life imposed itself on him, and he did what he could to accept it. And so he had come here.

'By who?' Michelle asked. 'Those people outside?'

He would have done his best to answer, had he not just then seen the wolf spider once again, crouched on the floor not far from Michelle's feet. It was facing the two of them, watching them. The world looked different, Adrien knew, when you had eight eyes on the top of your head. He shivered and touched his scalp, finding for once his thinning hair and bald spot reassuring.

'There's something you haven't told me, isn't there?' Michelle asked. 'Something on your mind.'

He waved a hand dismissively. 'Now really isn't the time to go into it.'

'It is. It's important. I can see that.'

For a moment he thought about blurting it all out, the story of the whisperers and the throne tree and Gweneth on the beach and the man in the pharmacy and the creature that had spun his mind full of things he kept remembering.

'Something for another day,' he said.

Michelle stood up. 'I don't know whether there's going to be another day for us.'

Adrien stood up too. 'Is . . . is this it, then?'

She shrugged. 'Maybe.'

'So how . . . how do we end it?'

Her voice was fraying at the edges. 'We try to remember the best bits,' she said. Then she wiped her eyes and departed the hall in a stumbling hurry.

Adrien opened his mouth to call after her, but no sound would come. He heard Michelle gasp for breath as she exited the room, as if she had just pulled herself clear of a freezing lake. For a few long minutes he remained as motionless as the wolf spider still crouched on the floor. Then he took a step and the spider rippled away. He drifted towards the exit his wife had taken, and his fingers brushed against the doorframe as he took it. Adrien wished there was something, anything, he could do to serve Michelle better than this. He felt like he had stolen a chunk of her life, one of the best parts of it, and tossed it to the dogs.

He stepped outside into the drab open space of the valley, and saw his friends and fellow travellers waiting for him just ahead. Hiroko had her fox on her shoulder, nuzzling her hair. Seb had filled out since leaving his home in England, and his new nose made him seem years older. Hannah looked exhausted by guilt and sleeplessness but was, just like the teenagers, still full of concern for Adrien.

His steps dragged and it seemed to take him an age to cross the mud to where his friends stood. He wondered how much longer it would take him to complete that simple favour his wife (his ex-wife, he now supposed) had asked of him. Work out what you really want from life.

A lowing creak came from the distant forest, and Adrien paused and looked up at the trees atop the valley's slopes. The sound could have been a braying stag, or that of falling timber, but he suspected it was nothing so ordinary. A flock of crows took nervous flight from out of the canopy, and were a black scatter rising through a murky sky.

He had a feeling that the woods had not yet finished with him.

6

Forest Law

Hannah knew things had not gone well when she and the teenagers watched Michelle leave the building, crying and alone. Michelle looked in their direction for a moment as she departed, and Hannah's heart went out to her. She had not expected to like Adrien's wife, for in all of his anecdotes she had sounded too beautiful and strong, too perfect to be somebody to care about. But here she was looking as lost as Hannah herself had done on the slopes above Zach's lodge.

After Michelle had hurried away, Hannah braced herself and waited for Adrien. She resolved that she would take him away from this lifeless valley as soon as possible. She would lead him miles and miles from Leonard, and there gladly do whatever it took to support him in moving on with his life.

When Adrien finally stepped out of the building, he looked as if he hadn't slept in months. He dragged himself the short distance to where they stood, pausing once to glance towards the woods, then looked so unbalanced that Hannah darted forward and grabbed him. He stood like that for a while, eyes on the dirt, before he spoke.

'I suppose you can tell how that ended,' he said.

After another silence, Hiroko was the first to respond. 'What a bitch.'

Adrien frowned. 'No, Hiroko. Please don't call her that. I don't think things could have turned out any other way.'

'But what did she say to you?' asked Seb. 'Is she really with Roland?'

'Yes . . .'

Hannah shook her head. 'That bastard Leonard must have known all along.'

'She isn't happy, though,' said Adrien, rubbing his eyes. 'Things certainly aren't perfect.'

'So what now?' asked Seb, sounding almost as defeated as Adrien. 'Is this really what we've come all this way for?'

They all waited for Adrien's response, but he didn't look up from the floor. In the mud there were bits of trampled litter. There was a ring pull. There were flattened cardboard boxes that might have been laid as a path before the dirt had subsumed them.

'She isn't happy,' said Adrien again.

'If she's chosen Roland,' said Hiroko, 'then her happiness is none of your concern.'

'But I owe her . . .'

Hiroko folded her arms. 'Owe her what?'

'*Happiness*. I'm the reason she doesn't have it. I want to be the reason she gets it back. And that's why . . . I'm going to stay here until I've figured it out.'

Hannah sighed, and thought of Leonard and his Alsatian patrolling the valley.

'Is it too early,' began Adrien, 'to ask what you three plan to do?'

Hannah looked at Seb and Hiroko, and they both nodded.

'Stay with you,' said Hannah, 'until you've done whatever it is you need to do.'

Hannah had to wait in a kind of queue to speak to Roland. When finally she received her audience, he informed her with a great show of magnanimity that she, Adrien, Hiroko and Seb were permitted to remain in the valley for as long or as short a time as they desired. They would be entitled to a share of what he called the place's luxuries, so long as they earned them by working each day for the good of the community, and so long as Adrien did not harass Michelle.

'This place is big enough for two people to avoid one another,' smiled Roland. 'So make sure he doesn't step on our toes.'

To such an end, the four of them were shown to a corner of a timber shelter on the edge of the settlement. There they were told they could sleep, along with seven or eight strangers, and were offered bedding made out of curtains, and a share of the broth being stewed in a huge tin pot over one of that night's campfires. The morning came grey as a gull, and they were given another bowl of the evening's broth for their breakfast, on the cold surface of which a thick skin had congealed. Then it was time to repay these luxuries with work.

It had become natural for the teenagers to go out hunting, but Hannah had no desire to forage. In the cold first light she'd seen Leonard striding off towards the woods, his rifle over his shoulder and his Alsatian skulking at his heels. She had turned away and hoped some wolf or bear would get him, for that would be his comeuppance in any just world.

Foraging would have been thankless work, regardless. The wood-fringe had been so scorched and trampled by lumberjack teams that no good food would be found growing there. Hannah would rather take on some other job, be it building the newest shelters, joining the kitchen tent's skivvies, salvaging on the scrapheap, or (and this was what she decided to do) helping with the livestock.

It transpired that Michelle was the one in charge of that duty, and Hannah found her gathering eggs from the chicken coop. 'Hey,' she hailed her over the fence, 'do you need any help in there?'

Michelle turned and looked up at her with red cheeks and her hair tangled. For an unguarded moment she looked suspicious, even jealous, then she stood up straight and smiled politely. 'Hello,' she said, 'I suppose I could always use another pair of hands.'

The coop stood in the corner of a large enclosure marked out by a fence. If it had ever had grass in it, none grew now. On the far side of the field, the five sorry cattle rubbed themselves against the fence. Behind them in the mud, eight hens and a cockerel squawked and strutted about in proud contrast. The cockerel was tall with resplendent plumage, and the hens golden-feathered with bright orange beaks.

'Where do you find feed for the chickens?' asked Hannah, climbing over the fence.

'We don't. We don't need it. Just look at the soil.'

The enclosure was a rectangle of mud, varied only by the pats of the cows and the dust baths the chickens had rolled in the drier places. But when Hannah looked for just a moment longer at the dirt, she found it to be crawling with movement. Worm after worm, squirming to the surface, and the hens happily pecking them up as they came, clucking with pleasure as they shook them down their beaks.

'I don't think they could go hungry if they tried,' said Michelle, putting her hands on her hips. 'These must be the most carnivorous chickens in all of Ireland.'

Hannah didn't mention how unfair she thought that was. Along with the worms she could see millipedes, beetles and crawling lice, but chickens needed more than just meat to stay healthy. 'Are you giving them any grit for their stomachs? You can even feed them their own egg shells, if you crush them.'

'Really? I'd have never thought of that.'

'A long time ago, I used to help keep some chickens. And cows, in fact.'

That had been at Handel's Wood, where they'd had more poultry but fewer cattle, and goats and a grand old pig called Ringo.

'That's going to be useful here, then,' said Michelle, although she still sounded wary.

Hannah thought it best to tackle the elephant in the field. 'Is it too weird? That I'm friends with Adrien, and . . . and . . . I mean, I could go and do some other sort of work.'

Michelle shook her head. 'Sorry, Hannah. It is Hannah, isn't it? I'm just being oversensitive. When I saw that you'd come all this way with Adrien, I thought that the two of you must be . . . must be . . . but he assures me you're not. It's just still a bit overwhelming that he's come here at all. Especially now that he's sulking.'

Hannah frowned. 'I don't think he's sulking. Believe me, I do know what it's like when he does.'

370

Michelle pointed across the valley. 'Look up there.'

On the opposite slope, made small by the distance, Adrien sat facing the woods. 'He was supposed to be helping in the kitchen tent this morning,' said Michelle, 'but apparently he just wandered off and plonked himself down on that stump. Roland isn't going to take it kindly. There's work to be done, and no time for sitting around and moping.'

'I'll talk to him,' said Hannah, 'but I don't think he's moping, not this time. He's been having . . . strange episodes, lately.'

Michelle smiled sadly. 'He's always had strange episodes. But maybe I am being hard . . . I don't really know whether I want to see him again.'

Hannah wondered if she should cross the valley and try to comfort Adrien. 'He's got a lot on his mind,' she said, deciding against it. 'I think he needs some time to work things out.'

Michelle sighed. 'That's what I told him. Over a year ago.' She gestured to the chickens loping around in the dirt. 'I always wanted to keep some of these, I thought it would be wonderful to have fresh eggs sometimes in the mornings. I'm sure you can guess what Adrien thought of that.' She put on a grumbling voice that was a perfect impression of her husband. '*They'll wake me up at some godawful hour. And even if I learn to like them, then they'll have put me off my roast dinner!*'

Hannah laughed. 'It's probably true that a chicken would get the better of him. He does have a habit of making himself inferior to everything.'

Michelle laughed too, then looked sad again and folded her arms. 'Sorry,' she said. 'I keep going up and down.'

'That's understandable.'

Michelle nodded. 'What was it like? Coming all this way with him. Did you find a way to put up with those episodes of his?'

'He did infuriate me at times, I can't deny it. But other times just having him there was a support. I always knew he cared, that he wanted to help, even if he struggled over how to express it. Some . . . bad things happened to me along the way. I needed that help. There was . . . one thing, something I did, that other people might have shunned me for. But Adrien didn't, and he gave me something new to head for.'

Hannah watched Michelle's reaction closely, wondering how she might respond should she tell her about the gunman. But she felt as if Michelle was owed honesty, and a chance to make sense of her husband's actions, no matter what she might think about Hannah afterwards.

'What was the bad thing?' asked Michelle. 'What did he help with?'

Hannah took a deep breath. 'To begin with, Seb and I were only heading to my brother's house. We never intended to come all this way. But, when we got there . . . my brother had been shot.'

'Oh. Oh, I'm so sorry to hear that. Was he . . . dead?'

Hannah nodded briskly. 'Yes. And so . . . and so . . . I killed the man who did it.'

At first the words seemed to fly past Michelle's ears. She looked puzzled, as if she had misheard them. Then she became serious. 'Tell me what happened.'

'He ambushed Adrien in the woods near my brother's house. Hiroko caught him and tied him up inside. I was all over the place. I didn't want any of it to be happening. And he was taunting us . . . saying all kinds of stuff, none of which showed a drop of humanity inside. I went for a walk.' Hannah took another deep breath. 'Saw some things in the forest. Got angry. Stormed back to the lodge. Took up his gun. Then . . . and then . . . I don't know what I would have done if I'd been thinking straight. Maybe I would have just done it anyway. Maybe I wouldn't have, if he hadn't told me that I didn't have it in me.'

Michelle pursed her lips. She was shifting her weight ever so slightly from foot to foot. 'Jesus,' she said, after a minute. 'That's . . . big.'

'There's a reason I'm telling you this,' said Hannah hurriedly. 'Believe me, I don't enjoy talking about it. Adrien was probably already planning to head home after that, but because of what happened, I needed some sort of direction. And so he kept pretending he was brave enough to come here, for my sake. To give me some sort of purpose.'

'Me?' asked Michelle. 'He gave you *me* as your purpose?'

'I suppose you could put it like that. Yes.' Hannah chewed her lip.

'You were brave, to tell me all that stuff,' said Michelle eventually. 'It can't be easy, and you have my condolences for what happened to your brother. I'm sorry I didn't say so right away, but it's hard to process everything right now. I think . . . I think I can trust you. Adrien obviously does.'

'That's kind of you to say.'

'Come on,' said Michelle, turning away. 'We have to fill the troughs up.'

They topped up, using rainwater collected in buckets, the animals' troughs. Then they had to go up to the forest to gather foliage for the cows to eat. With nothing but mud in their field, they needed sacks of leaves and grasses brought down to them to chew on. It seemed to Hannah a remarkably inefficient way of doing things. 'Why don't you just bring them up here to the woods and let them graze?'

'To tell you the truth,' said Michelle, 'no one here knows very much about keeping cattle. So Roland is worried they'll escape. Wouldn't you, if you were faced with a choice between a square of mud and all the leaves you'd ever wanted?'

Yes, thought Hannah, *if I didn't have a friend here who needed my help*. She smiled, and tried to sound as friendly as possible. She didn't want Michelle to think her too pushy. 'With all due respect to Roland . . . the problem is that the cows can see the trees from where they're standing. They're pining for them. If they had bigger brains they'd realise that they're strong enough to smash the fence down and escape, but they're not that bright. They'll settle for rubbing their bodies against it all day long.'

'I know . . . I know, it's sad to see. But we still do our best for them. Even if gathering the leaves ourselves isn't exactly labour-efficient. The cows are well looked after, I promise.'

'I've no doubt about it. I wasn't criticising you for it. I just meant that they're weakening the fence.'

'Well, if they weaken it too much we'll repair it.'

'They only have to weaken it a little. I can see places where they already have.'

'But you just said that they're not bright enough to smash it down.'

'They're not. I'm talking about the chickens.'

Michelle frowned. 'I don't follow you . . .'

'*I* can smell those chickens from here. There will be things with better noses than mine who come here at night, and they'll be checking every fencepost for a way in. They know when something's weak enough to take advantage, believe me.'

Michelle looked exasperated. 'Why does everything always have to want to eat something else? Okay, I'll talk to Roland about it. But I doubt he'll give it much thought. He's sort of . . . stopped looking at the little details, of late. He'll probably insist that we keep the cows in the field all day just to spite me.'

Hannah held her tongue after that. She followed Michelle's direction, and helped to gather leaves and shrubs the cows could eat. They had to go some way into the forest to find them, for where the trees met the valley their bark was hard as elephant hide, and what leaves they still possessed drooped dankly for the ground. Even the earth was ripped open there, the dead roots on show in the silt.

'Earlier,' began Michelle, once they had found some healthier growth, 'when you were telling me all that stuff about your brother . . . I wanted to tell you that I know nothing's ever simple. There's been . . . killing here, too.'

Hannah's fingers paused, gripping tight the twigs she had been pulling.

'You've met our friend Leonard,' said Michelle.

A branch cracked behind them and Hannah scanned the woods in its direction. There was nothing to see. Leonard and his dog had headed in the other direction that morning.

'When the trees came,' Michelle continued, 'those of us who stayed here were in two minds about what to do. Roland wasn't just put in charge instantly. There was another man, a big man called David, and he had his own ideas about how we should react. He'd been awake to see it happen, and I think it had unsettled him on some fundamental level. He said that what had happened was a sort of apocalypse, and that we were in a kind of hell now, and what we did would come back to bless or to haunt us. He was a very persuasive speaker. Lots of people believed him.'

'Not you, by the sound of it.'

'I threw my lot in with Roland, of course. David was making people hysterical, and Roland was the only one to challenge him. On that first morning, Roland found a fire axe in the hotel's ruins and used it to cut a tree down. He told David that, if the forest was so godlike, it could come right now and punish him. Nothing happened, if you don't count David's subsequent tantrum, but it was an important marker. It gave people someone else to look up to. Anyway . . . like I said, I think David had become unhinged somehow. He started saying we needed to appease the forest. I remember . . . I remember coming out of the hotel ruins one day, after salvaging what we could from the kitchen, and David had caught a forest hog. He and his followers had rounded it up and they'd stabbed it horribly with knives and it was bleeding to death and could hardly stand. They weren't even going to eat it, they just dragged it onto a tree stump and slit its throat and left it there as if it were on an altar. Roland told me right after that that we were going to have to deal with David.'

'What happened?' asked Hannah, noting that she had not encountered anyone called David in the valley.

'Well, first of all, more people started showing up. Some hoped there might be supplies to be had, some just stumbled upon us. Both Roland and David invited them to stay, saying we could use their assistance here. Roland wanted everybody he could to help with building and organising. But David's idea was to make us into a kind of congregation. When he started talking about building a church to the forest, that was the final straw for Roland. They had a blazing row in front of everyone.'

'A row I presume Roland won?'

'No. You'd think it, now, but back then people remained divided. David had a knack for touching a nerve. Things became unbearably tense, some people had actual fights, and there were countless heated arguments.'

'So what resolved it? Everyone here seems behind Roland now.'

'Leonard. He arrived on his own one day, along with his dog. He didn't even introduce himself to any of us. We were asking each other, *Does anyone know this guy? I've never seen him before.* Anyway, he arrived, and at first didn't really say anything. He just watched, and people were happy to stay out of his way. Then, when things reached a boiling point, we called a big meeting for everybody to attend. The idea was that we'd thrash out our differences, and choose to build either a community under Roland or a sort of crazy tree cult with David. Perhaps it was naive of us to expect consensus. When Roland suggested, after both he and David had said their piece, that we put the future to a ballot, David said there was no way he could agree to it. Probably he thought he'd lose, but he said something along the lines of voting being part of a system that had failed us. Voting had no authority, that's what he said. Only the forest. And that was when Leonard stood up.'

Hannah shuddered, and remembered the gunman. *You will either decide that you are your own authority or imagine a new one.*

Michelle carried on with the story. 'Leonard told David he was right. There were no authorities now, he said, and none of our old rules. He said the only law was survival and that therefore . . . therefore we would be doing things Roland's way, since it gave us the best chance of riding out the winter. And he said that was the end of the argument, and when he'd finished speaking even David seemed at a loss for words. I'm not even sure he'd ever noticed Leonard before. Eventually he recovered himself and rebutted him in front of everyone, but you could tell he was frightened by the way Leonard had addressed him. Halfway through his response,

Leonard just walked away, as if David had never even been speaking. And then, in the morning, David had gone.'

'He'd just left?'

'That's what we were supposed to assume. I mean, I know Leonard well enough now to be sure that's not what happened, but the official line is that David just packed his bags and vanished without telling anyone.'

Hannah gripped tight the bundle of sticks she had gathered. 'He said there are no policemen. That there are no judges now. But he's made *himself* into a sort of policeman.'

Michelle nodded thoughtfully. 'Who said that? Leonard? That does sound just like the kind of thing he'd say.'

'No . . . no, that was somebody else. But did nobody confront Leonard? Did nobody try to find David?'

'No . . . You see, after that, Roland was in charge. Things started to get done. It was hard work, but it wasn't long before people felt more secure, felt their chances were getting better. Those who'd followed David just sort of forgot about him. They began to see, I think, how Roland's plan could work out for all of us.'

'Someone should have confronted him,' murmured Hannah. 'He might do the same again.'

'You're right, of course,' Michelle admitted. 'But people are scared, and with good reason. There are children and old people here. Families. And Leonard has Roland's ear. In fact, if I'm honest with you, Hannah . . . Roland's always risen to the top, in everything he's done, but this time it's been different. Having Leonard at his side has made him . . . well, it's difficult to place my finger on it.' She swallowed. She looked very small, Hannah thought, beneath all those trees. 'Put it this way, now sometimes I don't trust him. Now sometimes I'm frightened. Now sometimes I wish I had somewhere else to be, other than in this damned valley.'

7

Fox

At night, in the valley, several fires were always kept burning. Chief among these was a bonfire in the middle of the settlement, provided for warmth and for cooking over. Smaller fires burned at four points around the perimeter, both to lend light and to act as sentry posts against anything coming out of the forest. People took it in turns to staff them, and stacks of wooden torches were stored at each, in case the lookouts needed to venture away from the flames.

One such sentry was just beginning to nod off, beside the eastern campfire, when Hiroko appeared out of the darkness. The firelight lit up her eyes like a cat's. 'I'm here for a torch,' she announced, then gave the sentry her best hungry smile.

'B–but,' said the sentry, 'they're not to be wasted.'

'Who says I'm going to waste it?'

'They're for emergencies only. In case we need to find our way.'

'Not this one,' she said, and skipped past to take it. She scooped its brand through the flames and it caught at once. The sentry didn't oppose her, and she couldn't stop giggling when she returned to Seb with the torch blazing in her hand.

'Idiots wouldn't be able to defend this place if they tried,' she told him. 'Now come with me.'

'Where are we going?'

'Anywhere,' she shrugged. 'I just can't bear to sit around in the mud.'

Soon they had found their way into the settlement's scrap yard. The sputtering light of the torch played over the junk mounds as if searching them, illuminating the hob of a gas cooker, the hubcap of a car, a half of satellite dish, a useless extension cable. Everything it lit it shadowed away again quickly, and all the time it crackled and spat as if disgusted with what it showed.

'What a lot of stuff we used to have,' muttered Seb, looking around him. 'And now it's all landfill.'

'There's got to be something worth finding, in one of these piles.'

A rumbling came from some way off in the darkness, and for a moment they both looked up. It was just a part of the hotel crumbling in, and when a second rumble came they ignored it. They had been getting used to that sound.

'I think I see something,' said Hiroko, looking back at the scrap. She thrust the torch towards him. 'Hold this.'

She danced up the side of the biggest scrapheap, lifted a broken chair and pulled something out from beneath. When she skidded back down, she was holding an intact laptop.

Seb's face altered as she gave it to him, and flickers of the boy he had been not so long ago came and went like the light of the flame. He had changed more than mere dirt and a broken nose accounted for. Handing her back the torch, he sat down cross-legged and opened the laptop on the ground before him. He touched the smooth plastic of the screen as if it were some priceless antiquity.

Instead of pressing the power button at once, he reached beneath his collar. From there he retrieved his memory stick, on its string, and plugged it into the appropriate socket. Hiroko bit her lip, finding to her surprise that she was excited. She wanted to at last be introduced to this website into which he'd invested so much of his youth: his online scrapbook and his webpage letters to his loved ones.

'Moment of truth,' he said, and pressed the power button.

Nothing happened. The laptop was dead.

'Oh,' said Hiroko, slouching. 'Damn. It was worth a try, Seb. I'm sorry.'

He shook his head. 'Don't be.' He stood up holding the laptop, with the memory stick still attached to it. Then he flung it onto the scrapheap. Hiroko's arm trailed after it on instinct, but it flew off like a discus and clattered against the other pieces of the demolished world.

'Seb! Your memory stick . . .'

'Don't worry. I should have done that ages ago. I should have dropped it into the sea. It's served its purpose, now.'

Hiroko stepped closer to him. 'That can't have been easy.'

'It's got no future. Best to let it go and keep sight of what does.'

She reached out and stroked a finger over the bridge of his nose. 'Which is?'

He grinned. 'Us, I hope. And speaking of the future, I've been thinking about what to do next. Once we're done in this valley, I mean. Actually, I've been thinking about it for some time, I just didn't want to jump in and suggest it before I'd had a chance to mull it over.' He licked his lips. 'So . . . here goes . . . Hiroko, what would you say if I suggested—'

'Wait,' she snapped, turning away with her nose twitching.

Seb deflated. 'What is it?'

Hiroko reached up and felt her empty hood. She patted her shoulder and found nothing there. 'Where's Yasuo?' She turned on the spot and swept the torch after shadows. 'Yasuo?' she called, and the name was swallowed by the night air. 'Where are you, Yasuo?'

Seb, too, became concerned. 'He was with us, wasn't he, when we started looking through the scrapheap?'

'I'm not sure. I think so. He's normally right here.'

There was no sign of him, so she tried to think when she'd last seen the little fox. She thought she'd heard him purring in her hood not a minute before, yet the harder she tried to remember the more blurred was the result. He was snuggled in her hood in so many of her memories that she couldn't be sure whether any given one had happened a minute ago, a day or a week.

She cupped a hand to her mouth. 'Yasuo!'

No answer.

They hurried back along the route they had walked, flashing the flaming torch at the scrap mounds. The orange light found picture frames and wheels without tyres, lampstands and bookshelves and a pot of paint, but no fox.

'Yasuo!' they both yelled. Hiroko kept expecting him to streak out of the shadows, to materialise from the firelight as he had on that first night when he'd introduced himself to them. There was only the stillness of the dark.

'Yasuo!' she cried, as they came out of the scrapheap and back into the settlement proper. She could not believe she had lost him.

From somewhere nearby, Leonard's Alsatian barked.

'Oh shit!' cursed Hiroko, spurring towards it. Seb broke into a run behind her, shouting the fox's name. Snakes of reflected fire shimmered through the mud, but all Hiroko could think of was the dog. It had cast hungry eyes at Yasuo ever since they'd met it, and Leonard didn't bother to leash it at night. Had Yasuo slipped away alone, the Alsatian could easily have followed up on its instincts.

'Yasuo?' she screamed. '*Please!*'

Somebody stepped irate out of their shelter and hissed at them to keep the noise down.

'Yasuo?' shouted Seb, at the top of his voice.

On Hiroko rushed, almost tripping on a tree stump. She'd grown used to the way they covered the valley, but in the streaming light of her torch they were like mutilated remains.

'Yasuo! Yasuo!'

'What's going on, kids?' called Roland gruffly, coming out of his hut beside the big wooden hall. 'People are trying to get some sleep.'

'Yasuo!' was all she could yell, hurtling onwards.

'Hiroko?' asked Adrien, appearing with Hannah alongside.

She dashed on past them all. 'Yasuo!'

Then, up ahead, somebody shouted something else.

It was not the name of the fox, but a voice raised in alarm. It came from the livestock enclosure, and something skittered through

Hiroko's heart when she heard it. She had a sudden vivid recollection of her grandmother standing outside her duck house, shaking in outrage.

At once she broke into a final sprint, her torch guttering out as she ran. She cast it aside and hurdled the enclosure's fence as soon as she reached it, heading for the chicken coop, around which five or six other people had already gathered with a torch of their own. Its light painted their shocked expressions red. They had lifted the roof of the coop and were looking in at its contents.

Hiroko skidded to a halt a few yards from them, but Seb overtook her and saw what they were seeing.

'Oh no,' Hiroko whispered, drawing closer almost at a tiptoe. 'No no no . . .'

Seb tried to make her turn back. 'You don't want to see this.'

She pushed him aside.

All of the chickens' heads were missing, and blood had sprayed the coop's walls as if it were paint spun from a bucket. The proud cockerel's neck of fine feathers was topped now by a festival of sticky red.

Roland was the first of those who'd followed them to catch up. 'What's going on?' he asked, and strode into the huddle around the coop. He stared for a long minute at the sight, then turned from it furious with dismay. 'Who the hell did this?'

'It had to be a fox,' said one of those gathered. 'This is what foxes do.'

Hiroko took a step backwards, into the shadows. It wasn't far enough for Roland's searching eyes to miss her. When he came towards her, she thought for a moment he was going to punch her.

'It wasn't Yasuo,' she said, before he had a chance to speak.

'You can prove that, can you?'

'It must have been some other fox.'

Roland turned to Seb. 'Can you vouch for that?'

Seb nodded. 'Yes. Yes, Yasuo was with us all night.'

'And what about just now? Is that why you woke us all up by yelling like you'd lost him?'

At first, neither Hiroko nor Seb could say a word. Adrien and Hannah had by now arrived, and Michelle and a half-dozen others, but they were all stricken spectators. Then Seb came up with something. 'He's not big enough.'

'Exactly,' said Hiroko, seizing upon it because it was all they had. 'He's too young to do something like this. Foxes don't learn to kill until they're older, and Yasuo is just a baby.'

Roland opened his mouth to disagree, but at that moment a little yip cut the air. Hiroko's heart froze, but it was already too late.

Yasuo crept out from under the chicken coop. Some of those gathered nearby cried out and backed off, as if he had the power to behead them too. He trotted over to Hiroko and purred contentedly, just like he always did when he wanted picking up. Even in the flickering light, she could see that his snout was a brighter red than usual, and something as thin and rubbery as an elastic band was caught on his teeth.

'Oh, Yasuo,' she said, crouching to huddle him up. He licked her nose when she lifted him, and his tongue smelled of gore.

She was aware that everyone was looking at her, but she refused to look back. She deliberately turned her back on them.

'You're not taking him anywhere,' said Roland.

She began to walk away from them. They were going to try to stop her, of course, but she knew she was faster and smarter than them.

'Come back here right now,' growled Roland.

All she had to do was get over the enclosure's fence, and then she could flee into the woods. She almost smiled at her own capability. Yasuo yawned and snuggled up against her collarbone and she held him there tight. She would run into the forest and live with her fox there, and Seb could come and visit and the others could find her when they were done in this place.

'Stop her,' said Roland, and his footsteps became heavier.

She broke into an instant run, glancing back over her shoulder to see Roland and two strangers doing the same. Yet no sooner was Roland in motion than Seb had stuck out a leg and tripped him.

He fell with a shout into the mud, and his lackeys hesitated before continuing their pursuit. Hiroko cackled with relief, for that had been all the extra time she would need to get away and over the fence. She was already too far ahead for them to catch her, racing across the field towards the valley's slope. She would scramble over the fence in seconds and be rid of them. Then she would be free.

Leonard was leaning on the fence when she reached it. His pose was a bored one, as if she were late for an appointment. His Alsatian stood behind him, the discs of its eyes reflecting her pursuers' torchlight.

Hiroko slowed down as best she could, but the mud skidded out beneath her and she fell to her hands and knees. Yasuo tumbled from her arms with a yelp, but she snatched him back up even as she regained her footing. Leonard straightened, and the approaching light glittered off the frames of his glasses. Then Hiroko spun around and found herself hemmed in by Roland and the others, although among them were Adrien and Hannah and Michelle.

'Stop!' yelled Seb, dashing between Roland and Hiroko. 'Cool off, everyone.'

'Whyever should we be *cool*?' asked Roland, wiping grime off his lips. 'You kids are a law unto yourselves.'

'This isn't Yasuo's fault,' objected Hannah, barging forward. 'It's in his nature.'

'She's right,' said Michelle, and Hiroko looked to her with sudden gratitude. 'Hannah warned us that the cows were weakening the fence.'

'I don't give a damn about what's in his nature,' snorted Roland, and pointed at Yasuo. 'Give him to me, girl.'

Hiroko held Yasuo all the tighter, looking from left to right for another way out. She could hear a faint growl in the Alsatian's throat.

Then, without any warning, Seb threw himself at the person holding the torch. He grabbed hold of it, wrenched it free and buried its fire in the mud. At once everything turned black.

Hiroko ran. Sprinting away to her right, absolutely blind and hoping she didn't collide with the fence in that direction, once she reached it. She raced as fast as she'd ever done, with Yasuo whimpering in her ear.

She collided with something and it floored her. She gasped for the air it had knocked out of her lungs, then regained her urgency and scrabbled back to her feet. When she picked Yasuo up once more he was trembling, perhaps sensing his predicament through the panic of his mistress.

Hiroko did all she could to steady both herself and the fox. But what she had collided with was not the fence.

'Hand it over,' said Leonard, his voice disembodied by the dark. He sounded casual, formal even, but of course he knew that Hiroko would do no such thing.

She turned to run again, but the blow came so fast to her back that it felt as if her shoulder blades had imploded. She fell and her mouth filled deep with mud. When she clambered back to her feet, retching cold soil, someone was bringing another torch.

'Can you see this?' asked Leonard, holding Yasuo up by the tail. The approaching light was still weak, but Yasuo writhed in such distress that it was impossible to miss.

Hiroko lunged for him but, before she could even raise her fists, Leonard dropped Yasuo.

The Alsatian's jaws clamped around the little fox before he hit the ground. The dog shook its head as it savaged him, its throat rumbling with a happy bloodlust. By the time it cast Yasuo aside, his body was like a thing unzipped, and the teeth of the zip were the pieces of his vertebrae. His neck was twisted so far round that his chest was like his back, and he stared at the night sky with dull eyes.

Hiroko dropped to her knees, but it felt like she fell much further. She clawed her way over to where Yasuo lay and lifted him up without blinking. The blood trickled warmly over her fingers and into the cuffs of her hoodie. The light was growing brighter, and there were voices raised behind her in accusation and argument, but she had no ears for them. She ran her forefinger down the length of Yasuo's face, and the end of his nose was still moist, as was the tongue in his mouth. She held her finger between his teeth and willed him to bite them, to leave another set of pinprick scars in her skin. He did not.

She laid his sorry remains gently on her lap, and his blood seeped into her jeans. Then her anger began to rise up, pulled from the depths of her as a tree pulls up water. She broke, and grabbed handfuls of her hair and pulled it as hard as she could until it made her scream. At some point Seb knelt at her side to restrain her, but everything felt far away. 'What have you done to me?' she choked at him, but he didn't seem to hear.

The Alsatian might just as well have bitten her heart in two. She missed her *sobo* and her *sofu* and she missed Carter. She even missed Saori. She missed the Tokyo apartment, the puppy wrestling its rubber toys on the carpet, and she screamed, 'Yasuo!' at the top of her voice. She missed her poor young mother, dead as many days as she herself had been alive. And most of all she missed her father.

She pushed Seb away from her and rose to her feet, pulling out her skinning knife and grasping its hilt in her fist.

Leonard waited, without his guard up. Maybe he wanted what was coming.

Hiroko launched at him, quick as a spark, but before she knew it she had been yanked back hard. Her knife flew to the ground with a slap. Seb, Hannah and Adrien were struggling to contain her.

'Hiroko!' shouted Seb. 'You can't just stab him!'

She punched one of them, she didn't know who, then elbowed another in the gut. Still they kept her back, while Leonard only watched without stirring. Even though he had not moved a muscle, he had his own blade out now, his knife as long as a machete. Perhaps he'd had it drawn all along.

With a sneer, he turned away and disappeared into the night. The Alsatian vanished after him.

Hiroko stopped fighting. She cried through clenched teeth, and she was just a little girl, and her daddy Inoue Naoki was holding her just so, after a wasp sting or a deep gash from a briar or even just a day of being picked on at school. '*Gomenasai!*' she sobbed, which meant *I'm sorry* in Nihongo. 'I'm sorry, I'm sorry! I was angry with you. Of course we couldn't have the forest house! Of course!'

'Hiroko,' Seb was saying worriedly. 'Hiroko . . .'

'*Gomenasai! Gomenasai!*' She looked up with a gasp and the night was underwater with tears. Seb and the others were huddling close around her and their arms were the only things keeping her upright. Leonard was gone, but what did that matter? Yasuo was gone too.

8

The Grave

After the events of the night, Hannah felt sicker than ever at the sight of Leonard. Come breakfast he lazed outside the settlement's makeshift kitchen, taking his time over a bowl of the gruel they served there. She couldn't eat that stuff (it was full of dead birds and rabbits, boiled until the meat floated off the bones), and had finished every supply that Seb had brought her, so she wasted no time in hiking up to the woods. So long as Leonard remained in the valley, foraging again felt like a wholesome pursuit. Before she entered the forest, she took one last look down the slope. The wind crashed about as it pleased, and even as she watched there came a groan from the hotel as another piece of roof caved in. A chimney dropped some twenty metres and exploded off a branch, showering the ruin in bricks and a weathervane.

She left it all behind her. Once she was beyond the forest's dead borders, the day seemed suddenly more alive. Granted there was no sun, few flowers and not much greenery, but the woods were full of autumn's boggy riches. Everything was tan or umber or meltingly dark, and she found enough edible mushrooms to fill an old carrier bag. Toads watched her from damp ditches, playing their throat music.

She was just breaking off another chanterelle at the stalk when a bray like a cow's stopped her hand. She looked up and saw it chewing on leaves: a calf kirin the size of a roe deer. Its pelt was far blacker than those of the adults she had seen, perhaps to better camouflage it from its predators. Its horn, yet to fully develop, was a fistful of stone still covered in a membrane of skin.

'What are you doing here?' she whispered. 'It isn't safe. He's already shot one far bigger than you.'

It brayed again, then began to wander away, deeper into the forest.

'Go on,' she urged it, 'keep going. Best to get away from here.'

It stomped its foot and gazed back at her along the length of its body.

'Oh,' she said, 'of course. I understand.'

She followed it. They headed north-west, through undulating land. Each orange leaf was a paper-cut fire, burning on the forest floor or adding its flame to the cold inferno in the canopy.

After some fifteen minutes of walking, the kirin came to a sudden halt. Hannah looked around for the reason and at first saw nothing out of the ordinary. Then she realised that a mass of ivy up ahead was not growing on a fallen tree but on a cracked stone wall. Stepping closer, she discovered it was part of a ruined chapel, a place that had been derelict since well before the trees came and was now not much more than three crumbling walls heaped with grass and the creepers. Despite that, someone had made camp between them, not too long ago, and the chewed ribs of some toasted animal lay in the ashes of a fire. More disconcerting, the place smelled of dog. Its excrement lay dried out and untidied in the shadow of the tallest wall.

She spotted the grave just beyond the chapel, and the calf kirin whinnied as she did so. A filthy brown anorak drew her eye to it, its hem flapping up from the soil. The grave it had been unearthed from was too new to have been made for any of the chapel's congregation. It was shallow and raked open by beasts, and Hannah looked away from it at once, even though she had already seen too much. Its ditch had not been dug deep enough to keep its incumbent safe from scavengers, and the animals that had opened it had devoured almost all of the soft matter from inside. The coat was a man's, Hannah would guess, but there was not much else to identify the corpse by. It was probably only a few weeks old, but that was a long time in the forest.

For a while, Hannah stood very still, unsure of what to do. Part of her wanted to dash away as quickly as possible, but another part of her felt like she owed this dead stranger some last token of respect. The kirin snorted, and turned its head to itch its shoulder with its horn. Then, with a nervous shuffle, Hannah dared to look again.

Bangled around the body's wrist bones was a watch. Its leather strap was cut and frayed by tooth marks, but the timepiece itself was unscratched, and it said that it had just turned ten forty-seven in the morning. It was an expensive watch, Hannah reckoned, perhaps the kind given as a gift, and upon seeing it a suspicion began to nag her, based on something Michelle had said. She held her breath as she approached the arm, choosing a stick to be her tool. The kirin began to chomp on the chapel's ivy.

She jiggled the watch loose with the stick. The bones were not well attached, so the task was largely one of stomach. When she had freed it she lifted it up at arm's length.

Engraved on the underside were the words *For David. Happy 50th Birthday.*

9

Forest Law

'What are you doing?' asked Roland, when he found Adrien sitting on a tree stump, halfway up the valley's north slope.

Adrien didn't answer, only buttoned up his jacket against a blustering wind that rolled downhill and made something fall with a crash from the roof of the ruined hotel.

Roland put his hands on his hips. 'You know this isn't the deal, don't you? You don't get to stay here if you don't pull your weight. Even the children do something useful with their days.'

'I did some chores in the kitchen tent,' said Adrien, 'but I couldn't concentrate, so I came up here.'

'Wow. You're really working your fingers to the bone. There aren't career breaks any more, Adrien. It's hard graft here, and that's only fair. While we're on the subject, what was your excuse for this yesterday?'

Adrien looked up at him. Roland's shirt was a fresh primrose, and he was wearing gumboots to protect his trousers from the mud.

'Yesterday you did exactly what you're doing now,' continued Roland. 'You sat on this stump, all day long. I hope you've got a good enough reason.'

Adrien's reason was this: someone had put a crow in the gruel pot. He had just about been coping with the steady slew of rabbits and other birds (and rats, there'd been a brace of rats that morning), all tossed in for the boil, but the crow had been too much. He had closed his eyes and felt the tickle at the back of his throat, that one

391

that came from too much cawing, in the roost or on serrated wing. Merely remembering it had made his lips feel pinched and stretched, hard enough to peck meat off the bone.

That was the reason why he had run up here with his stomach heaving. Thankfully, he had been too hungry to vomit. Roland could withhold his place at the settlement's tables all he wanted, since Adrien had not eaten anything in a day. His guts were aching now with hunger, but for that he was actually grateful. At least it was a human hunger, not a carrion one. Nor was it the hunger of worms, nor of leaves pining for the sunlight, nor the insatiable thirst of roots in the ground.

'I've got a good enough reason,' mumbled Adrien.

'Care to explain it?'

'You might not believe me.'

To his surprise, Roland took a seat on the stump ahead of him. They faced each other for a moment without speaking, then Roland smiled. 'I have a proposition for you.'

'Oh yeah? What's that?'

'You have to understand that it doesn't look good. You, just sitting up here. Nobody should get special treatment.'

'I can't go back to the kitchen, Roland. And I definitely can't chop down trees.'

Roland raised his hands in conciliatory fashion. 'Are you going to let me finish?'

'I'm listening.'

He stood up. 'Walk with me. This is a thing it's best if I show you.'

Adrien shrugged to himself and stood up, too. How much of a trap could a walk be? They set off alongside each other but at a distance. People looked up with respect at Roland, then with intrigue at Adrien, no doubt wondering what a hopeless case like him was doing in the company of their glorious leader.

Roland led him back down the slope, but not towards the scrapheap or the shelters. They headed, instead, towards the ruined hotel that stood apart from the settlement.

'I thought this place was out of bounds,' said Adrien, as they drew closer. 'Bits of it keep falling down.'

'We have to say it's a no-go zone,' soothed Roland, making his way towards a stone entry, an arch atop a run of steps, 'because we don't want the kids to try to play in here. But some parts are more stable than others. Stick close to me and you'll be fine.'

When they reached the archway, the hotel gave a long and ruminative groan, as if a giant foot had just pressed down on all its floorboards. Above the arch the split wood of the door had been lifted like a portcullis, and chained up there by brambles. Through this they entered, and found themselves in a cavernous lobby which might once have been impressive in its own right. Now the trees had risen through the flagstones and superimposed their own idea of grandeur. They were among the biggest Adrien had ever seen, their branches thick as trunks, their twigs thick as branches. They draped themselves with curtain upon curtain of autumn leaves, and among them there was no ceiling to speak of. There was just a nest of winding boughs, interspersed with brick and glass, rising as high as could be seen. When the breeze parted the foliage, it revealed sections of hotel room and corridor tipped on their sides or prised open for a craggy bough to pass through.

Roland led Adrien across the lobby floor, their footsteps ringing briefly off the flagstones. They passed through another doorway gripped by creepers and entered another hall, arched over by an ever-rising vault of orange vegetation. Here and there were the splintered remains of chairs and tables, and gilded ornaments dangled upside down or on their sides among briars. The branches groaned, and a sprinkling of brick dust sifted down between the leaves.

'You told me this place was safe,' said Adrien, craning his neck. The trees groaned again, and he wondered if it was due only to the weight of the architecture.

'It is,' said Roland. 'This part of it, at any rate. This was the hotel's restaurant.' He crouched to find a silver fork beneath the leaf litter. 'See? Before that, it was the banqueting hall for the

393

lord of the manor. Here, you can take that. It can be the first thing you find for us.'

Adrien took the fork and twirled it in his fingers. 'I get it,' he said. 'You want me to try to salvage things.'

Roland nodded. 'But stay in this hall and the lobby. I'd hate it if a chunk of bricks fell down on you.'

'You're a bad liar.'

'Oh please, Adrien, let's be grown up about this. Just because you and I see the world differently, doesn't mean I want you to die.'

All of the banqueting hall's decoration had been either faux medieval or genuine antique, although not much of it had survived the forest's attention intact. Plate mail busts with plumed and antlered helmets had been seized from their plinths and flung aloft, their visors gaping open for sprigs to shoot through. The sunlight fell almost at random through the levels above, waiting for openings blown between the leaves. Sometimes it found blue and ruby shards, remnants of stained glass that had once made the windows colourful.

'None of this is going to be much use,' said Adrien. 'Unless you're planning to go jousting.'

'Very funny. Although if you can rescue any of that stuff, I wouldn't consider it wasted effort. It would be nice to have something to look at that wasn't just huts and mud.'

You already would have, thought Adrien, *if you hadn't chopped it all down.*

Roland sighed and made a sweeping gesture to indicate the hall around them. 'Try to imagine it, Adrien. Sometimes I can't, any more. But this place was so grand before the forest spoiled everything. You really had to be here to believe in it.'

Adrien had visited a fair few overblown stately homes in his time. He reckoned he could imagine the opulence of this one.

'We dined like kings, that night the trees came, we really did. The hotel lavished everything on us. Then, after our evening meal, the staff moved the tables aside and there was dancing.'

Much to the dismay of some deeply buried part of himself (that part that Adrien nominally termed his dignity), he did his

394

best to picture it. The room's ornate tables and chairs would have been cleared aside in a far less unruly fashion than they had been by the trees. Likewise the floor would have been flat, not root-ridged, and the hotel guests would have been able to look across from one wall to the other without some imposter trunk looming in the middle of the dance floor.

'Now I look back on it,' said Roland with a contented sigh, 'I can't think of any better way to have spent my last night in the world we had before. Michelle, of course, was the most beautiful woman there. You should have seen her in her evening dress. Simply stunning. The epitome of beauty.'

Adrien thought of his own final night, spent with his chicken balls and his westerns. 'Why are you telling me this, Roland?'

'She's been rattled by your arrival. She's normally a cool customer, but things have been getting to her since you came. Last night, for example. She didn't react very sensibly to what happened last night.'

Adrien shook his head. 'Last night you made a mistake. That fox meant a lot to Hiroko.'

'Those chickens meant a lot to me. And not just me. I don't expect you to understand, but when you're in a position of authority you have to make tough calls. The people here need to know that I'll protect their interests.' Roland narrowed his eyes. 'What's that, Adrien? Are you *scowling*?'

'I think you went too far with Yasuo.'

'Go on, then, enlighten me. Why was that fox so special? How many eggs would it have laid? And, while you're at it, tell me what kind of system you'd run here. Would you have some sort of anarchy, Adrien?'

Adrien thought about that for a moment. 'I'm not very good at being in charge,' he said.

'Well there you have it.'

'But I wouldn't chop everything down and sit on top of what was left as if I'd made it better. And if somebody already had, then . . . then when I was put in charge I'd make sure that the trees could grow back. I'd fix the soil, if I could, and . . . and I'd protect each new sapling. I'd think long and hard about every last bit of timber I took, just like I'd think long and hard about how we could live *in* the forest, not in place of it.'

'Is that what you were doing on that stump? Thinking long and hard? Was it getting anybody anywhere? *My* priority is our survival.'

'I doubt that. And if it is, then you're going about it all wrong.'

Roland looked flabbergasted. Then, slowly, he began to laugh, and his laugh built into a snorting guffaw that echoed through the hall and made the leaves fall faster from their twigs. Adrien waited it out, for he had expected it. He hardly even listened. His ears were straining towards some other sound which he had just heard, coming from somewhere above him in the leaf-crossed ceiling. It was a whisper, faint and fluctuating.

'Let's forget this . . .' said Roland, dabbing his eyes with his fingers. 'Let's talk about Michelle. Like I said, you coming here has got her all in a flap. I need you to go and tell her that her place is with me.'

'Are you serious?'

'She told me you didn't love her any more.'

'That . . . that was a private conversation.'

'But it's the truth, isn't it?'

Adrien stared at Roland, and the whisper from above him lisped on the edge of hearing. Quite suddenly he could not believe he had used to find this man so intimidating. *Wolves* were intimidating, not this.

'Michelle is a very special woman,' said Roland.

'You think I don't know that?'

'I'm just trying to explain that I want to make her happy.'

'Me too. More than anything.'

'Then set her mind straight, Adrien, for God's sake. Go and talk to her and persuade her that you think I should have her now. And if you do that I can overlook all your shirking and so on, and we can both be adults about it.'

Faint as a tiptoe, the highest branches creaked. Something pattered along the length of one, but when Adrien looked up there were only the leaves in every shade of amber. 'You surprise me,' said Adrien, looking back down at Roland.

Roland took it as a compliment, and preened.

'You're even more ridiculous than I thought. *Have* her? What kind of talk is that?'

Roland gaped at him for a moment, before his gape twisted into a sneer. 'Jesus, Adrien, it was just a turn of phrase. And do you know something? If you want straight talking, I think it's high time that someone offered you a few home truths. And I tell you this for your benefit, not mine. I'm actually worried about you. What you've let yourself become. You're a very bitter man. A closed man.'

'My many failings aren't exactly undocumented.'

'But it's that precise attitude that so riles me. That way you just accept your own failures. Oh, Michelle has told me all about you. Your self-loathing, your stubbornness and rattiness and the way you kept her up all hours by worrying. Your mood swings. The way you abase yourself to pre-empt others from doing so. The meals you spoiled by fixating on the burning candles. The *bed times.*' He shook his head. 'You're a worm of a man, Adrien, wriggling around in the dirt.'

Adrien nodded thoughtfully. 'You're right. I was an appalling husband.'

Roland looked delighted. 'I'm glad I've hit the nail on the head. Michelle can hardly be blamed for deciding enough is enough.'

The whispering above peaked into a hiss. Adrien turned his eyes upwards and there one sat, a whisperer with a brassy yellow body, haired all over with dead, curled leaves. Its mouth was like that of an anglerfish, filling its face with teeth. Above it the trees' leaves were countless, and bright orange fungi grew out of both bark and plaster. The trunks themselves were heavier than Adrien could comprehend, dragging water up from the mineral deeps to quench the thirst in their arching limbs. They all looked so huge that standing beneath them felt like being in a mountain cave, with all those tonnes of natural weight suspended above him. Roland had eyes for none of this.

'Look at you, Roland. Your folded arms. Your smug sneer. How do men like you get put in charge of the world, when you don't know the first thing about it?'

Roland's face darkened. 'I get put in charge because I make the right calls. People can see that.'

'I think you ended up in charge here because, even when the world got destroyed by a forest, you thought you were a match for it.'

'That sounds like a bloody good reason to me. I *will* be a match for it. That's something Adrien Thomas can only ever dream about.'

'I don't think you've ever doubted yourself, have you? Even now, when the woods have made it so easy for you, when you could get lost among the trees at the drop of a hat.'

'You say that as if you think it's a healthy thing. That approach, Adrien, is precisely why you've never got anywhere in life.'

'You're too bloody full of yourself to have room to be scared. While everyone else is frightened and trying to make sense of things, you waltz straight in and seize control. That doesn't make you the one who's best equipped. That just makes you the first bloody loudmouth on the scene. Or perhaps you're genuinely convinced.'

'Genuinely convinced about *what*?'

'That the answer to everything is a man like you.'

'Have you been drinking, Adrien? You sound like you have. Are you quite finished? Good, because I don't expect to be spoken to like this. In fact, here's how things are going to work now. Take a tent, if you want, take some supplies. But if you haven't left the valley by, let's see . . . this time tomorrow, I'm going to ask Leonard to escort you away. Understood? And believe me, if that happens you'll see why *men like me* end up in charge. I won't suffer shirkers and drunkards here.'

Adrien hadn't been expecting quite so blunt a threat. Still full of unexpected confidence, he looked up to the whisperer for further strength.

It had vanished, and with it went much of Adrien's resolve. His shoulders sloped an inch.

'I think I've made myself perfectly clear,' purred Roland. 'Your friends can all stay, but it's high time you did some packing.'

10

Murderers

Leonard's shack was a cube of wood without windows, which he had built himself with no help or advice from those who had constructed the rest of the settlement's shelters. Those others might have been built crudely, but they had at least been given corner posts and roofs of overlapping planks that kept the rain out. Their builders had done their best to replicate construction methods they remembered, but Leonard had simply built his shack through force of will, hammering timber onto timber until he had piled up thick walls and a heavy ceiling. The door he had taken from the hotel, and the silver ampersand of its handle was an elegant thing at odds with the rest of the structure. There was no hinge or frame to hold it in place. The door simply had to be dragged aside to be opened.

Hannah had waited a full hour for the Alsatian to wander off, as it often did when it grew bored of the mud outside the shack. Never leashed, it sometimes roamed as far as the woodfringe, perhaps scenting some fowl or rabbit under the trees, but Hannah had never known it to actually enter the forest without its master. Wherever it was now headed, she was glad to see the back of it. If things turned nasty inside the shack (knowing Leonard, she thought she had good reason to suppose they might), she didn't want the odds stacked even further against her.

As soon as the dog was gone, Hannah hurried across the mud. She had stolen a steak knife from the kitchen tents and, to conceal it, pushed its blade through the lining of her trouser pocket. The cool metal against her thigh was not the reassurance she'd hoped for, but she stood before Leonard's lean-to door and took deep breaths to restrain herself from knocking. She had not come here to be polite.

The door was heavier than she'd thought it would be, scraping noisily against the wall when she moved it. That spoiled any element of surprise she might have had in her favour, and Leonard was waiting for her calmly when she stepped inside. The thick walls made the shack's interior even more cramped than Hannah had envisioned. There was space only for some bedding, a few boxes of clothes and other basics, and an antique dressing table with a large and tarnished mirror. At this sat Leonard, topless and with his back to her, for he had been trimming his beard. He didn't turn to face her, even as she dragged the door shut behind her, only watched her reflection.

He was not as muscled as Hannah had remembered him being, but nor was he as slim as the gunman. There were fine hairs on his shoulders, and a birthmark smattered across the small of his back. Hannah tried to ignore such details of his body and focus on what he had done. The kirin. Yasuo. David's grave.

'Evening,' he said eventually, then splashed water into his beard from a washbowl on the dresser.

Hannah stopped herself from returning the greeting. She took a deep breath, and tried to sound as fierce as she could. 'I've come . . . I've come to bring you a warning.'

Leonard chopped a tuft out of his beard.

'A warning,' she repeated, when he offered no response.

Leonard turned his jaw to look sideways at his reflection, his fingers probing the length of his beard beneath his ear. The dresser must have broken when the trees came, but he had since restored it using the same brute carpentry he'd used to build the shack. Its mirror was untrue, warping his reflection so that his shoulders were thinner and his features less blunt. 'Go on, then,' he said at last. 'Warn me.'

'It's concerning David,' said Hannah.

'I see.'

She darted forward and dumped the watch on the dressing table. At once she retreated for the safety of the doorway, but she felt her point was made.

Leonard considered the timepiece for a long minute, twirling the scissors in his grip. 'So what?' he asked, eventually.

'Don't try to pretend that you're innocent.'

'Of what? Killing him? What makes you think I'm pretending?'

'Is that . . . is that an admission?' Hannah slipped her nervous hands into her pockets, there to grip the handle of her knife.

'What have you got there? A blade of some sort? Did David mean something to you? Are you out for revenge?'

'I never met him. But I've come here to tell you that you don't get to ride roughshod any more.'

'Is that so?'

'And . . . and . . . you'd better listen to me, Leonard, because . . . I'm the same thing you are.'

That gave him pause. The scissors stopped moving mid-twirl. 'I'm not entirely sure,' he said, 'what to make of that.'

'I killed a man not so different from you.'

Leonard stared at her hard. He looked, for the first time since they'd found that rare pinkgill in the forest, enthused. Hannah couldn't help but shudder.

'And what makes you think,' asked Leonard carefully, 'that he was like me?'

'Because,' she said, against the tightening of her throat, 'he was a man who treated everything just like you do.'

'And how do you think I treat it?'

'Indifferently. As if it doesn't matter.'

Leonard made a show of putting the scissors down on the dresser. He took a towel off the back of his chair and dried his hands methodically. 'As if it doesn't matter . . .' he repeated, inspecting his fingers for any leftover moisture.

Hannah had spotted his rifle. It leaned against the corner of the room, far enough out of reach that he'd have to turn his back on her if he made a dash for it. She kept hold of the knife in her pocket.

'You're trembling,' he said, without looking up.

'Killing makes me angry,' she said. 'Doesn't it you?'

'Not any more.'

From a hook on the wall hung his shirt, which he took down and pulled on, then began to fasten the buttons. He gestured to another chair, beside the doorway. 'Please have a seat, Hannah.'

He retook his own and folded his hands in his lap, but Hannah didn't sit, only watched him intently.

'So . . .' he said, after a moment, 'are you just going to stare at me all evening? Or are you going to tell me how you did it?'

She squared her shoulders. 'I shot him in the head.'

'From a distance, or . . . ?'

'Close up,' she said, as casually as she could.

He raised an eyebrow. 'Why are you doing that?'

'Doing what?'

'Trying to make it sound like it was easy.'

'I . . . I . . .'

'That you shot him surprises me, though. I wouldn't have thought you'd do it with a gun.'

'Why? Why not?'

'I just had you pinned as the strangling type. You know, in a red mist.'

She stopped herself from objecting just in time. She wouldn't play into his hands. Yet what had he just insinuated? That he'd only deemed her capable of killing in a kind of thoughtless frenzy? Or that a gun was such an easy way to do it? Or, worse, that he was impressed? She hovered by the door, unsure of the way things were developing.

'So it was an execution,' Leonard said.

'No!'

He held up his hands. 'Who am I to judge?'

Hannah thought of the gunman, tied in the chair where it had fallen against the wall of Zach's lodge. Sometimes she wasn't sure whether he'd ever truly believed she'd go through with it. Perhaps there had been time for a flash of realisation, in that moment

403

between the movement of her finger and the bullet exiting the gun barrel.

'You can tell me what happened,' said Leonard, 'if you want.'

'Whyever would I want to do that?'

'Up to you. Perhaps it would help to talk to someone who knows what it's like.'

Hannah watched him reclining there in silence, as relaxed as she was agitated. She opened her mouth to tell him that she had her own confidants, thank you very much, and they had been good to her and had not judged her and had done their best to understand, but then she closed her mouth again and swallowed. She was lucky, she supposed, to have had confidants at all.

But none of them really knew what it was *like*.

'You . . . you admit, then . . .' she said, stalling for time. 'You admit to doing it.'

'That's the reason you're here, isn't it? You said I'd better listen to you, because of this thing we have in common. So go ahead and let me listen.'

Hannah didn't answer at once, only twisted the blunt side of the knife against her thigh, trying to make it a hard cold reminder of why she had come in here to face him. She had made a bad start, she knew, but she had prepared herself for an argument or an altercation, or both. Never a temptation.

She wetted her lips. 'Would it be a trap?'

'Nobody's forcing you to say anything.'

'Hiroko . . .' she began, speaking very hesitantly. 'Hiroko had him tied up. It was because . . . he'd killed my brother. That bastard killed my brother and he hardly seemed to think it mattered. I don't know if he even believed he was in any sort of danger. He didn't think any of us had the guts to hurt him.'

Leonard nodded. 'He underestimated you.'

'He killed my brother, and he was just so fucking *puffed up* about it! So smug! He said . . . he said all kinds of stuff, all kinds of things I can't shift out of my head, however hard I try. Do you

'. . . do you . . . I mean *since* . . . do you think about it all the time?'

'I used to. I can't say for sure if it's normal to do so. It probably is.'

She ran her hands back through her hair, then took the seat Leonard had offered her. 'Hiroko had him tied up, and . . . I went for a walk to sort myself out. Hah! When I came back I was seething. I was the angriest I've ever been. There was nothing I could do to calm it. Perhaps I didn't want to.'

'What was your brother's name?'

'Zach.'

'Maybe you felt like you owed it to Zach to stay angry.'

Her heartbeat was racing. 'You're right! I was just so angry and I couldn't . . . I refused to let it burn out, because wouldn't that be like saying everything was okay? So I . . . I kicked him over, in the chair. He was against the wall. And he kept talking. He was wedged against the wall but still he just kept talking.'

'He didn't think you had it in you.'

'Exactly. That bastard thought I would never go through with it. He said so himself, there and then. And I . . . I . . .'

Leonard gave her time.

'I shot him,' she said, through clenched teeth. 'I fucking blew that bastard's brains out, because he killed Zach for no reason. My brother never hurt a fly, and that man killed him for no reason at all. I shot him because he deserved it. I shot him and I'd . . . I'd . . .'

'You'd do it again.'

She burst into tears.

'Do you want a tissue or something? I could get you one.'

Hannah dragged herself back together and shook her head. 'He told me . . . Right before he died, he told me that he'd killed the second time just to try to forget the first.'

Leonard laughed. 'Idiot.'

She wiped her eyes dry. 'You . . . you said you don't remember any more. So how . . . how . . .' She swallowed her guilt. She needed this. 'How did you forget about David?'

'Him? I never thought much about him. It was the first ones that stuck with me.'

At that Hannah felt as if a trap had just sprung closed on her, seizing her in place. Yet there was something almost pleasing about its cold vice, as if a part of her had long needed its security. 'How many have there been?' she asked.

Leonard sat forward, and the shack seemed suddenly far smaller. 'Seven.'

'Seven . . .'

'And I have forgotten them all.'

'*Seven?*'

'Would you like me to tell you how I forgot? I won't, if you don't want me to.'

Hannah could hardly move. She wondered, with a frost lining her vertebrae, whether this, all along, was what the kirin had been leading her towards. This piece of knowledge that only a man like Leonard could impart. She offered him the stiffest of nods.

'What were you, Hannah? Before the trees came.'

'I was a nursery worker. At a flower nursery.'

'I was a landscape gardener.'

Hannah shrank against the back of her chair. She thought again of the pinkgill, whose rarity he'd spotted at once.

'You didn't like hearing that,' smirked Leonard. 'All the same, that's what we both were. Gardeners.'

'There are a lot of gardeners in the world.'

'Were,' he chuckled. 'Not so many any more. Did you enjoy gardening?'

Hannah chewed her lip. Even if the answer to that was that no, in the last few years she had begun to find the nursery another kind of chore, she felt suddenly protective of the place, and of poor Diane who had died there.

'I loved landscape gardening, to begin with,' said Leonard. 'But I was a young man, in my twenties when I started. I couldn't believe my luck to be paid to do something I enjoyed. So, you know, I thought I was happy. I don't know exactly when it all changed. Life just drifts along, doesn't it? Before I knew it I had people who depended on me, had all kinds of bills to pay . . . what I thought I loved had become just another way of putting money on the table.'

'What does this have to do with what you did to David?'

'And what you did to that man. Listen, have you ever had one of those nights when you guess how many healthy years you've got left and think, *Oh shit, that's not enough?* Call it a midlife crisis, if you want, but I looked at my gardening and I knew I needed something bigger. I'd always said I wanted to work with nature, not flowerbeds and decking and fucking *patios*.'

He shook his head, and the shack fell silent. Hannah clasped her hands in her lap. Yet it was true there'd been times when she'd longed for something bigger and more meaningful. Hadn't that been what she'd confused the trees with, on those first days after their arrival?

'I made it my mission,' said Leonard quietly, 'to work out what I really wanted. My family were . . . not supportive, but it was a compulsion. I had no choice. To begin with I went off on my own to the moors, to the bogs and the national parks. I taught myself how to get by, but it wasn't enough. This country, so many countries, I realised, had been tamed. No bears any more, no wolves. The worst dangers are ditches and fog. So I went abroad. I used to have a sister in Alaska, so I stayed with her until we fell out. I hitchhiked all the way across North America, and I crossed through Mexico and stayed in the Amazon for a while. I stayed in other places, too, and everywhere I went I saw . . . the faith other people had. Would you say you have faith, Hannah? Faith in anything?'

Hannah thought at once of the kirin, dead by this man's hand. She thought of her brother. Her mother.

'I know it's a funny question,' said Leonard eventually, still staring at the floor. 'And I'm not a religious man, believe me. I tried to be, when I first grew up, but I've always found faith a hard thing to understand. Then, like I said, I set out to see the world, and everywhere I went there were people putting faith in things. Faith in their gods, their countries, even in their fucking economies. But how few, I thought, put their faith in *this*.' He stomped his foot and the army boot he wore made a loud thud against the timber floor. 'Maybe I'm lucky. Down to earth, people have called me. I've always known that the ground beneath us is the only real thing we have.'

'But you killed the kirin as if it was just . . . just an insect to squash on a wall. Don't try to make it sound like you have any kind of faith in nature. I saw what you did.'

Leonard looked up with the same indifferent stare he'd met her with in the coal pit, when he'd had the kirin's blood all over his arms. 'I probably haven't been clear enough,' he said. 'I still don't give a shit about your kirin. That's what I've been saying to you.' He bent forward in his chair, and a kind of zeal was glistening in his eyes. 'People like you and me, Hannah, we know about the ground. Sounds like your brother did too, if he was a forester. We were the ones who tried to stay close to nature, when everyone else was sitting indoors. We were the ones who knew all along that the earth is all we have. What did you think, when the trees came? Back in those first days, before you found your brother, what was your response?'

'I thought,' admitted Hannah slowly, 'that nature might have come to save us.'

'If the trees had come five or six years ago, I would have thought the same. But I'm further down this path than you. Like I said, I travelled through the wilderness. I stood on the tops of mountains. I was among the elephants flapping their ears. I climbed a giant redwood. I sat in the wind that blew the cherry blossom. It was all very beautiful. Sometimes it even moved me to tears . . .'

Hannah waited, expecting him to go on, but a minute later he still hadn't said another word.

'I thought you were going to tell me how to forget.'

'That's exactly what I'm doing.'

'It doesn't sound like it.'

'I went to a chimpanzee colony. I watched two patrols of rivals clash. After the fight one patrol ran away, but there was a chimp who was injured and couldn't run fast enough. The victors caught up with him and tore his arms and legs off. Then they ripped open his belly and ate his lungs. They even ate his balls.'

It took an effort, but Hannah managed to shrug. 'Everyone knows that chimps are violent.'

'I was swimming in a reef and there were baby porpoises. Cute things, not much bigger than rugby balls. Some dolphins came. Swimming with dolphins and porpoise calves at once, can you believe my luck? People would have paid good money for that. Then the dolphins started ramming the porpoise babies with their noses. Charging at them through the water and smacking them to death. Those calves made a funny sound while they died, Hannah.' He made the sound with the back of his tongue against the roof of his mouth. 'I don't think I need to tell you about the worms that hatch in people's eyeballs, or all the other parasites under the sun.'

'Are you trying to tell me that I should be heartless, just because nature is?'

'I don't blame people for turning away from nature,' said Leonard pensively. 'It makes sense to want to put your faith elsewhere. But the fact remains that the real world is the only one we have. Even people like you and me and your brother, we used to live our lives as if nature was our fucking picture gallery, something to wander around in and admire.'

'This doesn't explain why you killed seven people.'

'You didn't ask me to explain *why*. You asked me to tell you how to forget.'

She held her breath.

Leonard clasped his hands and looked her in the eye. 'There is nothing, nothing real, to have faith in. Anything good you can think of is nothing but a dream, dreamed up by a human hoping. The truth says that you and I and your brother and the man you killed are just lives. You killed a man. You brought yourself face-to-face with the truth, whether you wanted to or not. Did that man have a family with him? Did his loved ones come leaping out from behind the trees to grieve?'

409

Hannah shook her head.

'You're probably the only person in the world who's mourning for him. And you had good reason to kill him, when nature, when *the real world*, didn't even ask for one. You know you could kill another man tonight, and it wouldn't matter. It's all just a few more lives.'

'It would matter to me. I'd break in half.'

Leonard looked unimpressed. 'Would you? I reckon you're tougher than you think.'

'I could never kill again.'

'You could. I'd even be happy to bet that you will.'

'Then you'd be mistaken. Besides . . . I came . . . I came here for the opposite. To demand assurances. That *you* won't do it again.'

Leonard sounded disappointed. 'You know I can't promise that any more than you can.'

'I can promise that right now, if it will help.'

He sprawled back in his chair, laughter all over his face. 'I've tried to explain it to you, but you won't allow yourself to see the truth.'

'I could never, ever, kill someone again. How's that for the truth?'

He watched her closely for a moment. 'Let's pretend,' he said eventually, 'that someone or other killed your son . . .'

Hannah stood up abruptly, and turned to the door.

'Killed him in cold blood,' continued Leonard, 'almost as if it was a *test*. Let's pretend you found the man who did it, and he refused to apologise because he didn't see anything to apologise for. He thought your son was just another life among a whole pile of lives. And let's say you had a weapon, and the man was saying all kinds of things that made your blood boil, and all you could think about was your poor little boy . . .'

Hannah dragged the door open. She didn't know whether what Leonard was saying was meant as a threat or cruel speculation, but it made her every follicle feel pricked by a needle. As she stepped out into the dusk, Leonard said her name, then said it again in a softer voice. She ignored him. She tried as best she could to walk away calmly, but after a few seconds she was running from his shack. To her great relief, Leonard did not follow.

Above the valley, the stars were beginning to glimmer. Tired groups of workers headed for their shelters, or the kitchen tents, or the fires beginning to blaze throughout the settlement. To north and south the bare slopes loomed, and atop each an evening haze had thickened, levitating the forest on its bank of grey fog.

Hannah strode as fast as she could, moving with no clear purpose other than to escape from Leonard. She only wished she could escape her own mind just as easily.

When she remembered Nora's seashell, she pulled it out and clasped it to her ear. The ocean rolled inside it, but when she looked up at the valley's slopes they seemed like two converging tidal waves, and the haze atop them the froth of their breaking. In a moment of horror, she flung the shell away, and the deepening dusk swallowed it whole. She threw after it the steak knife, which had proved such a useless defence, then she came to a halt and stood holding her hands to her head. After a minute she hurried after the shell to try to retrieve it, but all she could find was the knife, glinting in the early light of the stars.

II

Stargazing

After his confrontation with Roland, Adrien had not returned to the shelters at the bottom of the valley. He had stayed for an hour or more in the ruins of the hotel, although he had not spent any of that time salvaging on Roland's behalf. Instead he had pulled up a chair with an inch missing from the bottom of one of its legs and sat on it unevenly, to watch the leaves above him for some sign from the whisperers. The last light of the day had entered the hotel's upper stories without ever falling so low as the dining hall where Adrien sat. He had been swamped in gloom and shadow, while above him rays of golden light wove through the foliage. Every leaf had warmed in the sun and then cooled again, but Adrien had seen no further hint from any of the little figures who had watched him ever since the trees came. Eventually, he had pushed himself to his feet and trodden out into the dusk, feeling cold the moment he stepped out from under the hotel's branches and into the deforested valley soft with mud.

Still he did not return to the settlement, where in the near distance the fires that would burn all night were beginning to grow. He sat on a block of fallen masonry that might once have been the sculpted balcony of a hotel room, and turned up the collar of his jacket and stuffed his hands into his pockets. He wondered what had possessed him to pick a fight with Roland, and supposed he had to take seriously his threat to have Leonard escort him from the valley. There had been a moment, while he and Roland had argued in the hotel, when he'd had the notion that the whisperers were on his side. Now he wasn't so sure. He wished they would give him some clearer sign to put his faith in.

He was still sitting on the masonry, some time later, when he saw an agitated figure pacing through the gathering dark.

'Hannah?' he called out.

She jumped when he said it, and covered her heart with both hands. Adrien sprang up and hurried towards her, raising his arms so she could see it was only him.

'What are you doing out here?' she asked, when she'd recovered herself. 'I thought you were back at the shelter.'

'I've been watching the stars come out,' he told her, which was a version of the truth. 'What about you?'

'I'm . . . out for a walk.'

He could tell that was not the whole story, either, but nor did he question it. Instead, he said, 'Do you want to look at the stars with me? I think I saw one shooting, about half an hour ago. There might be more if we keep an eye out.'

'I'll try,' said Hannah, and shuffled alongside him to look up at the sky. 'Where do we have to watch?'

'Anywhere. But the last one was over there, by Pisces.'

She stared in the direction he was pointing, which was towards the southern horizon, but Adrien didn't think her mind was on the stars.

'I never really learned the names for them,' she said, 'although now I wish I had. I wasted all my time learning about plants and animals.'

'There's nothing wrong with that. I used to stargaze a hell of a lot, when I was a kid, and look where it got me. Did I ever tell you about that? I used to know all the names of all the constellations. Over there you've got Pisces, Aquarius, Capricorn.'

Hannah sighed and crossed her arms. 'That's what Eoin had tattooed on his back. A capricorn. He knew about the stars, as well.'

Adrien hoped a story might cheer her up. 'I used to want to be a comet, when I was a kid, or failing that an asteroid or a tiny moon. I sometimes used to draw a chalk sun on the school playground and run circles around it, spinning as I went, until I fell down dizzy and cut my knees.'

Hannah laughed at him, and it was a small pleasure to hear it.

'I was bullied at school,' he added.

'I'd kind of guessed that.'

'Are you going to tell me what's wrong, Hannah?'

'It's nothing,' she said, but her gaze drifted back towards the settlement, and the orange blazes of the campfires. A moment later she said, quieter, 'I should have been a stargazer, too. Or I should have been an ocean-lover, like Eoin. I'd have even been better off doing computers, like Seb. Anything but the woods.'

'Don't say stuff like that. We'd never have come all this way without you.'

She sighed. 'And what have we come here for? Why did the kirin keep showing itself, if this place is such a dead end? Or are dead ends all it ever wanted to show us in the first place?'

Adrien frowned. 'Tell me what's happened. You normally leave the pessimism to me.'

She sat down on another chunk of broken hotel, pressing her hands between her knees. Adrien sat alongside her and watched an ant crawl through the dirt at their feet, the starlight picking out the varnish of its carapace. Another ant followed it, and another after that, and so on in a tidy trail.

'I went to see Leonard,' said Hannah.

'Oh.'

Adrien thought she might elaborate but she did not, and when a shooting star sped down the sky she didn't notice it. 'Hannah,' he said, 'whatever he said to you . . . you should just forget it.'

Tears flashed down her cheeks as quickly as the star. 'But what if I agree with him? Because I didn't when he said it, but now . . . I sort of think I do. He said that nature is just a kind of mindless flow of killings, and he's right about that. Isn't he? He said I was

414

fooling myself if I thought otherwise and . . . and I *have* been, I think. Zach fooled himself, too. All of my green friends fooled themselves. For some reason I used to be able to cope with this stuff, far better than I can right now.' She gestured to the ants parading around their boots. 'We're all just . . . *just lives*, that's what Leonard said.'

Adrien closed his eyes and remembered a tunnel descending in a corkscrew through the soil, and the clatter of the feet of the ants before him and the ants following behind. In the queen's chamber the larvae smelled so pristine, their brand-new antennae tapping forth out of their egg sacs. He opened his eyes again, shook his head and tried to focus. Hannah was gazing morosely up at the sky.

'Of course I've always known the world is cruel, everybody does, but before the trees came I suppose I thought I had some sort of answer. Zach and me, we used to talk about it sometimes.'

'And what did you say?'

She shook her head. 'It feels like a long time ago.'

'A lot has happened.'

'We said . . .' Hannah shook her head as if in disgust at herself, and Adrien hated to see that expression, so familiar when it crossed his own features, crossing hers. 'We said we thought that people might change. That if we just . . . just . . . I mean, it all sounds so hopelessly naive now . . .'

'Tell me.'

'Zach always said . . .' Hannah pulled a stern face and did a tearful impression of her brother. '*We just have to get people to live hand-in-hand with nature. Then everything will work out fine.* But when I look at what rises to the top, what still does now just like it did before the trees came . . . then I start to realise *we already do*, and *we always did*. When I see men like Leonard and the gunman, and Roland and Callum and all the rest who I've never met but I'm sure are out there . . . then no wonder everything is so bloody cruel. To think . . . when the trees first arrived I actually thought things had changed.'

Adrien folded his hands together. 'Do you know what I always used to love about outer space?'

'Huh? Why do you ask that?'

'There isn't any way to feel big about yourself up there. I mean, looking at all these tiny lights from down here, the Earth feels so massive, but we know it isn't really. If we put it alongside a star it would just be a speck. And even the stars are tiny, compared with all that emptiness surrounding them. Nothing is allowed to call itself the biggest, in outer space. I always loved stargazing, because it made me feel insignificant. Sounds like Leonard likes to talk about insignificance, but a man like him can't really understand it. He's got too big an idea of himself.'

'He's seen a lot. He said he'd been around the world.'

Adrien thought of the thing *he'd* seen, creeping through the branches of the theatre in time with the whisperers' song.

'Nature's a creature,' he said quietly, 'made up of many branches. Some bits of those branches are big, others are just twig-sized. I don't think it really has a mind of its own, only a whole lot of smaller ones. Just lives, as Leonard would say. All the billions of lives going on in the world.'

Hannah looked surprised. 'Why can't you be in charge, Adrien? That's what we need. Someone who knows about small things.'

'I'd be awful. I can't even control a class of children.'

'Nonsense. I saw what a difference you made on the beach.'

'That was . . . under exceptional circumstances.'

'Everything is, now.'

He watched the ants pass by his toes. Neither he nor Hannah spoke for a minute. Then bricks scraped against bricks in the nearby hotel, and some part of it fell to the ground with a crash and the noise of twisting branches. Hannah flinched at the sound, but the ants marched on. Adrien closed his eyes and could remember a chamber, somewhere underground, where the eggs lay about like piles of rice. He and his fellow ants sorted them, tiptoed over them, checked for the nuclei beneath the white outer rinds. Beside him the giant queen crouched, many times his size, and strained her abdomen and laid another egg. He took hold of it in his teeth and carried it to its pile and came back and waited for the next egg to fall . . .

'Adrien?' asked Hannah. 'Are you okay?'

'Yeah,' he said, mopping his brow. 'Never been better.'

She looked unconvinced, but before she could press him another shooting star streaked quick and white to the south, and Adrien pointed to it and said, 'There!'

Hannah looked too slowly. 'I didn't see it,' she sighed. 'I don't think I'm going to see one tonight.'

She had her arms folded, and her trigger finger was tapping against her elbow. Adrien watched it for a moment, although Hannah was too preoccupied to notice. Then he reached out and took hold of her finger and enclosed it in his own.

Hannah turned to him at once and uncrossed her arms and he spread his wide and put them around her. She leaned against him and her hair was against his jaw and her breath came out against his neck.

'Give me one more day in this horrible place,' whispered Adrien. 'I still think there's something I have to do, if only I can figure out what. Then I'm taking you away from here. We're leaving Leonard behind. We're going to go south, and we can try to find Eoin if you want, and we're going to work everything out a step at a time. You're the one who got me here in one piece, and I'm the one who's going to get you safely out again.'

12

Gunman

Hiroko cremated Yasuo, because she wanted him to be in the air and not the earth. Without telling anyone where they were headed, she and Seb carried what was left of him out to the woods. In a quiet glade they built the fire, and let it burn and burn for hours, the two of them circling now and then to stand downwind of the smoke. The flames thrashed and floundered, like the tails of the magical foxes in the stories her grandmother used to tell.

'They all feel even further away now,' she whispered to Seb. Her hood was raised and her cuff was damp from where she'd chewed it to hold herself together. 'My *sobo* and my *sofu* and my *otosan*.'

'Talk to me about them,' suggested Seb. 'So they can feel that bit closer.'

She shook her head and watched the smoke rising. 'Words can't help, not this time. They aren't close, Seb. They're on the other side of the world.'

He didn't have an answer for that. The fire blazed. The sun laboured across the sky. The planet tweaked on its axis. 'I just wish,' Seb said at last, 'that I'd done something more to stop Leonard.'

'You did everything you could.'

'Did I? I thought I did. But I promised I'd help you, and now Yasuo's dead. So what good did I do?'

Hiroko grabbed his hand and threaded her fingers between his. She could feel the tension in his knuckles and wrist, just as she could see it in every other joint of his body. He'd not shown her such anger since he'd told her about his father, but she was grateful to him for feeling like this. It was as if he was keeping her own fury burning, while she had no strength left to tend it.

When, in the afternoon, Yasuo's pyre died out and the burned brands were left glowing and bursting in their wake, there was no sign left of the fox kit's bones. They would be mixed into the ash that the fire had made, or dispersing with the smoke on the wind. After a while Hiroko nodded and the couple made their way back towards the settlement. The trees they passed beneath were larches, their yellow needles falling steadily to lie on the ground in a decaying thatch. The canopy was the colour of wheat, the sky above it a drab old grey, but whenever Hiroko closed her eyes it was a fur-red blur that she saw. She had stared so long into Yasuo's pyre that it had imprinted on her vision like a sunspot.

They arrived back at the valley and Hiroko stayed quiet all evening, lying down early to sleep. Several times, that night, she woke up grasping at the empty space in her hood. Several times she felt whiskers tickling her cheeks, then when she opened her eyes saw only empty darkness.

In the morning, a cry of someone else's anguish woke her.

It was so loud it sounded like something prehistoric, and Hiroko sprang up with her knife out, blinking away sleep. Only as the cry subsided and turned into a steadily sobbed, 'No, no, no . . .' did she realise that it was coming from further off in the camp, and was that of a man.

Seb, Adrien and Hannah all followed her to her feet, just as did the strangers they shared the building with. Even the heaviest sleepers were rising, for the sobbing was too distressing to ignore.

Outdoors, the dawn light shone the pitted mud. A starling stretched a worm from the ground, and rooks traced overhead. Other people were emerging, too, Roland from his shelter and Michelle from hers, and two dozen more folk who all headed with Hiroko and the others towards the source of the noise.

419

They found Leonard kneeling outside his lonely shack, his shoulders trembling and his glasses removed. He had red scoremarks down his cheeks where he had tried to claw his tears away, but one by one they kept coming, welling on his eyelashes then dripping into the mud at his knees. As for his Alsatian, that lay on its side, its body taxidermied by rigor mortis, its head made strangely two-dimensional by its wounds. The bloodied brick that someone had used to flatten its skull lay alongside it, but the dog was no longer bleeding. It must have been killed at some hour in the night, and flies hummed around it now. Leonard swept a hand at them, but they carried on.

'Leonard,' said Roland, who for all his cool seemed as shocked as anyone there. 'What . . . what happened here?'

Leonard did not seem to hear. He spread his arms and said, 'This is our dog!' Then he bowed his head and pressed the back of his fist across his eyes.

How strange, thought Hiroko, to see him like this. He looked a different man in his open grief, as if he were some cracked and tumbledown statue now restored to its purer shape.

She still hated him.

Looking at the dog again, she entertained the brief fancy that Yasuo's spirit had done this. Yet it seemed unlike a ghost to bash a dog's skull in with a brick, and with a sigh she acknowledged that Yasuo was gone now to wherever the smoke of fires flew. She couldn't even draw any pleasure from the dog's death, even though it had been the animal who had killed her fox. The dog had been the weapon, not the wielder, and to blame it would be like blaming her slingshot for the kills she herself had made.

Leonard stood up. He drew his arm slowly across his eyes, but that could not prevent them from streaming. He put on his glasses and spluttered, and his bottom lip trembled out of control, as shiny with saliva as the morning ground was with the dew.

He spotted Hiroko in the crowd at once, and when he trudged towards her the people of the settlement parted and she was left with only Seb, Adrien and Hannah for support. She steadied herself and met the big man's eyes as he came to a halt a few feet away. 'You know what you've done,' he said, but his voice sounded uncharacteristically faint.

Hiroko shook her head. 'Not this. This wasn't me.'

'You did,' he said, nodding. 'It had to have been you. It was revenge for your fox.'

She looked from face to face of those assembled, and saw that they either all believed Leonard or had no guts to side against him. Of the people from the settlement, only Michelle dared meet her eye.

Hiroko tried to resist reaching for her knife. 'I didn't kill your dog,' she said as calmly as she could, 'and this is how you can know. If I *had* killed it, I would boast about it. Believe me, I would. And I wouldn't just leave it lying there. I'd break it in half like you had it break my Yasuo, and I'd nail the two parts of it to the wall of your hut.'

One or two people gasped, and some stepped backwards. The rest held their breath and waited for Leonard to explode. Instead he just watched her for a minute, then nodded. He turned back to his Alsatian, as if he hoped his vision had deceived him and that, at any moment, the animal would spring to life and wag its tail. He snorted and went to where the brick was, and picked it up and turned it over in his hand.

'Leonard,' said Roland cautiously. 'I think you're in some sort of shock. Go for a walk. Talk to someone, if you must. As for you, girl, I'd like to speak to you in private.'

'No,' said Hiroko. 'There's nothing to say. I didn't do this.'

Roland lowered his voice. 'Of course you did, and you'd best admit it. Like he says, it was payback for your fox.'

'I was with her all night,' objected Seb, 'we were in the shelter until just now.'

'You *would* say that. Of course you'd say that.'

'Shh,' said Leonard, striding back towards Hiroko with the brick in his hand. She faced him down, as best she could. Seb drew close to her side, and Hannah and Adrien were at her back.

Leonard held the brick so tight that his knuckles were white. His stare locked with Hiroko's and his irises were blue as ice, and she could make out her reflection in his glasses. Only the wind and the flies made noise, then a trio of crows who landed on the roof of Leonard's shack and eyed the corpse of the Alsatian.

Leonard turned away from her again. 'She's telling the truth. And she's the only one of you brave enough to do it.' His glare passed quickly across all the assembled faces, until it came to rest on Hannah's. '*You*,' he said, with an intake of breath, as if she had just there and then stabbed him. 'Is this how you follow up on your warnings?'

Hannah shook her head, and looked upset. 'It wasn't me either,' she insisted.

'What message did you hope this would give me? Did you think this would change anything for the better?'

'It *wasn't* me.'

He locked eyes with her, just as he had done with Hiroko. Then he turned away and raised his voice to address all those gathered. 'One of you. It had to be one of you. I'll find out, believe me. You know what happens, after that.'

Then he stalked away, between the rows of shelters.

For the rest of that day, a tense atmosphere hung over the settlement. Several times Hiroko overheard groups of people discussing the death of the Alsatian, then falling silent if they noticed her passing. Clearly they all thought she'd done it, regardless of what she or even Leonard had said. Leonard himself was nowhere to be seen, and he left his dog lying dead where they'd found it, and nobody dared so much as to cover it from the flies.

Hiroko did her best to sleep that night, and not to think of Leonard or the Alsatian, or of poor little Yasuo or her family so many miles away, or even of the snoring and rustling of the strangers in the shelter. Seb was her remedy. She pressed herself against him with their foreheads and noses touching, their arms around one another, their hair tangled up. Sometimes the movements of his feet stirred her, and sometimes she suspected his toes and hers of carrying out a romance all of their own at the foot of the bed.

Their nudging was the one thing she didn't mind waking her. If it did, she would focus on the soft flow of his breath against her cheeks and lips, and do her best to think of nothing else in the world.

Love was a trail through the forest of yourself. If grief and savagery threatened, you could stick to its course and hope it would prevent you from disappearing into shadows. Finding that trail in the first place was the hardest part, but now that she had found it she had no intention of letting it out of her sight. That night she dreamed of the forest house, but in her dream it was she and Seb who lived there, and her father came to visit them and he and Seb joked in Nihongo and were happy. She was not angry any more, she realised, at her *otosan*. She wondered if he realised that she missed him, wherever he was now, if he was even alive. She wondered whether parents had some inbuilt sense of whether or not their children loved them, no matter where the child was or how badly they had behaved. *Tochan*, she thought, at some waking point in the night, *I understand it all now*. And it was true. Her father's heartbreak had simply been too insistent to allow him to return to the beech woods in Iwate. She no longer thought of that weakness as dishonourable. In fact, she loved him all the more for his admission of it.

She smiled and lifted her cheek and laid it against Seb's. He smiled too, in his sleep, and she stroked the hair along the top of his neck. She wasn't even sure if she was awake or asleep but, regardless, she hoped she would soon dream again of the forest house. They had an orchard there, she and Seb, and he always chose her the sweetest of the apples . . .

All of a sudden there was a hand over her mouth and nostrils, and another around her waist. Before she knew what was happening, she had been lifted off the ground and was being dragged backwards, towards the door. All of her kicking and struggling did nothing to break her assailant's grip, and he had stolen her out of the shelter before Seb could even jump to his feet. Then the hand across her mouth tightened and all she could smell was old meat on rough skin, and she could not breathe. She could not breathe. She battled to do so, but she could not breathe.

She tried her best to bite, but the hand squeezed so tight that her jaw buckled. She was outside now, in the night, and she could not breathe and it made the dark turn bright. Her eyes rolled for want of oxygen. Somewhere Seb was yelling her name but everything was pitch black and blurring into blue-green and how fast she was moving, how fast, and she could not breathe.

Her head nodded in time with the bounds of her abductor.

She must be dizzy, or drunk. And she could not breathe. She was out of air.

Out of air.

13

Unicorn

Adrien, Hannah and Seb searched for Hiroko until the sun came up, grabbing a torch and following the trail of Leonard's footprints, which headed uphill through the mud. Among them were scrapes and gouges made by Hiroko's kicking heels, but halfway up the slope these petered out and there were only the lengthening paces of Leonard's army boots. As the mud grew thinner, the prints grew faint. Then they reached the forest and there was nothing.

Eventually, and after they had walked in circles for what seemed like hours, Adrien begged them to halt. An unwelcome dawn had arrived, shining its light on their useless search. Birds cawed throughout the forest, and the white tail of a running deer flashed across the middle distance.

Seb would not stop. 'Hiroko!' he tried to yell, but his voice was cracked from all the yelling he had done already.

'Adrien's right,' said Hannah, grabbing hold of her son. 'We're just burning ourselves out. We need to stop and make a plan.'

Seb screwed his fingers into the fabric of his top. 'If I'd only been quicker I might have caught him. I can't believe I wasn't quicker. This is all my fault.'

'You were asleep,' said Adrien, rubbing his eyes, 'and we're all exhausted. Let's not start blaming ourselves. We just have to think of a way to find her.'

That was easier said than done. They had been trying to think of ways to find Hiroko all night now. In the last hour, as tiredness had caught up with him, Adrien had caught himself muttering little prayers under his breath. 'Help us,' he'd implored of the forest, of the whisperers, of *anything*. 'Please help us to find her.'

A thrush landed on a nearby twig, and sang to him out of its spotted breast. Adrien watched it with worn-out hope, wondering if perhaps it might trigger a revelation such as those that had dogged him since his encounter in the theatre. He wanted a useful vision this time, not one of worm tunnels and the appetites of crows. He wanted to follow the thrush's flight through the woods, and by doing so find the place where Hiroko was being held.

Nothing happened. The thrush flew away. 'Please,' he begged again, under his breath, but there was no response.

'Alright,' sighed Hannah, 'We've stopped charging around, so let's reconsider. Is there anything we could be doing differently?'

'We could . . . we could look for that chapel again,' said Adrien, still watching the forest for an answer to his pleas.

They had already searched fruitlessly for the chapel where Hannah had discovered David's grave. It was possible, she'd suggested, that Leonard had dragged Hiroko there, but try as she might, she could not remember the way. She'd only found it the first time by following the kirin calf.

'Anything's better than standing around talking,' said Seb. 'Come on.'

They looked for the chapel all over again. Some landmarks Hannah thought she recognised, such as a dead tree spiralled by creepers or a tall trunk covered in domed fungi, each of which hung out of the bark like a miniature parachute. Before long, however, the stops in their search lasted longer than the starts.

'I can't bear this,' said Seb. 'We're getting nowhere.'

Adrien looked to the canopy and strained his eyes by trying to picture whisperers up there, or to pick out a huge and spidery silhouette. He could see nothing but sticks and withering leaves. *Help us*, he thought, but there was no answer.

'Okay,' he sighed, 'maybe it's time to spread out.'

'I'm not so sure,' worried Hannah. 'If Leonard is nearby, we don't want to get caught out alone.'

'We won't spread out that far. We'll go in a line, and carry on north-west, since that's where you reckoned the chapel might be. Keep sight of each other at all times, and . . . and look out for anything. Anything at all.'

That seemed like a safe enough compromise. Adrien walked on the right, with Hannah in the middle and Seb to the left. It was a beautiful autumn day, the kind of crisp, gold-lit morning when even someone like Adrien would enjoy a long afternoon ramble through the countryside. Every shadow, every twig, was distinct, as if the world had been drawn by an architect. Adrien glanced across at Hannah, as she passed in and out of view behind the banded bark of the trees. These were silver birches: he had learned that from her.

They kept going. Even Seb walked heavily now, and each of them tripped often. Adrien did his best to scrutinise every thicket and bush they trudged past, but there were only roots and mushrooms and endless bloody silver birches.

'You little bastards,' he muttered to the whisperers, feeling desperate and betrayed. 'Where the hell do you go when we need you?'

He called out to Hannah, to his left, to ask if she'd seen anything yet. She called back that there'd been nothing, and sounded just as tired as he. Adrien shook his head and kept on plodding, feeling like a fool for believing that, just because the whisperers had taken to haunting him, they might deign to listen to him also.

Then he stopped walking. *It's a test*, the man in the pharmacy had said. *A question.*

'So show me,' muttered Adrien, certain that if the whisperers were capable of hearing him, he need not raise his voice for them to do so. 'Show me what you want or what you're asking and I'll do it or answer if I can. I don't care what it takes. But you . . . you just have to help me help Hiroko.'

Nothing happened. Not so much as a creak or a murmur on the wind. He gave it thirty seconds, then delivered a tirade of every filthy word he knew in the English language, and three in Italian and one in French for good measure. After that, he hurried to catch up with his place in the line.

The sun winked through the treetops, dazzling Adrien's weary eyes. When he yawned, his head swayed as heavy as a pendulum, and he was just beginning to wonder whether he might, in fact, already be sleepwalking, when he saw something bulky away to his right. 'Wait!' he called urgently to the others, then veered towards it. It looked like a wall, but no sooner had he begun to hope it was the chapel's than it raised its head and snorted at him.

'Kirin!' called Adrien, over his shoulder, but the animal shied from his shout and trotted away. It was the calf Hannah had described, with its immature horn and its pelt dark as charcoal. Adrien hurried after it, his arms raised to try to convey peaceful intentions. When the calf slowed to a wary halt, he checked back to ensure that the others were following.

He could not see them. 'Hannah! Get over here!'

The kirin skittered away, and did not stop running until it had reached the edge of vision.

'Oh bloody hell,' snapped Adrien, glaring back between the trees and wondering if Hannah and Seb had simply crashed down asleep in the undergrowth. He was loath to go and fetch them and let the animal out of sight, but when they did not appear, he supposed he had no other option. He headed back towards them.

Something whispered in the undergrowth.

'Wait . . .' he said, realising that none of the trees surrounding him were silver birches. These woods had been thick with them not a minute ago, but now he was standing in a grove of squat and twisted vegetation, and he did not know the names for any of it. At once he broke into a jog, but after two or three minutes' running had seen neither a birch, nor Hannah, nor Seb, nor anything he recognised as having walked past.

A snort of breath sounded behind him. He turned resignedly to face it. The calf kirin had followed him, and was waiting with one hoof raised.

When Adrien took his first step towards it, it brayed and began to lead him on his way.

14

Slingshot

'Morning has broken,' said Leonard, when Hiroko roused from unconsciousness.

She turned her neck from side to side, trying to stretch the stiffness out of it. Her breathing was a wheeze and her cheeks bruised from where his hand had clamped them. She was sitting with her back to a lump of stone, in a roofless building that looked like it had once been some sort of chapel. It was small and built from uneven bricks, but it had clearly been derelict since before the trees came.

'Morning has broken,' he said again, indicating with a snapped branch a wooden panel still affixed to one of the chapel walls. The panel had cracked in several places, but it still carried the separate wooden plates of some hymn numbers. They alone in the ruin clean, pristine black and white. 'Number eight in the song book,' he said, and tossed the branch onto a fire he'd got burning in the middle of the floor.

Her hands were tied together by wire, just like her ankles, and both sets of bonds were attached to the stone behind her. She didn't try to struggle, for he had used trapper's wire and it would only cut her skin.

'Well then,' said Leonard, 'here we are. Bit like a family camping trip.'

At once she thought of her father, in the forests of California, in a time that seemed a thousand years ago. She wondered if she'd ever mentioned that around Leonard, and whether he had said that to goad her. She had no choice but to shove the memory out of

429

her head. Her old self was what she needed right now. The tough Hiroko.

Her larynx was swollen where he'd choked her, so when she spoke it was in a growl. 'Why are you doing this?'

Leonard opened a rucksack he had placed on a ledge. From it he took a steel camping kettle with a blackened base, then filled it carefully with rainwater from a bucket. He had a trivet over the flames, but he did not place the kettle on it yet. 'I'll have a cup of something when your friends arrive,' he said.

'I already told you,' said Hiroko, 'I didn't kill your dog.'

'I know. I believe you.'

'So why have you brought me here? Why am I the one tied up?'

'Two reasons. The first is that you were the easiest. Oh come on, don't look so angry about that. I think you forget that you're just a girl. The second reason is *because* it wasn't you. I've thought long and hard about it. They'll come now, your friends, and whichever one of them killed it will own up, because you don't deserve the consequences.'

'That's ridiculous. None of them killed your dog. None of them have a reason.'

'Maybe they took revenge on your behalf? We can place bets on who it was, if you want.'

'They'll never find us, here. You've wasted your time.'

'They will. They'll work it out, eventually. Hannah has already been to this place.'

'And even if they find it, what then? You should have just come and talked to us in the settlement.'

'Too many other people there. Oh come on, girl, don't pretend you don't know where this is leading. You, out of all of them, must understand how this works.'

'Is that supposed to be a threat?'

He laughed. 'What kind of position do you think that you're in? Of course it's a fucking threat. This entire situation is a threat, by its very nature.'

'You're crazy.'

430

'I doubt it. In fact, everything I'm doing is entirely predictable. If whoever killed my dog had employed just a bit more foresight, you wouldn't be in this mess.'

'They'll outnumber you.'

'Doesn't matter.' He held up another length of trapping wire, which he had bound into a simple noose. 'Have you ever done one of these?'

Hiroko recognised the kind of clip used to make the circle of the noose. It was threaded in such a fashion that the wire could not loosen, only constrict. Poachers sometimes used them in rabbit runs or at the entrances to burrows, where unsuspecting prey might pass their heads through the noose and get caught. Their struggles to escape would tighten the wire until it garrotted them. 'They're illegal,' she said.

He laughed again. 'Illegal . . . Jesus, I overestimated you . . .' He disappeared through the door of the chapel, and when he came back he was not holding the snare trap. 'You'd better dial nine-nine-nine. And while you're at it, tell them that I've laid a dozen more. I'm sure the police will come *rushing*.'

'Fuck you.'

'That's better. I expected you to be angry.'

Leonard smiled, and picked something up from next to his rucksack. It was her slingshot. He turned it around and around, sucking his lip.

'Where are you from?' he asked her.

'You know that already.'

'Where precisely in Japan, I mean. I might know it.'

'You wouldn't.'

'Try me.'

'It's in Iwate Prefecture.'

He grinned. 'I've been there!'

'No you haven't,' she said, loathing the idea of his boots trampling her homeland's soil. 'You're just saying that to upset me.'

'Why would saying that upset you? But I was on a kind of quest to understand the world, and I went to many places. I spent a month on the slopes of Mount Hayachine. Stayed with an old *ojiisan* there who liked to paint the alpine flowers. Nice place. Are you from near there?'

Hiroko neither said a word, nor moved a muscle.

Leonard nodded. 'So be it. Can I be honest with you? I'm still surprised it wasn't you. You were the only one with any reason.'

'You killed my fox. You and your dog. I'm starting to wish it *had* been me who did it.'

'But it wasn't. I don't think you even know how to lie. But if I were you, and you killed my dog, I would certainly kill your fox in return.'

'You *did* kill my fox.'

'That was because it killed our chickens.'

'And now what? Now you think you're going to get some sort of justice by . . . by hurting whoever did it?'

His lips bunched. He kicked life into the fire. 'I loved that dog. Do you hear? You should know full well I'm not planning just to hurt whoever took her from me. I loved that dog more than I loved any living human being. There was no one else left, do you understand?'

Hiroko swallowed. 'If you kill any of them, Leonard, I swear to God I'll kill you in return.'

Now, when he laughed, he looked genuinely delighted. 'And do you know what?' he chuckled, 'I'd *let* you, if there were only some way I could see you after. I'd let you, just to see what you'd do with a taste of it. You're ripe for it. It would fuck you up so thoroughly.'

'I've killed stuff before. Doesn't bother me.'

He shook his head, still chuckling. 'You haven't killed anything.'

When he had finished laughing, Leonard held up her slingshot. 'Did you make this? It's good.'

'It works.'

'You're a crack shot with it. I never really learned to use one myself, although I always wanted to try.' He bent down and selected a pebble from the chapel floor. 'Is there a knack? There must be techniques.'

For a moment, Hiroko imagined Carter coming out of the woods to save her. Carter could have shown Leonard's nose a technique or two, shown the gristle all the way back into the skull. But men like Leonard were why Carter had gone to live in the wilderness in the first place.

'A steady hand,' Leonard said. 'I bet that's more than half of it.'

He fitted the pebble to the rubber and stretched it back to his chin. He was concentrating very hard, and his fist was tight where he gripped the wood. He let go of the rubber and the pebble zinged through the air, then ricocheted off the hymn board. 'Not good enough,' he muttered, and reached down for another pebble. 'But how was my hand? Was it steady enough?'

Hiroko didn't answer.

The next time he fired, one of the hymn numbers leapt off the shelf and clattered against the wall. Leonard whooped and turned to her with the slingshot raised aloft. 'Not bad, huh? I knew I'd be good with this thing.'

'Give it to me,' she growled, 'and I'll teach you how to *really* shoot it.'

Leonard chuckled and looked in the direction of the sun, which was edging higher into the sky.

'Okay,' he said, coming back over and crouching beside her. His eyes looked tired and lined behind the lenses of his glasses. 'Maybe it's worth screaming now.'

'What do you mean?'

'I want you to scream for help. So they can find you. Scream their names, if you want.'

Hiroko would have bitten him, had he leaned in a few inches closer. She believed him about the snares, and what he was planning, and she didn't want the others to walk into his trap, Seb least of all. 'I'm not going to scream,' she said. 'I'm not even going to raise my voice.'

He struck her immediately. His knuckles cracked hard off her jaw and whipped her already sore neck sideways, but she let out nothing but a stifled grunt. She had been expecting him to do something like that.

He stepped back from her with a scowl on his face. 'You've misjudged your position.'

'No, I haven't,' she slurred, nodding slowly with her eyes closed, groggy from the pain in her jaw. 'You want me to draw them to you. But I won't. So . . . hit me again. Get on with it.'

Leonard whistled under his breath. She heard him walk away from her. When she dared open her eyes, he was on the other side of the campfire and he had a pebble pulled back in her slingshot's rubber. He was aiming it squarely at her.

He fired.

15

Unicorn

Adrien followed the calf kirin through the woods.

It trampled along at a pace that seemed infuriatingly slow, when losing his friends made him want to dash. He wanted to run, wanted to climb on its back and gallop. Once or twice he clapped his hands to gee it up, but that only made it stop and flap its ears at him, or raise a forefoot as if about to flee. Then he would be on tenterhooks, for the last thing he wanted was to lose the kirin along with everybody else.

It led him beneath clawed trees, whose branches snagged at his clothes as if trying to tear them to ribbons. It hopped over a gurgling brook that Adrien had to take a run-up to jump. It ploughed through a series of puddled ditches he would far rather have picked his way around, but into which he had no choice but to follow. Looking ahead, he could see no sign of where the beast was leading him, and as more time passed he began to wonder whether it was not just stamping its usual trails, leading him nowhere.

Then a scream rang out through the woods. Adrien froze rigid, while the kirin bridled and clopped the forest floor. It had been a girl's cry, defiant but full of pain.

'H-Hiroko?' whispered Adrien, then yelled it, 'Hiroko!'

He received no answer, and nor could he be sure exactly where the scream had come from. It had seemed to ricochet between the trunks, and the kirin grumbled and plodded on as if it had already forgotten it.

'Come on!' urged Adrien, waving his arms at the beast. 'We're supposed to be helping her!'

The kirin continued stoically, and Adrien began to fear that the scream had been Hiroko's final shout. What if Leonard had simply killed her? That would explain why he'd heard no further cries.

'Come on, come on, come *on*,' he begged of the calf, while trying his best to stay alert for any sight of the girl, or of the chapel, or even of Hannah and Seb.

The tree trunks moaned and creaked, and a rumbling of gas escaped the kirin's stomach. Adrien wondered if this was all a sick joke of the forest's, staged at his expense. Perhaps his promise to the whisperers had come too late, and this interminable journey was his punishment. He was busily composing another foul-mouthed rebuke to them when, finally, a change appeared in the woods up ahead. There the going looked brighter and clearer, and Adrien filled up with a sudden fear of arrival, and of what he might find at the chapel. The kirin turned its head sideways and looked back at him with one dozy eye. Upon seeing the blunt block of its horn, Adrien couldn't believe that he'd come all of this way unarmed. He had not even thought about choosing a dead branch for a weapon. When he cast around in the undergrowth, there was only a thatch of skinny twigs, and many of those bound up in thorns that nipped his fingers when he tried to reach among them. He snatched back his hand and sucked the cut skin.

The kirin didn't wait. It quickened its pace and cantered uphill until it reached the clearing ahead. At first, Adrien held back, his imagination already peopling the chapel with a dead Hiroko and a triumphant Leonard towering over her. Then he took a deep breath and forced himself across the final distance, up the slope to where the trees parted and the sun shone through.

It was not the chapel. It was the hotel valley.

'No!' he gasped, staring horrified at the kirin. 'No no . . .' He pointed down the felled slope to the ruined hotel, and his arm was shaking. 'Not this! Not *here*! You stupid animal! You cretin! We were supposed to be rescuing Hiroko!'

A wad of slobber escaped from the animal's lips. It reached down its head and scratched the side of its knee with its horn. Adrien took off his glasses and pinched the bridge of his nose.

From the base of the valley came a rumble and a crash, that familiar sound of a part of the hotel collapsing. A grating thump followed it, followed by an awful squeal and a sequence of pounding thuds. Adrien put his glasses back on and supposed that his only options now were either to hurriedly muster help or to strike back into the woods alone.

When he looked at the hotel again, it was under a parting haze of dust. The wind blew and teased the smoke away, and revealed that the roof and upper floors were all gone. One wing of the building had caved in with such force that it had felled a tree beneath it. That trunk now lay almost horizontal, a mirror image of another that had grown that way on the far side of the building. All of the thinner, higher branches had been stripped by the avalanche, and the trees that remained upright were joined together by sheets of wall and flooring. The overall effect was of one colossal patchwork trunk, with two symmetrical arms.

Adrien stared from the building to the kirin, then back to the hotel.

Its shape was that of the throne tree.

'Oh shit,' he said.

He looked back over his shoulder at the forest, expecting to see whisperers at his back. There were only the trees, and nearer than them the stumps. The kirin rooted vacantly through the dirt on the edge of the wood, then looked up at Adrien with a huff of breath, as if surprised to find him still present.

'Okay,' he said, 'okay . . .'

He started down the slope. Then he broke into a jog. And then he ran.

16

Murderers

'Adrien?' cried Hannah. 'Adrien, where are you?'

'I can't believe this,' said Seb, rubbing his eyes. 'I can't believe any of this.'

'He was right there. Right there. And then he was gone.'

Hannah's first fear had been that Leonard had got him too. She'd grabbed Seb and stayed very close to him while they'd checked the place where they'd last seen Adrien. She had whispered his name a few times before she'd dared to call it, at any moment expecting Leonard to spring out on them with his rifle.

'Do you think,' suggested Seb, 'I mean, I don't want to accuse him of anything, but . . . do you think he might have just chickened out?'

'It's possible,' she said, although she didn't think it likely. One thing she had learned about Adrien Thomas was that he could find running away just as terrifying a prospect as staying put, especially if running left him alone.

The morning sun brightened every detail of the forest, revealing every crease in every tree trunk and every blemish on every leaf. Still they saw no sign of Adrien, and were calling out his name when they heard a scream.

'That was Hiroko!' gasped Seb, and launched himself in the cry's direction. It had been faint and distant, but undoubtedly the noise of a girl. Hannah looked around the birch woods one last time, then dashed after Seb. She supposed Adrien would have to fend for himself, wherever he had gone.

They'd been blundering in the direction of the scream for several minutes before they found the path. When Hannah reached down and sank her fingers through the leaf litter, she felt hard paving underneath. 'This way!' she exclaimed, and they hurried along it, jogging wherever it was firmest underfoot. They had not gone far before they tasted cinders on the air. A moment later they spotted the chapel up ahead, and both ducked into a crouch.

The nearest of the building's stone walls was just visible between the trees. A trail of smoke drifted from within, although they could not see the flames from their vantage point.

'Someone must be there,' whispered Seb.

Hannah couldn't see anybody, but she nodded agreement. 'It's probably a trap. We should be as quiet as we can.'

As they crept nearer, more broken masonry revealed itself, but they still didn't have a clear view of the inside of the chapel. They could see a campfire's glow buffing a fringe of greenery that over-hung the western wall, and could hear logs spitting out of sight.

'What now?' whispered Seb.

Hannah looked in every direction, but could see nothing unto-ward. She took a deep breath. 'Your call, Seb. I'm almost certain that Leonard's got this planned.'

'Maybe he's asleep in there. Maybe he's just gone to the loo, and this is our best chance. We might be able to slip in and out again before he even notices.'

Hannah wasn't convinced, but they sidled around the chapel to try to get a better look. The north wall had crumbled away entirely, so they made that their target. When they reached it, they could finally look into the chapel's interior, which was an overgrown rectangle beneath a hymn board and a few rotten planks of pew. There was no Leonard. There was only the smouldering campfire and, beyond it, Hiroko.

She was lashed to a stone with her back to them, but no sooner did Seb see her, and see she was alone, than he sprang up and rushed towards her. Hannah tried to grab him but he was too quick, off like a dog after a stick. At the sound of his accelerating steps, Hiroko turned and looked over her shoulder. She was gagged, but her eyes were wide with warning.

In the same moment, Hannah saw the kettle. It sat on a trivet in the fire but, although the flames licked its base, no steam was rising from its spout. Either it had boiled dry, or someone had placed it there not a few minutes before.

'Wait!' she screamed, but Seb already had too much momentum and Hannah not enough to catch him. He'd just set foot in the chapel when his ankle stuck in place as if it had been cemented to the floor. He lost all forward momentum and fell hard, his skull bouncing with a crack off the flagstones. Hannah shrieked and, full of instinct, forgot all traps and dangers. She hurtled after him but had not gone two bounds before her right knee jerked out from under her. She fell sideways with a hard thud, feeling like her kneecap had just exited her leg. Only when she pulled herself back up, panic for Seb overcoming her pain, did she realise that she had been shot and not snared as he had been.

The second stone hit her in the hip. It could only have been airborne for an instant, but her ear picked out its approach like the noise of a hornet. The muscles and the bone in her hip juddered at the impact, and she fell again, the fall making the pain ring out doubly. She looked up and saw Leonard stalking towards her. He was not carrying his rifle, but Hiroko's slingshot, and he was approaching from the very patch of forest she and Seb had just passed through. Perhaps they had stepped within a whisker of him, so fixated on the chapel that they had missed altogether the danger in the woods. He had another pebble fitted to the slingshot's rubber, keeping it trained in her direction while he looked left and right between the trees.

'Where are you?' he called out to the woods. 'Game's up! I'll kill them if you don't show yourself.'

Nothing answered. Only a song thrush which had landed near the hymn board.

'Seb?' hissed Hannah.

He moved, and her relief was so great it was anaesthetic. He tried to prop himself up, but squealed at once as his left arm skidded out from under him. He flopped down again holding that arm at a peculiar angle, and Hannah could tell it was broken. Blood dribbled from a gash in his forehead and more seeped from his trapped ankle, but he was alive and that was what mattered.

Leonard stepped urgently into the chapel. 'Where is he?'

'Where's who?' gasped Hannah, holding her hip.

'Don't push me.'

'Do you mean *Adrien*?' She shook her head to try to cast the pain away. 'He didn't come with us.'

'Bullshit. He would want to help his friends.'

Hannah's pelvis had filled up with tiny explosions. She dug her teeth into her bottom lip, to try to keep herself focused. 'Adrien just vanished. On the way here.'

Leonard stared into the woods, and the rubber strained in the slingshot.

'Hold out your hands,' he said.

She didn't suppose she had any choice. He slackened the weapon and tied up her wrists with the same sharp wire that had bitten Seb's ankle. While he was busy doing so, Hannah seized the chance to meet her son's eyes. Seb was panting from the pain of his wounds, but he managed to nod at her, to show he was coping. Even in these circumstances, she was incredibly proud of him.

Leonard finished tying the wire.

'Why are you doing this?' demanded Hannah.

'I already held that conversation with the girl.'

Hannah looked to Hiroko, who was straining to turn her head far enough to see them. A bruise had swollen the line of her jaw and a small gash bled on her shoulder, but she didn't appear to have suffered any serious injuries.

'Ankles,' said Leonard, motioning to Hannah's legs. Reluctantly, she shifted position so that he could tie them. He crouched and reached into his pocket for more wire, but his hand came out empty so he reached into the other one. 'Damn,' he said, 'no more wire.'

At that Hannah seized her chance, rocking back onto her hips despite the agony of putting weight there. When she swung forward again she kicked Leonard with both legs, hard as she could.

He caught her ankles before she made contact. She wriggled to try to escape him, but to no avail.

'Stop,' he said, and the fight went out of her.

Leonard lowered her feet to the ground, but did not let go. His grip was firm and warm without hurting. *A gardener's touch*, she thought with a shiver.

'No wire,' he said again, then placed both hands around her right foot.

He snapped it sideways, ninety degrees, and Hannah bellowed at the sudden shock of it. Seb tried to rise to help her but could only flop back towards the snare that held him, spitting with pain of his own.

Leonard stood up. 'Calm down, Hannah. I've only sprained it.'

It didn't feel like that to her, it felt four times its normal size and expanding, and as hot as an oven inside. Her eyes were streaming, but she clenched her bound hands together and sank her finger-nails into her skin, forcing herself to think straight.

Leonard stood up and scanned the woods in the direction they'd come from. 'I'm not happy that he's still out there, but it probably wasn't him anyway. Chances are it was one of you two.'

Hannah tried to picture Adrien charging out of the woods to save them. It was almost impossible. Even if he came, he would never best a man such as this.

'No matter,' said Leonard, scowling again at the forest.

'You've got it all wrong,' grunted Hannah. 'None of us killed your dog!'

Leonard's rucksack and gear were tucked out of sight beneath one of the window ledges. He picked something up from between them and held it outstretched on his palm like a crystal ball. 'Recognise this?'

It was the block of brick that had killed the Alsatian, stained almost black around one corner.

'I know your dog meant a lot to you . . .' began Hannah, battling to keep the hurt in her ankle in check, 'I know that but . . . doing this . . . it's . . .'

'It's *what*?'

She screwed shut her eyes as a wave of pain crashed up her shin and the underside of her thigh. 'Not going to achieve anything.'

Leonard regarded the brick in his hands, then tossed it disgustedly to the floor. It rolled to a clunking halt between her and Seb. 'Both of you take a long hard look at that and see whether it jogs your memory. I want to know why you did it. What you were thinking. Was it not obvious that I'd catch you?'

Hannah scanned her surroundings for some kind of escape. The chapel was like a scene from a postcard, its walls overgrown with flowering greenery that honeybees explored. Birds sang. Sun shone.

'How . . . how do you expect us to tell you anything,' puffed Hannah, 'when we weren't . . . the ones who did it?'

With a groan, Seb pushed his back upright against the wall. His face was smeared red from blood and sweat combined, and he had a lock of hair stuck to the gash along his forehead. He held his broken arm with his good one, but the shape of the bone looked wrong. After drawing a long breath, he said, 'Leonard . . . I did it because I wanted you to know what it was like.'

Hiroko closed her eyes and groaned through her gag. Hannah immediately felt sick, the sickest she'd ever been. 'No!' she said, full of adrenalin at once. 'No, Leonard, don't listen to him. He's trying to be brave, because . . . because really it was Adrien! Yes, it was Adrien who killed it! He confessed it to me on the way here.'

Despite the obvious pain he was in, Seb's voice was calm. 'It was me, Mum.'

'No, Seb,' she said, staring at him. 'No it wasn't . . .'

Seb looked up at Leonard. 'I did it because you killed Yasuo. That fox was all Hiroko had to link her to her family, to everything

443

she's lost that mattered to her. You took it from her. And you enjoyed it. I wanted, at the very least, to take your enjoyment away.'

Hiroko's head drooped, and her shoulders sloped away.

'Do you understand what you've done?' growled Leonard. 'Do you understand that you took away the one thing that—'

'Yes,' interrupted Seb. '*Yes* I understand. Don't lecture me.'

Leonard clenched his teeth. There was a long silence, and during that silence the kettle began to whistle.

'No doubt, then,' said Leonard, 'you've anticipated what happens next.'

Seb nodded. Blood dripped from his chin. When Leonard turned his back on him and crossed to the fire, Hiroko began screaming through her gag. Hannah tried to push herself up, despite the agony in her ankle. The wire teased open the skin of her wrists and her hip made a noise like a key turning in a lock, but despite the pain she was in she managed to climb, while Leonard picked up the kettle, onto her good leg. When she tried to put weight on her right foot the tendons screamed and it was all she could do to stay upright. Blood traced out of the cuts along her wrists but she paid it no heed. She knew she would only get one chance at this. The moment Leonard turned back from the fire, she made her move. The nerves in her leg were a cracking whip that somehow she pushed to her advantage, charging at Leonard with a furious scream.

When she neared him he raised a leg and kicked her over. She came easily off balance and, with her arms tied in front of her, had no way to ease her landing. Her ribs cracked off the brick Leonard had dropped, and her back muscles spasmed and made her ribs burn all the more. She rolled onto her side and the pain coursed into her hip.

Leonard watched for a moment, then flipped the cap up on the kettle's spout. Hiroko was sobbing, but the noise was muffled by cloth and spittle. Seb sat as still as he could, white now as well as red, blinking up at his captor through blood-encrusted eyelashes. Leonard locked eyes with him, then slowly outstretched the kettle until the spout hung over Seb.

'You brought this on yourself,' he said, and poured.

17

Heart of the Forest

Fifteen minutes before Leonard poured the kettle, Adrien arrived in the lobby of the hotel.

It was quiet in there. Not quiet as a cathedral or a grand old library is quiet, but quiet like the depths of the subsoil where only the lonely roots sink (Adrien wished he didn't know what that was like). With the leaves hanging in silence, the sole noise was that of his puffing. He leaned with his hands on his knees, trying to regain his breath after hurtling down the valley's slope. Above him the maze of branches intertwined, with phantoms of dust following their paths. The tree trunks divided into many leaning columns, rising and rising to become lost amid the brassy foliage. 'Well?' he said to them, and to the whisperers if they could hear. 'I'm here, aren't I? So what now?'

His question echoed away into nothing. The tree trunks dwarfed both the lobby's stone pillars and the grand staircase, carpeted by moss, that led to the hotel's upper floors.

'Adrien.'

He spun around in alarm. 'Oh! Oh . . . hello Michelle.'

She stepped into the lobby through the door he'd just used, and she looked the weariest he'd ever seen her. A lump formed in his throat, for he felt responsible for those bags under her eyes. All through their marriage he had guzzled her love and generosity and now, when she looked drained and in need of restoring, he didn't even have the time to help her. The trees creaked above him like scraping saws, as if to underline the point.

'I just saw you sprinting down the hill,' she said, with a nervous laugh. 'What on earth are you doing in here? Can't you see the whole place is collapsing?'

'Michelle . . . I wish there was time to explain.'

She raised an eyebrow. She always did that when he withheld things from her. 'So you're not going to tell me why you just came belting in here, as if your life depended on it?'

'You wouldn't believe me, even if I could.'

'Try me.'

'My . . . my friend is in trouble.'

'Hannah?'

'Maybe her, too. But Hiroko's been taken by Leonard. Hannah and Seb are looking for her.'

Michelle only had to hear Leonard's name to look terrified for the others. 'Where has he taken her?'

'I don't know. Hannah thought there might have been a chapel.'

'Where she found David . . .'

'Yes! Do you know where it is?'

Michelle shook her head. 'If I did I'd be there in a flash. But you've come running in here . . .'

'Because,' said Adrien, and took a deep breath. 'There's something here I hope can help us.'

'There's nothing here but ruins. I don't understand.'

'I don't even know if I do either.'

'Adrien . . .'

'There's no time to persuade you,' he said, 'but there are things in this forest that whisper, and that showed me . . . maybe they showed me something that can help.'

Just as he'd expected, Michelle looked lost for words. Then, although Adrien hadn't heard any wind blow, the branches stirred. A scattering of sunshine fell between them, and brightly lit the moss-covered staircase.

'You should be out there with Hannah,' frowned Michelle. 'Leonard is a dangerous man. You know that as well as I do. Why on earth would you come running in here if—'

The trees above them whined, and things skittered through the foliage. Michelle heard them too, and they both craned their necks. 'Adrien,' she began, suddenly nervous, 'can you see a . . . a . . .'

'Yes,' he said.

The leaves parted and a whisperer crawled headfirst down a trunk, pausing midway to regard them. It had eight bulbous eyes, each like an embedded acorn.

'It's okay,' said Adrien, as calmly as he could. 'I expect it's come here to show me the way.'

'It's come here to *what*? What is that thing?'

'There was a vicar we met in the forest, who reckoned they might be devils or angels. They're definitely some kind of servants.'

Again she could only gape at him, but this time the whisperer had given him some hope. It had scared the disbelief out of Michelle.

Long, sinewy moans came out of the trunks. The leaves stirred, rustling in their thousands as they parted wide enough to let even more sun fall on the staircase. A path of intense light ran up the steps, turning the mosses a sickening green, and it was as if the trees strained to hold themselves open and reveal it.

'I think I have to go up there,' said Adrien, as the whisperer scuttled around the trunk and disappeared from sight.

'Why?'

'Because they want something from me, or at least I hope so. If there's nothing I can do for them, I don't know how I'll get them to help *me*.'

It was clear that Michelle didn't know what to say, and nor would Adrien expect her to. He only wished she didn't look so small and frightened. He was supposed to be the small one.

'Listen, Michelle . . . I know I've no right to ask anything of you, but will you gather up anyone you can and try to find Hiroko? Try to find Hannah and Seb.'

Michelle gave a tiny nod. 'But what are you going to do?'

'I'm not really sure,' said Adrien. 'I'm just . . . following a hunch, I suppose. Acting on instinct, and all that.'

She shook her head. 'But you don't. You never do that.'

447

He raised an arm to gesture to the trees all around them. 'I think the whisperers played a part in this, Michelle.'

'In what?'

'The forest. In why it's here. Maybe they're even the reason.'

Michelle only stared at him with such puzzlement that it was as if they'd been decades apart, not months.

Adrien shook his head. 'I wish I had time to explain everything. I wish I had time to somehow make things up to you. But I haven't, so that's why I'm going to say this instead . . . It wasn't so bad, walking all the way here. With Hannah and the others, I mean. Even if we only had mushrooms to eat, we still ate most nights, and that was because those three knew how to get by.'

'Adrien . . . why are you telling me this right now?'

'Because if you get the chance, after all this is done, I think you should stop and think about where things are headed here. Roland, I mean, and how he's running this place.'

'Roland is already history,' she said quietly. 'I finished with him this morning. What he let happen to Yasuo was the last straw.'

Adrien was so grateful that for a moment he could hardly breathe. The trees creaked urgently above him.

'Hadn't you better get going?' whispered Michelle.

He nodded, took off his glasses, wiped his eyes, then pushed the glasses back up his nose. 'Yes,' he said. 'Yes, I suppose I'm going to climb that staircase now.'

'I suppose,' repeated Michelle, folding her arms tight.

Then, with a tremor that shook the floor beneath them, the hotel rumbled and collapsed further. Two huge blocks of mortar fell out of the branches where, a minute ago, the whisperer had crawled. They exploded against the flagstones and both Adrien and Michelle ducked their heads from the shrapnel spray that followed. A third block, the biggest yet, a right angle of bricks that had once been two walls of a hotel room, plunged through the foliage and crashed into the staircase. Steps snapped in half and flew into the air, and the sheer force of the impact carried the block through the planks and banisters and into the very foundations of the hotel.

Only when it became clear that no more debris was falling did the two of them straighten up. Dust swirled in the lobby air. Sunshafts shone through it, like spotlights in smoke. Loose leaves twirled towards the floor.

'What now?' asked Michelle, looking at the place where the damage had been done. There was no longer any way up, for the falling walls had left only a cavity where the staircase had been.

Adrien watched the floating leaves drift and ebb and, one after another, disappear down the hole the bricks had made. 'Oh,' he groaned, 'of course. That makes sense.'

'What does?'

'Down. Where the soil is. That's where they want me to go.'

'You're actually going to go through with this, aren't you?'

He nodded.

'It isn't like you.'

'But that's . . . good, right?'

Michelle tried to smile. He looked her in the eyes. She only seemed appallingly sad, and he could hardly bear that he was going to leave without fixing things with her. 'I've got to go,' he said.

'Of course you do.' She reached into her pocket. 'So take these. I was saving them, using them sometimes when I needed to find things in the night. There's not much fuel left in the lighter, but . . . here, just take them.'

She handed him a cigarette lighter and a stub of white candle, and they both let their hands touch when he took them.

'Are you going to be alright with those?' she asked.

'Why wouldn't I be?'

'Because of the candle.'

'Oh . . . yeah. I think I'll be able to cope.'

She smiled.

'Goodbye, Michelle,' he choked.

'Yep,' she said, in the tiniest voice.

He teetered towards her, and she to him. They each held the other as if they were two fragile vases, and then they stepped apart.

'Okay,' they both said at once.

Adrien took a deep breath and walked across the hall, to stand on the brink of the cavity. The broken staircase entered into it, but he could not see the bottom. He looked back over his shoulder, and Michelle was watching him from the place he had left her.

The loose leaves danced into the hole. The branches squealed overhead.

Michelle turned and stumbled out of the hotel.

Adrien was expecting the sudden loneliness that hit him, so he absorbed its blow and took his first downward step, onto the broken boards of the staircase. Together with chunks of brick and other rubble, they formed an unstable slope he could descend. As he got lower, everything became murkier, but he resolved to save the candle until he really needed it. For now, the faint light from above would have to be enough. He edged into some sort of basement room that smelled of tannins and alcohol. When the light unearthed green glimmers in a hundred places, he realised it had been a wine cellar.

In a crater of smashed glass lay the fallen chunk of bricks, but it was not the only intrusion in the cellar. There were also many roots, each of them giant enough to support the great trunks they nourished. He could see only their beginnings here, for they bulged into the floor without narrowing.

'So what now?' he whispered to the forest, peering around for some other exit. It took his eyes a minute to find it. Another hole, beyond which the light gave out entirely. Its entrance lay below an archway, formed by part of a root, and it was not man-made. It was simply a rend, a seam which the trees' growth had left torn in the earth. He approached its opening and struck the lighter. The flame wavered yellow and showed him a path, just wide enough for him to walk down and almost precisely his own height. He touched the fire to the candle's wick, then proceeded in its faint and dancing light.

The passage curved as he went, and squelched underfoot. It was no long-established tunnel with dried-out floor and walls, but more of an accidental seam, a narrow air pocket running through denser soil. From somewhere nearby came a constant dripping. From somewhere else something slithered. The tunnel continued as far as the candle would show, progressing steeply downhill. Out of its walls poked more twists and turns of enormous root, moisture slicking their pale surfaces as if they were sloppy drinkers. The soil they had bored through was spongy and soaked, but that was all Adrien could take in before a chill air current blew and the flame quivered out.

Slow music, deep notes played by the creaks and groans of plant fibres and the weight of the earth, began to make itself heard from somewhere deep below him. Adrien's thumb jittered at the lighter's button, but before he could get it sparking a drip struck the back of his neck and he flinched as if it had dropped from a guillotine. Then there was a sound as of something pattering across the ceiling. Something else brushed his ankles. He finally got the lighter working and, in the moment of touching its flame back to the candle, saw a diminutive silhouette tottering away from him down the tunnel. Then it was gone around a bend.

'Okay,' he nodded to himself. 'You should be used to them by now. You can just let it lead the way.'

He plodded on with all the bravery he could summon, and the air grew even colder and damper against his cheeks. When the candle blew out again he spent a frantic minute flicking his thumb against the lighter. Michelle had been right that there was not much fuel left inside. When he got it burning the flame was small and weak, and the wick took what seemed like an age to catch.

The tunnel wound gradually downward with no end in sight. Adrien plodded on as bravely as he could, and once more the air shifted, becoming the coldest so far. The next time the candle went out, he could not get the lighter to spark. He had no choice but to continue blind, one arm outstretched and the other clenching the useless wax in the ball of his fist. A worm writhed against his fingers when he pawed at a wall.

And then there was light.

At first he thought it was some trick played on him by his retinas. A green smear on the otherwise perfect dark. Yet as the tunnel bent it became steadily brighter, until he came upon its source.

It was a fungal colony, some two dozen ears of gelatinous matter growing out of the wall. Theirs was a delicate luminescence, no more powerful than moonlight, but when Adrien looked down at his body it was lit up in phantasmal greens, as were the contours of the tunnel, along which more of the strange fungi shone. He began to walk quicker again, and was just passing one particularly bright stack when it detached from the wall. It slopped onto the path in front of him and propped itself up on doddery legs. It was a whisperer with a glowing head of mushrooms. It loped ahead of him, showing him the way in a viridescent aura, and he followed it until the tunnel reached its terminus.

The space it opened into was a yawning cavern, its ceiling rising high overhead like a cathedral's. Adrien was surprised to have come so far below ground, then immediately wary. He felt the same seasick sensation he'd had upon leaving Hannah's nursery, when the road had been stolen from them for the first time on their journey.

All the way up the vaulting walls, hundreds more of the mushroom lights twinkled. Some were fat globes and some small as stars, but they were all reflected in a shallow subterranean pool that was the polished floor of the cavern. Adrien had emerged onto a ledge of soil, some six feet off the water's surface, and in other circumstances he might have stopped to admire its serene beauty. Instead, he arched his neck and stared upwards, at an enormous chandelier of roots that hung all the way down from the ceiling. Each giant tendril was as pale as the wax of his candle, and descended tangled with the others to within a few feet of the water. 'Are these the roots of the throne tree?' he asked, but the reply he received did not come from the glowing figure who had guided him.

It was a chorus sung without melody, an anthem hummed by bone-dry throats, and now Adrien realised that none of the mushroom lights that covered the walls were ordinary growths. They were all the haloed heads of countless whisperers such as his guide, and in turn they lit up a host of thornier figures, who clung to the dirt in between those that shone. The longer Adrien looked, the more of them he saw, gathered like choirs on every ledge and vantage point. Some of them were pallid things with corkscrewed limbs, and others were brittle and gaunt. Every last one had its gaze bent on the same thing, something caught at the very bottom of the flow of roots.

It was the creature. Like some immense squid dragged up in a net from the ocean bottom, it hung limp above the surface of the water. It had been easy to miss at first, for compared with the roots its bark was dim as shadow. Nor was it moving, and several of its legs drooped so lifelessly towards the water that Adrien wondered if it might in fact have perished in this cavern.

'What . . . what's wrong with it?' he asked, looking up at the audience of whisperers.

They responded with urgent sibilance, but he had no idea what they were saying. Then the one who had guided him down the tunnel brushed past his ankle and walked straight over the ledge, to fall with a plop into the pool. It bobbed back to the surface at once, breaking the calm water into circles. Then, using its own body as a raft, it headed for the pool's centre, above which the creature hung. There it paddled to a halt and stayed floating on the spot, like an eerie green prayer candle pushed out onto a lake.

Adrien took deep breaths of the underground air. He suspected he was being asked to follow but, more than ever before, he was aware of the limitations of his body. Aware of how his legs ached after walking all this way, of the elasticity in his spine that had always stopped him from standing upright, of the cold air against his bald spot, even of the fillings in his teeth. He didn't like one bit the look of the water, and didn't think he could find the strength to step into it. Surely the whisperers knew he was a coward. He had never pretended to be anything but.

'Maybe this isn't such a good idea,' he said, trying his best to raise his voice. 'Maybe I should just . . . just go back up the tunnel and find someone better. That's what I'll do. I'll come back here with someone far more capable.'

But by then, he supposed, everything would already be too late.

Adrien slid down the banked dirt of the ledge and landed with a splash in the pool.

The water only came up to his knees, but it was instantly freezing. He gritted his teeth and waded after the floating whisperer. As his steps stirred the pool they made its remaining reflections vanish, but as he sloshed closer to where the creature hung he began to get a better view of it. The rot in its wood looked worse now than it had in the theatre. Each cut in its bark had widened, and the air this close was thick with the reek of decay. Adrien covered his nose and mouth with his sleeve, but the smell still got through. Mould and sulphur and sap and blood on the tongue. He could feel it in his lungs and stomach like the settling layers of some filthy sediment.

'What's happening to it?' he asked.

The whispering from above him intensified. When Adrien looked up, he saw a thousand tiny arms twitching and gesturing nonsensically.

A dry wheeze began, somewhere in the body of the creature. Then, with a torturous groan, it shifted a dozen of its legs. They rose up in a kind of crooked salute, before flopping aside. By the time they had stilled with an exhausted creak, the thing had re-arranged itself among the dangling roots, revealing its great dark mouth.

The mouth was wider than Adrien remembered it. The lips of it were mounded with blistery bunions and oozing pustules that bled out sap. It reminded Adrien of a wound that had festered, and the rank darkness inside was far too deep for the lights of the whisperers to penetrate. Yet at the same time it seemed less terrible than it had in the theatre. It did not command Adrien's gaze as it had done there. Neither did the stink of its breath overwhelm him, although he kept his nose covered with his sleeve.

'Is it sick?' he asked.

When he looked to the whisperers, he found that all of their gazes were fixed on him.

'You can't expect me to help it,' he said, 'if I don't know what to do.'

With a dry rattle, like the sound of dead leaves scuffing over stone, the creature exhaled again. Adrien's lips curled and he nearly gagged as the smell floated down from where it hung, but it was nothing like as irresistible as it had been before.

'Show me what to do,' he asked of the whisperers, but they gave no response. Then it occurred to him that there might be a way to show himself, could he only summon the courage.

At once he did not want to. He wished he'd never even thought it. Yet it was the only plan he had, and he tried to remember that he was here to help his friends and had to do whatever it took. When the creature wheezed one further time and its sigh of decay wafted over him, Adrien dropped his arm to his side and inhaled as deeply as he could.

It was as if he had snorted up worms.

His vision rolled and the insides of his skull felt full of pulsing movement. He staggered backwards, tripped and fell, but by the time his body hit the water the splash already sounded like a faraway tinkle. His thoughts squirmed away into darkness.

Darkness where he drank.

He drank below ground with innumerable buried tongues, and when the sun shone he was above ground lapping the very light out of the air. Drinking in the grandeur to which he was entitled, drinking for endless miles, shoulder to shoulder with himself across lands, across continents. Like a wave his thoughts rushed around the sunlit half of the world and swooned for the fireball blazing in the sky. He basked in it, and spread out his leaves. To wear a ruffled flower on his cactus he endured the roasting heat and the bombarding sand, and the next moment in another part of the world he dropped his pine cones to better shoulder huge weights of snow. In the mangrove swamps he felt the tides wash around him and the countless teeth of the fish nibbling his roots and he let his attentions roll on, further and further afield. Just as with one gesture he surrendered his leaves to insistent winter, with the next he touched spring and unpacked tight new buds. In the greenest parts of his being he was fanned by the flipbook thrum of the hummingbird's wings. His fingers tapped time to the monkey's maniac dance. He lost track over and over of the padding tiger who rubbed itself against him like a house cat rubs its master's legs. In the cold realms where he had to hold his breath for the light, he gave up his mosses to the teeth of the reindeer herd. He had lived five thousand years as a bristlecone pine on an arid mountain summit. He was the mighty giant and the waifish sapling both, and all the bellies of the trees were his full bellies, their strong arms his arms, their straight backs his straight backs, their contortions his feats. He put up a toadstool, speckled fat and red. He put up a million bluebells and let them chime in silence on a windy day. He lent his disguise to the moth, to the shield bug, even to the jaguar with closed emerald eyes dreaming fang dreams in the aftertaste of blood.

A wasp landed on his petal tongue and crawled a little deeper, and he slammed shut his lips and he was the wasp, melting alone in perfumed saliva, cut off from the hive and the free air. He poisoned a tamarin for stealing his berries and he was the tamarin who had cherished those fruits as dear as gemstones, and he choked to death curled up among them. Caterpillars ate him, and he pincered the caterpillars with his beak, and then out came his golden talons to catch himself. He was swept up high into the eyrie and there he was crushed and torn apart and regurgitated for the chicks in his nest, and he was the chick side-by-side with his hated sister, seeing the world in nothing but shades of blindness, already scheming for the moment when he could push her overboard. He wrapped tight the faun in a scaly constriction, and hissed as he listened for the snaps. He was the spring-loaded mantis, lunging at the song-bird's breast, spearing its heart with his claw.

The orangutan seated in his branches pondered him. The dolphin playing in his coral stopped and nudged him with its bottle nose. The studious rat watched and bided.

Along forking paths of root and branch he flowed, just as he flowed in nerves and veins. Every tree trunk was his signature, and so was every beating heart with stems and shoots of artery and every patterned leaf blowing in the wind. Round and round he blustered, and when the wind lulled and he tired of his crackling dance he settled down in layers on the dirt. The soil was his bed and he tucked himself in, and he rested under wilting sheets and crumbly quilts. His was the brown dissolving sleep from which nothing ever wakens. He slept himself into a moisture, a gift of wine for the eyeless denizens of the soil. Down into the dirt he drained, and sometimes he filtered as far as the bedrock and the secret caverns, and within one such chamber he was in a bead of fluid welling out of an earthen ceiling, and he dropped onto the first root of a vast descending tangle and ran from bristle to bristle all the way down until he swung from the lowest tip.

He fell.

He was a thought in a watery sphere, spinning through darkness . . .

. . . and he landed on the forehead of a middle-aged man, slumped on his knees, waist-deep in a pool.

With a drawn-out shiver, Adrien returned to himself. He clutched his hands to his shirt, confused to feel his own heartbeat under layers of goosebumped skin and muscle. His breathing was rapid and shallow. He felt put together wrong, with not enough pieces.

'Wh-what just happened?' he stuttered, although already he was beginning to remember.

It took his eyes a minute to refocus, but he could tell that the creature had not vanished as it had done in the theatre. It still hung in the web of roots, looking even more wretched now than before.

457

Above it the walls of the cavern arched, but the lights of the whisperers were all gone from their perches. Instead they shone, in one great green glow, from the pool all around him.

While Adrien's mind had been spinning through whatever places it had just been, every single whisperer had descended from its vantage point on high. Too many of them to float, they had piled into the water submerged or stacked on each other's bodies, surrounding Adrien in a heap.

Adrien heaved himself to his feet. 'I still don't understand,' he said in a small voice. 'What do you expect me to *do*?'

The whisperers gave no response, so Adrien looked again to the creature. He was starting to doubt it was even aware of him, if it possessed any awareness at all. It had no mind of its own. It was just lives.

'I can't help it,' he repeated, 'if you won't even tell me what's wrong.'

A sound came from out of the creature's shoulders, like that of cut timber squealing before a fall. Adrien began to retreat, wading backwards as fast as he could while the whisperers scrambled and splashed to part the way for him.

With a scrape and a rattle and a final capitulating squeal, the creature slid out of the roots and dropped into the pool. When it hit the surface it threw up a sheet of spray that struck Adrien's face cold as hail. He wiped himself dry with his sleeves, while the ripples from the splash lapped past his knees.

The creature lay motionless where it had crashed into the pool, its legs bunched up in a swatted pose. Adrien held his breath and waited for it to move, but with each passing moment when it did not, he felt a curdling sense of despair.

'No,' he muttered, 'this can't be right.'

He supposed that, since the theatre, he had come to think of the thing that had just collapsed before him as powerful and ancient. It had seemed wounded, too, but surely it was too potent a being to simply wither away. He held his hands to his collar and thought of Hiroko dragged off by Leonard, and of Hannah and Seb staggering after her. It was the power of the creature that he'd hoped could be somehow entreated, tweaked or diverted, to offer mercy to his friends, but now it did not even twitch. When Adrien looked to the whisperers they were as motionless as a heap of mannequins, and he began to wonder if there had been some sign of theirs that he had missed from the start, some signal they had tried to impart that had been lost on him.

'It's dying, isn't it?' he asked.

Nothing in the cavern moved, save the ripples on the pool.

'But . . .' Adrien shook his head despondently, 'I needed it to help me.'

He looked back towards the tunnel he had come down. He felt, not for the first time in his life, like an abject failure. It would be a cold, difficult walk towards the surface, and all of his muscles already ached in so many places. How tired he was. The backs of his eyes felt like slices of glass.

'I have to do what I can for my friends,' he told the whisperers, as firmly as he could, then began to wade back towards the tunnel. They did not try to stop him. Instead, those in his way parted before him like rats scrambling out of a sewer. He reached the pool's bank and dragged himself out of the water, dripping his way up the soil. He did not let himself speculate on what the creature's demise meant for everything he had seen in that strange state brought about by its breath. All of his energies were needed for getting back to the surface, and for trying to help Hiroko, Hannah and Seb.

Something split behind him.

It was a brief, sudden crack, like the sound of an axe slamming through a log. When Adrien looked around, the creature had broken nearly in half. The rot surrounding its mouth had finally given way and its entire body looked snapped at the jaws, its branches divided into two wretched portions.

Despite that, none of the whisperers were looking at it. They were all watching Adrien go.

All except for two.

Adrien did not think he had seen any quite like them before. They had climbed atop the remains of the creature, where they were busying themselves with some sort of labour, bending their heads close to its frame and inserting their fingers like keys into its rotten bark. They were half as big again as the rest of their kind, and their skin was silver, and each had a single wooden antler screwing out of its scalp. The prongs of those antlers were decked in black clumps of moss, as were their wooden skeletons, which were shaped as if the bones of some nimble deer or leaping hare had been forced into an approximation of human form.

With a dead crunch, the body of the creature slouched further into the water. One of the two silver whisperers glanced up for a few seconds, black ribbons of vegetable matter strung from its mouth, then ducked its head again and continued its work. Adrien bit his lip. At first he'd assumed they'd been trying to fix the great creature, but now he could see they were picking the last of it apart.

With one last feeble groan and then a glug of water, what remained of the creature's core sank into the pool. The silver whisperers, however, had separated a trophy from its body, and now held it aloft between them. It was a ring of jagged black wood, its circumference not much wider than Adrien's forearm, its bark glazed all over by a dripping gel of resin. It was some part they had cut from its mouth, and Adrien fancied it might be whatever passed for the creature's throat or gullet. Holding it in their fragile arms as if it weighed no more than an ounce, the whisperers turned to face Adrien.

'What is that?' he asked. 'What are you doing with it?'

They began to limp towards him, down off the carcass of the creature and onto the bodies of the other whisperers, who only purred when used as stepping stones. The silver pair moved at an unerring creep, bearing the circle of wood as if it were some torc or relic at a coronation.

Adrien backed away. He had reached the tunnel mouth but he felt no safer there, even if none of the whisperers had tried to prevent him from leaving. In the pool, the two silver relic-bearers drew to a halt, their circle of wood still raised above their antlers.

'I . . . I came down here for my friends,' he spluttered. 'If you can't do anything for them then . . . I've got to go.'

None of the whisperers responded. Nor did they stop staring at Adrien.

'I needed your creature to send a . . . a bear or something. Anything, to rescue them from Leonard. That was what I was asking for, in the woods, when I said I'd do whatever it takes.' He pointed to what was left of the many-legged creature. 'But *now* look at it.'

Not one of them did.

Adrien cleared his throat. 'Goodbye,' he croaked, and turned to hurry back up the tunnel.

No matter the otherworldliness of the scene he now left behind him, Adrien felt an all too familiar despair to have come down here when his friends needed him most. The rush in which he'd charged after the kirin now seemed at best a fanciful miscalculation and at worst raw cowardice. How like Adrien Thomas, he told himself, to find the deepest hole to hide in when the going got tough. How like Adrien Thomas to look for something he could beg to save him, before he had even attempted to fight his own fight.

He looked back over his shoulder. The silver whisperers were watching him go, their circle of wood still held aloft between them. Adrien only shook his head and toiled on up the slope. He could hardly bear to imagine what had happened while he'd wasted so much time down here. He thought of Hiroko, not strong enough despite all her bravery to win out against a brute like Leonard. He thought of the heartbreak that waited for Seb if he lost her. He thought of his dear friend Hannah, who had lost all her faith in second chances. He doubted he could be of much use to any of them now and, for an awful moment, he pictured himself burying them. Yet, with the creature crumpled away to nothing, their only hope left was Adrien Thomas.

'Oh,' he said, ten steps later.

The vision is a test, the man in the pharmacy had said. *A question.*

'Ohh,' said Adrien again, feeling the blood run out of his cheeks.

And now he could remember something else that poor, broken man had said. At the time Adrien had thought it nothing but a plea for company, in the final hours of his life.

Can I keep you?

Adrien turned slowly to look back down the tunnel. Right at the bottom, lit by the eerie light of their kin, were the silver whisperers with their circle of wood. 'You can't be suggesting . . .' he began, clasping his hands to his collar. 'I mean . . . I'm not even close to strong enough.'

Yet even as he protested, Adrien knew it was not a strong man whom the whisperers had been searching for. Strong men only drove the world to ruin.

He would have liked to have paused and taken even so little as a minute to consider things further, but he suspected he had wasted too much time already. This was his chance to make a difference, perhaps his only one. Slowly at first, and then at a terrified scamper, he headed back down to the pool's edge. He nearly lost his balance when he slid into the water, for his heart was pounding and the pool seemed even more freezing than before. He steadied himself and took a deep breath and began to wade towards the silver whisperers as determinedly as he could.

They awaited him with their circle of wood raised. It had a shape like a shark's jaws, but there were buds packed beneath its resin rind just as there were rotten roots and stalks as tight as tendons. 'Will it hurt?' gulped Adrien as he approached.

The whisperers tilted their heads and changed their noise to something hymnal.

Adrien knew every moment was precious, but he stopped within arm's reach. It took him several seconds to find the bravery to say, 'Do it, then.'

The silver whisperers lowered the wooden ring over his head.

It came to rest against Adrien's neck and shoulders. It was lighter than he'd anticipated, hardly weighing a thing, but the sap in which it was coated began at once to glue to his flesh, and he could feel it hardening there and binding, and he shuddered. Other than that, nothing happened. He had expected something overwhelming, such as the first time he'd looked into the creature's mouth, but all he felt was a tickle behind his left knee. He turned to see a whisperer climbing his leg, then a second going up the other one and another pair following those. As nimbly as beetles, and with more flowing behind, they hurried up his trousers, over his hips and onto his back. Adrien clamped his jaws and tried to stay still, fighting the urge to thrash around and try to bat them off. They weighed next to nothing, and even as more of them swarmed onto him he hardly had to stoop to bear them. None climbed any higher than the wood around his neck, but on his back they milled and grappled and, if they could find no part to cling onto, simply grabbed another whisperer by the limb and dangled from there. All the way down to the pool they hung, like the patchwork of a leafy mantle.

When the two silver whisperers climbed onto his shoulders to join the rest, Adrien had to swallow a scream. With spindly arms they caressed his cheekbones and forehead, and up close he could see that they were whiskered by the thinnest white twigs, and the bark around their eye sockets was cragged into something like crow's feet. They reached out to lock limbs around his skull, and he only managed to stave off his panic by thinking of the people he still somehow hoped to save. They would not understand that he'd done this for them. They would never infer it from Michelle's account of him entering the basement. That didn't matter. He had never really known any glory, and he was content to finish things that way.

The silver whisperers pressed their crooked lips to Adrien's ears, and their whispers were rough kisses against his skin. Tears dashed down his cheeks, while his veins felt stiff with fear and the pool even colder than a moment before and his legs almost numb below the knees. An ache developed between each of his fingers. A pain like a stitch underlined his every rib. He shut his eyes and wished with all his heart that Michelle would turn away from Roland and look to Hannah for how to live in the woods, and that Hannah would find her love for it again and in doing so be there for Seb, and that Seb would not be heartbroken because Hiroko would still be alive.

When next he tried to move his feet they were too numb. All he could feel was a strange sensation of flowing water, as if it were moving *in between* his leg bones. Adrien had never been able to remember how many ribs a man had, but he seemed to have double the number he was used to. His spine felt misaligned, as if his shoulder blades were the two ends of a broken zip.

He opened his eyes and looked down, and felt very tall. His arms appeared stretched, and the veins of his hands were bulging. Then, with less pain than the prick of a needle, the end of one ruptured. It was not blood that flowed out but a shoot, a worm-sized stalk with a tiny leaf already growing from the end of it. When Adrien tried to shout his lungs were soundless hollows, and he blinked and there were flakes of green among his eyelashes. He reached up an arm to brush them away, but his elbow creaked and would not bend far enough. He tried to move one of his other arms and in that moment realised he had at least three.

Hanging like a cape around him, else staring up from where they swarmed on the surface of the pool, were the whisperers. Their faces were eerie and haggard, full of warts and varnished blisters, but as Adrien stared at them their warts all split. Their blisters burst and from beneath them opened pallid flowers, tinged green by the luminescence. Every wooden face filled up with petals, and then with a lisping crescendo they all blew free. Adrien tried to watch them swirl but he could not. It was becoming too hard to focus. His eyes were fixed and drying out.

He had forgotten what it was to be cold. He had forgotten the quantity of his arms and legs. Each of his thoughts was a sycamore seed, spinning lonely in the air. The last few things he remembered, as if they were the only memories permissible, were the faces of Hannah, Hiroko, Seb and Michelle. But he also knew, at last, what it was the whisperers had been saying, all this time, and it was the silver ones at his ears who whispered it the loudest.

Grow.

With a rhyming creak, and with at least two dozen wooden arms, he reached up for the dangling roots of his throne.

18

Wolves

Seb squealed as the kettle water seethed onto his wounded ankle. He screamed and kicked with his other leg and arched his back in agony, but Leonard only kept the water flowing steady. The sun, climbing higher above the chapel, cast the big man's shadow over his prey. He moved the kettle with engrossed precision, so that a scalding hot ribbon traced its way up Seb's shin and onto his knee. Here Leonard let the water pour a moment longer, so that it pattered onto the kneecap. Seb screeched and sobbed and tried to kick his bound leg to no avail.

'Got to make sure there's still enough,' said Leonard, moving the water again, letting it hiss against the denim along Seb's thigh, 'for you to have a nice refreshing drink at the end of it.'

The brick hit him where his beard met his jaw. Leonard grunted and staggered sideways, the arc of water swerving off its course. It was the brick that had killed his Alsatian, and it clunked now to the floor and rolled to a halt beneath a pew. Hannah had flung it with both hands, swinging it through the air with all the strength she had, but she knew she couldn't stop there.

With a howl of agony, she threw herself up onto damaged feet and bowled into Leonard to knock him to the floor. She crashed down on top of him, and he punched her hard in the ribs and she barely felt it. Adrenalin had set her alight, and filled her tied-up fists with the fire she needed to hammer them hard against Leonard's head. He hit her again and she rocked sideways, and one of his hands grappled at her face and she bit it. She could feel her blood rushing through every vein in her body, and slicking red her hands where it flowed from the cuts in her wrists. Leonard was clubbing her hard, but she pushed, pushed down between his blows to seize hold of his throat. He would not murder her son. If another member of her family had to die, it had better be her next in line. Leonard hit her again, throwing her off balance, but she clung on to his neck because Seb's life depended on it, and she did not care if her own was lost in saving it.

She pushed her thumbs deep, into the soft spots on either side of his oesophagus. When next Leonard struck her it was with less force, and less direction. She leaned all of her weight into her thumbs, and knew he was flagging because his face turned darker and his eyes widened and rolled back beneath his glasses. Knowing she would burn out at any moment, she put everything she had left into her thumbs. She could feel the gristle of his windpipe in her grasp, and she did not let go. Leonard made a strange noise like toads sometimes make. He tried, one last time, to throw her aside, but she had anchored herself with hatred, and with fear for her son, and with the loss of her brother and her mother and her father too, and she was gasping for breath and hot with blood and sweat, all because of monsters like this one. His final two blows knocked against her head and made her skull pound like a drum, but still she held on. She put everything she had into her thumbs. It mattered too much to let go.

Leonard stilled.

His eyes closed and his shoulders sank against the chapel floor.

His face had filled up purple, and perhaps it was that change that made Hannah notice its details. Faint freckles on the sides of his nose. An eyelash stuck to the lens of his glasses. His beard was soft and fine against her fingers in a way she'd never have thought, but that only made her think of Zach, and the struggle she'd had to try to close her brother's eyes after she had found him, and in the end she had been too overcome and Hiroko had done it for her.

She would not be overcome this time.

'Mum,' wheezed Seb, from where he lay snared behind her. 'Mum, you have to stop.'

'No, Seb. I mustn't.'

An impatient fly had arrived and was buzzing at Hannah's ear. 'Mum!' gasped Seb, again, but still she clung on.

The fly kept buzzing, bouncing against her nostril as it zoomed its figure-of-eight around her head. Hannah ignored it and held on to Leonard, but when she next felt something brush her face it was not the insect but feathers, and the air filled with a sudden squabble. She looked up in surprise to see sparrows swerving back and forth from wall to wall, shrieking at her with every pass. Yet the moment she let them distract her she thought she felt the pulse in Leonard's artery and restored her attention to the task in hand. Even when she heard a padded *thump* against the stone floor she did not look up, and it took a second *thump* and a third to draw her attention.

Three hares sat equidistant from each other in the entrance to the chapel. Their ears were flat against their skulls and their feet were drumming an urgent beat against the overgrown flagstones. They had amber irises and deep black pupils, and all three of their gazes were fixed on Hannah. In surprise, she lessened her hold on Leonard's neck. At once he drew a pitiful, rattling breath, and she clamped her hands back round his throat again.

'Mum, please . . .' begged Seb very softly.

Tears dashed down Hannah's cheeks. She could feel their heat where they welled on her chin.

'No,' she said. She had no room in her thoughts for what the hares were doing here. She put all of the force she had left into her thumbs.

As she squeezed the remaining life out of him, some of her tears dropped onto Leonard's cheeks and forehead. They were not for his sake. They were for her own. Leonard would be in her head when this was over, just as the gunman was there already. She doubted she could cope with both of their ghosts inside her, but nevertheless she held on. It was for Seb that she did this. For everyone.

Then, from somewhere nearby in the woods, there came a canine growl.

The wolf pack slunk into the chapel with bright eyes and their tongues out like dogs. Their sides rose and fell sharply, as if they had been sprinting to get here, but they were calm now and fearless. At last Hannah let go and fell away from Leonard, crawling backwards towards Seb.

There were seven wolves, and they padded into the chapel in formation. For a moment Hannah remembered the Alsatian, and panicked that Leonard was somehow kin to these cruel animals, and that all of the predators of the world were in league with one another.

As if to prove her right, Leonard spluttered. He pawed at his neck with his hands and rolled onto his side groaning. Hannah saw his eyes open and squeeze shut again as he tried to make sense of where he was and what had just happened to him.

The lead wolf lodged its jaws around his throat while a second tore open the cloth of his shirt, spat it out then ripped wide his belly. The bite was so powerful that Hannah could see Leonard's ribs raised like outstretched fingers. She didn't know whether to watch or to screw up her eyes. Seb began shouting, and Hiroko started struggling at her bonds to no avail.

Leonard did not scream, probably because the first wolf had its teeth through his larynx. The worst part of it was that his arms and legs kept moving, long into the pack's meal. Maybe he died quickly, when the first wolf opened his throat. Maybe those movements were all just electric afterthoughts. Or maybe it took longer, for the beasts made no further effort to still him. Two ravens sprang greedily down from the treetops, and croaked to one another like an elderly couple out for their walk.

When the wolves were done, the nearest looked up and met Hannah's eyes.

Now it's my turn, she thought, and turned her head to look at Seb. She tried to show strength for him, but he was too busy trying to do the same for Hiroko.

The wolf barked, as if to command Hannah's attention, and she looked to it obediently. Its maw was smothered in Leonard's blood, and the scarlet gore made its green eyes look all the greener. The wolf watched her with no readable expression, even as a red string of its slather dripped neatly to the chapel floor. *There are no policemen and no judges now*, thought Hannah, but here was a judge like no other. She became almost calm as she waited for its verdict.

It nodded to her and walked out of the chapel. The other wolves padded after it, licking their teeth as they went. Then the ravens bustled in.

It took Hannah some time to find any strength remaining. She was amazed, in the end, that she had enough to drag herself close to what remained of Leonard and find his knife. This she used to saw through the bonds at Hiroko's wrists, after which she collapsed and let the girl take charge.

Hiroko freed herself and cut Seb loose while Hannah lay back on the stone and hurt all over, and looked up at a sky so blue above the branches. The ravens kept sneaking looks at her from their feast, perhaps wondering if she'd soon become their next meal.

'I'm going to look for branches,' said Hiroko. 'Ones we can use as splints and crutches.'

The girl dashed off and left mother and son alone for a minute. Seb slipped his hand through Hannah's, and their blood dried their palms together.

Hannah smiled at him. 'Do you love her?' she asked.

'What?'

She giggled, before the giggle turned into a splutter of pain. 'Do you love Hiroko?'

'Are you really asking me this *now*?'

'Good a time as any. Well? Do you?'

'Yes,' Seb said, with conviction.

When Hiroko returned, she helped Hannah get to her feet by means of a long stave of wood. Then she helped Seb with another

470

crutch, and did her best to support them both as they flung their arms around her and tried to walk away from the chapel. It was agonisingly slow, but none of them could bear to stay in that place.

It was Michelle who found them, in the end, along with some of the kinder souls from the settlement. They gave Hannah and Seb water, and sat them down while they organised bandages and a sling, and stretchers to carry them back to the valley. Only when they were safely returned, and propped on bedding in Michelle's more spacious shelter, did Hannah begin to ask about Adrien. She had expected to find him waiting for them in the valley, perhaps seated pensively on some stump or other, and although she would have been furious with him had he been so, that would have been better than his absence.

'He must still be up there, in the woods,' Hannah said urgently, 'you'd better go back and look for him before it gets dark!'

Michelle shook her head. 'Adrien isn't up there. He came back this afternoon, and it's because of him that we set out to find you.'

'I don't understand . . .'

'He went into the ruined hotel. And now . . .'

Hannah propped herself up, just enough to look out through the shelter's window. She could see nothing of the hotel besides a heap of bricks and broken trees.

'It all fell down not long after I left him in there,' said Michelle, with tears in her eyes. 'I . . . don't think he got out.'

Hannah could scarcely believe it. 'What was he *doing* in there?'

'He said he was going to follow the . . . he called them the . . .'

'Whisperers,' said Hannah, eyes widening, and at once she thought of the look the wolf had given her, and the hares and the sparrows and the fly that had preceded it. She remembered Adrien trying to explain what it was like to be a lichen, and she thought perhaps she understood some fraction of what had happened. 'Oh, Adrien,' she said, with a sad shake of her head. Then she added, almost without breath because her voice was cracking, 'Thank you.'

19

Slingshot

The news of Leonard's death spread quickly. Rumours flew as only rumours can: that Hiroko had dragged him out to the woods as he slept and there murdered him with his own rifle; that Hiroko and Seb had killed his dog and then him as part of some twisted act of nature worship; that Hiroko was a witch and Leonard her sacrifice. The girl didn't care what people thought about her, although when Roland came to talk with them and demand the truth of the matter, she suspected he had been the one to start the rumours. He became flustered when Michelle calmly told him the true details of what had happened, but if he didn't believe her he didn't say. He looked smaller and more agitated without Leonard's menace at his side.

They set Seb's arm with sticks and made what compresses they could for the scalds along his leg, which came up in huge blisters big as toadstools. For several days he said hardly anything, and drank almost as much water as he sweated out again. Michelle kept apologising that the people of the settlement had already used all the painkillers from the hotel's medical supply, but Seb bore the pain with the same determination he had shown after Hiroko had broken his nose. She was proud of him, and told him so with caresses.

As for Seb's ankle, the cuts there were very deep and the worry was infection. Yet, to what seemed their great fortune, no poisonous bacteria took hold. Slowly his ankle began to heal, as did Hannah's as she kept her weight off it. Neither Hannah's ribs nor her pelvis were cracked, which she confided to Hiroko had been her great fear in the moment. Bruises bloomed as big as roses on her flesh, but after a week turned a sickly yellow and then faded.

Whenever she was not tending to Seb or Hannah, Hiroko wandered up into the forest. She found, however, that she no longer enjoyed being alone. Hunting was joyless without her partner in crime, and besides she had thrown her old slingshot into a river. The weapon had dropped from Leonard's pocket in his tussle with Hannah, and so had avoided being on his person when the wolves set upon him. Although that had kept it clean, it might as well have been blood-stained every inch, as far as Hiroko was concerned. She had watched the river carry it away on frothing water and rubbed her shoulder where Leonard had shot her.

She had already found a fine fork of wood to cut into a new catapult. Its fibres were the perfect union of the robust and the supple, and the grip was just the right thickness to grasp in her fist. Yet whenever she tried to work on it, to do as little as strim away the bark with her knife, she thought of her grandfather Yasuo whittling wood on the deck of his forest house, and the blade in her hand became as immovable as the dead.

Without the slingshot she had focused on trap-making. Remembering Ruth and her family by the lake, she had set about not only frog-catching but snail-farming, and had found an eager pupil in Michelle. The two of them rummaged in the debris of the hotel for bath tubs to use as their snail farm's foundation. They found three, and lugged them clear of the ruins, but although they tried to laugh and joke about washing with invertebrates, Hiroko could tell that Michelle was thinking about Adrien, and praying not to find his body in the rubble. For her own part, the site of the hotel was doubly painful. If ever she pictured it falling, some cruel path of the mind led her to imagine the tower blocks of Tokyo. Then she'd screw up her fists so hard it felt like her knuckles would burst, just to stop herself from thinking of the city coming down.

'I'll make sure to fatten up these snails,' Seb volunteered, once they had brought the bathtubs back to the settlement. 'Until my ankle's fixed, I'm doing everything at their pace anyway.'

'Well, you're in luck,' said Michelle. 'We found a grand old armchair in the hotel. It's missing a leg, but we can prop it up on a stump for you.'

'Great,' said Seb with a clap of his hands, 'I'll sit in it and watch their every slither.'

Michelle, for her own part, was even more enthused by frog-trapping than Hiroko had been when she'd first discovered it. To her frustration, however, her efforts were met by little reward in the great barren trench of the valley. Worms were easy to come by in the mud, thick squirming red ones they hung from the handles of the buckets, but in the mornings they were limp and untaken and the traps remained empty of frogs. It was not until Hiroko roamed some distance west of the settlement that they had a break-through. She had gone where her boots had led her, notching the trees with her knife as she passed, and so had come to marshy land that burped with every footstep. There the creaks of bent and rotting willows were mimicked by frogs in the rushes, and on a lime-green cushion of algae Hiroko spied a giant, rotund female. Its blotch-marked skin and horn-rimmed eyebrows were a match even for Ruth's Cleopatra, and Hiroko was almost trembling with concentration when she stalked towards it and, lightning fast, shot out her hands to imprison it in her grip.

They called that frog Nefertiti, and she lured hordes of lovesick males down to the traps in the valley. At night sometimes Hiroko would hear her would-be suitors, and one time she even slipped out of bed to watch them springing to their doom in the moon-light. That was the night when the strange thing happened. She had been awake, in the first place, because she had been missing her family. During their journey to the hotel, even if they'd been heading west and not east, they'd always had some direction to distract her heart with. Now that they were stuck in the valley there was no such reprieve. Hiroko slipped out of bed and went outside, and stood in the cold dark with the male frogs leaping past her down the slope. She could feel the immensity of all the mud and stone and bedrock beneath her feet. The sheer magnitude of the planet, somewhere on the far side of which was Japan. Seb had helped her learn to cope with it, but a weight didn't lighten just because you found the strength to carry it.

Closing her eyes in the darkness, Hiroko tried to conjure up her father's face. She couldn't do it without placing him in the Tokyo apartment, in profile, gazing out of the window with Saori at his side. They were looking out at the surrounding tower blocks, just as Hiroko had seen them do on countless occasions. This time, however, Tokyo's high rises stood up amid a sea of leaves. Every glass pane of every tower had filled up with green reflections.

Ribbet, went a frog at her ankle. *Ribbet*. Hiroko wiped her eyes and looked down just in time to see the amphibian jump boldly onto the toecap of her boot. There it shuffled ninety degrees and tilted its head to look up at her, the moon a miniaturised reflection in each of its eyes.

Ribbet, it said, almost like a query, and for some reason Hiroko thought it was trying to tell her something.

She crouched down and lifted it off her boot. It sat almost motionless on her palm, as light as a thought.

'What is it?' she whispered. 'What is it you have to say?'

It didn't say anything.

'Don't go any further down the slope, little frog. It's all a big trap that we made for you. We're going to cook you if you fall for it.'

The frog only blinked and looked queasy. Probably it was just a fancy of the moonlight, but there seemed something familiar about its worried expression. She returned it to the soil, placing it facing uphill, then stood and headed back towards the settlement, where the moonlight picked out shards of metal in the crumbled ruins of the Caisleán Hotel.

She staggered to a halt, pushing her wrists hard against her eyes. The tears found their escape routes, all the same. Her father and

Saori were with her like ghosts tonight. Standing at the apartment window, looking out at all that green . . .

It was as if her subconscious had long been rehearsing it while she strove to turn her thoughts elsewhere. Branches had broken the tower blocks' struts and girders. Roots had bent the deepest foundations. The towers' own mass had done the rest. They had packed themselves down, floor by floor, with neatness. Near the ground they had billowed out dust clouds that had hidden the city and the forest as one.

Hiroko had to crouch. The trembling in her legs was the trembling of the floor beneath her father's feet.

What would have gone through her beloved *otosan*'s mind, in that final moment before everything gave way? Saori, beside him? Something remembered from his days in America? The face of his wife, whom his daughter had killed at her birth?

No. Hiroko knew, as certainly as she knew the layout of the bones in a prey animal's skeleton, who her father would have thought of in those final seconds of his life.

Ribbet.

She opened her eyes and was momentarily appalled to find that the frog had returned, to crouch right there in front of her. Couldn't it see that she was grieving?

The frog's tongue shot out and dabbed her nose.

A moment later it was gone, hopping away while Hiroko remained too stunned to reach after it. It did not head any further down the valley, nor back up the slope. Instead it hopped *along* it, away from both Hiroko and the settlement and the pheromone lure of Nefertiti.

It was not until a day later, in a moment of idle speculation with the compass in her hand, that Hiroko realised that the frog had hopped due east.

'Adrien?' she asked, and the branches of the trees atop the valley's heights shook in a breeze she could not feel blowing against her skin.

20

Direction

A month and a half passed by. Someone at the settlement had been keeping a calendar, and in mid-December Hannah began to move on her ankle again. At first she did so only for short spells, and with the aid of a walking stick, but she was desperate to rebuild her strength. She had no desire to stay put in the valley, and if the year had not been against her she would have left as soon as she could limp.

The leaves were all gone now from the trees and in most parts of the forest the undergrowth was a black mush laced with ice. Treading tentatively through such wintry woodland, Hannah sometimes let out a heartfelt sigh, wishing that the planet would turn a little faster, and spring arrive in weeks instead of months. It pained her to admit it, but she knew that leaving at this time of year would be madness. The world would be far too cold and barren to travel in.

On Christmas Eve a hoarfrost etched every skeletal leaf into the forest floor. Hannah was once again out walking, enjoying the crunching ground she slowly trod. Frozen water feathered every twig, and some branches looked as white as the pinions of swans. The trunks, on the other hand, remained resolutely dark, and even the mosses had turned black. When, plodding into an open glade, Hannah saw red shapes strewn among the blacks and whites, she paused and held her breath, expecting them to be the innards of some poor murdered animal. Then she yelped, and almost forgot to use her walking stick in her hurry to get closer.

They were wild strawberries. It was impossible, but they were. She gathered them incredulously, half expecting them to transform into mould in the blink of an eye. Yet when she tasted them they were as sweet as high summer's best crop.

Back at the settlement, she shared what she had found with nobody except Seb, Hiroko and Michelle. She had brought masses of the fruits back with her as a treat as well as proof, and they ate them with wonder and red juice bursting over their lips.

'An early Christmas present,' declared Michelle, when they had finished the last of them.

'But from who?' wondered Hannah, looking up the slope towards the forest.

The next day, Christmas Day, all four of them went looking for the strawberry glade. It was nowhere to be found, so they returned to the fires in the valley and sang, along with several others, every festive song they could remember. Roland appeared and wished everybody season's greetings, then urged them not to forget their daily chores. Michelle said that everyone deserved a day off, on this of all days, and the two began to argue. They had been arguing whenever they crossed paths, since their split.

Just as she had sought Hiroko's advice, Michelle sought Hannah's on a good many things. In defiance of Roland's orders, she did as Hannah had previously suggested and took the cows up into the forest. There they roamed for a while and ate what little they could find, then let themselves be ushered back down to their paddock. Likewise Michelle was fascinated by herblore. Hannah drew for her the best pictures she could to create a sort of forager's field guide, and it felt good to do so. It reminded her of time spent with Zach, long ago.

Early in January, Michelle and Roland had their most ferocious clash yet, and several other people from the settlement took Michelle's side over his. She had discovered that Roland had been hiding a secret stash of alcohol, retrieved from the hotel's bar, and this flew against everyone's idea of community. When he tried to apologise he slurred some of his words, and people began to mutter about a change of direction for the settlement.

Hannah began to practise walking without her stick's assistance. She was always on the lookout for flashes of colour amid the drab of winter, but the next time that she encountered something extraordinary it was not red but black and white, with a dash of blue across its wing feathers.

She was walking beneath a mesh of grey branches, with the colourless sky cold up above, when she became aware of a magpie hopping along a branch to her left. She had thought she had seen it earlier, but magpies were common birds so she hadn't paid it much heed. This time, however, she had a hunch that it was following her, and five minutes later it was still on her trail. She paused and thought for a moment, then turned to face it and whispered, 'What is it you want?'

It squawked and took off from its branch, flapping closer and beating hard its wings to hover in the air before her. In its claws it grasped something small and shiny. Hannah reached out a tentative hand and it dropped the object onto her palm. Then it flapped away laughing.

It had given her a silver key, from a child's jewellery box.

'Adrien?' she asked, under her breath.

That night, Roland picked another fight with Michelle. He had uncovered a secret ballot in circulation, a petition for someone else to take charge, and he accused her of orchestrating it. She knew nothing about the ballot, having been too busy learning woodcraft from Hiroko and Hannah, and she told Roland as much. Then he revealed a copy of the petition and asked her to explain why, therefore, her name was foremost among those being suggested to take his place. At that Michelle was stunned, but a crowd had heard their raised voices and gathered round, and began to murmur their support. An hour later, Michelle was made leader of the settlement.

It was Michelle, therefore, who led the farewells when Hannah, Hiroko and Seb set out again into the woods. 'I can't believe you're doing this,' she said, shaking her head. 'It's tantamount to suicide.'

'It will be alright,' said Hannah. 'I know it will be.'

'It won't be,' said Michelle. 'It's January, Hannah. It's the worst month for doing anything.'

Hannah twirled between her finger and thumb the silver key the magpie had given her. 'We'll wait and see,' she said.

Michelle offered them all the supplies her community could spare, but Hannah refused them politely. And with that, and after each of them had embraced the bemused Michelle, they began to walk south.

Their journey was a surreal experience, nothing like as trying as the one they had taken to get to the valley. Whenever Hannah's foraging pack became empty, and she began to wonder when next they would eat, they would stumble upon splashes of colour. A plum tree, fruiting in defiance of the season. A bed of crow garlic, its aroma made doubly pungent by the crisp winter air. A grove of long, floppy leaves sprouting all over the forest floor, whereupon Hannah laughed and cried at the same time and would not tell the others what they'd found, insisting that they, 'Dig! Dig some of them up!'

They dug and found leeks. Fat leeks too plentiful to carry them all.

Food might be taken care of, but good firewood did not at first prove easy to come by. The damp made most timber too moist to burn, and on their first rainy night when the drizzle sieved down through the canopy, Hannah worried that they'd all catch a chill and fall sick. At once a speckled songthrush appeared, warbling with insistent jubilation before darting away to their right, slightly west of their course. From a branch there it sang to them, and they all looked to each other and shrugged and then followed where it led, which within fifteen minutes transpired to be an abandoned cottage. Its roof was intact enough to give them shelter, and by a hearth that had lost its fireplace they found a sealed stash of logs and kindling.

In ways such as these the journey was made smooth for them, and Hannah began to recover her optimism: optimism, it seemed, restored from a past self, a self from before Zach had died. By the start of February they reached the coast some thirty miles east of Dungarvan. From there they struck west, asking everyone they met whether they'd encountered a sailor with a capricorn tattoo and a vivacious little daughter. One or two people had, and on an overcast day they found him, waist-deep in water as he waded back to the shore. He had a filled pot of shellfish in his hand, but he dropped it with a splash when he saw Hannah. She beamed at him (and a robin sang from out of the woods), and then Nora came hurtling out of nowhere and flung her arms around Hannah's waist.

Eoin had been repairing the house of his parents-in-law, who he said he had buried at sea. The travellers helped him to complete the work, just as they had with his boat, and they lost sight of the days passing by as they did so. The rain fell heavier and often, and on one bitterly cold morning the icicles hung like glass roots from the eaves of the house. When it snowed they built a life-sized snowman, and Seb lifted Nora so she could place pebbles for its mouth, nose and eyes. Then she used her finger to draw spectacles into the snow and said it was Adrien Thomas, and Hannah nearly choked on the sudden tightening in her throat, and the woods made a creaking noise like the snow underfoot.

One evening, after the thaw, while Hiroko was playing wild beasts with Nora and a salt-starved Eoin had gone for a dip in the ocean, Hannah and Seb sat alone on the sand. After a while, Seb said, 'I'm glad we got this chance to talk with you in private, Mum.'

'Why's that?' she asked. 'Have you got something to tell me?'

Hannah was excited about this. For weeks it had been obvious that Seb and Hiroko had a secret in their lives. Seb was far better at concealing it than Hiroko, but he was still her son and she had learned how his face worked as only mothers can. She'd become so excited, in fact, that she had already begun planning a little party. What could be more appropriate, given that the new life of spring would coincide with their announcement? They were going to be good parents, she knew, and it would be a pleasure to think of Hiroko as her daughter-in-law.

481

Seb was struggling to say it. She nudged him with her elbow, trying to hold back her smile. 'Go on,' she said, 'you can tell me.'

'Okay,' he said at last, then cleared his throat. 'We're going . . .'

'Yes?' She could hardly bear to wait one moment longer. 'Going to have a what?'

'Going,' he said.

She waited. 'Going to . . . ?'

'Going, Mum. Um. I've been trying to tell you since we got here. But I haven't been brave enough. Sorry.'

'What . . . ?' she asked, although she had heard him full well. 'What did you say you were doing?'

'Leaving, Mum. Once the summer's here.'

She held her hands to her head. *Leaving*? It made no sense. None at all.

'Blame me if you're upset, not Hiroko. It was my idea.'

'But . . . where? Where could you possibly want to go?'

Seb puffed out his cheeks. He ran his hands back over the top of his head. 'Japan.'

Hannah was silent for a minute. And then, despite her distress at the thought that she'd be losing him, losing both of them, she gasped with a proud laughter, and reached out for him, and they embraced so tight that he winced in pain from his newly unslung arm. They held each other gentler for a minute, and then she went and found Hiroko and hugged her too, and after that, no more words were needed.

Seb and Hiroko left on the first truly warm day of the year. Eoin gifted them the boat, the one that they had helped him to build, for they planned to retrace his route along the coast, and so eventually back across the water to Wales, and then perhaps around Land's End and the south coast of England until they were ready to brave the crossing to France. They were in no hurry, for of course it would be foolish to be. Their journey was going to take them years and years.

Years, Hannah hoped, were something they had on their side.

At the hour of their departure, the trees creaked and seemed almost to strain to be with them on the beach, as if they wanted to be closer when their farewells finally took place. Hannah and the others stood in a stiff huddle to wave them off. There were tears in all their eyes, but Hannah's most of all. Yet when Seb and Hiroko began to row she felt, despite her sorrow, something that was bittersweet and apt. The two of them had a path to follow, and whether that path proved as straight as they hoped for or a tangled thing without any bearings did not matter, so long as they could keep their feet on it.

Seb's eyes stayed locked on his mother's as the boat shrank into a haze that eventually concealed it. Then Hannah closed her eyes and for a minute kept fixed, in her mind, a picture of that face she had first seen laid down on her breast not minutes after he had breathed his first. His eyes had sought out hers on that day just as they had on this, and now she felt as if all of her struggles to be here in this moment, waving him farewell, were steel preparing her for what he needed, which was the right and natural commencement of his adult life. And now he was gone, and Nora clung to her leg, and Eoin took hold of her and clasped her close, and she felt both a sorrow and a pride, which she imagined might in past lives have been saved for aisle days and days of white dresses, and among the trees the green leaves were whispering, and above them wheeled countless birds of many species and above those the deft clouds. Life was changing into something new, in keeping with its ancient motions.

Acknowledgements

Thank you to Sue Armstrong for your dedication and positivity, and for long patient sessions hearing out story ideas.

Thank you to Helen Garnons-Williams for your faith in me and your incredible insight, and an office full of leaves and whisperers.

Thanks most of all to Iona Shaw, for listening through each draft of this thing and always having the words to say when I have none. I seem very good at getting lost in the woods: thank you for leading me out of them every time.

A Note on the Author

Ali Shaw is the author of *The Girl with Glass Feet*, which won the Desmond Elliott Prize, was shortlisted for the Costa First Novel Award and was longlisted for the *Guardian* first book award. His second novel, *The Man Who Rained*, was published in 2013. He grew up in Dorset and graduated from Lancaster University with a degree in English Literature. He has since worked as a bookseller and at the Bodleian Library. He now lives in Oxford, with his wife and baby daughter.

@Ali_Shaw
alishaw.co.uk

A Note on the Type

The text of this book is set in Bembo, which was first used in 1495 by the Venetian printer Aldus Manutius for Cardinal Bembo's *De Aetna*. The original types were cut for Manutius by Francesco Griffo. Bembo was one of the types used by Claude Garamond (1480–1561) as a model for his Romain de l'Université, and so it was a forerunner of what became the standard European type for the following two centuries. Its modern form follows the original types and was designed for Monotype in 1929.